Sarah Ball is getting a little bit older, dispro-
portionately greyer and has now moved to
Cambridge with her husband David and two
children Ellie and Sam. She is getting through
an awful lot of wine and sweets these days but
still manages to write for ten minutes every
other Thursday.

For more information about Sarah you can visit
her website at www.sarahball.co.uk

*Also by Sarah Ball*

**Nine Months**

# Marry Me

*SARAH BALL*

**PIATKUS**

## Visit the Piatkus website!

Piatkus publishes a wide range of exciting fiction and non-fiction, including books on health, mind, body & spirit, sex, self-help, cookery, biography and the paranormal. If you want to:

- read descriptions of our popular titles
- buy our books over the internet
- take advantage of our special offers
- enter our monthly competition
- learn more about your favourite Piatkus authors

visit our website at:

### www.piatkus.co.uk

First published in Great Britain in 2003 by
Judy Piatkus (Publishers) Ltd of
5 Windmill Street, London W1T 2JA
email: info@piatkus.co.uk

**The moral right of the author has been asserted**

*A catalogue record for this book is available from the British Library*

ISBN 0 7499 3379 8

Typeset in Palatino by Palimpsest Book Production Limited, Polmont, Stirlingshire

Printed and bound in Great Britain by
Bookmarque Ltd, Croydon, Surrey

# ACKNOWLEDGEMENTS

Another book, another page of thank yous (although I'll try not to do a Gwyneth this time!) Firstly thank you Dad, who's been invaluable and whose knowledge extends to the most surprising of subjects!

Again thanks to Mary and Mel for always encouraging, helping and nagging me to get on with it. To Simon my brother and great web designer, Ellie and Sam, and to Gillian and all at Piatkus, a huge thank you.

Additional praise must go to; Liz Kynoch (my brilliant legal adviser), Mum, Mike, Jane and John, Kerrie and Charlie (this book is not for looking up rude words!), and Steve Fletcher and friends for their extensive knowledge of words for getting drunk (I was shocked and appalled!).

For the musicians that inspired this book, particularly David Gahan and Brett Anderson, in the words of Sweden's finest, thank you for the music.

And lastly an obvious thank you but one not to be overlooked is to those of you who have bought, begged, borrowed or found this book down the back of a sofa – thank you for picking it up! And a big thank you to those readers who have emailed me over the past year with words of praise and encouragement, you always put a smile on my face and motivate me to put down my wine, turn off the telly and write a little bit more.

For David, for everything.

# CHAPTER ONE

I could only just glimpse Nathan in a gap between the rows of guests that lined the pews in front of me. He had his back to me, as you would expect, but I could still sense that he was nervous. His shoulders were unnaturally straight and motionless, his neck stiff and his hands looked lost as they hung empty, resting close to his thighs. An unnecessarily large pink hat bobbed into my line of vision obscuring the view altogether, probably a good job as my eyes had already been lingering on Nathan's thighs for longer than was socially acceptable in situations such as these.

Rocking back onto my heels I closed my eyes, blocking out the chessboard of grey suits and pastel sundresses. As the minister spoke I felt as though I could have been standing in my kitchen at home, listening to a play on the radio. I wished I was. Not that I ever listened to plays – Radio One had not to my knowledge ever made a habit of broadcasting them – but you know what I mean.

I caught the minister saying, 'But first I am required to ask if anyone here present knows a reason why these persons may not lawfully marry, to declare it now . . .' and I turned to peer at the door behind me. A woman with a little girl perched on her lap frowned at me and I realised I must have looked a little too eager for the kind of eleventh hour showdown that soaps can't resist throwing in. I turned back, blushing furiously and fixed my eyes on the parquet flooring. I could tell that Vicky was looking at me, wanting to share a conspiratorial smile, but the herringbone pattern on the floor really was fascinating.

A tune had been playing over and over in my head and it was really beginning to niggle at me, tempting me to sing it out loud. I wasn't sure what the song was, but words were forming, teasing me. I cleared my throat and tried to concentrate on what is going on up ahead.

'Nathan Jack Priestly, will you take Rebecca Frances Conway to be your wife?'

God, what is it? It's on the tip of my tongue.

'Will you love her—'

It was a woman singing.

'—comfort her—'

Something to do with marriage and socks smelling of Brie.

'—honour and protect her—'

I think it was the Beautiful South.

'—and, forsaking all others—'

Of course. I remember now.

'—be faithful to her as long as you both shall live?'

It's 'Don't marry her, have me'.

'I will.'

Oh bollocks!

Vicky looked at me quizzically and whispered, 'Did you say something?'

I shook my head vigorously and gave her a wobbly smile. This seemed to convince her, as she bent down to whisper something to her son who was now shuffling from one foot to another, holding his crotch with one hand and tugging at his shirt collar with the other. This morning, when Vicky had told him that he would have to wear his best shirt, he perplexed us all by crying, 'yes!' and punching the air. It wasn't until he returned clutching his favourite football shirt that we clicked and a scene not dissimilar to the Battle of Britain then emerged in Vicky's living room. When Jack looked up in my direction I rolled my eyes skyward as if to say, 'Bo-*ring!*' and he giggled until Vicky nudged him then looked around to see why he was laughing. Looking forward again I saw that Nathan and Rebecca were now holding hands, gazing at one another as they said their vows. I swallowed hard as my head pounded and I fought the urge to vomit right there in the pew.

Years ago I used to dream about this moment, standing in a beautiful lofty church decorated with flowers at the end of every aisle, Nathan looking incredible and gazing at me as we repeated our vows. This was not what I had in mind at all, something had gone horribly wrong. Mind you, it had also been Rebecca's fantasy back then too, and Vicky's. The three of us were relentless in

3

our pursuit of Nathan at school, and united in our appreciation. We never fell out over him or became competitive. Even Rebecca didn't try her usual tactics to ensnare him, although in hindsight maybe she had been all along. Still, at the time we thought it was pointless to fight over him, we never really believed he would want to go out with any of us.

I first really noticed Nathan at Little Beat, a record shop that had recently opened on a back road between Clifton and Bristol city centre. He was leafing through records in the second-hand room at the back of the shop, nodding his head in time with a Cure song. I vaguely recognised him as being in the year above me at school. He was one of the boys that hung out in the computer room rather than go out into the courtyard so I didn't know his name or much about him. I was fourteen then and he was the same height as me and, being skinnier than most of his peers, possibly the same size as me as well. He had an old grey bag slung over his shoulder that I noticed was scrawled with names of bands that read like my bedroom play-list. This boy, I decided, was a kindred spirit.

From then on I hung out at Little Beat every chance I could. I befriended the owner, Ed Little, who was only twenty-two and attractive in an inaccessibly older and cooler way. He took it upon himself to educate me on my music taste, introducing me to bands he knew instinctively that I'd like.

4

I didn't often see Nathan there, and when I did he was always preoccupied, absorbed in the music, but I liked that. I found him mysterious and intense.

Vicky and Rebecca didn't share my enthusiasm then. Vicky agreed that he was cute, but not her type, and Rebecca was more interested in the already nearly-six-foot-tall, Michael McCallister. Michael was the popular choice for girls at school, with his thick blonde flick, Don Johnson in *Miami Vice* dress sense and his hilarious ability to take off Rik Mayall from *The Young Ones*. They couldn't see what I saw in Nathan and teased me for having unique taste in boys.

The year Nathan returned from the summer holidays ready to join the sixth form he must have grown a foot in height. His jaw had developed a sculpted masculinity and his hair was cut back enough to see that his rich hazel eyes were framed with incredibly long, dark eyelashes. Time had also caught up with him and his charity shop dress sense and army boots were no longer a reason for him to be teased. His individuality earned him respect and he was suddenly deemed fashionable, with alternative edge.

Vicky and Rebecca noticed the change in him almost immediately. We were walking arm-in-arm to school on the first day back after the summer holidays, discussing how unfair it was that the year above us were starting their A levels. They were losing compulsory PE, and instead acquiring free periods and a common room. We had heard rumours that, in the sixth form, the teachers treated

5

you more like adults and not like the spotty plebs our maths teacher always referred to us as. We longed to feel grown up and taken seriously.

'Nisha's brother told me that her Humanities teacher swears in front of them all the time,' Rebecca whispered.

Vicky looked horrified and gaped at us, making us laugh.

'Did you know they can play music on the common room stereo?' I asked.

'Erm, I think you may have mentioned it once or twice,' Vicky said sarcastically.

'Oh God Abby, I hope you go off those dreary Smiths albums before next year, they'll do my head in,' Rebecca moaned, riffling through her bag for a lipstick.

We were standing at a pedestrian crossing, waiting for the lights to change, when I spotted Nathan approaching us on his mountain bike. He had a personal stereo on and was obviously so involved in the music that he hadn't noticed the road ahead. He braked hard just before he reached the curb, clipping Rebecca's arm and knocking the lipstick out of her hand and into the road. His bike slid at a dangerous angle and he toppled off, skidding along the tarmac on his side.

'God, are you all right?' Vicky cried, rushing to his aid.

Rebecca and I stood watching as he got up and brushed off his black Levi's.

'Cheers,' he mumbled as Vicky picked his bike up and handed it back to him. He took his ear piece out and I caught a snatch of the song he had been listening to. 'The Boy with the Thorn in his Side' by The Smiths. I stared at him open mouthed. I had been listening to that song whilst I had been getting ready. My eyes travelled down to his legs and I wondered if he had indeed got a thorn in his side, just to complete the coincidence. Fate, I decided, had engineered this moment. It was a sign.

We watched as he mounted his bike and, with a brief wave and a shy smile, he rode off, bunny hopping a curb.

'Oh my God, was that really Nathan?' Vicky whispered, looking from me to Rebecca with a twinkle in her eye.

I smiled, proudly. 'He's different, isn't he? Taller, and kind of manlier.'

'Just a bit!' Rebecca whistled and grinned at me. 'He's looking *good*. I have to hand it to you Abby, you're a bloody good talent spotter. Who'd have thought he'd, er, *develop* so well.' She raised her eyes scandalously and I laughed, glad that they could finally see where I was coming from. Now I could talk about Nathan without them pulling faces. They would be my allies.

I wasn't quite so thrilled later that week, when I realised every other girl in the school had also come to the same conclusion about Nathan. Rumours were rife that his talents on the bass guitar had earned him a place in the school band, Reverb, that played in the theatre room at the end of every term and was occasionally offered gigs in local pubs. When these rumours were confirmed, his popularity was sealed and his status elevated to 'man of the moment'.

The first time Rebecca, Vicky and I went to see them play was in the Hat and Feather, a grotty pub out of town, one Thursday night. We walked into the pub laughing nervously, only to be greeted by the vacant stares of half-a-dozen locals and an enormous sheepdog that lazed under a bar stool.

A group of Reverb's friends sat on the table opposite where the band had set up. They looked over as we walked in then turned back, sharing a private joke. The rest of the pub was empty. We stood out like sausage rolls at a bar mitzvah.

Rebecca looked the oldest so she bought each of us a bottle of Diamond White and we tried to make ourselves invisible in a corner as the band started their next number. Nathan stood at the front mike and I realised that although he wasn't the lead singer of the band, this song was his. They started into a rendition of Velvet Underground's 'Pale Blue Eyes'.

Nathan's voice wasn't perfect; it wavered and broke, but with a soulful style which suited the song and the way Lou Reed had originally sung it. I watched him transfixed as he sang with his eyes half shut, his lips almost touching the microphone. His arms were dropped loosely and his hands were touching the microphone stand at waist height. Not grabbing it tightly, the way singers often do, but gently, his fingers only just touching the stand and moving unconsciously as he sang. It was the most sensual thing I had ever seen.

The icing on the cake for me was that being the only one of the three friends that had blue eyes, I could be lulled into thinking that the song was mine. That nobody else existed in that dingy pub and he was singing directly to me. Whatever I had felt for Nathan before paled into insignificance at that moment and I knew then and there that I loved him.

That was more than ten years ago, and the memories of his voice and the feelings it stirred in me are as clear as they have ever been. I had bought a Velvet Underground album the following day, and the song 'Pale Blue Eyes' was on my play-list for that night's disco.

I stood on the lawn outside the church with Vicky and her husband Alistair, watching as the bride and groom gathered their family together in various unfathomable sequences for photographs. It seemed to be taking forever, yet the smiles on their faces were still convincingly genuine and spontaneous.

Rebecca looked incredible with her hair pinned up elegantly with delicate flowers woven into the back. Her dress reminded me of a BBC Jane Austen adaptation as it was fitted around her bust with a low scoop neck that showed off her round cleavage. From just under her chest, folds of silk fabric fell loosely in a simple empire style. Nathan was also dressed in traditional wedding attire. He wore a grey morning suit and even had a top hat, although I noticed he never wore it for long, opting, instead, to hold it in front of his trousers like a footballer waiting for a penalty kick. He tugged at his cravat and I was reminded of Vicky's son Jack in the church, a lad at heart, not wanting to be restricted. Marriage doesn't suit him, I thought, then immediately flushed with shame. *Bitch, bitch, bitch*, I silently chastised, trying to drum it into my thick skull how completely out of order I was. How could I think that about my own friend's husband? How could I look at him and wish he was mine?

I turned away and looked at Vicky and Alistair instead. They were laughing, their arms wrapped tightly around each other, enjoying the romance and excitement that was in the air. I wondered if it had been Vicky that had finally ensnared Nathan, would I have been more capable of switching off my feelings for him? I had always been closer to her. I cared a lot for Rebecca, but Vicky was different. I loved her like a sister. But although the thought upset me, I still couldn't imagine feeling different about Nathan, no matter who he was with. After all, I had decided Nathan was the one when I was just fourteen years old. How could I just switch that off?

'Can I have all the friends now please, no family, just friends of the bride and groom,' the photographer announced, clapping his hands then waving them in the air, directing people over to the church entrance. I looked at Rebecca, she was grinning, gesturing for us to hurry up.

Vicky grumbled, 'Oh God, I hate being in wedding pictures, I either get moved to the very front where everyone can see me, or I just end up with the top of my hair bobbing about in the middle somewhere.' She was only five foot two and after having had two children she had been left feeling self-conscious about her figure.

'You'd better hide at the back then,' Alistair said taking her hand. 'You don't want to upstage the bride.'

'Flatterer,' Vicky said, laughing as Jack ran behind us shouting, 'Daddy, why are you touching mummy's bottom?'

Vicky and Alistair were so sweet together, always touching and kissing.

'You're very quiet Abby, are you all right?' Alistair said, looking over at me.

I smiled at him, then looked away, pretending to be distracted by watching Jack, who ran up to the gathering ensemble and jumped about singing a Robbie William's song, emulating his hero to a captive audience.

Vicky gave me a withering look. 'He is just too embarrassing,' she whispered. 'Maybe I should have left him at home with Clarice and mum.'

'Oh, you don't mean that,' I said, watching him affectionately. For a four-year-old, Jack had an amazing amount of confidence. He charmed everyone.

Clarice, Vicky's two-year-old, was quite different. She shied away from strangers. Almost every time I saw her, she would clamp herself to Vicky's leg like a big shin pad and not let go until she was sure I wasn't going to do anything sudden or scary.

We joined the group of people by the church steps, trying to worm our way near the back.

'Can the lady in the pale-blue suit and the little boy come and stand at the front?' the photographer called out, pointing to Vicky and Jack. Vicky rolled her eyes and reluctantly trudged to the front, where a group of children had already gathered.

After a couple more rearrangements, the photographer was ready to take the picture, Rebecca and Nathan turned to each other and kissed and I sighed a little too loud.

'OK, smile everyone!'

Alistair bent down to me and said, 'Don't you worry Abby, it'll be your turn soon I'm sure.' He gave my shoulder a consolatory squeeze just as the camera clicked.

The photographer looked up from his lens. 'OK, let's just try this once more, only this time can the girl at the front try not to fiddle with her skirt, it looks beautiful as it is, and the lady at the back there, the one with the suede jacket . . .'

I looked around me.

'Yes, you. Try to smile this time, I want happy vibes. Think wedding ring, not boxing ring,' he quipped, laughing at me, then looked back down through the lens of his camera.

Everyone's a sodding comedian, I thought, blushing to the roots of my hair.

# CHAPTER TWO

'I can't believe Alistair said that to you,' Ed said, tutting and looking at me with sympathy in his eyes. This only succeeded in making me feel more embarrassed and I stared at my coke, avoiding his gaze.

I was having a drink in the hotel bar with my two friends, Ed and Harriet, before I had to start setting up the equipment for the reception disco. Ed and Harriet only knew Rebecca and Nathan through me and so had just been invited to the evening reception. They had agreed to help me set up and give me some much needed moral support in the process.

Harriet was my oldest friend. Her dad had worked with mine for a brief period in the early 70s and had hit it off immediately. They introduced their wives over dinner and a lifelong friendship begun. Harriet being older than me by about three years can remember me being brought home from the hospital, she apparently used to help my mum bath and dress me and sometimes jokes that that was when she first developed an aversion to babies.

We went to different schools but remained close, and when I wasn't with Rebecca and Vicky, then I would get together with Harriet after school and in the holidays. We would play 45-and-in, in the long grass of the meadow that Harriet's house backed on to, until the sun went down and my parents fetched me home.

When I first befriended Ed, I had this romantic notion that he would meet Harriet and they would fall in love. Two of my most favourite people, the two people I looked up to and admired. It would be so perfect. Harriet was closer in age to Ed than I was. Ed, to me, was just the most knowledgeable, worldly person I had ever known. Maybe if I had been older I would have fallen for him myself. Perhaps in the early days I did have a mild crush on him, but it didn't last long. He took on the role of an older brother figure, teaching me, protecting me and ruffling my hair affectionately whenever I said something daft. My crush was pointless and Nathan soon became the only person I could imagine myself with.

Of course the idea of Ed and Harriet together was also crazy and if I had been older I would have realised immediately just how unsuited they were. They were poles apart. Harriet was serious, goal orientated and smart. She knew exactly what she wanted out of life and saw no reason why she couldn't have it. Ed was laid back and loud, with the sense of humour and the dress sense of a fashionably scruffy teenager. Occasionally he would let me see the Ed underneath, the confused and sensitive Ed who couldn't even decide on his own sexuality, let alone his future. They were very different people, and when they met sparks flew all right, not from any romantic frisson, but instead from the verbal sparring they fell in to and have kept up ever since. I had only agreed to let them both help on the condition that they would behave, be nice, and keep the playful insults to a minimum.

The handy thing about being the wedding DJ was that it gave me the perfect excuse to get out of that afternoon's sit down meal and speeches. I couldn't bear the thought of sitting and listening to Rebecca's dad tell the tale of how the happy couple had first met. I knew they would all be laughing at the way we used to follow him around like faithful puppies and how Nathan's friends used to call us the 'fan club'. How Nathan had always dismissed us as silly kids until years after he returned from university and bumped into Rebecca at a bar, where he started chatting her up, without even recognising who she was. Everyone would expect Vicky and I to laugh along at our own foolishness, and the daft things we got up to, to try and make him notice us. Well, it was easy for Vicky to laugh along, she had forgotten Nathan as soon as she went to university and met and fell in love with Alistair. And as far as they were all concerned, I had moved on too. I'd had a string of boyfriends, my most serious being Chris, who I had been with for a year when Rebecca brought Nathan back into our lives. I couldn't keep it together with Chris after that. Nathan was always turning up at the pub and when we all went out as a group I couldn't help comparing the two of them. Chris's bad points seemed to magnify themselves and he began to complain that I seemed distracted, as though I had lost interest. Eventually I let our relationship fizzle out.

'I can't believe Vicky hasn't guessed how you feel about Nathan,' Harriet said. She downed her gin and tonic and proceeded to suck the juice out of the lemon she had fished from the bottom of the glass. 'I mean, you've been on edge for weeks now.'

I cringed, feeling utterly ashamed of myself. 'I feel like I must be the most evil woman on earth. I mean, it's the ultimate sin against feminism isn't it? We're supposed to stick up for each other no matter what. Our women friends should always come before men. I can't believe you don't hate me for this.' I was tempted to go and order a large Bacardi to lace my coke and dull the pain in my heart, but I knew I wouldn't be able to do my job properly if I'd drunk more than one or two that night.

Ed took one of my hands and Harriet took the other. 'We love you babes,' Ed said affectionately.

'Of course we do, you're one of my only true friends and I would trust you with my life,' Harriet agreed. 'You know how intolerant of people I am, if I thought you weren't trustworthy I wouldn't be living with you, would I? You've got to stop beating yourself up about this. You can't help being attracted to Nathan and it's not as if you've done anything about it either. You don't even flirt with the guy, which, let's be honest here, is pretty damned controlled of you, you have to admit. The guy is so sexy I'd find it hard not to flirt with him myself,' she said with an uncharacteristically wicked glint in her eye.

'I'll second that,' Ed said, faking a camp accent and licking his lips. 'But you'll get over Nathan, you just need to find someone that matches up to him and you haven't yet.'

I smiled gratefully at him, secretly thinking that no one could match up to Nathan.

'Besides,' Ed whispered, leaning in towards us. 'You know what I think of Rebecca, she's the one that shouldn't be trusted. If you ask me she's a bit of a cow!'

'Ed!' I cried, feeling disloyal for just having this conversation. 'You're about to go to her wedding do, I hope you're going to behave yourself.' I was beginning to worry that he would get drunk and say something out of turn. He did have a habit of being outspoken, a side of his personality that was reflected in his dress sense, I thought, eyeing his loud, short sleeved shirt. 'Besides, you don't know her like I do. She's actually a really selfless person.'

Ed just arched his eyebrows and took a long, thoughtful drag on his cigarette.

I checked my watch. 'Shit! I can't believe the time already. They'll be arriving in an hour and a half!' I leaped up, downing the last of my coke and grabbed my jacket. 'Come on you two,' I cried to Ed and Harriet, who were still lingering over their drinks.

Usually, for a big gig like this, it took two hours

to set up all my equipment, although granted I normally did it on my own. Still, I wanted everything to be perfect tonight and go without a hitch. It would be my way of showing Rebecca and Nathan that I was capable of being big about this, that I could handle them being together and just wanted them to be happy. And it had nothing, absolutely nothing, to do with the fact that I wanted to show Nathan how talented I was and impress him with my collection of fantastic, eclectic music, because that would be wrong – wrong and shallow, which I was not.

When I discussed the play-list for the disco with Nathan and Rebecca, they had chosen maybe a dozen songs that they wanted played, songs that were special to them. The rest, Nathan insisted, was up to me. He knew from all the discussions we'd had about music in the pub that we shared very similar tastes. Rebecca had never been really into music and only asked for 'Chaka Khan' and 'Crazy for You', which Nathan reluctantly agreed to. The song they chose for their first dance together was, 'Kiss Me' by Sixpence None The Richer, a song I had always loved. Nathan wasn't a big fan of traditionally slow love songs, but Rebecca hadn't minded. She told me how Nathan had played it to her one night when she was in the bath and now it always gave her goose bumps. I didn't even want to think about that.

The room where the disco was to take place was huge. I had never been inside the Country Hotel before now and was slightly intimidated by how grand it was. It had been decorated beautifully with large vases of white flowers and white and silver balloons. An enormous banner was draped from the ceiling saying CONGRATULATIONS! and they had left baskets of party poppers on the few scattered tables at the far end of the room. I didn't expect they'd last long. The windows were floor to ceiling and backed onto the hotel gardens. The glass doors were propped open as it was a warm and sunny evening, and a marquee was set up in the grounds with a long table where some hotel staff were busying themselves with the final touches to the most delicious looking buffet food. The room we were in had a high ceiling and a heavily polished wooden floor that didn't help with the acoustics. I clapped my hands and frowned at the echo.

'Don't be so fussy Abby, no one will know the difference,' Ed said, looking up from my cases of records.

'It's really beautiful isn't it?' Harriet said, returning from the toilet. She looked around and whispered, 'They've got all kinds of goodies in the ladies, you've got to go and see. Sweet little bottles of lotions and perfume.'

Ed rubbed his hands, grinning. 'Hey, do you think they do the same in the men's? Maybe they do complimentary cologne.'

Harriet laughed. 'Hey, I walked past the men's and you should just count yourself lucky it doesn't smell as bad as the one in your local. I heard they had to move the tables away from the toilet door because people were worried that if they lit a cigarette the whole place would go up in smoke!'

Ed grabbed Harriet's handbag and held it up to

her crying loudly, 'Ooh, hark at Miss Uptown Girl over there, can't handle a downtown man!'

'Down and out more like,' Harriet joked, ducking as Ed took a playful swing at her.

'Ladies, ladies, please,' I shouted, eyeing my watch for the hundredth time in a matter of minutes. 'We've only got a quarter of an hour before they're supposed to start arriving. Now behave; I'm starting the music.' I selected a Massive Attack record and put it on, setting the volume quite low until the place started filling up. When I looked up I saw Nathan walking through the doors. I froze.

'Hey Abby,' he called out and started nodding along to the beat. 'I love this song.' He walked over to me and I sensed he was ever so slightly drunk. His tie was loosened and the top couple of buttons of his shirt were undone. His jacket was nowhere to be seen and his hair looked as though it had been ruffled half-a-dozen times. He had the look of a loveable puppy dog. He leaned over and kissed me lightly on the cheek. 'I haven't had time to speak to you since I got married, have I? It's such a shame you couldn't come for the meal. Rebecca was disappointed. Still, I guess that's our fault for making you work.'

I hesitated for a moment, my throat felt suddenly parched and my knees were threatening to yield to gravity. I leant forward, holding on to the table, finally managing to say, 'Oh, that's all right. Congratulations by the way.' I gave him my biggest smile. 'Do you feel any different yet?'

'Actually, you know, I think I do. I didn't think

I would but I definitely feel different to the way I did this morning. I don't feel sick anymore.' he laughed. 'And not so terrified. And I suppose I'm a bit drunker.' He grinned at me, rubbing his cheek thoughtfully. 'Seriously though, I definitely feel more respectable, more responsible.' He looked bashful and said quietly, 'And happy, definitely happy.'

My heart flipped. I could see in his eyes how happy he was and it made me want to cry. I looked away from him, picking out the next track to play.

'So, is it OK to let people in now?' Nathan said, gesturing to the door. 'I think they're all dying to let their hair down. Bec's dad gave us the speech of a lifetime . . . in fact he's probably still waffling now, so we're going to need some loud music to drown him out.'

'Hey, if that's what you want, then I'm your girl,' I said and nudged up the volume.

Nathan gave me a wink and wondered off to begin showing people in.

By ten o'clock the guests had had enough of finger food and chit-chat. The luxuriously liberating effects of alcohol had loosened everybody up, putting them in the mood for celebration and the dance floor was packed. I was playing back-to-back, up-tempo disco music and even I was beginning to feel happy as the music lifted me up.

Hundreds of coloured paper streamers were now everywhere you looked. They were draped around people's shoulders, hanging from the many ornate

21

crystal chandeliers and they littered the floor and tables. Every now and again one would flutter onto my decks like ticker tape at a carnival or I'd have to fish the soggy tendrils out of my coke.

Rebecca and Nathan were dancing together, laughing at some friends I didn't recognise who were egging each other on to see who could do the most convincing moonwalk. One of them fell over, knocking into a couple of older women, who looked down at him in disgust and side-stepped away. Rebecca looked at Nathan and burst out laughing. They moved together, dancing to the music, their bodies perfectly in time.

I found the song I had chosen to play next and put it to one side, then picked out Heaven 17's 'Temptation' instead and put it on the turntable ready. When it started I saw Nathan recognise the song and grin at his friends, who danced harder, reaching their arms in the air. Rebecca pulled a face and kissed Nathan, mouthing that she was going to sit that one out. She wandered off to find where she'd left her drink.

If I hadn't felt guilty enough already I was certainly feeling it now. I knew Rebecca wouldn't like that song. I wanted to switch the records back but the deed had already been done. I moved away from the decks, sitting on a stool. What kind of person was I turning into? If this was a film, I would definitely be the baddie. If I was in a pantomime, this would be the bit where I get booed off the stage.

'Boo!' a voice cried behind me and I jumped off my seat, arms poised in a defensive stance. 'Abby

Jenson, what are you acting so edgy about?' Ed said, handing me a glass of champagne.

I sat back down and took the drink, downing half of it with one large swallow.

Ed followed my gaze across the dance floor and saw Nathan dancing with his friends. He raised his eyebrows and looked knowingly at me. 'You're not doing that subliminal messages thing again are you?'

I looked at him quizzically. 'I don't know what you mean!'

'Yes you do, with song lyrics.' He wiggled his body like a pole dancer and looked at Nathan, singing 'Temp-ta-tion' with the music.

I slapped his arm, warning through gritted teeth, 'Stop it Ed, someone will see you.' Then looked guiltily away. 'Of course I'm not, I wouldn't do that.'

'No?' he retorted. 'What about that poor lad that kept coming in the shop trying to chat you up? You put on Beck's "Loser" and Radiohead's "creep" one after the other, hoping it'd give him the message.'

I couldn't help but smile. 'Didn't work though, did it? He bought them both and came back the next day to see if I could recommend anything similar.'

Ed snorted with laughter. 'Then there was the time you took a fancy to that huge guy with the dreadlocks and you put on Depeche Mode's "Stripped" and then just stared at him over the counter, undressing him with your eyes no doubt!'

I laughed with him, finishing the champagne and enjoying the subtle head rush it gave me.

'Hey Abby, how's it going?' a voice cried over the music.

Ed and I turned around and saw Rebecca beaming at us. Her cheeks were rosy from dancing and her hair was starting to wind itself out of it's elaborately pinned style becoming looser and more natural looking than it had been this morning. She looked incredibly feminine.

'I couldn't carry on dancing anymore,' she continued. 'My dress is so heavy I was convinced all that bouncing around was going to pull the front down.' She gave the bodice another tug upwards, looking down to make sure there was nothing on show that shouldn't be.

'You've got nothing to worry about. You look stunning, Bec. If I could look half as good as you when I get married I'll be over the moon,' I said, almost choked with jealousy. It was plain to see why Nathan had fallen for her, what red blooded male could resist?

'Oh Abby.' She squeezed my arm affectionately then began to giggle. 'Can you remember when you went through your "alternative" phase and swore blind you'd get married in a green mini dress and white Doc Marten boots?'

I smiled at the memory. 'You forgot that I insisted I'd turn up on a motorbike.'

Rebecca laughed then shook her head, looking at me. 'I always thought it would be you that married first. You were always planning how it would be and what you would look like,' she mused.

'Thank God I've got a little more refined in my

old age,' I said, fingering my hair, which was now a natural shade of brown. When we were at school it had alternated between a vivid henna red and raven black.

'Always our favourite romantic, weren't you Abby?' Ed said, wrapping his arms around me and giving me a fond squeeze.

I had a sneaking suspicion that Ed thought Rebecca was laughing at me, rather than with me, and was acting protective. He was always defending me when there was really no need. I knew Rebecca was just reminiscing, nothing more. I busied myself with the music, ignoring Ed.

'Hey, that reminds me,' Rebecca said, clicking her fingers. 'I think I'd better warn you that Chris is here.'

I nodded, nonchalantly, without looking up. I had expected Chris to be there. We had, after all, met through Rebecca as they worked in the same department together. Before I glanced up at Ed I could tell exactly what expression he was pulling, and when I checked, there it was. He looked as though he had just bitten into an apple then noticed half a worm wriggling in what was left.

'Don't say it.' I held my hand up to his mouth but he still managed a muffled, 'What, Chris De Bleurgh?'

I tutted and looked back at Rebecca apologetically. 'Ed doesn't like many people, do you Ed?'

He looked like he was going to say something unpleasant then stopped, thinking better of it.

'No, it's all right,' Rebecca said. 'He did kind of

make a bit of a fool of himself over you didn't he? But don't worry, he hasn't talked about you at work in ages, keeps going on about how he's in the market for a new woman.' I heard Ed snort with laughter behind me but Rebecca ignored him. 'In fact, I noticed he has been talking to your friend Harriet a lot tonight.'

Ed cracked up laughing at that point and even I couldn't resist a wry smile. His chances with Harriet were less than minimal.

Rebecca grinned. 'I know, from what I gather of Harriet he hasn't got a hope in hell. He asked me for some tips on her and I said that, in all honesty, she wasn't really his type.'

'She'd have to be blind drunk I reckon,' Ed said.

'Funnily enough, that's more or less what I told him,' Rebecca said. 'Only with a tad more tact. At least I hope I was tactful. God, this whole day has been like a whirlwind. A mad dream. I'm not sure what I've said to anyone. I've only had one glass of champagne as well. I don't know how I'm going to be able to get it together enough for a night of unbridled passion, or is that now bridled passion?' She laughed, holding up her hand and gazing at the band of gold that now adorned it.

One of Nathan's drunk friends wandered up to table and leaned across it towards me, grinning drunkenly. 'Ave you got teen schpirit?' he slurred.

'Have I got "Teen Spirit"?' I repeated, checking I'd heard him correctly.

He nodded, still beaming stupidly.

'I like to think so,' I joked, making Rebecca and Ed

laugh, but Nathan's friend just continued to stare at me blankly. I put him out of his misery and waved a Nirvana record under his nose which perked him up like a dose of smelling salts.

'I'll put it on next,' I said. He turned on his heel, waving his hands triumphantly in the air at Nathan and his friends, who cheered and put their thumbs up at me.

As soon as the unmistakable intro to 'Smells Like Teen Spirit' blasted across the room, a swarm of people flocked to the dance floor. Mostly male, mostly my generation and mostly po-going like lunatics, arms flailing and hair obscuring their faces. I got this reaction every time I put this record on, without exception. It was always a good one for energising a crowd, and I would say, if you discounted Motorhead's 'The Ace of Spades', it was also the most likely to produce injuries.

'Oh my God, he's going to be sick if he keeps that up,' Rebecca said, eyeing Nathan through the heaving crowd with disbelief.

Ed slipped off, unable to resist joining in with the dancing any longer and left me alone with Rebecca.

'So, are you enjoying yourself?' she said. 'I was a bit worried about you not wanting to work tonight.'

'Bec, if anyone else had DJed for you tonight I would have been offended. Besides, you know how I feel about it. It's not work as such, it's what I love and I'm glad to be a part of your day, you know that.'

She smiled at me, satisfied and looked back to the

27

crowd where a fight was threatening to break out between a couple of teenage boys, vying for space to fling themselves in. A middle aged lady in a leather mini skirt waved at Rebecca from the sidelines and beckoned her to come over. 'Duty calls,' she said under her breath and turned my hand over to check the time on my watch. 'Give me about ten minutes then Nathan and I will be off to our hotel. If I can drag him away from the music that is. We'll make a quick speech before we go so I'll give you the nod, okay?' She pecked me on the cheek again then swept off to join the woman that had called her.

'Everybody, can I have your attention please?' Nathan said into the mike.

I faded out the sound, much to everyone's displeasure, but when they saw Nathan by the mike they quietened down and waited expectantly. I noticed Vicky near the back of the room and gave her a wave. She looked tired. Alistair was holding Jack in his arms. He had been asleep for some time and was a picture of trust, slumped against Alistair's chest, arms hanging loosely by his sides.

'Okay, I just wanted to say to you all, thanks for coming and celebrating this special day with us . . .' There was a spattering of applause and whistles. 'Rebecca and I are going to leave you now and retire to our hotel, and no, I'm not going to tell you where it is, thank you very much!' Many of the guests began to laugh suggestively and wolf whistle. Nathan held his hands up to quieten them. 'Yeah, yeah, all right. Before we go, we just wanted to thank one last person as she couldn't be at the meal this afternoon. In fact, as she missed my now-father-in-law's speech, I wrote it all down for her and would just like to go through it all again for Abby's benefit.' There were incredulous groans and objections from almost everyone in the room. Nathan took a roll of paper from behind his back and let it unravel. Reams of paper dropped to the floor and gathered in a heap by his feet. Everybody cracked up laughing and Rebecca's dad cried out, 'Yes, thanks Nathan, very funny!'

'Seriously though. We did just want to thank Abby for doing the honours tonight. I'm sure you'll all agree that she's done us all proud and we do appreciate her hard work, don't we everybody?' There was an eruption of cheers and applause.

I waved modestly to them, an involuntary smile spread across my face.

'Right, with that said, I won't keep you any longer. The taxi's waiting, so have a wonderful night. Keep on dancing, we have an extended licence so no slacking now, I want to hear that you partied hard on our behalf!' Nathan turned to Rebecca and stooped down, sweeping her up and into his arms. Everybody cheered and clapped them, throwing confetti as they passed by, and Nathan carried his giggling new bride through the parting crowd and out of the room.

Having known that Rebecca and Nathan were planning to leave at eleven, I had made up a mini-disc of songs, an hour long, to play after they had left. That way I got to have a good break and mix with friends before the end of the night. Many of the guests had gone home when the happy couple did and only several dozen remained in the huge room I was in. There were probably more in the marquee and gardens but as it was now pitch dark outside, I couldn't see out through the windows any longer.

Vicky and Alistair had taken Jack home when Rebecca and Nathan left. Ed, meanwhile, had been dancing with some girls that looked about twelve, until their parents insisted they go home. He staggered over to me, sweating and panting. 'I'm getting too old for this caper,' he said and wiped his brow with the back of his hand.

'Ed, I haven't seen Harriet for ages, do you know where she is?'

He shrugged and took a cigarette from the top pocket of his shirt and lit it, taking a long, drawn out drag. 'A decent head rush at last,' he said in a cloud of smoke. 'I didn't want to spark up in front of the Connor twins, can't set a bad example can we?' He linked arms with me. 'Come on you, let's find H. I bet she's outside.'

The marquee in the garden was surrounded by huge willow trees and softly lit with lanterns. It looked magical and inviting. I could hear the rhythmic thud of bass from the music I had left playing in the hotel and the disco lights lit up the grass in pulses of red, blue and green, fading as we walked further from the building. Behind the marquee the gardens were shrouded in darkness, yet I could still hear voices emanating out of the night.

Ed and I walked into the marquee. There were only three tables occupied. One by a couple kissing passionately, hands all over each other. A group of men occupied the table beside them, one I recognised as Rebecca's uncle. They were all in their fifties or sixties and were supping pints as though they had all the time in the world. The table at the back was where I found Harriet. She was all alone, slumped forward with her head in her arms and looked half asleep. My heart went out to her. She had never been good at socialising and mixing with others. Nor was she used to going out late. She worked so hard that she rarely had the energy.

'Hey H,' I called, ruffling her hair affectionately. 'Wakey wakey.'

'Wha? Wassup?' she drawled, looking up and squinting at me. 'Abs, hey friend! My bez girl.' She slung a heavy arm around my shoulders and made a badly coordinated attempt at a hug.

'Bloody hell,' Ed said. 'She's pissed!'

'Oh, hi there,' a voice said behind us. I turned around and saw Chris walking over to the table, a glass of wine in each hand. He put a drink in front of Harriet and drew up a chair beside her. Harriet giggled and waved at Chris then guzzled on the wine, spilling half of it down her chin and onto her white shirt.

I tried to breathe calmly and leaned on the table. 'Chris, do you think that perhaps Harriet's had

31

enough to drink now, and might appreciate a coffee or a coke or something instead?'

Chris looked at me, surprised at the tone of my voice, then looked at Harriet, who was giggling and trying to make a face out of a handful of pretzels she'd scooped off the floor.

'Abby, I just got her what she asked for. She's a grown woman you know, I can't see the problem.' He watched Harriet blow raspberries at the face she made then flicked it across the lawn onto the buffet table, doubling over with laughter. 'Anyway, she didn't seem this drunk when I left her. She was fine then. It must have just hit her.'

'Doosh!' Harriet cried, slapping her forehead with the palm of her hand to illustrate Chris's point.

I knelt down beside her, whispering, 'H, you want to come with me? I'm going to pack up soon. I'll take you home in the Scooby.'

'Shcoobydoobydoooooo!' Harriet yelled and looked at me sniggering, then blinked and said seriously, 'OK.'

I helped Harriet up and Ed, who had been standing with his arms folded, staring at Chris with a face like thunder, snapped out of his menacing trance and took Harriet's other arm. We started back towards the hotel.

'Look's like Chris took Rebecca literally when she said he'd have to get Harriet drunk before he had a chance with her,' Ed said with his teeth clenched.

I shook my head, fuming at Chris. I couldn't believe he'd sink that low.

'Chrish's a nish guy,' Harriet said.

'H, he tried to get you pissed so he could jump you, nice guys don't do that,' Ed snapped.

Harriet stopped and looked at Ed in surprise. 'He wanted me?' she said quietly then turned back to look at Chris, who was sitting on the table watching us leave. 'You wanted me?' she shouted back at him incredulously.

Chris looked away embarrassed. The men with the pints turned to look at him and the kissing couple also broke away to see what all the commotion was about.

Harriet pointed a wobbly finger at him and laughed. 'I know all abou' you Chrish, Abby toll me.' I tried to hush her up but she carried on regardless. 'You wear a black leaver thong coz you wanna be awl rock n' roll and Abby sez you got too much bum hair n she dumped you coz you wanted to do it in funt of uh mirror an she did'n like seein your bairy hare, hairy bare bum bouncin.'

At that point I was able to wrestle Harriet out of the marquee, leaving Chris staring after us, his face flaming red as the guests stared at him curiously.

Ed was laughing so hard he had to wipe a tear from his cheek. 'I can't believe you never told me that!' he said, gulping for breath.

# CHAPTER THREE

The next morning I woke up squinty-eyed as sun streamed through the gaps in my curtains, illuminating the room with beams of dusty light. For a fraction of a second my mood sank at the memory of Nathan vowing his heart to one of my oldest friends. Then I remembered the resolution I had decided on after hours of sitting up late that night, going over old ground. Today was the beginning of a new me. Nathan was gone, off limits, trespassing punishable by complete social alienation. It was time to accept this and put Nathan down as one of the great untouchables, just as I did with George Michael when he announced to the world he was gay. I had done it before and I could do it again. It was time to enjoy my search for a new man.

In the manner of a woman with a new sense of purpose, I threw back my duvet cover and leaped out of bed. I drew my curtains, reeled backwards, half blinded, then returned to the window, my eyes gradually adjusting to the sunshine. I opened the window wide and leaned out, taking in a lungful of the dewy morning air. Already there were couples walking dogs on the green outside the house and what looked like a group of male students were kicking a football in the distance. I toyed with the idea of putting on some running shoes and jogging by, but quickly decided that the chances of humiliation outweighed the possibility of pulling a student by quite a majority. I was due to go over to dad's house for Sunday lunch and, remembering the state Harriet was in last night, I figured I'd better go and check on her before I went out. I quickly got washed and dressed then stepped out of my flat and down the stairs to Harriet's house.

Harriet had bought her house when she earned herself a hefty bonus and promotion at the marketing agency she worked for. She came up with a catchy slogan that secured a contract with the South West tourism board to promote Bristol to young people on their new website. It was a huge campaign and she played a significant role in its success, but, unfortunately for Harriet, the managing director was a friend of her dad and several of Harriet's colleges saw her early promotion almost as a form of nepotism. There was jealousy amongst the staff she left behind, but Harriet was tough and worked hard, always trying to prove herself. She didn't care what they thought of her, she knew she deserved it and the house she loved more than made up for any atmosphere at work.

Harriet bought her 'white-fronted, three-storey, Georgian mid-terrace, with imaginative decor, fabulous outlook to the front and enchanting garden to the rear', seven years ago, when house prices in

Clifton were simply *high*, rather than the *highly laughable* they had now become. It had turned out to need more work than she could ever dream of taking on herself. The agent had been right about the outlook, but the enchanting garden's lawn was waist height and if you tried to wade through it you would step on discarded beer cans, bottles of Thunderbird and a whole plethora of rotten unmentionables. The house had previously been split up and rented to students who appeared to have partied hard and spent the rest of their time painting rooms black, chipping holes in the plasterwork and blocking up the plumbing with old pants. But Harriet hadn't been phased by what she called 'small cosmetic glitches' and talked at length about her new favourite word, 'potential'. She split off the third storey, insisting that she rent it to me for a modest price and had been transforming the house ever since. She had made a wise investment and despite not being finished yet, the house was worth twice what she paid for it. She lived in one of the most desirable areas of Bristol and, fortunately for me, I couldn't imagine that she would ever want to leave.

I tiptoed downstairs and knocked quietly on her bedroom door. No answer. I pushed it open and peeped into the room, her bed was unmade and empty. There was a crash and a groan from downstairs and I went down to investigate.

Harriet was kneeling on the floor, picking up shards of broken glass and collecting them in a cereal bowl, as spilt milk formed a steadily growing puddle on the lino. She looked up as I walked in and groaned again. 'How on earth could I have let myself get that drunk,' she said, putting the bowl on the kitchen table. She leant over the puddle to fetch some kitchen towel to mop it up with.

'Let me help you with that,' I said. I took the paper towels from her, sat her down at the table then started mopping up the mess. 'How are you feeling this morning?'

She shook her head slowly. 'I was sick in the shower. I've decided they don't make plug holes big enough,' she said, looking as though she might be sick again.

'Poor thing.' I threw the soggy kitchen towel in the bin and wandered over to the kettle. 'Do you want me to make you a drink?'

'Coffee, no sugar. And you'd better make it black,' she said, nodding to where the milk had spilled.

'Flat coke's excellent for hangovers.'

She looked at me grimly and held up a limp hand. 'Don't mention food or drink of any description again, please. Coffee will do just fine.'

I put the kettle on and busied myself making drinks.

'So, exactly what did I do?' Harriet said eventually.

'Can't you remember?'

'No.'

'Nothing at all?'

'Nothing after picking at the buffet food with Rebecca's granny.'

'Can't you remember talking to Chris then?'

'Chris who?' she said, taking her head out of her hands and looking at me.

'Chris, my ex of course.'

'Oh, *Chris* Chris. Oh dear, he was there was he? I hope he didn't go making another scene over you again.'

I set Harriet's coffee in front of her and sat down opposite. 'Not exactly, no. I think he might finally be over me now.'

'Actually, I think I vaguely recall him buying me a drink.' She thought for a moment then smiled, remembering. 'Yes, I'm sure it was him. Can't remember past that though.'

That was probably a good thing, I thought, but said, 'I haven't seen you drunk like that in ages. It's not like you.' Harriet was always very self-controlled and never normally drank more than a glass or two of wine when we went out. I often wished she'd drink more so that I wouldn't look so self-indulgent in comparison. Ed once said I'd probably drink four-star petrol if it came with ice and a slice. I wouldn't have said I was quite that bad, but next to Harriet I was a raging wino.

She rubbed her eyes with the sleeve of her checked pyjamas. 'Are you going over to your dad's house today?'

I nodded. 'We're going to the pub for lunch, then I promised Vicky I would call in at her place for a post-wedding dissection.' I grimaced at the thought. I wanted to pretend it never happened and just get on with the future, but I knew if it had been anybody else's wedding we would have enjoyed going over it afterwards. I didn't want to make her suspicious.

'For goodness sake Abby. Vicky is one of your best friends, why don't you tell her how you feel about Nathan?'

'Look,' I said, putting my drink down on the table. 'Vicky wouldn't understand. She's very happily married. Happily married people don't empathise with women that go for "taken" men.'

'You're hardly "going" for Nathan though are you? You make yourself sound like some kind of home-wrecker, and you know you're nothing like that.'

I shrugged. 'Well, maybe, but Vicky's quite traditional about this sort of thing. I couldn't bear it if she judged me. And besides, she sees Rebecca more than I do, I don't want to put her in an awkward position. At least if she doesn't know and Rebecca quizzes her she can plausibly deny it.'

Harriet blew on her coffee. 'Well, it's your choice, but I think she'd be hurt that you're not confiding in her.'

'Hey, there's nothing to confide. It's finished now. Nathan's gone. I think I've just taken this "you always want what you can't have" thing a little too far. It's time I started looking forward. I'm on the hunt for a soul mate,' I said, raising my eyebrows and grinning.

Harriet looked stony faced at me. 'Are you quoting song lyrics again? Because you're beginning to sound like James Brown.'

I laughed and grabbed a biscuit from the tin on the table and got up to go.

After I had said goodbye to Harriet I skipped out of the house to the Scooby. The Scooby had been aptly named by Ed, who was convinced it resembled Fred and Daphne's 'Mystery Machine' in Scooby Doo. It was originally a rusty white transit van that I had bought cheaply and decorated myself. I had sprayed it blue and painted the side panels with bright flowers. In the middle of the panels I had written ABBY J . . . FOR YOUR PERFECT DAY with my telephone number underneath. Ed insisted that I write MOBILE DJ on the back doors in case people fell under the false impression that I was a flower shop delivery girl or something similar. Dad helped me to patch up the rust and get it to a roadworthy condition, and although it has trouble chugging up the steep hills that surround Clifton, it has been with me since the beginning. Give something a name and a sentimentality develops; that was certainly true of my Scooby.

I climbed in, turned up the radio, and set off for dad's house.

Dad lives just a mile away, in the same house I was born and brought up in. It was eerie going back to a place so steeped in memories, most good, some terrible. I often wished that dad would move on, find himself a place that wouldn't be a persistent reminder of what he had prematurely lost. I could never bring myself to tell him this though, he seemed happy enough to stay, comforted by his memories of my mother.

There was no answer at the door so I wandered around to the back garden, calling out to him. He wasn't in the shed or the greenhouse so I tried the backdoor and found it unlocked. The house was silent, which was unusual for dad. I had inherited my love of music from him, despite our tastes being worlds apart. He always had a record playing if he was in the house, or he listened to the world service on an old Bakelite radio upstairs. He was too young to remember the war in a lot of detail, but still loved wartime tunes by the likes of Glenn Miller or Vera Lynn, and if he wasn't sitting in his old armchair listening to these, then it would inevitably be Dixieland and Ragtime jazz.

'Dad!' I called out in the hallway, my voice sounding strangely isolated in a house that was usually swinging with old time rhythm and blues.

'Up here,' Dad called with a voice that sounded far away. I breathed out with relief, realising that my heart had quickened with fear. 'I'm in the loft,' he called again.

When I found him, he was sitting on the ledge of the loft hatch, his slippered feet dangling through the ceiling on the landing. There were dusty old boxes and bin bags piled up on the floor outside my old bedroom. 'Hello love, sorry, I lost track of time. I'll finish in a minute.' He swung out, feeling for the ladder with his feet.

'Careful!' I cried, holding the ladder for him as he climbed unsteadily down, holding a shoebox under one arm.

'Abby, you fuss too much. I am not a doddering

41

old biddy yet you know,' he said, looking at me with wise amusement. He was right, I did worry unnecessarily about him; after losing my mother, dad's own mortality seemed all the more real to me.

'What are you up to anyway? What is all this stuff?'

'Oh, it's mainly just things of your mother's; clothes, jewellery, books. All the bits I hated to part with. I put them in the loft for safe keeping, but they were appealing on the radio this morning for those poor families in Russia, where the earthquake was. Most of them have only got the clothes they're standing up in.' He wandered into my bedroom where there were several more bags and sat down on a desk chair, leaning over to start sorting through the bag closest to him. 'Anyway, I got to thinking how your mum was always so good at giving to charities. Every year she'd clear out your cupboards and give the things you'd grown out of to the Sally Army. She could have sold a lot of it but she was never keen. She always said we had so much given to us when you were a baby, it was only right to pass it on. She wouldn't have liked the thought of all this stuff going to waste up there.'

I stared at him, aghast, as he took out mum's old clothes and started to sort them into piles. I snatched up a purple sweatshirt that he discarded. 'What are you going to do with this?'

'I think that ought to go in the bin, don't you? It's looking a bit too raggedy.'

'Mum used to do the gardening in this.'

'Exactly.' He added a couple of T-shirts and a

42

ripped pair of jeans to the pile destined for the bin.

'Dad!' I gathered them all up, holding them to my chest. I couldn't believe he was being so callous. I held the clothes close to me and buried my face in them, breathing in the scent. I was expecting to catch a hint of mum's perfume but instead all I got was old mothballs and the characteristic damp, musty smell that lofts always exude.

Dad looked at me sadly. 'Abby, those things have been sitting in the loft for over two years now. *Two years,*' he emphasised. 'That's too long. I've never got them down and looked at them, they're no good to us now . . . they're just clothes. They'll freshen up in the wash, some of them, but the others . . . I should get rid of them now. I have my memories, I have photos, her special things, but these . . .' He picked up another bin liner and showed me the colourful fabric inside. 'They're just clothes Abby.'

We sat staring at each other for a moment. Dad was beseeching me with his eyes, asking me to be reasonable, to allow him to do this.

'OK,' I said eventually. 'I think I'll wait downstairs though, put the kettle on. We can have a brew before we go to the pub.'

It was pandemonium at Vicky's house when I turned up later that afternoon. Some of Jack's friends were over and they were all playing in the garden, fighting with the water from Clarice's paddling pool. Clarice was standing in the pool, naked, with her hair hanging in bedraggled bunches. She was crying as she watched the boys steal her water, helpless to do anything about it.

'Boys, come on now, that's enough,' Vicky said, her voice trailing off. I could tell she had been trying to keep the peace all afternoon and was suffering from 'negotiation fatigue'. This is what Vicky described as that end of the day feeling where you've tried so hard to stay calm, and ended up so exhausted by it all that you fight the urge to dump their dinner on their heads and order them to 'bugger off to bed'. Of course, Vicky assured me, she would never do that, but it didn't stop the urge from boiling inside her on those particularly long days. Vicky picked up a towel from the back of a garden chair and wrapped her daughter in it, rubbing her back to get her warm again. Clarice giggled and hunched over, feeling suddenly ticklish.

'Come on then lads, time to go home,' Alistair called through the living room window.

'Oh, Dad, can't they stay a bit longer?' Jack said, his water pistol suspended in the air, aiming towards his smaller, ginger-haired friend.

'No, come on now, I told David's parents I'd bring him home by six.'

'What's the time?' Jack said, always astute in his thinking.

'Nearly six,' Alistair said, clearly taking advantage of the fact that his son was not able to tell the time well enough to contradict him. The tone of his dad's voice suggested to Jack that it was pointless arguing and so the boys trooped dejectedly back into the house.

Vicky couldn't hide her relief as she said goodbye to them and turned to me, grinning. 'Thank God,' she whispered. 'I could have throttled those little monkeys if they'd stayed much longer.'

'Ooo ooo ooo,' Clarice cried, jumping out of her towel and hopping around in the garden, delighted that she was making us both laugh. She stood on the lawn, her legs apart, and, grinning broadly at us, proceeded to wee on the grass.

Vicky groaned. 'Clary, that's naughty. Just because your daddy does it, doesn't make it right,' she joked, looking cheekily at me and got up to take Clarice into the house.

When Clarice had finally been bathed and tucked into bed, radiating warmth and fragrance, Vicky and I settled in the living room with a bottle of wine. Their house was the other side of Clifton Bridge to mine, and only a short walk away. I often left the Scooby outside their house and walked back so Vicky and I could enjoy a drink. If Alistair was around he would insist on walking me home, but I never minded going alone. I enjoyed those quiet, alchoholically hazy moments where I would lean on the railings of the bridge and look across the deep wooded valley that cut dramatically between our houses, the lights of the city glittering nearby. It cleared my head, gave me a sense of perspective.

Visiting Vicky and Alistair's was always a treat for me. Their house is noisy and cluttered to the point of disorientation, but it is a reassuring chaos, a Kansas City whirlwind that picks you up, sucks you in and transports you to the heart of their family. I loved the fact that if I ever accidentally called around during their mealtime, they would invite me to their table, where I would be presented with a plate and a glass of whatever they were having. If I called when they were putting the kids to bed I would be roped in to brushing teeth and reading stories. If they were in the middle of a family feud they would inevitably fight to get me on-side until they all fell about laughing at the look of torn anguish on my face. They had everything I always wanted for myself and I often wondered impatiently when it would be my turn. At least I could console myself by knowing that Vicky and Alistair thought of me as a part of their own family, and at their house, there was definitely no place like home.

The living room window was open and the air resonated with the punchy sounds of Alistair and Jack kicking a ball in the garden as they laughed and cheered each other on. Vicky was curled up in an armchair, her feet tucked up under her bottom. She hugged a glass of wine to her as though it was a hot water bottle on a chilly winter night. 'Yes, it was a lovely night wasn't it?' she said, carrying on the conversation we had started whilst Clarice was splashing in the bath. 'They did really well to get everything organised so quickly, Rebecca is so efficient. God, remember the hassle Alistair and I went through? We planned our wedding for well over a year.' Vicky smiled at her wedding photograph that sat on their mantelpiece. 'Thinking about it, I don't blame them for doing it quickly, not having all the build up and anticipation. It just ends up getting stressful.'

'That's Nathan to a tee though isn't it? A laid-back type. In fact I'm surprised he agreed to wear the full three piece. I think if he'd had his way he would have got married on a beach in a pair of shorts.'

'I know what you mean,' Vicky said. 'But I think that Rebecca's parents wanted her to have a traditional day. They've always been quite old fashioned haven't they? The kind of people that take occasions very seriously. Remember going to their house at Christmas?' She laughed to herself. 'They used to have a separate seasonal dinner service, didn't they? All their dishes and mugs had holly on them. God, I'm only surprised they let Rebecca get away with such a simple do. Although what surprises me even more is that she agreed to get married in the first place. If only her parents knew what a secret rebel she was really. Sneaking a bag of make-up and a change of clothes to school then changing in the loos. And all the boyfriends she had, especially at university. I never saw her as the marrying type.'

I sighed into my glass. 'I don't know. Nathan was special for all of us at one time. He was like the ultimate catch. Everyone wanted to know him. You know Rebecca, she's always been competitive. She was given the opportunity to fulfil a dream we all shared. I'm not at all surprised she went for it. They make a gorgeous couple.' I said this, not sure if I really believed it. I couldn't help thinking that Rebecca was too fiery for Nathan, too ambitious.

Vicky pulled a face. 'If I'm being completely honest, Abby. Don't tell anyone I said this but I'm surprised he didn't go for you. You're so alike. Always chatting away about music, so easy with each other.'

I stared out the window. 'Nah, I could never compete with Rebecca, and besides, Nat and I are like brother and sister now.'

The truth was, I never would have had a chance with Nathan anyway. Rebecca hadn't even told us who she was seeing until they were securely in love. She had phoned Vicky and I up one day, telling us about a guy that had chatted her up the night before. How they had stayed at the pub till they were thrown out and had agreed to meet up the next day. She sounded exhilarated, thrilled that he had chatted her up, which was unusual for Rebecca, she was so used to being approached by men that she didn't usually take it as a compliment, more as a matter-of-fact. But this time Rebecca sounded keen. Really keen. She wouldn't tell us his name and was cagey about who he was, only saying that she wanted to surprise us, hinting that we would be 'shocked'. When Vicky and I talked about it, we speculated that it must be someone famous. Maybe a member of the cast of *Holby City* who we had seen out drinking in Bristol several times before.

It took a month for Rebecca to finally agree to let us meet him, by which time they were a couple. We all arranged to meet at a pub in town. Rebecca had relished keeping us in the dark for so long. She loved to shock people, loved the drama. She couldn't wait to see our faces.

When he walked in I didn't recognise him immediately. I had held on to the image of him at school, of him as a boy. The man that stood in front of me in the smoky pub was very much a man. He was broad shouldered and muscular, his hair was shorter and he had a slight stubble on his chin. But he was still handsome, with the same sculpted jaw line, soulful hazel eyes and full, kissable lips.

When I realised that he was the man Rebecca had told us about, the one she had fallen in love with, I was lost for words. I wanted to run away and hide but I was rooted to the spot.

Vicky had saved me from speaking and cleared the air straightaway by saying, 'Nathan! The one we used to follow around at school? How embarrassing! Were we sad then or what?' She cracked up laughing and we all followed her lead, laughing with relief that the subject had been brought up and dismissed so quickly.

We spent the rest of the evening reminiscing about our school days, about teachers and school friends, wondering where everyone was now. Nathan was charming and sweet, commenting on how much we had all changed, how he never would have recognised us. I was glad that he didn't equate us with the lovesick girls that had followed him around at school, it was embarrassing enough as it was.

I sat watching him as he talked, hating Rebecca for doing this to me, hating the way she was looking at him and just praying that their relationship would go the same way as all her others. I could barely speak. It was too much of a shock. I excused myself early and went back to the flat where I reminisced alone, wallowing in melancholy music as the image of Nathan in the pub played over and over in my mind.

'Hey, they'll be back from their honeymoon next week won't they?' Vicky said, breaking my chain of thought. 'I bet Rebecca will want us to get together and catch up.'

I smiled then changed the subject, telling Vicky what had happened at my dad's house.

'Aren't you pleased for him?' she said later. 'I mean you always worried about him didn't you? You thought he would never get over your mum, and it can't be good for him to wallow in the past like that. At last he sounds like he's looking forward again. It's a positive thing.' She smiled kindly at me and I looked away, feeling mean.

'I know. It was just a surprise seeing all mum's stuff. It brought it all back. And time has gone so quickly. Two years have flown by and sometimes it feels like it only happened yesterday.'

'It must be hard.'

I nodded.

'I remember when you first told me your mum was sick, that summer. I couldn't believe how well you handled it. I think I would have gone to pieces. You know, when you're seventeen you think you're just about ready for anything, that you're as adult and free as it's possible to be. We were all set for Uni, ready to take on the world. Then that happened and it really made me think, made me realise how naïve I still was. And how much I needed my parents. I could never have dealt with it the way you did. You were amazing, the way you took control. You were so strong.'

'I had to be, I suppose,' I said, shrugging.

Vicky and I had talked about my mother many times and it didn't hurt so much now; it had become an integral part of my life that I didn't know any different from. The day my mum got sick I changed, I no longer saw the world through young eyes. From that day on I felt like an adult; I had responsibilities, I was forced to face a harsh reality and I knew I couldn't be shielded from it. I realised that I couldn't change the future, I couldn't make her well again, but I could deal with it a lot better if I recreated some normality in my life; a routine, a sense of stability – a distraction.

Besides, she didn't seem seriously ill at first. She had been losing weight for months, but it was such a slow and gradual change that took a while to notice. She was tired a lot. I think that was what first concerned me, because she had always been so full of energy. I had never known her sleep in the afternoon before or have to be coaxed out of bed on a Saturday morning. Looking back I sometimes think I should have realised sooner, but it just never occurred to me that she could ever be anything other than full of life.

By the time the lymphoma had been diagnosed it

was the summer that I was set to go to university. She was upset when I deferred and eventually gave up my place, begging me to reconsider. I wanted to go, to make her happy, but I just couldn't leave. The thought of her getting worse was scary. Mum was always supposed to be there for me. I decided instead, that I would always be there for her.

She needed chemotherapy, which made her ill and caused her to lose her hair. It was a frightening time. She seemed tiny all of a sudden, and frail. But she refused to let it get her down. Her determination was what kept dad and I going during the years of treatment and tests. But even when she went into remission I couldn't relax. I had read about the survival rates, the possibility of the cancer returning and I spent as much time with her as possible, watching her constantly for signs of illness. Five years on and I still hadn't completely relaxed my guard, but mum was adamant that she was fine, better than ever. She hated the medical intervention and being seen as a patient. I often wondered if she hid her discomfort, pretending to feel better than she really did.

Then, one week in January, not long after Christmas, she seemed to be declining rapidly. She was pale and washed out, her sparkle had gone. She protested at first, saying that Christmas had just taken a lot out of her and the weather wasn't helping. She wouldn't see a doctor until dad couldn't stand it any longer and called one to the house.

She was in hospital for three days. The tests showed up an aggressive form of leukaemia that was too advanced to respond to treatment. Seventy-two hours later she was gone. I received the phone call from dad late in the night. I had gone home to get some rest and also to give mum and dad some time alone together. She passed away in his arms, he told me weakly.

I stood holding the phone, hearing his words, my body rigid and defensive as if not wanting to let the news in. I didn't cry at first, I was numb. I didn't cry until I saw Ed, late the next day. The sadness he felt for me was so evident in his eyes, I couldn't block it out any longer. Ed understood better than anyone how I was feeling and without him to confide in I think it would have taken me a lot longer to get over my mother.

'So, you're not upset about your dad then?' Vicky asked.

'No, no. Of course not. More than anything I want him to be happy. He deserves that. It just made me think that's all. He's moving on . . . *everyone*'s moving on . . . life is changing, yet I've been doing the same thing since I gave up Uni. I have a teenage boy's job, I'm still single, and I work in someone else's shop. I'm hardly a candidate for an "achiever of the year" award, am I? If mum could see me now I think she'd be disappointed.'

'Oh Abby, you're too hard on yourself. You love your job, and Ed's shop, you're in your element being surrounded by music all the time.'

'Of course I love my job. I've never been the ambitious type,' I joked. 'But, don't you ever get

moments where you wonder where you're headed
. . . what's your purpose in life?'

'Oh, I get those all right,' Vicky said, nodding
furiously. 'Usually when I'm scrubbing sick off the
living room carpet, or looking out the bedroom
window, watching everyone go off to work, while
Clarice is trying to make a flag with a pair of my
knickers and the cat's tail.'

I laughed. 'Well, maybe that's how I feel at the
moment. I started off this morning excited about
the future, but somehow seeing dad just brought
me back to reality, and now, the more I think about
it, the more daunted I become.'

# CHAPTER FOUR

I was leaning on the counter, humming to the Carpenters CD when Ed marched up to the hi-fi and switched it off abruptly. 'Abby, it's time you stopped being miserable,' he said, replacing the CD with one he had been hiding behind his back.

'I'm not being miserable!' I protested.

He waved the Carpenters CD at me. 'I know you're feeling miserable because whenever you are, you always play this stuff and get all melancholy.'

He was right of course. The Carpenters had been my mum's favourite group. Every Sunday morning when Dad was in the living room listening to jazz or show tunes, she would always be in the kitchen, cooking Sunday lunch and singing along with Karen Carpenter with a singing voice I wish I'd inherited. I think I must be one of the only people who cries when listening to 'Calling Occupants of Interplanetary Craft'.

The infectious rhythm of Supergrass's, 'Alright' suddenly blasted out into the back room of Ed's shop. He executed a perfect Madness-style walk between the rows of LPs and I couldn't help but laugh at how daft he looked.

'You're so good at that it's actually scary,' I joked, laughing even louder when a man walked into the room, raised his eyebrows at Ed, then deftly avoided the aisle Ed was in, opting instead to riffle through the bargain section, hidden in the corner.

The back room of Little Beat was mostly devoted to second-hand vinyl, although several years ago, Ed had grudgingly agreed to allow us to buy and sell second-hand CDs as well. The front room of the shop was devoted to chart and current music. Ed and I could mainly be found in the back room, where we weren't required to promote the 'next big thing' and serve the queues of teenagers, clutching the latest boy band offering with eager fingers. Ed hired students and school leavers for that particular job. Not that we are music snobs – God forbid. You couldn't be a mobile DJ if you were a true music snob. It would be impossible, like selling your soul to the devil. There are too many requests for the likes of Celine Dion, Wet Wet Wet, Boyzone and countless other populist pop tunes for a music snob to be able to stomach. I don't sneer at 'manu-factured' groups and make no apology for playing the Spice Girls second album whilst driving to gigs in the Scooby. Although, like most music lovers, I prefer the sound of vinyl to CD. Anybody with a tuned ear could recognise that records sound better, but I don't think CDs are only fit to be used as coasters (Ed's opinion) and look down on those who disagree. I don't ridicule midi-systems or believe them to have offered as much to the appreciation of 'real' music as the bread bin (also

Ed's opinion). I don't think you *need* to know that Madness weren't the first people to sing 'It Must Be Love', or that to say you love The Who, for example, you would need to know that Jimmy Page played lead guitar on the studio version of 'I Can't Explain', and own every foreign import and unreleased demo they ever made. I don't even think you need to know who the hell Jimmy Page is. These are facts that music snobs love to know, it gives them a misjudged feeling of superiority over those who don't. Fortunately, despite being a self confessed hi-fi snob, Ed could never be a music snob, he wasn't selective or anal enough, but he had plenty of customers frequenting the back room of his shop that were. Ed may not share their taste or expanse of trivia but his passion and willingness to launch into an opinionated tirade gained him the respect of these people, whether he liked it or not.

'Stop staring at him,' I whispered to Ed, who was hovering behind the counter under the pretext of leafing through a catalogue. He looked flustered at having been sussed.

'I can't help it, he's sexy.'

I checked out the man still lurking in the corner of the room to see if there was something I had missed. He looked about the same age as me and maybe an inch shorter. He was scruffy, and I could tell by his body language that he was awkward, lacking in confidence. He had a few days growth of stubble which he scratched absently at as he leafed through the records. 'He looks as though he needs a decent meal.'

'He needs a decent something . . .' Ed said, raising an eyebrow and smiling devilishly.

'Shhh, he'll hear you,' I said, trying to look stern but finding it too much effort.

I secretly liked it when Ed checked out guys. I'm not too sure why this would be, and often questioned my own motives. I didn't believe it to be a perversion on my part. Maybe I liked having a fellow conspirator, someone to talk to with a unique take on men that I couldn't get from my girlfriends. Or maybe it was the fact that whenever Ed showed an interest in someone, a hint of vulnerability showed through the surface of his high volume façade. Ed was the most wonderful, devoted friend you could wish for. He was jolly and colourful, with an enthusiasm usually only reserved for canines and the under tens. Kids were drawn to him, he could have old ladies clutching his arm and crying with laughter and had such a magnetism with women you could dress him up in a tux and call him 'Bond'. He was gorgeous, although not in the classic sense that Nathan was. He was wiry rather than butch, but he still looked fit. He had the body of someone that practises martial arts, in that there wasn't an ounce of unnecessary fat on him, and his muscles were well defined but not obvious. His thick scruffy hair reminded me of a little boy and there was often a sparkle in his blue eyes, hinting at his wicked sense of humour. They won most people over, yet he seemed to make some men nervous, and he knew it. Hence the vulnerability; well disguised, but there, detectable only to those close to him.

Ed shot me a wide-eyed look of panic when the man he had been watching put down the battered Erasure's *Innocence* album and, after a brief hunt through the Indie A-D section, approached the counter.

'Can I help you?' I said, beating Ed to it by a fraction of a second.

The guy took hold of the strap of the record bag that he wore diagonally across his chest and lifted it over his head. As he did so, the hood of his top, that was poking out from under his denim jacket, was picked up by the bag's wide strap and was momentarily pulled up over his head, giving him an almost boyish appearance; like a sweet little urchin, protecting himself from the cold. He pushed it back, embarrassed.

I looked at Ed, who had a hand placed close to his heart and his eyes crinkled up as if to say, 'Oh, bless him.'

'You buy old records don't you?' he checked, his hand on the bag, ready to present us with something. I nodded and Ed leaned over the counter, intrigued. The guy pulled out a pristine copy of Pink Floyd's, *The Wall*.

'Jesus!' Ed whistled, taking it off him and turning it over in his hands. 'There's no writing on this.'

The guy looked around the room, then shrugged at Ed, his face a picture of 'it wasn't me' innocence.

'That's a good thing, means it's an original.' He took one of the records out of its sleeve and inspected it, did the same with the other, then checked inside the cover. 'Ha! Look at that,' he said, pointing inside and holding it right under my nose. I spotted an old shop sticker.

'Oh yeah, look. Ha ha, look at the funny Woolworths sticker, look at the way it's written, it looks ancient.'

'Not that, look at the numbers. Twelve, twelve, seventy-nine. Fucking hell, you can't sell this, are you fucking nuts?'

'Here we go again,' I muttered, rolling my eyes at the poor guy who was about to get the full force of Ed's passion for music right between the eyes.

'This is a fucking classic. It's a work of the *highest* genius. Honestly, this—' he tapped the record, holding it as though it were a divine offering '—THIS, is one of the greatest stories ever told. A story of psychological barriers, neurosis, death, sex, mental breakdown, you can't *fail* to be touched by this.' He waved the album under the nose of his captive audience.

His audience just blinked regretfully, his eyes as wide and round as dinner plates.

'Did you listen to "Mother"?'

The audience nodded his head, obviously growing increasingly concerned.

'Did you cry?'

Audience shook his head like a child admitting to his mother that he hadn't wiped his bottom after visiting the toilet and braced himself for another tirade.

'You're telling me you listened to "Mother" and you failed to cry?'

Audience blinked six times in quick succession.

Ed looked up to the ceiling and scratched his head

in bewilderment. There was a long pause in which I noticed that Ed was beginning to gain some interest from the other people in the shop. A small handful of customers were now gathered in the back room, obviously eager to know what he would say next, yet mindful not to gain eye contact in case they got dragged into the discussion. Ed breathed slowly and deliberately then leaned on the counter and spoke with a renewed sense of calm and charity. 'OK, not to worry,' he said gently.

Audience physically relaxed and smiled slightly.

'You obviously haven't listened to it *properly*. For an album of this . . . *calibre*, it's pretty essential that you hear it how it was intended. What's your system like?'

Audience, after stuttering slightly, found his voice and said, 'I've got a Linn Sondek record player, a Mission Cyrus II amp and Mission 770 Freedom speakers.' A momentary hint of pride flickered in his eyes then faded when he saw Ed's reaction.

Ed looked as though he had just been slapped and sucked his cheeks in. 'But you didn't listen to it on that right?'

Audience nodded then whispered, 'I wasn't really all that . . . keen.' His face was colouring before my eyes.

'*Keen*?' Ed repeated, unable to comprehend this statement.

Audience looked as though he was about to pee his pants and made an attempt to recover his album from Ed's grasp. Ed, now sensing all eyes on him, anticipating his next move, paced the length of the counter, twice, then turned to the guy and said quietly, 'I'm not going to buy this from you, not because I don't want it—' he snuck another peak at the inside cover '—but because I *love* it. I have faith in you . . . you've got a good set up, you've got the potential to have great taste. I know you'll do the right thing . . . you just haven't given it a chance. You've got to invest in it, *feel* it, and it'll pay you back time and again.' He handed the album back reverently, and his audience took it, grateful to be pardoned. I thought I heard him whisper a meek 'sorry' before he scurried away.

'And you'd better not go straight to Select-A-Disc and sell it to them. I'll check, you know!' Ed shouted after him. The people in the shop busied themselves, making like nothing had just happened. I was going to point out that Ed would find it hard to check if Select-A-Disk had bought it, since he had been banned for life just two months earlier, but I didn't think it was quite the right time. Ed sat back on a stool, shaking his head in disbelief. 'Fucking hell Abby,' he said, hunting for a cigarette in the pocket of the coat that hung on the wall beside him. 'What's happening to our generation? Couldn't you just fucking weep for them?'

Ed was not his usual self for the rest of the morning. He wandered about quietly, dealing with customers with the minimum verbal exchange. I knew better than to try and jolly him out of it. I knew Ed too well. He was sensitive and introspective. Music was his life support, and his favourite albums were loved like substitute babies. The guy that had brought in Pink Floyd's *The Wall* had committed a heinous crime in Ed's eyes. It was like someone telling Vicky that her children would never amount to much. It's got to hurt. I let him work in relative peace and by lunchtime he was beginning to perk up again. He shut the till drawer hard and leaned against it, letting out a drawn out sigh. 'If I don't have a coffee and a bacon sandwich soon I'll just die right here on the counter,' he said, smiling at me and batting his eyelids.

'No way! I got them last time, remember?' I wagged a finger at him. 'And don't you look at me like that. Why don't you ask Tasha or Pete, I bet they'd like a break from the front counter?'

'Yeah, and they'll bump into about fourteen of their student friends on the way, have fourteen conversations about going out and which pub they'll meet up in, say "mad" and "sorted" about three hundred times and, by the time they get back, my sandwich would be smelling like a pigs armpit.'

'Do pigs have armpits?' I asked.

Ed shook his head at me then grabbed his coat. 'I'll get it myself. Do you want your usual?'

I nodded, smiling triumphantly and waved as he walked through the archway to ask Tasha and Pete what they wanted.

Five minutes after Ed had left Vicky phoned.

'Hey Vic, how are you?' I said, glad of the distraction.

'Good, good,' she said. 'Well, bored actually. Looking forward to Jack going back to school, wishing I was still on holiday, fed up of treading on Lego . . . it bloody hurts that does. My life isn't just humdrum you know, it's become mumdrum!'

'Poor love,' I said, wondering how on earth Vicky managed to stay so consistently calm. She never seemed to get a moment's peace. 'Aren't you doing anything exciting today then?'

'Nope. Just taking Jack to his friend Robin's house, then taking Clarice to a birthday party, sneaking off to do some food shopping – if Clary will let me – picking her up again, then picking up Jack, feeding them both, dropping Jack off for a karate lesson . . . I won't continue! I've got slimming class tonight, Alistair's working late and I doubt I'll have a chance to have a shower first and my hair will smell of cooking oil because I promised Jack he could have chips for tea and all the ladies'll think I've cheated.' She paused for breath then continued. 'Just a regular day in the Biddles household. Which is why I was wondering if you were busy on Friday. Have you got a gig on that day?'

I thought for a minute. 'Nope, I'm free. I've got my regular "Eighties night" gig at The Venue on Wednesday and a wedding on Saturday, so Friday's fine. Why?'

'Weeeeell,' Vicky said. 'Alistair and I are having a dinner party. Just some people from his work, and I really wanted you to come. You know how I hate all that grown-up work chatter.'

'Right, so you need a child-like, non-ambitious type to make up the numbers,' I joked, pretending to be offended.

'Damn, you got me.' She laughed. 'But you know

what I mean. I would be happier if you came too. You can bring a friend. Harriet or Ed if you like?'

I raised my eyebrows in surprise. I had always got the impression that Vicky didn't like Harriet. She had never invited her over before and usually went quiet if I mentioned her. A lot of people found Harriet hard to get on with. She came across as being stand-offish and serious, with a sharp tongue. She was well-spoken and public school educated, which had at times been falsely interpreted as snobbishness, but I knew different. She was shy of relationships but was loyal and giving in the few she had. OK, she was blunt and didn't suffer fools gladly, but at least she was true to her heart, you knew where you stood and she would never talk behind people's backs. I admired her for that.

'Sounds lovely, I'll invite Harriet if that's OK. So, who are the people from work, anyone I've met before?'

Vicky paused briefly, just long enough to arouse my suspicion.

'You're not trying to pair me off again are you?' I asked wearily.

'Not at all! There's Dave and Trish, you met those two once before at a Christmas do I think, then a couple of guys that have just started working in Alistair's department, who are funnily enough called, now don't laugh . . . Ben and Jerry.'

I stifled a giggle. 'Are you being serious?'

'Yes,' she said with a mock defensive tone. 'They don't really know anyone yet, so Alistair thought it would be nice to get to know them better and give them a chance to meet a few people at the same time. I've met them once already and they're really lovely. Plus I'm doing a special favourite of yours; my famous poached salmon.'

I ignored her attempt to subtly divert the conversation. 'So, you are trying to pair me and Harriet up with this *tasty* twosome are you?' I said, smirking.

'Look, Abby, don't see it like that. We would have invited them anyway, they're nice guys. Plus they're good looking, intelligent and not short of money, you and Harriet could do a lot worse!' She laughed, attempting to put her comments under the guise of a joke, but I knew it was what she really thought. Vicky knew how much I wanted to settle down and have children, she was only trying to steer me in the right direction.

'All right,' I groaned. 'But don't have high hopes for Harriet, she's been seeing some guy called Robert. It doesn't sound really serious yet but I think Harriet wants it to be, so she might not be interested. And promise not to embarrass me. No winking when I'm talking to them, I hate that!' Finally, I could resist it no longer and cracked, 'And Ben and Jerry better not go straight to my thighs and bum like they usually do!'

That night Harriet and I slumped together on the huge old sofa that I had rescued from a junk shop the previous year. I had hidden the threadbare upholstery with a deep pink throw that was so soft you couldn't sit down without stroking the fabric like a well-loved pet.

'This is so comfortable, you could have a bottom the size of a barge and it would still feel accommodating,' Harriet said with a lazy smile.

Today, like most days, Harriet had come straight upstairs when she arrived home from work. It was an unspoken agreement that if we were in the house at the same time then we would most likely be found together. Recently, Harriet had been working hard on a project for the marketing firm she worked for and about once a month she would meet up with Robert. She had been away a lot and staying at work until late so we hadn't shared as many evening meals as we would normally. Until recently we would eat together most nights and occasionally, if we had been drinking, had a marathon video session or been chatting into the small hours, either Harriet would sleep on my sofa or I would sleep in her spare bed. Our living arrangements were ideal. We had the close bond of flatmates yet were physically separate enough so as not to jeopardise our friendship with gripes about washing-up or one another's mess and bathroom habits. Tonight we were settling in for a night of wine and chat.

'You know, last night, Vicky and I got through a bottle of wine between us,' I said, uncorking the bottle Harriet had bought on the way home. 'Tonight we'll most likely do the same, if not more. I can't remember the last night I didn't have alcohol.'

'Don't,' Harriet said. 'I used to be so self-controlled, but just lately I don't know what's got into me. I mean I don't mind getting tipsy at home with you occasionally, but drunk in public, that's bad! The wedding was only the second time in my life I've done that.'

'Hon, you have nothing to worry about, I used to do that every Friday.' I remembered Vicky's invite then. 'Speaking of Friday, Vicky's invited us to a dinner party on Friday night with some guys from Alistair's work.'

'Us?' Harriet asked, looking at me dubiously. 'You mean you and Ed?'

'No, you and me. What do you think?'

'Me?' she repeated. 'Are you sure?'

'The name Harriet was definitely mentioned. Of course I'm sure.'

'Gosh, I never thought Vicky liked me that much. I mean how long have we both known you? Me, since you were born, Vicky since you were at school together, and not once has she seemed keen to get to know me. Everything I know about her is via either you or Ed. I'm surprised, that's all.'

'To be honest with you, I could be wrong, but I think Vicky has always had a slight self-confidence thing. She probably sees you as a bit of a high achiever . . . a career woman. She probably thinks – *wrongly* thinks – she would suffer by comparison. I think if she got to know you, you could be great friends. Very complementary in fact, because your strengths are in such different areas you'd get a lot from one another.'

Harriet nodded slowly and frowned at her glass. 'You're telling me that on her sixth birthday, when I was eight or nine or whatever, and she had that enormous birthday party when her cousins came over from Australia and she had a bouncy castle and a roller disco, and she invited everybody under the sun, including that tiny little girl from your tap dancing class that you only went to for two weeks before you dropped it . . . even she was invited, but not me. Not your oldest friend in the world that she had met a hundred times at *your* house and *your* parties. You're telling me that was because, at the age of nine, I was a career woman?'

'Well, no. You've got a good memory haven't you? I'd forgotten about that. That was some party . . .' I caught sight of the expression on her face and laughed affectionately. 'H, you can't bear a grudge against her for that. It was over twenty years ago! Come on, give her a chance. Please come.'

She sighed, defeated and eventually said 'OK.'

Two hours later Harriet and I were showing an alcoholic lack of inhibition. We were laughing uncontrollably about a guy at Harriet's work that had been hassling her, flooding her with over-familiar e-mails and leaning on her desk a lot.

'Your trouble is you want perfection,' I said.

'No, Abby, that's your department. I'm not fussy, I just frighten most of the men I like and attract the ones I don't. A victim of circumstance, that was always my problem. I don't expect that when I meet the right man, everything will be just right. There are always complications. That's why you haven't found anyone yet. You have set your standards at an unreachable height. You want to feel like you did when you were a teenager, when you were

69

pulsing with hormones and a vivid imagination. I don't think you'll get that again. You know that bit more as an adult. You've experienced enough to see that reality is never black and white. People are never consummately perfect. I don't think you can recreate those feelings.'

'So you wouldn't say that Robert was perfect then?' I looked at her slyly. I still hadn't met Robert and I was bursting with curiosity. She was being characteristically private about her love life, but what wasn't like her was allowing a man to really get under her skin, and I suspected that Robert had.

Harriet looked suddenly serious. 'No. He's definitely not perfect. But the good things about him are so wonderful, they kind of overshadow the bad. Everyone is flawed, you just have to accept that. I don't get the breathtaking feeling, the wow factor that you always talk about, but then I don't think I ever will.'

I shook my head, not so sure, and disappointed with her resignation. 'I know what I want, how I want to feel. I've felt it before and I will again. I won't settle for less.' I grinned at her, trying to portray a confidence that I didn't really feel.

'But how do you know you haven't met someone who can make you feel like that already. Perhaps you have, but you gave up on them before you got the chance. You found out that they liked Mariah Carey, played air guitar or whatever else you might regard as a musical faux pas. They were history before you had a chance to really get to know them. You're a music snob,' she accused, waggling a finger at me.

I laughed at Harriet, knowing she was only playing devil's advocate. 'I am not! Music snobs are a different category altogether. It's just my thing, you know that. Like you and manners. You like men to be well-groomed and charming. You wouldn't be attracted by anyone that scratched their crotch in public or pronounced the letter h, "haitch".'

Harriet recoiled as though I had just scraped my nails across a blackboard.

'Well, it's a similar thing for me. I could never be with a man who played air guitar, it's ugh, it's just so unpleasant to watch. It smacks everso slightly of a sad, desperate man. And that guy, Luke, you were referring to. The student I met at the eighties night. He played Mariah Carey incessantly. Hers were the only CDs he owned and every time he put one on he raved that she had the "voice of an angel" no less. I couldn't have a future with someone who listened to her that loud all the time, no matter how wide her vocal range. She has the oral equivalent of a nervous twitch with all that wobbling up and down squealing all the time. It just gives me a headache. I don't think it's fussy to want someone who shares your taste. Who, essentially, is compatible. It's what most people want, isn't it?'

I put my drink down on the coffee table and got up from the sofa, determined to make Harriet see what I was getting at.

'Oh no,' Harriet groaned when she realised I had headed over to the hi-fi and flicked it all on.

'You're going to make me listen to stuff, aren't you?'

I didn't say anything but shuffled about, clearing the clutter off the floor and lighting the candles that were placed around the room on tall, silver holders. I closed my colourful draping curtains that I had made from a length of bright sari material. When I turned the main light off the room glowed instantly with warm pink light and the candle flames picked out the curtains gold trim, making them shimmer with luminescence.

'Sit there,' I instructed, ushering Harriet over to my 'listening chair'. Harriet knew better than to argue with me. I had taught her a long time ago that to hear the full power of a song you needed to sit directly between the speakers. I had an old armchair placed in the optimal position in the room. It was a completely different shape and style to the sofa, similar only because it too was hidden with a soft pink throw. It was one of those chairs you sank deeply in to.

'Right, don't make me move again,' Harriet purred, taking another sip of wine. 'This is heavenly.'

'Now, I want you to close your eyes, and you have to concentrate, OK?'

Harriet dutifully closed her eyes and nodded, smiling.

'I want you to really listen to the voice in this, it's unbelievably sexy. But you've got to *really* listen OK?'

Harriet nodded again and I picked a Suede CD from the bookcase behind me. I turned the volume up high and put the CD on, picking my favourite track, 'The Wild Ones'. A guitar started, followed by Brett Anderson's deep, resonating voice which rose and broke plaintively. The sound was so clear you could hear his breath. Even hear his lips parting.

I turned the volume down after the introduction. 'What do you think?'

Harriet snapped her eyes open. 'Wow! Play the rest,' she said, sitting forward in the chair.

'Don't you think he's got a sexy voice?'

'Unbelievable. I've never really listened to a man's voice like that before. It was amazing! So sensual, it was as though he was in the room with us. You've got to play it again. At least the start bit, it was gorgeous.'

I happily obliged, then picked Depeche Mode's *Black Celebration* album off the shelf. 'Now listen to this,' I said, swapping the discs over. I skipped through the beginning of the song until I reached the bit I wanted Harriet to hear. The bit halfway through where David Gahan implores you to kiss him. When I was younger, I would play this on a loop, over and over, imagining that he was singing to me. His voice was so urgent, so powerfully attractive. I would defy any hot blooded female to refuse a plea like that. Once more Harriet looked up, grinning from ear to ear. 'Who the hell was that?' she said.

'That was David Gahan from Depeche Mode. Now, is it just me or does he have the most incredibly sexy voice?'

'I would say that that's the most exhilarating sexual encounter I've had in many a long year,' she joked. She picked up her glass, which had been sitting empty by her feet, and carried it over to me by the hi-fi. She reached out for the bottle of wine and topped up both our glasses before sitting down and scouring my CD shelf. 'Play me another one like that,' she said.

An hour and a half later and I was beginning to get a headache from the excesses of wine and music we had been revelling in. CDs and records were left littering the floor around us in our quest to find the ultimate male voice. We had agreed that they didn't necessarily have to be the best singers or songwriters, so long as the passion was there. Harriet had also pointed out that one consistent feature in all the voices we chose were that they all sounded as though they had a cold. I preferred to think of them as being breathy with raw emotion, but had to admit she had a point.

'I wonder if it's a universal thing,' Harriet was saying. 'You know, like looks. I mean, obviously people are attracted by different things, but generally good looking men have similar qualities, don't they? A symmetrical face, square jaw line, good skin, thick hair. I would have thought that a sexy voice would be even less subjective.'

'Probably,' I said. I was lying on my back, watching the shadows of light flicker on the ceiling. 'Mind you, I could never see why Barry White was dubbed "The Walrus of Love". That guy leaves me cold.'

Harriet laughed. 'I know what you mean. But we agreed on practically every voice, no matter what the music was like. I never liked EMF, for example, but now you've played it for me, I have to appreciate he's got that voice, hasn't he?'

'The main man for me though is David Gahan. His early stuff gives me goose bumps.'

'You know what you should do? You should put together a compilation like you played for me tonight. You could sell it to women as a sex aid, you'd make a fortune!'

I laughed, rolling over on to my front so that I could see Harriet in the dim light. 'The thing is though, H, when I heard Nathan sing, it was like David Gahan, Brett Anderson, Paul Weller and that guy from Gene all rolled into one then multiplied a hundred fold, because he was real. OK, his voice wasn't outstanding, that's why he mainly played the guitar, but when I saw him singing . . . it was so, so incredibly intimate, does that make sense?'

Harriet nodded and I wished I hadn't detected a glint of sympathy in her eyes. She knew I was holding on to something I could never have.

'He just . . . he just captured me that night. I'll never forget it.' I rolled back and stared once more at the ceiling. The record I had left on came to an end and I lay still, listening to the rhythmic 'schoop, schoop' sound of the stylus waiting for me to free it. When I finally stood up I realised that Harriet had fallen asleep in the middle of the room. I picked a throw off the chair, placing it gently over her like a blanket, then I wandered over to the window. I pulled back the curtain and looked out across the green to the rows of houses beyond. I thought of the families tucked up together under those roofs; I thought of Vicky and Alistair and the security that compounded their lives; I thought of Nathan and Rebecca, and the excitement and discovery that were stretching out in front of theirs. I wandered back to the hi-fi and quietly, so as not to disturb Harriet, I put on a U2 album and sat down again, selecting the song, 'Stuck In A Moment That You Can't Get Out Of'. I hugged my knees tightly to me, resting my chin on them, and wondered how long this moment would last.

# CHAPTER FIVE

By Friday I had come to a big decision. I needed a new look. How could I break a pattern when I looked in the mirror and saw the same me every time. I had to convince myself that this was different. This time, I was really going to change.

My style, for too long now, had consisted of whatever was comfy. Trainers, combat style trousers and T-shirts acted like a form of camouflage, hiding me away, blending me comfortably in the background. It wasn't that I had a hang up about my body. I was an average height and neither noticeably skinny or chubby. I was perhaps just lazy. Stuck in this eternal, ever deepening groove. Lugging disco equipment was hard work, it would be made harder with heels on, or with a short skirt to worry about when I seemed to be forever bending over. My hair was a shoulder length, straight bob, no fringe, no layers, no fuss. Except that whenever I was working my hair always slipped forward over my eyes when I was looking down at the decks. Because of this I always twisted several strands of hair away from my face and clipped it back.

Always the same, and always for a practical rather than a decorative purpose. My only indulgence – if I can steel myself to call it that – was jewellery, and I'm not talking the sort Harriet wears, classy and expensive, that would never suit me. My jewellery was always what my dad would describe as 'cheap and cheerful'. I always make a bee-line for Mickey and Accessorise in town, but my favourites were one-off places, little craft shops and flea markets. I have thousands of colourful beaded bracelets, armlets and anklets, rings for fingers, thumbs and toes, chokers and beaded belts. When I take them off at night I feel naked and exposed, and no matter what my new look consisted of, my jewellery was going nowhere.

With Friday being the day of Vicky and Alistair's dinner party, I figured it was the perfect occasion for outing a new look. I decided if I was going to do this, I was going to do it properly and arranged the afternoon off so I could fit in an appointment at Toni&Guy. I had never been there before, opting instead for a salon two doors up from Little Beat. Trendy salons had always frightened me; their men seemed to have an uncanny knack of knowing exactly where you bought your clothes from, looking at you as though it just wasn't the 'right' place, and the women either sported incredibly long, glossy 'Friends' hair or a quirky short fringe and arty oblong glasses. They were always impossibly gorgeous. But today I was feeling brave, I was going to rediscover the woman in me and stop hiding my femininity. *Vive la différence!* My new motto.

*

When I arrived home, I unpacked my bags, laying my new purchases out on the bed and looking at them as though they were the component parts of some alien gadget I didn't understand. There was a flirty, pale blue Jigsaw skirt and a thin, almost silver, sleeveless knitted camisole. They were so delicate they weighed practically nothing. My under-wired bra alone was heavier. Next to them I put my new strappy sandals and the tissue wrapped package that contained a wide bracelet, made up of tiny green blue and silver beads woven into a spiral pattern. I opted for a wide bracelet as the top I bought exposed so much of my arms I had to find some way of feeling more covered up. Everything looked so pretty on my bed it seemed a shame to wear them and spoil the flawless outfit with my many imperfections. Then there was my hair. I looked in the mirror, frightened of even touching what had turned out to be a work of art. An expensive work of art. The stylist had advised me on a choppy, Meg Ryan style, with some 'sun-kissed' highlights. I had to admit, it looked pretty good; shorter than I was used to, and stripier, but very funky. She had blow dried it so that the ends flicked out and stayed there. On my way home I had toyed with the idea of sitting in a photo booth to capture the moment when my hair had never looked so groomed, as I was certain that it never would again.

I had just over an hour to prepare myself before I said I would find Harriet. It had been hot and still all day, so we had decided to walk to Vicky's house and get some fresh air. I skipped off to the bathroom with an armful of bottles and potions.

'Wow!' Harriet said, standing back to take it all in. I stood, feeling foolish, waiting for Harriet to compose herself. 'You look amazing! I love the outfit. It's so . . . so girlie! And the hair! So cute!'

I started blushing and told her to 'shush'. When I had looked in the mirror earlier I had to admit it all went together well, but I felt self-conscious. If it hadn't been so hot I would have put on my hooded fleece to dampen down the girlie image. My confidence and resolve for a 'new me' had dissolved and now I felt as though I wasn't being myself, I was trying to be someone else. I remembered Rebecca and how I had always envied her effortless femininity. I flushed, feeling foolish and transparent. 'I feel like an idiot,' I moaned.

Harriet took my arm and linked it with hers before I turned on my ever-so narrow heels and got changed. 'Darling, you look so gorgeous, you have nothing to worry about. It's just a culture shock that's all. You'll soon relax.' She looked at the expression on my face then added, 'Maybe a drink or two will help?'

I provoked a similar reaction from Vicky and Alistair when we arrived at their house. Alistair opened the door and whistled immediately, then drew me into a bear hug. 'You look terrific Abby, you should scrub up like this more often,' he joked. Instead of slugging him, as I would normally, I just smiled shyly. He greeted Harriet with an easy smile and took us through to the kitchen where Vicky was almost obscured behind the breakfast bar by bottles of wine, olive oil, packets of flour and other, more indefinable ingredients.

'Thank God it's you two,' she said, hurriedly bunging a baking tray in the oven. 'I don't want anyone else to see me like this.' She wiped her hands on her apron and blew a strand of hair out of her eyes. She hadn't got dressed yet and she was spattered with food. Her curly hair had frizzed out, the way it so often did when she had been rushing around getting hot. The kitchen was in a terrible state, yet the complementary mixture of smells that filled the room hinted at something delicious to come.

'Oh my God! Look at you, you're all womanly!' she cried when she finally looked at me properly (it was an improvement on girlie, I suppose). 'Oh hell, you look so gorgeous. Both of you,' she added, looking at Harriet. 'Right, I'm sorry, I'm going to have to dash upstairs to shower and change. Do you mind? I'm afraid I got really behind. I wanted to get the kids into bed early tonight, make it an adult night for a change. Sorry, promise I'll be as quick as a flash.'

We shook our heads, claiming firm protestations that it was all fine and she should take as long as she needed. 'Alistair will get you both a drink, won't you love,' she called as she bolted up the stairs, her bare feet leaving little floury toe-prints on the stairs.

Dave and Trish arrived whilst Harriet and I were helping Alistair tidy up the kitchen. Dave shook my hand, a gesture I had never found myself comfortable with. I guess it became second nature when you worked in a formal environment, but I didn't get it much; only with salesmen at Little Beat, who would offer me their hand as soon as they could, as though, by being the shaker, rather than the shakee, they were taking control of the ensuing conversation and reducing me to a form of submission. When I DJed at weddings, I found that fathers-of-the-bride were also keen hand-shakers, although they bothered me less; their motives weren't so dubious. Dave's was more the father-of-the-bride variety than the salesman shake, but I still felt silly doing it, aware that my hand had gone limp and was just being wobbled about. Harriet, ever the business woman, wasn't phased by this at all and got straight in there. She once told me that she liked to shake a person's hand, as by doing so you were setting a boundary, keeping them at arms length and confirming your personal space. Harriet rarely liked people to get too close to her. The only person I had ever seen kiss her in public was Ed. Ed was naturally affectionate and playful, he often hugged or kissed Harriet, as though he was teasing her for being uptight; she pretended to be irritated and swot him away, but I knew her well enough to know that she enjoyed it.

Ben and Jerry arrived together but, fortunately, introduced themselves separately. Ben looked like a student with aspirations to become a musician. He was good looking and trendy, wearing a pair of dark blue Diesel jeans and a close fitting T-shirt. Looking at the two men together it was obvious who Vicky

82

had paired Harriet and I up with in her mind. Ben was typical of the guys I usually go for, a casual dresser with a pretty-boy face and thick messy hair. Jerry was older, he looked about thirty-five, was smart, dressed in trousers and a Yves Saint Laurent shirt, the sleeves rolled partly up to expose a manly forearm and an expensive watch. If Harriet had been on the market for a new man, he would have been the ideal candidate.

Ben had brought a bottle of Beaujolais and a four pack of bottled ice lager, and Jerry brought two bottles of 'top shelf' wine that he put on the counter in front of Harriet. Harriet, I noticed, read the labels and nodded approvingly, which gained her a warm smile from Jerry.

We were all standing chatting in the kitchen when I looked up and saw Vicky walking down the hall to join us. She stopped briefly to check her reflection in the hall mirror and frowned at what she saw, although I couldn't see why, she looked lovely. She caught my eye and smiled with a pretend grimace then came in to join us, where she was welcomed affectionately, kissed by everyone except Harriet and Ben, who smiled shyly on the sidelines.

My hunch, unsurprisingly, was correct. Vicky had insisted on seating us all, with her and Alistair at either end of the table; Dave and Trish sitting opposite each other on Alistair's side; Harriet and Jerry facing each other in the middle and Ben and I, likewise, on Vicky's side.

Harriet and Jerry struck up a conversation from the onset of the meal, which looked as though it would have continued unbroken if the others hadn't often drawn them into their own discussions. I watched them, intrigued, as they chatted easily with each other. When Harriet talked about her job, Jerry listened intently, leaning in towards her and nodding, encouraging her to tell him more. When Vicky cleared away the plates to make way for dessert, I followed her into the kitchen to help serve up. We grinned at each other, knowing exactly what the other was thinking.

'Jerry's a nice guy isn't he?' Vicky started off.

'From what I can tell. I haven't had much chance to get to know him really though. I think his attention has been pretty much monopolised.'

'Oh, why does Harriet have to be seeing someone else?' Vicky groaned. 'They could be so perfect together. There's definitely a spark there.'

'I know, especially from Jerry's side. But still, Harriet has been acting a bit cagey when I quiz her about Robert so you never know, I wouldn't completely rule it out yet.' I grinned and counted out eight plates, spreading them out on the counter whilst Vicky searched the kitchen for a jug to put the cream in.

'And what about Ben?' she asked, fussing about in a cupboard in an effort to disguise her question as simply general chit-chat.

I checked the door, listening to make sure that the other guests were all absorbed, oblivious to us. 'He's not really my type Vic, he's nice enough but, well, just not for me.'

Vicky shut the cupboard door, jug in hand. 'Really?

I'm surprised at you. I thought he was just your type. He looks straight out of an Indie band for starters, and he's fun, trendy, has a nice firm bum, and is so laid back. Like most of the men you've been out with.'

'But that's just it, isn't it? None of them worked out; he'd be just the same. It's about time I stopped making the same old mistakes. Besides, the guy's really young. My biological clock is ticking so loud I'm surprised it doesn't wake me up in the night. I have to start looking at men as potential fathers and although Ben would make a great pub date, a father figure he's certainly not. He's told one drinking story after another. I've never heard so many words to describe being drunk. Tonight he's described himself as being—' I counted the words off on my fingers '—blasted, leathered, tanked, hammered, wrecked and steaming. For God's sake, the guy makes himself sound like he's been decorated!'

Vicky and I fell about laughing.

Alistair wandered into the kitchen at that point, making us squeal guiltily then laugh with relief when we realised we hadn't been overheard. Alistair looked at us blankly. 'What's so funny?'

'Nothing!' We both said at once, busying ourselves with the job of cutting up the layered meringue Vicky had made and sharing it out between the plates.

'God!' Alistair said, looking at us with bemusement. He wandered over to the fridge to take out the lagers that Ben had brought. 'We're not even on the dessert yet and you pair are plastered already.'

Vicky and I collapsed into another fit of giggles as

Alistair looked on in confusion asking, 'What? What did I say?'

Drinking coffee in the living room an hour later, I was beginning to get nervous that Ben had got the wrong impression. His eyes were glazed from the alcohol he had drunk. I, despite what Alistair might have thought, hadn't been drinking a lot. I had stopped at three glasses of wine (after three I usually lose all sense of when to stop and just keep going until somebody puts the kettle on or the pub shuts). I didn't want to have a hangover the next day as I was DJing for a wedding at a seafront hotel in Weston-Super-Mare. It was further afield than I would normally go and I knew it would be a long night. I needed a clear head. This clear head also served me well when it came to Ben, who had parked himself on the sofa next to me and was developing a nasty habit of letting his hand drop onto my knee. I was listening to a conversation that Trish and Vicky were having about their experiences of childbirth. I was morbidly fascinated to hear more, but Ben kept drawing me into a conversation that excluded all others. I tried to catch Harriet's eye, but she was absorbed in a serious discussion with Jerry and Alistair about work. Eventually I stood up, letting Ben's hand drop back onto the sofa with a thud. I announced that I had a long day on Saturday and needed to go home and get some sleep.

Vicky looked disappointed and asked if I was sure, then Alistair and Jerry tried to talk me into having a whisky with them. I declined with a smile.

Harriet stood up to join me, saying, 'I'll get my coat.'

'Why don't you stay?' Ben interrupted, talking to Harriet. 'I can walk Abby back. I have to go that way to get to my house anyway.' He stood up before I could argue.

Harriet faltered, unsure what to do. She hadn't been watching closely enough to be able to gauge whether Ben and I were getting on well enough to want privacy. But, with her still not knowing Vicky and Alistair that well, she would have felt awkward staying without me. She also glanced regretfully at Jerry, as though she would have liked to spend more time with him.

Jerry confirmed my hunch that he was a true gentlemen by sensing Harriet's awkward pause and jumped up, putting his whisky down on the coffee table. 'Why don't I walk you back, Harriet? I've always wanted to see the view from the bridge at night.' He turned to Alistair. 'I'll just drop Harriet off then come back here if that's all right. I can get a taxi when I get back.'

With that all settled we said our goodbyes. Vicky shot me an apologetic look but I reassured her with a smile, thanking her for yet another lovely evening and promising to call her the next day. Alistair led the four of us to the door and kissed me goodnight.

Walking down the drive I turned back and saw that Alistair was still there, grinning from the doorway. He winked at me and I frowned back, crossing my arms against the chill breeze.

Turning on to Sycamore Lane, Ben and Jerry appeared to be having a silent who-can-walk-the-slowest competition, each trying to drop back, presumably to gain some privacy with their chosen evening's date. Harriet and I weren't playing ball though, falling into step together and talking about Vicky and Alistair's house.

'They seem so happy don't they? Such a traditional family in many ways, but it just works doesn't it?' Harriet said.

'I know. I went upstairs and peered in on the kids when the guys were washing up. They're so cute, Clarice was sucking her thumb and Jack was snoring, bless.' This broody talk wouldn't normally be cool in front of a guy I'd just met, but tonight I didn't care about first impressions. I had no intention of wanting to impress Ben. Harriet, I noticed, snuck a backward glance at Jerry and smiled. I wondered if the decent thing for me to do would be to let Ben walk with me and give the two of them some more time to get to know each other.

Ben solved the problem, rather unconventionally, by suddenly dumping a pile of leaves on my head then running off up the road laughing, obviously expecting me to retaliate and chase him. 'Oi!' I cried, looking disbelievingly from Harriet to Jerry. Ben was possibly even more immature than I had first given him credit for. I toyed with the idea of watching Ben continue up the road, thinking what a prat he would seem if I just ignored him, but the sexual tension between Harriet and Jerry was so blatant I decided the best thing for Harriet would be to give her a break. I picked up a stick from the grassy bank that bordered the road, shouting, 'Right, you little sod!' and much to Ben's delight I chased him up the road and into the distance.

I caught up with Ben in the middle of the suspension bridge, where, laughing and wheezing, he tried to wrestle the stick off me. Feeling a little foolish without the alcoholic sense of fun that Ben obviously had, I felt I had to do something now I had caught him. I playfully whacked the stick across his backside and watched, impressed, when the stick broke in half. Vicky was right about this guy having a firm bum! I held the stick up, laughing at the short stump that was left in my hand. Ben was grinning at me, his eyes wide, like a kitten about to pounce on a ball of wool. 'You little minx,' he whispered naughtily. His hands were on my hips and I could feel him moving in closer. Realising that he was about to kiss me, I had no alternative but to take off up the road again. I turned on my heels and fled.

Twice more I had to fight Ben off, who had upped the ante by pinning me down on the grass and pretending to tickle me. My jaw was hurting from laughing loud, trying to cover my awkwardness at dealing with the situation. I was also paranoid about my skirt riding up, there was little covering me up. I wished I had worn my combat trousers after all.

If Ben had been Ed, I would have behaved completely differently. I would have let Ed catch me rather than pounding up the street for all that I was worth. Ed and I were always mucking around like this, but then we knew each other inside out and were completely at ease. Plus, with Ed nudging on the gay side of bisexual, there was never an undercurrent of anything more than friendship. Tonight was different though and I was dreading arriving home. I doubt it would be deemed acceptable for me to flee in to the house, lock the door behind me and set the burglar alarm.

When I did reach the house I leaned against the wall, gasping for breath. Ben's footsteps slowed down to a trot and he finally caught me up, leaning next to me on the wall. His breath was coming fast, his chest rising and falling quickly as he panted and laughed simultaneously.

'You're pretty fit aren't you?' he said eventually, grinning at me.

I smiled shyly, looking down the road to see if I could spot Harriet. She was nowhere to be seen. 'Right, well Ben. It's been fun. Really it has, but I've got to go in now. I've got a long day tomorrow. I need some sleep.'

'Sure, I understand,' he said. His breathing was reverting to normal and he turned, leaning on the wall and looked at me intently.

He was attractive, I assessed quickly, looking at his face that now glowed with warmth from running. His hair was tousled and messy. I had always been attracted by men with messy hair. Forget it, I thought. I could never have kids with a man like this, he was too excitable. I needed to stop complicating my life with second-bests. I had to keep searching.

'So, can I call you sometime Abby?'

I stammered, looking away, searching for inspiration to get me out of this tricky spot. I caught sight of the Scooby and realised that my phone number was written on the side panel, underneath my name. Please don't turn around, I silently pleaded.

Ben turned around to see what I was looking at. 'Oh, right I get it. Nice one. Cool van, Abby J. You know, I did have a perfect day.' He smiled at me and to my relief turned around and started walking down the road. 'Later,' he called out.

Half an hour later I was pacing the flat with a cup of tea, desperate to know how Harriet was getting on with Jerry. I heard voices in the street below and looked out. Under a street light I saw Jerry and Harriet. They were facing each other, Harriet's hands were in Jerry's as they looked into one another's eyes. They seemed calm and poised, the opposite of Ben and I half an hour earlier. I caught my breath, sure he was going to kiss her and dying to know what Harriet would do. I knew I should look away and grant them their privacy, but I was too curious, too excited for her. Jerry leaned in for a kiss and was about to touch Harriet. He's going for the lips, I thought grinning. Harriet looked away then and Jerry's kiss went wayward, landing instead on her cheek. She made an awkward attempt at fumbling for her keys then waved goodnight and walked into the house. Jerry stayed put for a moment, looking at the door then walked slowly away.

As I predicted Harriet came straight upstairs to find me. When she walked in I noticed that instead of being flushed with excitement as I had hoped, she looked defeated. She flopped down on the floor, silently kicking off her shoes.

'What happened Harriet? He really looked like he wanted to kiss you then. You two were getting on so well and he was perfect for you. A proper gent. Weren't you tempted? Is it because of your thing with Robert?' The words tumbled out of my mouth. I was aware that I sounded disappointed and shouldn't have got my hopes up when I knew she was in a relationship with Robert. She was still the same traditional Harriet that would never start something whilst she was seeing someone else. It wasn't her way.

'I know, I know,' Harriet said, holding up her hand to silence me. She sighed then said, as if talking to herself, 'I wait for ages for someone and get nothing for years, then all of a sudden two men come along at once.'

I grinned at her. 'So, you're admitting there was something there then? You sensed it too.'

Harriet bit her lip and smiled regretfully at me. 'Abby, don't. It wouldn't work. Look, I should have told you this sooner. I wanted to, but I wanted the time to be right. I wanted you to have met Robert first, but he's been away and . . .' She stopped herself from rambling and clutched her hands together, a wide and involuntary grin suddenly breaking on her face. 'I'm engaged!'

# CHAPTER SIX

On Monday I had spent the morning lost in thought.
I was desperate to tell Ed about Harriet's news but
wasn't sure whether it was something she wanted to
keep quiet. That had never been discussed. Actually,
the more I thought about it, the more I realised
that a lot of things hadn't been discussed. If it
had been anyone else, I am sure I would have
heard every little detail of the relationship until
I felt I had practically witnessed the whole thing
for myself. But Harriet had always been different in
that way. Her private life was exactly that; private.
It wasn't out of character for her to skirt around the
details, which was exactly what she had done that
evening.

We had sat up talking for half an hour before she
began yawning and became too tired to stay up any
longer. She had left me with a burning curiosity
about Robert. He had to be something special for
Harriet to want to marry him. I had never known
her fall in love with anyone before now. What made
him so different?

Ed was out of the shop almost all afternoon so I

never had the chance to talk to him anyway. Before he left he invited me back to his house for dinner after work and I jumped at the chance. Harriet had been away with Robert on Sunday and was unlikely to be back. I didn't fancy going home to an empty house and it would be the perfect chance to talk things through with him, get it off my chest.

'So, tell me everything,' Ed said, pouring me a cup of coffee.

'What makes you think there's anything to tell?' I teased, knowing full well that I was going to tell Ed. I couldn't hold out any longer.

'Come on. Something's going on, I know you well enough by now to tell when you've got something on your mind. You were acting dreamy all morning. Have you had a fall out with Harriet?'

I waved a dismissive hand. 'No. Nothing like that.'

Ed was thoughtful for a moment then his eyes grew wide. 'Something happened at Vicky's when you went for dinner. I never did ask what happened.' He looked at me suspiciously. 'Have you met a man?'

'I wish,' I joked. 'I'm becoming a social pariah. You should see the men Vicky's been trying to fix me up with. They get younger and younger. Anyone half decent my own age has been snapped up. I've either got to start dating boys or the divorced generation.'

'Charming!' Ed said. He reached into the oven and took out the potatoes, bringing them down hard onto the kitchen work surface so that they split open. He put them on the plates and punched them again then put a plate in front of me. '*Voilà!*'

I laughed. 'You're an artist,' I said, eyeing the pulped potato on my plate.

'You have to do that. It makes them fluffy, you should know that by now.' He shrugged then sat down opposite me rubbing his hands. 'So, if it's not a man, then what is it?'

I helped myself from the bowl of salad and began to explain what Harriet had told me on Saturday.

'No!' Ed said, his jaw dropping. 'Why didn't you tell me this sooner?'

'I don't know. I wasn't sure whether it was supposed to be kept secret.' I bit my lip guiltily. 'And anyway, when I tried to call you yesterday you were pretty much permanently engaged.'

Ed laughed. 'Ah. I was downloading music from the Internet.'

'And you're rubbish at switching your mobile on.'

'I know, I know. Sorry.' He bit into a piece of bread and chewed thoughtfully for a moment, saying finally, 'So, what do you know about him? Have you met him yet?'

I shook my head. 'I'm still in the dark there. All I know is he's called Robert, he's thirty-four and he was a client with the marketing agency Harriet works for when he was living in Bristol. He's got a job in London now though and has been travelling here for business reasons a lot. I knew that much already and she hasn't told me much more.

He's mature, intelligent and successful. Sounds like just the type I would have guessed Harriet would go for.'

'A posh suit,' Ed said nodding, a wry smile on his face.

I refused to smile at that. 'I guess I am just going to have to wait until I meet him. But I think that should happen soon. She seems pretty serious about him. I just hadn't realised how serious until Saturday.'

'Abby, she'd have to be if she's agreed to marry him,' Ed said.

'And that's the other weird thing. She says that it was her that asked him. That's why she hasn't got a ring yet. She said it was a spur of the moment thing. They were in a restaurant and she just said it.'

A look of surprise flashed across his face. 'Now that is out of character. Harriet's never spur of the moment about anything.'

'I know. Perhaps that's what love does to you?'

We ate slowly, comparing notes on the kind of man we thought Harriet would finally settle on. I couldn't remember her ever having a serious relationship. Not even at university. She had certainly turned down plenty and scared off more. He would have to be resilient. Harriet was proud of her independence. Her mother had never worked outside the home, giving up any chance of a career to look after Harriet and her older brother until they had left for university. As soon as her parents thought their children were forging their own lives away from the family home, the truth came out. Harriet's parents had put on a brave front, staying together for the sake of the children, but behind closed doors it transpired that their relationship had finished years earlier. Harriet's mother, Patricia, had discovered that her husband had had a secret affair with a man when he was in his thirties. She could never forgive him for the betrayal and was left paranoid that everyone he met and chatted with, male or female, was a threat to their relationship. She withdrew, put her head down and carried on regardless, a mess of insecurities. When Harriet was safely ensconced at Strathclyde University, her dad packed his bags and left Patricia. At the time I couldn't believe how well Harriet took it. She stayed in touch with her father and didn't seem to bear any grudge, I guess she had always known something wasn't right, that it would end eventually. If her experiences had left any lasting scars they were very well disguised. The only change I saw in her was an even stronger resolve to make it on her own and not base her life around the stability of a relationship.

When we were little, our parents used to laugh at how different we were. When we used to share a holiday cottage in Devon, Harriet would be trying her hand at sailing, beckoning me to join her, whilst I sat drawing circles in the sand, lost in thought. When I wanted to sit under a tree and read the *Famous Five*, Harriet had turned her Dad's shed into a pretend shop complete with priced stock and cash register. Occasionally we argued. I would get stroppy and Harriet would berate me by saying 'Oh don't be so childish!' but it didn't happen often considering how different we were. She was the leader, I was the follower; she was the doer, I was the thinker. Maybe it was the age gap between us, maybe it was the very different schools we went to or the fact that our parents had labelled us from an early age and we were just acting out the roles they expected us to play. Whatever it was, it seemed that the character traits I always admired in Harriet had by-passed me on a road marked 'wide berth'. If one of us was going to get married first, I had naturally assumed it would be me.

Later that evening Ed and I were slouched on his sofa, watching *American Graffiti* yet again. We knew it almost word perfectly but Ed, in particular, never tired of it. I lay at one end of the sofa, my legs up so that my feet rested on Ed's lap. Ed was chewing on some popcorn from a bowl we had balanced between us. I wasn't really watching the film, I was daydreaming. The film's nostalgic soundtrack was making me feel romantic and melancholy. Ed kept catching me looking at him and he'd flick some popcorn in my direction, which, if I had been in more feisty spirits, would have been the catalyst for a food fight. But instead I ignored him and looked at something else. Ed's flat, like mine, is covered in clutter. The shelves crammed with books and videos, the kitchen surfaces littered with gadgets; Alessi containers with little men dangling from the lids, one of those lemon squeezers that looks like a rocket, an ice-cream maker, a popcorn maker, a juicer – the list is endless. But unlike my flat, Ed's house has an underlying theme that ties these objects together. His kitchen is painted in the ice-cream pastel colours of a 1950s diner. All his appliances, units and furniture are either chrome or pastels. He has a porthole window in the dividing wall between the kitchen and living area which I love; it reminds me of *Playschool* where they peer through the shaped windows and are led into another world. Ed's living area is more subtly nostalgic, but for a later, more indefinable era. The walls are painted a bold red that is broken up by large black and white stills from Ed's favourite films; *Rebel Without a Cause*, *American Graffiti* and *Goodfellas*, amongst others. But he didn't just like the American classics and we both loved coming-of-age films from all decades and spent many evenings watching and dissecting our favourites. We had both watched and cried over *The Outsiders*, *Running on Empty*, *Stand By Me* and countless others so many times we really ought to be getting a discount on tissues by now. It was one of my favourite ways to spend an evening. Ed's love of nostalgia, with a modern twist, was reflected all around his flat, and even in the retro 70s clothes he wore. He was one of those people who are easy to buy Christmas presents for because his style is so easy to pinpoint. I would often see something in a shop and think, 'Ed would just love that.'

In my daydreams, the more farfetched ones I indulged in where I was married and rich, living in a beautiful country home with countless rooms, I would often plan how it would look. I loved so many different styles I could never just settle on one, so I would have to have themed rooms to incorporate all my favourites. Maybe a Moroccan bathroom with deep reds and coloured tiles and a huge mosaic mirror; a rustic French kitchen painted in an earthy terracotta, dotted with wicker baskets full of fresh vegetables; a modern living room with pale, natural colours and furniture with clean lines and chrome. And in this vast mansion of opposing tastes there would have to be an Ed room. It would certainly be an entertainment room, devoted to hi-fi listening and film nights; a cosy red room with giant fake fur cushions to cuddle into, and a giant, framed black and white photograph of a troubled teenage boy, taken from a film, because even though Ed was neither a teenager, nor troubled, I imagined that he once was, and now was intensely empathetic to those who were. My friendship with Ed was such a huge influence on my life I would always have a part of him with me now. Although I'd draw the line at a lava lamp or an inflatable plastic armchair.

Curt's plane took off to the sound of 'Goodnight Sweetheart' and the shadow of his plane passed over the Thunderbird that was travelling down the thin grey strip of highway. I sat up and stretched my legs, yawning, knowing it was the end of the film, but not talking, because even though we've seen this film dozens of times before, Ed always liked to read the characters epilogues at the end of the credits. I turned around and stretched out again, this time with my head on Ed's lap and he absently stroked my hair, his eyes fixed to the television.

When the last of the credits had disappeared Ed snapped off the television abruptly and looked down at me. 'Babe, you're nearly asleep, do you want me to take you home?'

I groaned and sat up, rubbing my eyes. I didn't really relish the thought of going home, I was so comfortable and I didn't fancy the idea of returning to a dark, empty house. Harriet would still be out with Robert. The need for sleep got the better of me though. If I didn't go now, I would end up sleeping on Ed's sofa and I didn't fancy waking up in the same clothes without even a toothbrush. 'OK,' I yawned and reached across the floor for my bag.

Ed drove the short distance home pretending he was 'cruising down Third Street' like the characters in *American Graffiti*, looking across to the next lane whilst we were waiting at the lights and grinning at the occupants of the neighbouring cars. His arm was resting on the ledge of the open window and he had a cigarette hanging, unlit, from corner of his mouth. I kept hissing at him to stop embarrassing me as he was attracting some puzzled looks from drivers, unsure if Ed was trying to pick them up or race them away from the lights.

'Look, maybe in Northern California, in a Hotrod, OK,' I snapped, as we pulled onto my road. 'But Bristol in a Vauxhall Astra, Ed. It really doesn't work. It's just weird.'

Ed was still laughing as he parked his car opposite the house and switched off the engine and lights.

We looked across the road at the house and I noticed that Harriet's front room light was on.

'Looks as though Harriet's back early from her date,' I said, reaching to the back seat for my bag.

Ed gasped with excitement. 'Look, Abby, I think I just saw Robert.'

I whirled back around and looked again at Harriet's window. Sure enough, through the muslin curtains that dressed the bay window, I could make out two silhouettes moving in the room. I looked at Ed, who was grinning mischievously.

'Are you thinking what I'm thinking?' he said.

'Possibly.'

'Oh, please Abby, I've just got to see what the man who finally broke Harriet looks like. Please let me.'

'I'm not letting you in,' I said. 'It'll just embarrass her. It'll be obvious that we're just checking him out.'

'Let's peek through the window,' Ed said and jumped out of the car before I could protest. I scrambled out after him, shutting the car door as quietly as I could and crossing the dimly lit street.

There is a wall outside the front door, close to the bay window, and when I caught Ed up he was already sitting on it, leaning as far forward as he could, trying to make out the people in the room. I sat next to him and spotted them both on the sofa, kissing.

'They're kissing!' I whispered to Ed and pointed out where they were.

Ed strained to look then pulled a face. 'He's got his back to us. I can't really see what he looks like.'

Robert's hand started wandering up Harriet's

skirt. 'Steady on,' Ed whispered. 'Hey, what if it's not even Robert? What if Harriet's actually had more men than Elizabeth Taylor and she's leading a sexy double life?'

I nudged him hard. 'Don't be so ridiculous.' Then, seeing the couple on the sofa, lost in a passionate embrace, I cringed. 'Maybe we shouldn't be watching this. It doesn't feel right.' Just as I spoke, Harriet broke away. Ed and I ducked our heads down and when I peered up again she was standing up next to her hi-fi, picking out a CD. Robert sat back, unbuttoning the top buttons of his shirt and we managed to get a clear view of him at last. He was medium height, medium build, smart, and was dressed like a typical business man. He looked older than Harriet although it was hard to pinpoint an age. His hair was cut very short and was slightly receding.

'Oh my God,' Ed said, shocked. 'He looks like Phil Collins!'

As he turned to me he lost his balance and slipped off the wall, taking me with him. I let out a squeal as we both dropped to the small patch of lawn below. I landed on top of Ed, winding him, and we both cracked up laughing. I heard someone walking towards the front door and we both froze, trying to dispel our giggles by shushing each other. The dew on the grass was soaking through the knees of my jeans but I couldn't move for fear of being seen.

'Oh, Abby it's you!' Harriet's voice broke through the quiet night. I jumped off Ed and looked up to the front door guiltily. Harriet was leaning over the wall. 'Oh, and hello Ed, I didn't see you there,' she added with a hint of amusement. 'I think I'll just leave the pair of you to it.' She turned away, smiling to herself.

'Hey, hang on, it's not what you think.' I looked at Ed, mortified, but he was just laughing as he brushed the grass off his back.

After I said goodbye to Ed I let myself into the house, planning to go straight up the stairs, partly out of embarrassment and partly as I wanted to give Harriet some privacy. I was about to sneak upstairs when Harriet poked her head around the living room door. 'Where are you going?'

I stood on the bottom step, unsure what to say. Harriet beckoned me over saying, 'Come on Abby, I want you to meet Robert.'

I followed her into the room, where Robert was standing, leaning against the fireplace as though he was the Great Gatsby. When he saw me he wandered across the room and shook my hand saying, 'I'm delighted to meet you Abby, Harriet has spoken very highly of you.' His voice was deep and refined, and he appeared to be better looking when not seen through the pattern of a muslin curtain. His face was tanned, his cheeks full, and I was drawn to his eyes which were a vivid blue, framed with the soft creases of laughter lines. His hair was thinning slightly and its light brown colour gave the impression it was fading, slowly and gracefully into grey. He had a confident air about him, something in the way he stood, the way he took my hand and looked me straight in the eye. It was the kind of worldly confidence that left me feeling uneasy and foolish by comparison.

'You must have a drink with us,' he said, fetching a bottle of champagne from the coffee table, then plucking an extra glass from Harriet's cabinet. It struck me just how at home he seemed in Harriet's house. I suppose it shouldn't have bothered me. I mean, they were going to get married so it would look odd if he acted like a guest. But it still took me by surprise.

We sat and shared a drink, talking mainly about work. I tried to skirt around the issue of what I did for a living, embarrassed at how little I had achieved in terms of a career compared to the two of them. Robert showed a polite interest when Harriet told him about my DJing.

'She's got the most massive music collection,' Harriet said, proudly. 'She could cater for any taste.'

'What sort of music do you like Robert?' I asked. It was a question I loved as it always gave me a good indication of a person's personality. A bit like looking at the contents of someone's fridge.

He thought for a long time, then said, 'I like a whole range of things really, although I have to admit I don't listen to the radio so much now so I am a bit out of touch. I've got a Chris Rea and a Genesis album in the car. And I love Kate Bush, she has a fantastic voice.'

Thank God he redeemed himself with Kate Bush, I thought smiling. Otherwise I would have been worried.

'Abby has a thing about the guy from Depeche Mode's voice, don't you?' Harriet said as she wandered out of the room to the kitchen, leaving us alone.

Robert laughed, finishing his champagne. 'They played at the Bridge House Hotel the year I finished my degree. That was before anyone had really heard of them. I think I was too drunk to remember much about them though.'

I nodded, noticing that Robert had visibly relaxed his politely formal façade now that we had found some common ground, or perhaps it was the champagne he had drunk.

As the conversation continued I found myself acting guarded, and I felt unnatural, as though I was talking to a friend's dad, who was trying to win points by pretending to be something he wasn't. Harriet returned with a pot of coffee, smiling when she saw we were deep in conversation.

I excused myself after one hurried cup of coffee, telling them I was too tired to stay up any longer. When I was sure Harriet had gone back into the living room I launched myself up the stairs two at a time. Robert seemed nice enough, I thought. Quite charming in fact, but there was something niggling me about him. Something not right. When I walked into my flat I went straight for the phone. The light on my answerphone was blinking and I played the messages.

'Hi Abby, it's Ben here. I met you at Vicky and Alistair's house the other night, remember?' There was a pause and I wondered why people asked questions on a machine, it just sounded awkward. 'I was just wondering if you wanted to meet up some time, go for a drink perhaps.' He left his phone number and I groaned, not really wanting to get back to him but feeling obliged. The next message was Rebecca.

'Hi Abby it's me, Mrs Priestly. I got back from the honeymoon a couple of days ago and I've been dying to talk to you. I've invited Vicky and Alistair for a meal at the Star of India, for a week on Saturday. I thought it'd be nice if we all went out for a meal and caught up. Of course I'd love a chat before then if you want to call me back. But I thought I'd give you lots of notice in case you have a gig or something. I hope you can make it. Speak soon.'

My heart sunk. Whilst they had been away I had been able to put thoughts of Nathan behind me. It was going to be hard now they were back. I wished I had a boyfriend I could take with me, someone who would be a match for Nathan, someone who would make me look at Nathan and make me glad I wasn't with him, glad that I had someone even more perfect beside me. If it were possible. I pushed those thoughts aside when I remembered Harriet and that uneasy feeling returned. I picked up the phone and dialled Ed's number.

'Hello?' he said, his voice thick and sleepy.

'Ed, it's me.'

'Abby, what's up?' he sounded worried for a moment and then the penny dropped. 'Of course, you met the mystery man, what's he like?'

'Ed, Depeche Mode. Before they were famous

they did a British tour, played at the Bridge House Hotel in London.'

'Abby, have you gone mad? What are you talking about?'

'Please, this is important, just help me OK. The Bridge House Hotel?'

'Yes, that's right,' he said. 'The 1980 tour. What of it?'

That was what I had suspected. I went quiet for a minute, thinking. Harriet told me Robert was thirty-four. The 1980 tour was twenty-two years ago. That means – that means – Robert would have to have been about twelve when he finished his degree, when he was 'too drunk to remember much about them though'.

'Ed, I think I have a bit of a problem with Robert,' I said finally.

# CHAPTER SEVEN

'That's really odd,' Ed said after I explained what Robert had told me. 'How old does he look?'

'Oh please, Ed, you know I'm crap at guessing ages. If I met you in a pub I'd guess you were younger than me.'

Ed made a noise that sounded like a snort.

'Look, all I could say is that he looked older than me, older than Harriet, and younger than my dad. He's one of those people that has that kind of confident older man appearance, but could be anything between thirty and fifty.'

'Well, if he really did see the band when he said he did, that would make him about forty-five wouldn't it? But why would he lie?'

I sighed. 'You don't think I'm just being silly do you? Blowing it all out of proportion. I mean, he might have seen a different band and got them confused.'

'It's possible, Abby, but I doubt it. It sounds as though he was quite specific, and it would be a big coincidence if he had been mistaken. I mean if he really is thirty-four, he couldn't have seen them at the Bridge House, or if he had he'd have been so young it would have been a big deal and it would stand out more in his memory. We know that they did play there in that year. Only that year, and he said it was before they were famous. What other explanation is there?'

'Maybe Harriet just got his age wrong, or lied about it because she was embarrassed about going out with someone so old,' Ed said.

'No,' I said with conviction. 'Harriet wouldn't lie.'

'Did he say what other music he liked?'

'He's got Chris Rea and Genesis in the car.' I knew exactly what Ed would say to that.

'Well there you go then. What more proof do you need?'

'But then he did say he also liked Kate Bush.'

'Ah,' Ed said, thinking for a second. 'Which album though?'

I looked at the phone in disbelief. 'Would it matter?'

'Possibly. Although I'd still say the guy has extremely suspect taste for a thirty-four year old.' Ed was thirty-four himself and refused to admit he was getting old.

'Oh, Ed, I don't know what to do. I just have a bad feeling about him and it's niggling me like crazy.'

'Try not to worry,' he said calmly. 'Find out how old Harriet thinks he is again. But if he's lying, it'll come out eventually. It's not the kind of thing you can hide for long.'

'Yes, but if he's lying about that, what else could

he lie about? And in the meantime Harriet gets in deeper and risks getting her heart broken. If she isn't already in too deep.'

'Abby, I haven't seen you in ages,' Vicky whined down the phone. 'It feels like forever.'

'I know. I'm sorry. I've had a few more gigs than normal. I guess people must be cramming their parties in now, making the most of the last days of summer. It'll slow down in the next couple of weeks I'm sure. It usually does.'

'Are you still going to this meal at the Indian on Saturday, with Nathan and Rebecca?'

'Well, I was planning to. I'm not working so I can make it.' I had toyed with the idea of excusing myself but it felt petty. I would have to get used to them being married sooner or later, and it wasn't as though much had changed. They had been living with each other for six months before the wedding and I had been over to their house many times. I had already seen how their shared lives melded together. The furniture that they chose together, the twin toothbrushes in the bathroom, the photograph of them in a boat off a Greek island that sat on the bookcase. All of those bitter pills I swallowed months ago, and the taste had been getting more bearable, more normal every time. If I was completely honest I guess I always thought of them as a non-permanent arrangement. Not through wishful thinking, but through my experiences of Rebecca's previous relationships. It wasn't the first time she had lived with someone and had told Vicky and I

111

that she was 'absolutely sure he was her future'. I can't remember Rebecca ever having been single. Nathan was the same. It was a bolt out of the blue when they announced they were getting married, and with only four weeks notice, it was a major piece of news to digest in such a short amount of time.

I had tried to call Rebecca several times over the past week since her message, but without success. Most of the time I got their machine, sometimes the machine didn't even click on and it just rang and rang. I called Rebecca at work but they told me she was booked off until the beginning of the following week. The one time I did get through, Nathan answered. He sounded out of breath and when I asked him about it he told me he was just on his way out. Normally he would have chatted to me about what we had been up to, how we were feeling, the way any friends do, but this time he treated me, not like an equal friend, but like Rebecca's friend.

'I'm sorry you haven't had a chance to speak to Rebecca,' he said, in an almost formal tone. 'She's had a lot on her plate since we got back. I'm sure she'll want to talk to you though. I'll get her to give you a call soon.' I was so taken aback by the tone of his voice that I didn't ask about the meal. I rang off quickly, feeling stung. Maybe now that they were married they were going to start cutting me out of their lives. OK, I could be analysing it too much but the way Nathan had said 'I'll *get* her to give you a call'. It was as though Rebecca needed to be pushed to call me, that she was trying to avoid me. I could imagine her standing behind

Nathan and mouthing 'tell her I'm out'. Perhaps she had finally realised that I still had feelings for Nathan and didn't want anything to do with me. I felt sick at the possibility that they could have discussed me. Nathan might have mentioned how I make him feel uncomfortable; Rebecca could have said that she feels she can't trust me anymore.

Ed, of course, told me I was paranoid. 'How could anybody want to ignore you?' he cooed, pinching my cheeks, like a father who believes their child can do no wrong and is irresistible to everyone they meet.

'Actually, I was going to ask you if you'd spoken to Rebecca or Nathan this week,' Vicky said. 'I've been trying to contact them, without much joy. I left a message but no one has called me back, which is very unlike them.'

I sat up on my bed, puzzled. 'Same here. I thought they were trying to avoid me.'

Vicky laughed out loud. 'Abby, you're so funny. Why would they want to ignore you?'

'Well, I don't know. I just thought it was strange I suppose.'

'Well, I'll keep trying and I'll let you know if I get through. Anyway, how did you get on with Harriet? Have you asked her?' I had told Vicky my suspicions about Harriet's fiancé. She was more dismissive than Ed and put it down to a misunderstanding, advising me to ask Harriet again how old she thought Robert was as she suspected I had simply misheard her.

'I did, she said thirty-four, I was right.'

'Odd,' Vicky said. 'And what do you think? Still suspicious?'

I plucked my cup of coffee off the bedside table and took a sip. 'Definitely. Did I tell you Ed thought he looked like Phil Collins?'

Vicky sighed and crooned in the voice of a love-sick teenager, 'Tarzan!'

I virtually spat my coffee out onto the receiver. 'Tarzan? Have you got the right Phil Collins? I'm talking about the man that has a universal look of "dad" about him. The short, middle-aged, balding guy?'

'Don't,' Vicky said. 'I just have to think of him and I feel like I could cry.'

'Eh?'

'Tarzan, the Disney film. I watched it with Clarice the other day. Phil Collins sung the soundtrack and, don't get me wrong, I'm not usually a fan or anything. But, oh, the songs were so lovely, all dramatic and powerful. And when Tarzan's falling in love with Jane, and beginning to see what he is, that he's a man. Phil Collins sings "Show Me", and they're swinging through the vines together, and then the pipes start up, and they are twisting in the air, looking into each other's eyes and oh, I just go all . . .' Vicky's voice got higher and higher until it sounded like a squeak and she trailed off emotionally.

I stared at the phone in disbelief and I could hear Vicky collecting herself, clearing her throat. 'Anyway,' she said defensively. 'I think he sounds nice. I don't think there's much reason to worry. Shame it didn't work out with Jerry though. He has been talking about her a lot to Alistair apparently. He's been asking if we can have another dinner party soon so that they can pick up where they left off.'

We chatted idly for another half an hour, mostly about Vicky's weight loss programme. She had done fantastically well and in two months had lost a stone and a half. Half of the amount she wanted to lose altogether, but she had now reached a plateau, and for the past few weeks had not managed to lose anything at all.

'I don't think you should worry about that,' I said. 'It's just your body's way of resting. It'll start dropping again soon.'

'Yes, I'm sure you're right,' Vicky said, not sounding too happy about it. 'I just get fed up when I've been so good and resisted so much and then nothing happens. It makes me think, well what was the point in that? Perhaps I've found my natural weight and no matter what I do I'll always be the podgy side of normal.'

'I really don't think so. What you need is a boost; a halfway treat. You should reward yourself for all that hard work. How about getting your hair done, or a manicure, something like that?'

'Oh, Abby, I would like nothing more, but when would I be able to fit that in? I couldn't take the kids with me to hairdressers, and by the time Alistair gets home most places are shut.'

'Look, why don't you let me have the kids? I can easily wangle an afternoon off with Ed. I haven't had many days off this year. It'd be a treat for me too. You know how much I love the kids. I could take them out somewhere.' I grinned at the phone and I could tell Vicky was smiling back, tempted by the idea of an afternoon's luxury. Only a mother's guilt was stopping her from jumping at the chance. 'That's settled then,' I said resolutely. 'You book yourself a treat and I'll treat the kids. Everyone's a winner. How does Thursday grab you? Then you'll look all polished for the meal on Saturday . . . if there still is one that is.'

Walking with kids takes forever, I thought as I took Clarice's hand, guiding her away from yet another pigeon feather she was trying to pluck out from the gutter. We had walked around some of the shops in town where I bought Clarice a baby-doll and Jack, a Lego kit. I knew Vicky would worry about me buying them presents but I just couldn't help myself. Walking around the toyshop I had been caught up in the kids' excitement and taken back to how it felt as a child when I went shopping with my mum. She used to spoil me rotten and was always buying me toys and gifts. It felt great to turn the tables and be the provider for a change. We wandered through the centre of the city, swinging our shopping bags and headed out to the harbour-side where I planned on buying us all lunch by the water. There was a new interactive science centre set behind the cafés where I thought I might take them after lunch. But first I needed somewhere to sit down and recharge.

We walked past a crêpe stall next to some steps, where water cascaded down from the pools by a statue of Neptune and out into the river. It was a glorious sunny day. Only a few little puffy white clouds dotted the sky and the sun was reflecting in the water and warming up the wooden slats of the walkway we were standing on. The smells of food from the bars and stalls were filling my senses and making my mouth water.

'Come on you two,' I called out to the kids. They were dawdling, fascinated by a couple of boys who were skateboarding across the water-covered steps, making mini-waves arc out in front of them. I leaned against a railing, waiting for them to catch up with me and watched as a ferry full of sightseers docked below me. I looked up, squinting into the sun and saw a lone figure of a man also leaning against the railings, his head bent low. My breath caught in my throat and my legs turned to jelly. It was Nathan. I watched him for a few seconds. He was miles away, lost in thought. I could have walked straight past him and he would have been none the wiser. I considered it. If he and Rebecca had been avoiding me then he wouldn't be pleased to see me now. But then Vicky hadn't spoken to them either, and Vicky was closer to Rebecca than I was. I was in two minds whether or not to risk it. If he looked disappointed to see me I didn't think I could bear it.

'Uncle Nat,' I heard Jack shout out from behind me. He raced past me over to where Nathan was standing. Nathan looked up in surprise as Jack threw his arms around his legs.

'Hello mate,' he said, bending down and ruffling Jack's hair. 'Where's your mum?' He looked up and saw Clarice and I approaching. 'Oh, hi Abby.' To my relief I saw that he was smiling. 'What are you doing here with this pair of rascals?' he said, laughing as Jack tried with all his might to wrestle Nathan to the ground, succeeding only in pulling his trousers down an inch.

'Oh, I said I'd look after the kids for the day. Give Vicky a chance to pamper herself. She's been run ragged recently.' I picked up Clarice who had been trying to lose herself in the folds of my baggy trousers.

'Don't be shy, Clary,' I said. 'You remember Nathan don't you? Nathan and Rebecca?' Clarice didn't look up from where her head was now buried into my neck. I smiled an apology at Nathan. 'I was just going to get the kids some lunch actually. Do you want to join us?' I said this hurriedly, without any advanced planning and I was surprised as the words tumbled out of my mouth. It wasn't until after I had said it that it occurred to me he was most likely here shopping or lunching with Rebecca. 'Where's Rebecca?' I asked, before he had a chance to answer my lunch invitation.

Was it my imagination or did Nathan's face cloud over as I said that?

'She's at home, having a lie down,' he said, then quickly changing the subject, added, 'Course I'll join you. I could do with a drink actually.'

We found a table by a big window at the Piano and Pitcher. A saxophonist was standing on the bridge outside playing Gershwin's 'Summertime', a slow jazz song my dad often played. The sun was streaming in, bathing me in warmth and sitting in a soft leather armchair, looking at Nathan across the table, I decided I wanted to stay right there for the rest of the day. Jack and Clarice were happily making dens on the wooden floor and playing with the toys I had bought them. We had ordered burgers and fries for the kids and a tapas with fat chips and dips for Nathan and I to share. We ate slowly, basking in the lazy afternoon atmosphere and chatting about their wedding and honeymoon. Nathan was relaxed in his chair, and I watched him as we talked, amazed at how different he looked compared to the last time I saw him at the wedding. Nathan usually had a slightly unshaven appearance and a casual dress sense. But today he looked almost scruffy. His trousers were well worn, his hair was standing up in multidirectional peaks and he had almost grown a beard as he looked as though he hadn't shaved for a week. Although he was smiling and chatty, the sparkle in his eyes was dulled and he spoke quietly, as though he was nursing a hangover and animated chat would hurt his head. He drunk his first bottled lager quickly and ordered himself another. After the waitress had left it on our table and walked away I asked him how Rebecca was.

'Not good,' he said. I looked up in surprise and he caught my gaze. He said nothing for a while but the sadness in his eyes was painfully apparent.

'Nathan, what's wrong?' My heart plummeted. Something awful had happened. I just knew it. Perhaps she was ill, seriously ill. I would never forgive myself if she was. I was such an awful friend to her. What if they had split up? Realised they had made a big mistake? I felt no excitement at the prospect. Only shame. Even as I sat there looking at Nathan, and, even in his current state, finding him almost irresistibly attractive, I couldn't be happy about anything that caused the hurt in his eyes.

Nathan glanced up, checking that the children were playing happily, oblivious to our conversation. They had pushed two armchairs together to make their den and were sitting in the middle, playing with the Lego. Clarice was watching every move Jack made. Neither of them looked interested in what Nathan was about to say, but I was, I was rooted to the spot.

'Rebecca had a miscarriage last week,' he said. I gasped. After a long swallow of lager he continued. 'She was pregnant when we got married. Thirteen weeks pregnant. She was over the twelve weeks that they say is critical. Not that we even thought it was a possibility. We were just getting used to the idea of being parents. I suppose that's why we got married. Once we knew she was going to have a baby, that was it. She wanted to be married, partly because she thought, well, we both thought, that the baby would be more secure if its parents were married, sharing the same name; and partly because of Rebecca's parents. She knew they would be happier about the baby if we were married, a proper family unit. She didn't want their disapproval. We didn't tell anyone because we thought that people would take our wedding more seriously if they didn't know. We didn't want them to think that that was the only reason we were getting married. Shotgun wedding and all that,' he said with a wry smile. 'We were going to announce it in the restaurant on Saturday.'

I sat stunned and silent, just letting him talk.

'She bled a bit on the plane back from Cyprus. She said it was nothing, that she wasn't worried. She spoke to a doctor who told her she needed bed-rest. Then on Wednesday last week I got up in the night and I found her in the bathroom. She'd been bleeding again. She knew that she'd lost it then. I took her in to the hospital and they gave her a D&C.' His eyes were brimming with tears and I swallowed hard, trying to rid myself of the lump in my throat. I reached over and squeezed his hand. He smiled back and breathed out heavily. 'It's OK, I'm all right. You'll probably think this is terrible, but, with us planning the wedding, it was hard to really think about the baby. It never really did sink in. To me, it's not like the way you see it happen in films or on TV. It wasn't like she even had a bump. We hadn't seen a scan yet. It didn't feel like a baby. It doesn't feel as though I've lost a child. Do you know what I mean?'

I nodded, although I couldn't really imagine how they must be feeling. 'How's Rebecca taking it?'

'She's just very quiet. I don't think she really wants to talk about it. She did have a long chat to Vicky on the phone a few days ago.'

My heart skipped over. Vicky knew and she didn't tell me?

'I think that helped her. She says that she's OK. That she hadn't got used to the thought of having a baby; like me I suppose. She wants to just carry on as normal. She's tired and was a bit tender from the anaesthetic, but physically, she's pretty much recovered. I think she's probably also worried that it was something that she'd done. She had champagne at the wedding, maybe flying or even the whole stress of getting married effected her, but the doctor said it most likely wouldn't be that, that no one knows why it happens. It just wasn't meant to be.'

He looked out of the window and I sat quietly, thinking over what he had told me, not knowing what to say that could help him. For the first time, I noticed that the saxophonist had finished playing and in his place were a group of drummers, hitting out a fast and thumping rhythm that was breaking up the peaceful ambience, making me feel jumpy and tense.

'Thanks for listening, Abby. I haven't really told anyone about this. I feel better getting it off my chest.'

I smiled, touched that he had confided in me. 'Anytime. And if there's anything I can do . . .' I trailed off lamely.

'Perhaps we will still go for a meal. Just a few of us. I cancelled the Indian, but maybe we should do something. I think Rebecca could do with a few close friends around her right now. And we need to have a bit of fun. It hasn't exactly been the best way to start married life, I think we need some light relief.'

Jack wandered back over to the table. 'Are we going to the science place now?' he said, looking desperate to go.

I checked the time. 'Oh crikey, it's half-past two. I

said I'd have you two back by four.' I saw Jack's face fall in disappointment and felt guilty that I hadn't taken them anywhere really special or different. 'Oh Jack, I'm really sorry. I'll take you soon I promise. Come on, I'll get you an ice-cream on the way back to the car.'

'Ice-cream!' Nathan said, jumping out of his chair and smiling at the children. 'What a perfect way to finish the day.' He bent down to gather up the toys and I got ready to leave, glad of an excuse to get away from the noise of the drums below us. I could see that Nathan also wanted the sober mood to be forgotten. He needed to take his mind off what had happened.

Walking across Millennium Square, Clarice was drawn to the giant steps that were set in the middle. Water was falling over them, creating flat, shallow pools. There were what looked like metal sheets sticking up like statues at either end. Water poured down them, creating dancing patterns of light. I suspected that the hot summer sun had warmed the water and a couple of older children were sitting on benches at the far end, dabbling their toes onto the step nearest them. We still had an hour before I said I'd have the kids home so, after a moments hesitation, I bent down and helped Clarice take her socks and shoes off. She laughed with delight and jumped straight onto the steps, pounding her feet in the puddles and splashing us. She marched up and down the walkways, kicking the water up as she went. Jack took off his trainers and rolled up his trousers, joining his sister and they splashed each other, laughing and squealing. I sat down on one of the benches and took off my own trainers. I was wearing cut off khaki trousers which finished just below my knees so I didn't need to roll them up. I leapt onto the first step, feeling the warm water flood around my toes, then as Nathan laughed with disbelief, I ran after the kids.

'Come on Nathan, the water's gorgeous!' I shouted from the top of the steps. He looked around, checking to see who was watching. There were only half-a-dozen people milling around. He shrugged his shoulders then took off his trainers, rolled up his trousers and joined us, chasing after Jack who kicked up water in retaliation, wetting Nathan's trousers and T-shirt.

Half an hour later we were all drenched and my jaw ached from laughing so much. Clarice had eventually taken her dress off and sat down in the water with her knickers on. Jack and Nathan had splashed one another so much they were completely sodden, and I had tried to walk through a narrow corridor made of metal sheets that acted like two walls of water. Of course I didn't fit through easily and the water had soaked me to the bone. I was beginning to feel cold and suggested we should head off. We rung out what clothes we could and squelched back to the carpark.

Fortunately I had borrowed Vicky's car to take the kids to town, so there was enough room for me to give Nathan a lift home. I turned the heating up, feeling guilty that I was returning the kids back home in such a state, but I knew Vicky wouldn't mind. They were happy and had enjoyed themselves, that was the main thing.

Nathan was smiling at me as I pulled the car out of the space. 'You were so funny, I can't believe you did that.'

'Why not? It was fun.'

'Rebecca would never do that. She'd be too worried about people staring at her, or getting her clothes wet.'

My mood deflated a fraction at the mention of Rebecca. I remembered what had happened and felt bad that we had had such a good time without her. 'Do you think she's been OK on her own?' I asked, biting my lip.

'Abby, don't feel bad. She wanted to be alone. That's why I walked into town, to give her a bit of breathing space. And besides, you did me a power of good.' He patted my leg with his hand briefly and I stiffened. His hand felt warm and strong through the wet material of my trousers. I tried to concentrate on driving but Nathan made me laugh by taking his hand away, saying 'yeuch' and trying to wipe it dry on the front of his T-shirt.

I dropped him off at the end of his road as I wanted to get the kids home as quickly as possible. He kissed me on the cheek before he left, brushing me with his stubble. I told him to give my love to Rebecca and that I would see her as soon as I could then I sat watching as he jogged down the road to his house.

'Has the car broken?' Jack asked after a while and I laughed, pulling away from the curb.

# CHAPTER EIGHT

On Friday I had been lost in thought for most of the day. Ed put it down to 'post-child-minding-stress-syndrome', assuming that Jack and Clarice had worn me out. I didn't tell him about seeing Nathan and what he had told me. Vicky had known about it and said nothing, so I presumed they didn't want it to be common knowledge. I also didn't want Ed analysing me. He was well aware of my feelings for Nathan and I didn't trust my ability to hide a smile if I told him about paddling with the kids. About how special I felt knowing it was me Nathan had turned to, and it was me who had turned him from the solemn, melancholy man at the harbour-side, to the man who was splashing us, laughing until he bent double. I knew it was wrong; I knew my thoughts should be with Rebecca, and they really were, I wanted to do everything I could to help her. But Nathan was my friend too. And try as I could to concentrate on the pain they must have gone through in the past week, I couldn't stop the image of him, wet and grinning, reappearing in my mind, making me smile. Ed, knowing me as well as he does, would see this a mile off. And although he was understanding and had told me a million times over that 'you can't help who you fall in love with', or how he understood what it felt like to 'fall for the wrong one', I knew that it wasn't the same. I knew Ed had never been attracted to a friend's husband, or wife; he wouldn't consider it. He was fiercely protective of me and despite all his words of understanding, I suspected my feelings for Nathan disappointed him, and that's the last thing I wanted to do.

That evening whilst I was picking out the last few records and CDs for an eighteenth birthday party I was booked to DJ for that night, Harriet came upstairs with two mugs of coffee balanced on a tray.

'Mmm, just what I needed, thank you.' I put mine on the coffee table and continued to hunt through a pile of CDs Ed had lent me.

'I wish you weren't going out tonight,' Harriet said, flopping down at the floor by my feet.

I smiled at her guiltily. Robert had not come over at all during the past week. He was over in Germany for business meetings until Sunday and then would be stuck in the office writing up reports and heading follow up meetings with his collegues in the London office. Harriet wasn't going to see him for a fortnight and had been spending more time upstairs with me. She had even fallen asleep on my sofa a couple of times. Displayed in the bay window of Harriet's living room was an enormous bouquet of roses. The card, which Harriet showed me proudly, read

WE SHOULD NEVER BE APART. R, beautifully scribed in fountain pen. A medium only the old or the very traditionally educated had got to grips with, I thought with uncharitable suspicion. I knew that there was every possibility Robert could turn out to be a decent man, the right man for Harriet, but sadly once my suspicions had been triggered about his age, I was looking for any kind of sign that would give him away. I said nothing to Harriet about these doubts. I needed something more concrete first, I couldn't just tell her I thought he had suspect taste in music.

'I'm sorry, H. It won't be a late one. The licence ends at eleven and it's only a small do, not much to pack up. I'll be back by midnight.'

Harriet grimaced. 'That might still feel early to you, but some of us like to be tucked up in bed by the end of the ten o'clock news.'

'We'll do something tomorrow, I promise. I don't think I've got anything on after tonight.' I saw the CD I wanted wedged under my hi-fi rack and wiggled onto my stomach, straining to reach it. Just at that moment the phone rang. I groaned. 'Please would you get it? Tell them I'm busy, I've got to leave the house in ten minutes or I'll be late setting up.'

Harriet padded over to the phone. 'Hello? No, no, it's Harriet, her house-mate. Abby can't come to the phone at the moment.'

I smiled to myself. Harriet never referred to herself as my landlady. She always said it sounded horrible, as though our friendship was a business arrangement and gave the impression to strangers that she was a fifty-year-old divorcee with empty nest syndrome – one in her family was plenty already, she would joke, referring to her mother.

'Oh right,' she continued. 'Hello there. How was the honeymoon?'

I banged my head on the rack above me. She was either talking to Rebecca or Nathan. I froze, listening for further clues.

'Excellent, I'm so pleased. It was lovely to see you too. Saturday? Abby didn't mention it, no. Right, oh I see. Well, I'm sure that would be fine. I'm not doing anything. Yes, I agree. I've been feeling a bit like that myself.'

It must be Rebecca, Nathan would be too shy on the phone to tell Harriet how he was feeling about anything.

'OK, well unless she calls you back, take it as a yes and we'll look forward to seeing you tomorrow.' She rang off and I jumped up.

'Was that Rebecca?'

Harriet nodded.

'What did she say?'

'She said she's been going mad in the house lately and thinks it would do us all good to have a big night out. Apparently there's quite a few people going out to a meal and then going to a few bars afterwards. She wanted to know if we could come. She said "bring whoever you want", and that she wanted to be "surrounded by friends, because now she's got married she doesn't want people thinking she's going to stay at home and cook vegetables".'

Harriet said this in a cheerful, enthusiastic tone, taking off the way Rebecca often talks.

'That sounds like Rebecca, always the life and soul. Doesn't want to be forgotten.' I was surprised though. It sounded like she was in good spirits and planning a big night out. From what Nathan had told me, I expected her to be more in the mood for an intimate night with close friends. But then that was never her style. She was never down for long and rarely dwelled too hard on anything, a good laugh and a night out with friends was always her cure in the past. I thought this time she might feel differently, but obviously I was wrong.

'Hey, you could bring Ed along,' Harriet said, grinning widely at me.

I frowned at her. 'Don't look at me like that. I've told you, you have the wrong end of the stick.' Ever since Harriet caught Ed and I on the front lawn, she had teased me about what we were up to. I hadn't protested a great deal, worried that she would figure out that we had really been trying to sneak a look at Robert. I just told her we were play fighting and left it at that. 'And you had better not say anything. You'll only embarrass us.' I dropped the last CD in my record case and snapped the lid down shut.

'Don't worry, my lips are sealed,' Harriet said. 'But I just want you to know, I think it's sweet.'

'Look,' I said seriously, standing and facing her. 'Ed is gay. End of story. He's like a big brother to me. I love him, but not in the way you think.'

Harriet laughed. 'Abby, Ed is bisexual, you know that.'

'Oh, come on, he's as good as gay. He never eyes up women, he hasn't had a relationship with a woman since he was in his early twenties, as far as I am aware. The only reason he doesn't call himself gay is so his mother can live in hope of a grandchild. And she'll have a long wait I can tell you.' I picked the keys to the Scooby off the table and waved Harriet goodbye. I wasn't going to discuss it anymore. The last thing I needed was to have my friendship with Ed tarred by salacious gossip, however well meaning it might be.

Chilli Manilli's was a new Mexican restaurant on Whiteladies Road and it was about as party-like in atmosphere as you could get. It was packed with people and the air hummed with a vibrant happiness as they laughed, chatted and cheered. Admittedly our table was contributing to a large proportion of the noise. We sat on the centre table, which was filled with about twenty of Rebecca's friends. Most of us were sampling cocktails whilst we waited for the food to arrive. We 'ooed' and 'ahhed' at the spectacular creations that were being brought to our table, decorated with fizzing sparklers or speared tropical fruit. My drink was presented in a glass the size of a cereal bowl and was a deep cherry red, gradually paling to pink and then, at the bottom, turned the colour of rosé wine. It was deliciously fruity and despite being served ice-cool, it was still making my cheeks glow with warmth.

Rebecca and Nathan made a very attractive couple. Rebecca looked gorgeous in a little black dress that stopped mid-thigh. Her hair was down and curling slightly at the ends to give it a sexy, tousled appearance. She made me feel underdressed by comparison, in my denim knee length skirt, T-shirt and green flash trainers. I suspected that Rebecca had dressed Nathan tonight. He was wearing a smart shirt, open at the collar, a pair of neatly fitting black trousers and was well groomed, the opposite of the last time I saw him. Rebecca was chatting animatedly with a huddle of work friends, faces I recognised, but people I didn't know very well. Nathan was sitting back watching, a cool observer, smiling as Rebecca laughed. He wasn't participating in the cocktail experimentation and was instead, as always, drinking bottled lager. He was the complete opposite of Ed, who was drinking something the colour of washing up liquid whilst writing his name with a sparkler.

'Harriet, I've got to congratulate you on your engagement,' Vicky said leaning across the table to see her better. 'I want to hear all the details.' Her eyes were bright with excitement. Vicky always loved a good romantic story.

Harriet shook her head, smiling coyly. 'Oh, there's not much to tell really. I don't even have a ring to show off yet. It all just happened so quickly. I think he has really swept me off my feet. I still don't think it's sunk in.'

'Well, I can't wait to meet him. It's such a shame he can't be here tonight.'

'I know,' Harriet said sadly. 'But then duty calls I'm afraid. He works very hard, and you know what the pace is like in the city, he rarely gets a break.'

'So what are you going to do in the future?' Vicky pressed on. 'Who's going to move to be with the other, or are you going to meet in the middle somewhere and both commute?'

I sat up straight, suddenly very interested to know what Harriet's answer would be. I had been so wrapped up in the present, getting used to the idea of Harriet being engaged to someone and pre-occupied with just what kind of someone he was, that the future implications of their engagement had never entered my head. Surely she wouldn't sell her beautiful house? She had spent so much time making it perfect. Her 'haven', she called it. She couldn't leave Bristol, I would lose one of my best friends, my house mate, my *house*. Jesus, I'd be homeless. I could never afford to live in Clifton if it wasn't for Harriet. I would have to move away, to a part of Bristol that could never be as close to my heart, my friends, my dad, my life, as where I lived now. I bypassed the curly straw and took a large slug of my drink.

Harriet shrugged and thought for a moment. 'We haven't really discussed the future yet. It's more a case of, we love each other, we want to be together and what happens next, well, we'll be together one way or another, but I'm not sure when. I suspect we'll have a long engagement. See how it goes.'

OK, no need to panic then. All's right with the world once more. Well, for the time being at least.

'Are you all right Abby? You're looking a little

pale,' Vicky asked, scrutinising my face. 'You're not coming down with something are you? Clarice has been a bit off colour today. Maybe you caught something off her on Thursday.'

'Oh, Thursday,' Rebecca joined in, rolling her eyes. 'The state that Nathan came home in, I couldn't believe it!'

I felt the colour return to my face as Nathan caught my eye.

Some of Rebecca's friends looked at her curiously, wanting to hear more and Rebecca obliged. 'Nathan bumped into Abby at the harbourside on Thursday. She was looking after Vicky's kids. They ended up actually *in* the fountain at the Millennium Square, and had a water fight. He came home absolutely drenched. Nathan walked in the door and I went, "Is it raining?" and ran out to bring the washing in!' Rebecca joked, making her friends laugh and look at us with amusement. Nathan and I shared a sheepish smile and it felt good that we had been linked together, like mischievous children; partners in crime. I caught Ed looking at me with a puzzled expression and realised he must find it odd that I hadn't told him about seeing Nathan. We spent so much time together that I usually told him about every fragment of my life.

Vicky laughed, joining in with Rebecca as though she was pretending to disapprove. 'You should have seen Jack and Clarice. They looked like they had taken a swim in the harbour. And I swear Abby has been playing them garage music in the car.

Clarice asked me to "Re-rewind" her Disney video this morning.'

Everyone burst out laughing and I pretended to be distracted by the menu.

As our food began to arrive at the table, the topic of conversation stayed on a musical theme as Harriet told Vicky, Alistair, Nathan and Rebecca about the night we had gone through my collection, looking for sexy male voices. 'Honestly,' she said, to Vicky in particular. 'You have to get Abby to do that for you. I can really see what she means about the power of a voice now. There are some songs that can just blow you away.'

'I know what you mean,' Vicky said, taking a plate of salad from the waiter. 'I always had a thing for Jim Kerr's voice. You know, the Simple Minds guy? There's something about the way he sings. All breathy, and . . . urgent.'

Alistair's eyebrows shot up and he looked at his wife in surprise. 'That's the last time I let you play *Street Fighting Years* during one of our romantic dinners.'

Vicky patted his hand playfully and speared a slice of avocado. 'Come on love, I know all about you and Blondie.'

We all laughed and Nathan joined in. 'For me there is only one truly sexy woman singer and that's the woman from the Cardigans. God, her voice is something else.'

I vowed never to listen to that album again.

'I don't really think I have a favourite,' Rebecca said, looking as though she wanted desperately to think of a name in retaliation to Nathan's comments, but Harriet cut in. 'What about you Ed? Do you have any favourites?'

'God, that's a point Ed,' Vicky said. 'If you fancy both men and women, do you find a man or a woman's voice sexy to listen to?'

All eyes shifted to Ed, who was chewing slowly, enjoying being the centre of attention. 'Good question,' he said, chewing some more. 'Women,' he said finally and everyone looked surprised. 'Yes, definitely women. Kylie when she did that "Confide in Me" song, definitely. And Madonna's "Justify My Love". They're both really sexy songs. But I don't usually listen to music for that reason.'

'Diva's. We should have known,' Nathan said, nodding. 'But is that because you fancy them or want to be them?' He winked and there was a smatter of laughter. I looked at Ed, checking that he had taken the comment in good humour, but he had and he balled up his serviette and threw it at Nathan. 'Oi! I'm no queen you know,' he said, grinning.

'Funny that you chose Kylie and Madonna though. They're gay icons aren't they?' Alistair said, sampling Vicky's cocktail when she wasn't looking.

'Everybody loves Madonna though don't they?' I said. 'I mean even I wouldn't say no.'

Ed looked at me grinning. 'Now that I would have to see.'

I felt Harriet kick me under the table and when I looked up she was smiling knowingly. I ignored her.

'Abby and I have countless discussions about what's our favourite Madonna look,' Ed continued, sparking off another lively debate.

Everybody had a preference and it was interesting to hear how different they all were. Vicky loved the 'Ray of Light' look where Madonna's dancing in a club. This, she revealed after much dissection, was due to the fact that it was just after the birth of Lourdes and it gave Vicky hope that after a baby you can still look fabulous and be taken seriously as a sexy, modern women. Rebecca liked the straight blonde hair scraped back into a ponytail which she had for the Blonde Ambition tour. Ed loved the Vogue video where she had a curly bob and wore a trouser suit. This, everyone agreed, was because she was less feminine and was going through a phase of gender 'experimentation', but Ed denied this profusely and swore that it was the way she danced in the video that really appealed to him. Harriet had a preference for the 'Material Girl' look, where she was dressed like Marilyn Monroe and again, we all laughed because Harriet had always been the kind of woman who would turn away men offering her diamonds and more. She was quite capable of going out and getting them for herself.

I could never choose a favourite as it depended on my mood, but the look I always went back to was her original 'Holiday' gear. The ragbag layers, skirts and leggings, lace and gloves with messy hair, bangles and of course, the crucifix.

Ed groaned and said, 'Abby you're such a purist.'

'Didn't she have hairy armpits then?' Alistair said

pulling a face. 'I could never really see why people fancied her.'

Vicky ruffled his hair playfully. 'She'd eat you for breakfast.'

'But if you saw her without the make-up and the clothes she'd be really quite ordinary, don't you think?'

'Madonna could never be ordinary, I think she's incredible,' Vicky said, chewing on a lettuce leaf.

'I didn't fancy her much when she was bleached blonde,' Nathan chipped in. 'She looked gorgeous in "Like A Prayer" when her hair was dark brown. Really feminine and sexy, with just a hint of raunch.' Again it was brought home to me just why he was attracted to Rebecca and not me. I sat up and crossed my legs, in an attempt to look more ladylike.

Harriet slapped her hands on the table. 'Hey, I've just had a great idea. It's my thirtieth at the end of October. We could have a Madonna fancy dress party. We could all dress up in one of her different looks or as one of the men she's been linked with. Let's face it, there's been enough of both. Abby could make a montage of Madonna songs, or songs linked with her. Maybe eighties compilations as that was her best era. It'd be a great laugh.'

Vicky grinned from ear to ear. 'Excellent! Count me in.'

Alistair looked less sure. 'I don't know,' he said warily. 'I don't know that much about her.'

Everyone looked at him then burst into a chorus of, 'Oh go on Alistair' and 'Don't be so boring', until eventually he nodded, smiling and warned,

'So long as I don't get lumbered with the conical bra.'

By eleven o'clock we had left Chilli Manilli's and found ourselves in a late night bar a few doors further down the road. By this time everyone was either drunk or getting that way, even Harriet, who seemed to be making more of a habit of drinking these days. Rebecca was standing at the bar talking to half-a-dozen people from her office. Only one of them was a woman. The men were giving Rebecca their fullest attention and Rebecca was lapping it up and flirting outrageously.

'I see marriage hasn't changed her much then,' Ed muttered under his breath. We were sitting together on a sofa, sharing a table with Vicky, Alistair and Harriet. I could just make out Nathan, standing across the room, talking to a man I didn't recognise. It seemed that whenever I looked up, he was glancing over the man's shoulder, watching Rebecca from a distance.

Vicky was slumped against Alistair's chest, her eyes half shut. 'God I'm drunk.'

'Come on you, I think I'd better take you home,' Alistair said, kissing the top of her head.

'Yeah, take me, take me,' she slurred, looking up into his eyes.

Alistair looked down and pulled a face. 'Vicky, you've just dribbled on me. That's disgusting!' He sat Vicky up and she wobbled then slumped down onto the other side of the sofa. After about ten minutes of giggling and drunken fumbling they finally managed to get up and say goodbye to us. They wandered off to tell Nathan and Rebecca they were going and disappeared into the heaving mass of people between us and the bar.

'Right, well, I think I'll be heading off as well if you don't mind. I'm pretty tired,' Ed said, downing the remains of his drink and standing up.

I looked up at him, surprised. It wasn't like Ed to leave the pub before last orders. We often joked that he didn't feel he'd had a successful night out unless he had been walked to the door by a butch bouncer.

'What's up Ed, don't you like the look of the doormen in this place?' I teased, grinning cheekily. My humour was lost on him though and he waved wordlessly, heading for the exit.

'Is Ed all right?' Harriet said. 'He seemed unusually quiet tonight.'

I shrugged. I was beginning to feel tired myself and was losing my own staying power at a rapid rate. It appeared Rebecca didn't need our support after all. She was the life and soul of the bar and I had barely spoken to her all night. I felt no sense of duty to stay and suggested to Harriet that we made a move.

'I'm so glad you said that,' she said, putting down her drink, that was only half finished, and picked her coat off the back of the chair. 'Let's go.'

I allowed myself one last look at Nathan as I followed Harriet to the door. He was still talking to the same person and, at the very moment I was looking at him, he glanced up and caught my eye.

He held up his hand, gesturing for me to wait and I faltered as Harriet was already reaching the door. He left his drink on the bar and walked over to me, reaching out for my hands.

'Don't go Abby,' he said, looking at me with a drunken, glazed expression.

'Oh Nathan, I've got to. I'm walking back with Harriet and she's already gone.'

'But I was just about to come and find you, oh, please stay.' He cocked his head to one side and I felt myself quickly becoming putty in his hands. I was racked with disappointment that I'd chosen this time to leave. I looked over to the door and saw Harriet stepping outside, rubbing her hands as the cold air hit her. I couldn't let her go home alone.

'Nathan, I can't, really. You go find your wife,' I said, smiling. The words pained me as I spoke them, but also made me proud of myself for showing restraint and loyalty.

He made a noise, like a whimper and his eyebrows creased up in the middle. God, if he was mine, I thought. If he was mine, there's no way I could ignore that face. There's no way I could stop myself from holding him, touching him.

'No, really, I've got to go,' I said quickly, glad I was still sober enough to be in control of my actions. I squeezed his hands and let go, then turned away and concentrated on walking out, without looking back. When I got to the door I spotted Harriet leaning against a lamppost, her eyes drooping with the effects of tiredness and drink. I pushed my way past the bouncers and as soon as I was outside my cool façade left me. I walked out onto the pavement, covering my face with my hands. 'Piss, piss, piss, piss,' I cried, jumping up and down in frustration.

'Oh Abby, you always need the toilet when we've just left the pub. You should have gone earlier,' Harriet grumbled, then set off up the road in the direction of home.

I lingered briefly outside the pub, tempted to press my nose against the chilly window and see if Nathan had joined his wife, but I thought better of it and jogged off to catch up with Harriet.

# CHAPTER NINE

Dad's kitchen is always a comforting place when things are getting me down. We had lived in the same house since I was four years old so it is the only house, apart from Harriet's, where I have a sense of home. The kitchen in particular is my favourite place. Especially on Sundays. The day's papers are always spread over the table to be looked at with a large jug of freshly brewed coffee. If we weren't going to the pub for lunch then the kitchen would be emanating those homely, familiar smells of chicken, roasting with sage and onion stuffing and home grown vegetables steaming on the hob; comfort food at its best. I hadn't seen dad since the day I came over and found him sorting out mum's things and although we had spoken on the phone, I felt guilty. I didn't want him to think I was upset about what he had been doing and so I had set aside the day to spend with him, just pottering about and keeping each other company.

Dad walked into the kitchen holding a white plastic bowl. 'Plums,' he said, waving one at me proudly. 'They're ready early this year. I thought we could make a crumble for pudding.' He put the bowl down on the table and I eyed the fruit suspiciously, looking for bugs and beasties.

'So, what's little Harriet up to these days?' Dad asked as he started to weigh out the ingredients for a crumble topping.

'Dad, she's hardly "little". She's three years older than me and she'll be thirty in a month or so.'

'Thirty, hey?' He shook his head. 'And I hear she's engaged now, is that right?'

I nodded and got up to wash the plums at the sink.

'So, what's the lucky fella like?'

I pulled a face which Dad wouldn't have been able to see. 'He's all right I suppose. I've only really met him once so it's hard to say. Harriet seems happy enough.'

'Good, good. Harriet's a lovely girl. I always liked her. And what about you?'

'Well, I'm a lovely girl too, and as far as I know, you've always liked me. Unless there's something you want to get off your chest.' Of course I knew full well what he was really asking, but I didn't feel like admitting I was single. It made me feel as though I had failed; like being jobless or having no friends to see on a Saturday night. Hardly the kind of topic I wanted to offer up for parental scrutiny.

'So there's no nice men you want to bring over and introduce me to then?'

I looked over my shoulder at him, raising my eyebrows in mock surprise. 'Men? I can really only handle one at a time, but if I ever bag myself some triplets you'll be the first to know.'

Dad made a 'Hmm' noise, then, admitting defeat, he dropped the subject.

Throughout lunch I noticed that Dad was pensive and serious. He was chewing his food slowly and waving his fork in the air, waggling it as though he was thinking about something, perhaps wanting to broach a subject but not sure how to go about it.

By the time we had nearly finished eating I was starting to get paranoid that he was about to drop a bombshell on me and decided to broach the subject first. 'Is everything all right Dad?'

He smiled, embarrassed. 'Actually, I was going to ask you the same thing. You've been very—' he sighed, struggling for the right words '—pre-occupied, lately.'

'Have I?' I hadn't been aware that I was acting any differently than normal.

Dad put down his spoon and rested his arms on the table. 'Listen, Abby, I know it's none of my business what you do with your life, and I will always trust your decisions. You know that, don't you?'

'Da-*ad*,' I moaned, concentrating hard on the pudding before me.

'I just want to know that you're happy. That's all.'

'I am happy.' I forced a smile.

'I'm not sure that you are though. It worries me. You see Abby, ever since your mother died . . .'

This sentence made me stiffen. I didn't want to talk about this now.

'. . . perhaps even since she first got sick, well, you haven't really allowed yourself to move on. You seem to be frozen in time. You gave up your place at university when you only really needed to defer for a year. I understand how hard it's been for you and of course I'm grateful to you for wanting to look out for us, and now for me, but I'm a grown man. I know I'll be OK. And you were always so excited about your English degree, I worry about what you've sacrificed. You're a bright girl; I don't want to see you wasting your life. You've turned your teenage hobbies into a job and I'm just not sure if it's right for you.'

'Dad, I love DJing. You know that. Music is my first love. If I could sing or play an instrument, then I'd be making it, but as I can't, I play it, sell it. It doesn't matter to me. I'm happy doing what I'm doing, and I'm good at it because I'm passionate about it. I know it's not some great career, but honestly Dad, I am happy. It's great to see people getting up and dancing, celebrating in an atmosphere I've helped create, especially at weddings. I get to share in their happiness, their special day.'

'But when will it be your turn? You can't live your life through other people's happiness, you should be creating some of your own.'

I sighed, why wasn't I able to convince him? 'Dad, I think that short of becoming a Blue Peter presenter and tap-dancing down your drive, there's not much I could do to stop you worrying about me being happy and fulfilled. It's your job to worry, and you're very good at it,' I teased, waggling my finger at him, then stood up to start collecting the dishes.

Dad stayed sitting, watching me for a moment. I got the feeling that he wasn't happy about me ending the discussion so flippantly and wanted to take it further, but I really didn't feel like a discussion on where my life was heading, I was confused enough already.

'Hey, Harriet's planning on having a Madonna theme for her thirtieth birthday.' I was noisily stacking the dishwasher and making an effort to look cheerful. Dad pulled a puzzled expression that made me laugh. 'She sang "Like A Virgin", and no, before you ask, it's not a hymn,' I teased.

'I know who Madonna is,' he said, casting a nonchalant eye over the paper. 'I could even tell you who S Club 7 and Norman Cook are.'

I grabbed a handful of cutlery and felt a sharp pain in my thumb. 'Shit!'

'Hey, there's no need to swear, it's not that shocking you know,' Dad said and started an off key rendition of 'Reach For The Stars'.

'Not that, this!' I held out my thumb for him to see, and a deep red rivulet of blood trickled down my hand, collected in a pool then dripped onto the carpet.

He put down his paper. 'Oh, darling, you're going to need a plaster on that. I'll get you one from the bathroom cupboard.'

'Don't worry, I'll go.' I blotted up the blood with a piece of kitchen towel then walked upstairs to the bathroom, also humming the S Club 7 song. 'God, Dad's started something now, I'll be humming that for days,' I muttered, swinging the bathroom cupboard open.

Rooting through the bottles at the front I saw a little first aid kit hidden at the back. I pulled it out, knocking an electric toothbrush and a pot of cream onto the bathroom floor. I bent down to pick them up and when I did a familiar label caught my eye. 'Space NK Night Cream?' I stared at it for a moment, turning it over in my hands. What was Dad doing with this? It was the most recent style of packaging that Harriet liked. I opened the lid and peered inside. It had only been used a few times and there were indentations in the cream where someone had taken out little amounts with their finger. A small, dainty finger. A woman's finger. It suddenly dawned on me that Dad had got a girlfriend.

'It could be your dad's,' Ed said. He was ripping open a box of CDs that had just been delivered and didn't even look up when I divulged my shocking bathroom find.

'Ed! What's up with you? This is my dad we're talking about. He's just not the moisturising type, and even if he was . . . well, it's not worth thinking about because it blatantly *is* a woman's moisturiser.'

'Well perhaps he just had a female visitor, you know the amount of stuff women take into the toilet with them. She probably just forgot to take it away.'

'It was a *night* cream. The kind of thing women only put on before they go to *bed*,' I snapped. Why couldn't he just agree with me and give me some support, instead of disputing the bare facts of the matter?

'What's so wrong with him having a girlfriend anyway, Abby? You should be happy for him,' Ed snapped. He looked at me for the first time since I had started the conversation and I felt as though he was challenging me.

'I am happy for him, of course I am. I just wish he felt he could talk to me about it, that's all,' I said in a small voice. 'And last time I saw him he was packing mum's stuff away, and now I can see why, and I swear I'm OK with it. I want him to find someone, but it just feels weird, you know? It's like mum really has gone now, it's the end of an era and . . .' I was aware that my voice was sounding progressively wobbly and I fought to keep it under control, but the more I tried, the more my throat felt tight, until I felt I couldn't breathe.

Ed's face softened and he walked over, wrapping his arms around me. 'It's all right,' he said, and the kindness that I needed was there at last. 'I'm sorry,' Ed whispered.

'What do you mean sorry?' I lifted my head up off his chest and looked at his face, but he just smiled and relaxed his grip. 'Hey, let's listen to the new Coldplay single,' he said and I felt the waft of a CD being waggled under my nose.

We spent the morning making each other laugh and talking a lot about the old days. Ed was making me cringe with embarrassment, teasing me about how much time I spent in his shop and the mad clothes I used to wear; the brightly coloured stripy tights and the big old army boots with mini-skirts that made me look as though my feet were ridiculously out of proportion to the rest of me. I would wear my dad's old cardigans with the sleeves practically trailing on the floor, and so many rings that Ed said my hands could have been classed as lethal weapons.

'Those were the days,' I said, fondly.

Ed laughed at me. 'What are you on about? Nothing's changed. We are still where we were ten years ago, only now you get paid to be here. Oh, and your dress sense is a bit less Gothic.'

I looked at him harshly. 'I was never a Goth. I was far too colourful. I prefer "experimental".'

Ed smirked and after a fresh bout of teasing we finally agreed on 'alternative'.

'You haven't changed a bit though. Same hair, same clothes, you just don't seem to age at all.'

Ed beamed at this. 'Hey, just call me the Peter Pan of pop.'

'Like Cliff Richard,' I joked. Tasha walked in then, saving me from being chased around the shop with a rolled up Limp Bizkit poster. 'Abby, phone for you,' she called.

'Who is it?'

'Didn't say. Nice voice though,' she said with a wink.

I followed her to the front desk and picked up the phone. 'Hello?'

'Hi Abby it's me.'

'Oh, hi Nathan. How are you?' I was taken aback to hear his voice. He rarely ever phoned me. Well, try never.

'Oh, not bad. Bored in the office. You know how it is. I was just wondering if you wanted to meet up after work. Rebecca's got some kind of works night out organised and I didn't fancy going straight home to an empty house.'

'Oh, right. OK, well, I've got no plans.' I could feel butterflies grouping together *en masse* in my stomach.

'Great, well, why don't I come and fetch you when you finish? What time are you off tonight?'

'About five-thirty.'

'Excellent, I can finish at five so that gives me enough time to come and find you.'

'OK, well, I'll see you then, then.'

'Yep, bye Abby.'

I kept the phone to my ear long after I heard him hang up. I couldn't believe he had called me up like that. Hundreds of thoughts flooded my brain in a jumble; Why me? Does Rebecca know? Should I tell anyone? I had a nauseating feeling that I was doing something wrong, but then why should I? I wouldn't question it if any of my other friends had called. Why should Nathan be any different? Because you love him, that's why, a devilish voice in my head taunted.

I put the phone down and returned to the back room where Ed was watching me, ignoring the customer he was halfway through serving.

'Well?' he said, expectantly.

'Oh, it was just Nathan. He's picking me up after work.' I tried to make myself sound as indifferent as possible.

Ed said nothing, slamming the till drawer so hard he made the customer jump with alarm.

Ten minutes later a lad in his late teens came in. He was wearing an old grey jacket that had been customised with patches on the shoulders to give it a military look. He was chewing gum lazily like a cow chewing cud and held an old carrier bag, scrunched up tight in the ball of his fist. He approached the counter and tipped the contents of the bag onto the surface. They appeared to be a collection of fairly recent chart CDs, mostly pop and dance. The lad looked Ed in the eye, still chewing, and said cockily, 'Thirty quid the lot.'

Ed barely looked at the CDs that were spread across the counter in front of him. He looked at the lad and with a bright, fake smile said. 'Done. *You* give *me* thirty quid and I'll dispose of them for you in a safe and controlled manner.'

Here we go again, I thought to myself and stepped back from the counter, not wanting to be drawn into the ensuing discussion.

The lad stopped chewing. 'Look, do you wanna buy em or not?'

Ed stared at him, his arms crossed, tapping his fingers on his biceps. The lad looked at me, then back at Ed. Ed looked at his watch then said, 'Do you want me to start charging you for my time as well?'

The lad gathered up his CDs. 'You'd better watch it, mate,' he said, staring Ed menacingly in the face then turned to walk out of the room, muttering 'Wanker!' under his breath.

I saw that on the back of his jacket he had drawn a balled up fist displaying a middle digit. Under this unpleasant, but really rather well drawn artistry, were the words KISS THIS. I wrinkled my nose and watched him walk away. When he was safely out of earshot I turned to Ed and hissed, 'What on earth did you do that for? That guy looked like a right hard nut, I really thought he was going to flatten you then! What's wrong with you? You're not invincible you know. One day you really will get punched, talking to people like that.'

Ed just shrugged. 'I don't do business with guys that look like they'd bash their own granny for a fag and a packet of sweets.'

Not long after that, Ed put on his coat, announcing that he had an appointment and asked if I wouldn't mind locking up the shop on my own. I agreed gladly, Ed wasn't exactly the best company when he was in a mood and it also gave me the chance to be alone before Nathan arrived. I could do my hair and make-up and prepare myself better without Ed there to see me getting myself into a flap.

After practising about a hundred different 'natural' poses I could be in when Nathan arrived, I finally decided on the sitting-on-a-stool-leaning-on-the-front-counter-opposite-the-window-doing-paperwork pose. Tasha and Pete had gone home at five so it was just me for the last half an hour. I turned the sign to 'closed' when they left as there had been no customers for the past twenty minutes and the street outside was looking empty. Then I sat still on the stool, my back arched, my chin in one hand and waggling a pen with the other, to suggest I was thinking deeply about something. I had spread paperwork out before me, and switched everything in the shop off apart from the hi-fi behind me. I had chosen carefully so as not to look too obvious and had settled on Morcheeba's *Big Calm*. Cool and chilled for the end of a working day, funky enough to appeal to Nathan and girlie enough to make it look as though I hadn't chosen to impress him and, more importantly, had feminine taste. I left the door unlocked so Nathan could just wander in and I could do my 'Oh, I had forgotten all about you coming,' look that I had practised in the mirror earlier. I adopted my on-the-stool pose at about a quarter past five, just in case he was early, and by five thirty my right leg was going numb. Another five minutes later and I was getting pins and needles in my foot. I waggled it about, massaging my toes. I wonder what Nathan plans on doing tonight? I thought. Neither of us will have eaten so maybe I should invite him back for dinner. I let my mind wander, thinking of all the meals I could cook for him, trying to think of something impressive, yet quick and easy enough to look as though I wasn't going to a lot of effort. All I could think of was Ed's baked potatoes so I turned to the idea of going for a meal somewhere.

God, me and Nathan out for a meal on our own, I thought naughtily. Where would it end?

'Abby, are you there?' A soft voice whispered in the darkness then footsteps resonated on the floor, causing my head to vibrate. Coloured lights cascaded before my eyes as though I was staring into a kaleidoscope. My head was throbbing painfully. What was going on? Where was I? The floor felt cold and hard and the voice was echoing. I tried to open my eyes but they felt heavy and unwilling.

'Can you get up?' the voice was asking. It was a male voice.

I pushed a helping hand away and half sat up. When I slowly opened my eyes the vision before me was blurred. Everything appeared to be moving with a sickening motion, as though I was at sea in a tiny boat. There were papers all around me and a stool balanced precariously across my leg. The man with the voice took the stool away and I realised it was Nathan.

I groaned. I must have fallen off the stool and knocked myself out.

'Abby, are you OK? What happened?' He leaned over me, trying to help me sit up.

I felt the back of my head and could feel a bump the size of a grapefruit under my hair. The last thing I could remember was waggling my foot, trying to shake off my pins and needles. I must have overbalanced. How cool am I? I thought with embarrassment.

I got up slowly, holding on to the counter to

steady myself. 'I think I fell over,' I said meekly. My head was swimming so much I thought I might be sick. My legs were shaky and I looked around the shop, trying to focus. Nathan held onto my arm and I leaned into him. 'It's all right. Everything's going to be all right,' he was saying, soothing me. He reached into his pocket and took out a mobile phone. 'I'm going to call the police.'

For a second this sounded ridiculous. Why on earth would Nathan call the police because I fell over? It was like some surreal dream. Then I realised for the first time just what I was looking at. A window display had been knocked over, spilling CDs across the floor. Some of them looked as though they had been trodden on as the cases had shattered and splinters of plastic were kicked across the floor. The cash register had been forced open and the drawer was pulled out as far as it would go. It was completely empty. The hi-fi behind the counter looked as though it had been attacked with a baseball bat. It was dented in places and the glass LED display was smashed. I looked around me in silence, trying to understand what had happened.

'Abby, perhaps you should sit down, you've had quite a knock on the head, I think,' Nathan said. He took my hand, ready to guide me over to a chair, but I didn't think I could make it that far. I slumped back down on the shop floor and closed my eyes.

# CHAPTER TEN

It must have only been a matter of minutes before the police arrived at Little Beat. Nathan had been waiting at the door for them. 'She's over there,' he said when they arrived and motioned to where I was sitting on the floor, leaning against the counter.

Two enormous, uniformed officers walked into the shop. Both men were well over six foot and I watched them from the floor. My angle of view gave the scene an added sense of unreality, as though I wasn't a part of what was happening and was instead watching an episode of *The Bill*. One of the men approached me and the other started to look around the shop. He bent down to get a better look at me and said, 'I'm PC McKillop. Are you all right?'

'I think so, my head . . . I think I had a bang on the head. I don't know what happened, I didn't see anything.'

'OK, I think I need to call an ambulance for you, get that checked out,' he said.

'No, don't do that. I don't want to go to hospital.' I looked anxiously at Nathan. I only had a headache and felt a bit dizzy, nothing a large drink wouldn't numb. All I wanted to do was carry on my evening with Nathan, but he was looking at me and nodding, agreeing with the officer.

The policeman frowned at me. 'I think it would be wise,' he said firmly and I sank back, knowing it would be fruitless to bother arguing with them.

Another man in full leathers walked into the shop, a helmet under his arm. I looked at him in surprise and PC McKillop told me he was a motorbike officer. There was the thud of car doors outside and two more uniformed officers hurried in. I couldn't believe it. The shop was now swarming with men and I couldn't help but feel a warm sense of security and importance that they had all come to my aid. I was *woman in peril*. Ed would be so jealous.

The thought of Ed quickly brought me back to my senses, if he could see what was going on he wouldn't be jealous, he'd be distraught. This wasn't just some small thing, it was serious. Ed had been robbed, his shop turned over and someone must have hit me from behind. I felt tears welling in my eyes and I fought not to cry in front of the policemen. I didn't want to be a victim, I needed to be brave.

'I need to call Ed,' I said.

The policeman took a notepad and pencil from his pocket. 'Ed?'

'Ed Little. He's the owner of the shop. And my friend.'

He nodded, writing something down. 'Do you know his number?'

'It's written on the list by the phone, over there.'
I nodded to where the phone was and winced
in pain.

'Right. Don't worry about that, one of us will
contact him shortly. Firstly I need to get some details
from you. Do you have any idea when this incident
took place?'

I thought hard. 'I remember looking at my watch
at twenty-five to six because Nathan was five minutes
late. That's the last thing I remember.'

Nathan looked away, his hands on his hips and
sighed heavily. 'Shit!' he said between his teeth.

I closed my eyes for a moment, wishing I hadn't
said that. I had made Nathan feel guilty and made
myself look seriously uncool in the process. I looked
at the clock on the wall, it was still only six o'clock.

The latest arrivals on the scene walked quickly
through the shop into the back room and it occurred
to me that they were checking to see if the person
who did this was still in there. I felt a chill travel
down my spine.

PC McKillop turned to Nathan. 'Are you the
person who reported this incident?'

He nodded.

'OK, well, we will be wanting to talk to you
separately. If you could accompany PC Tyler to
the station.' He gestured to the officer who was
now standing behind him then looked at me. 'I'll
travel with you in the ambulance and we can talk
on the way.'

I looked nervously from Nathan to the officer.

'I *do* need to talk to you separately,' he stressed,

before I could ask if Nathan was allowed to come with me. Then, so as to avoid further discussion on the matter, he led into a series of questions about CCTV cameras. Ed had been looking into having them installed after he had heard about a recent spate of burglaries in the area, but he hadn't had a chance to do anything about it yet. I knew he was going to be kicking himself.

When the ambulance arrived I insisted on walking out without help. The thought of having to lie on a stretcher in front of Nathan was too awful for words.

Nathan smiled regretfully at me. 'Don't worry Abby, I'll find you later. You'll be OK.'

I watched from the ambulance as he climbed into the backseat of a police car, which was parked at an angle in front of the shop. The paramedics shut the heavy ambulance doors behind me and through the tinted window I saw Nathan sitting in the car, staring at the shop. He ran his hand through his thick, dark hair and sat back in the seat, shaking his head.

It was dark outside when I was driven home in the police car. I sat in the back, leaning my forehead against the window, watching the streetlights flash by.

At the hospital, I had only waited for two and a half hours to be seen by a doctor. This, apparently, was preferential treatment, most likely because I was accompanied by my own personal police officer. As all I was capable of doing was sitting very quietly and speaking in short, unelaborated sentences, I didn't mind the wait. PC McKillop had exhausted all possible avenues of questioning, and after an hour of a complete lack of mental stimulation, appeared to have turned to stone.

I spent the remaining time trying to take my mind off what had happened and what Ed must be thinking, by concentrating hard on the obscure hospital objects that surrounded me in my cubicle. Piled high were trays that looked as though they had been made by nursery school children out of papier mâché; to my left was a bin marked BIOHAZARD with a big yellow triangle, the sort you might see on a nuclear warhead, and straight in front of me were stacks of neck braces with the sizes written on them in bold ink, they ranged from TALL to NO NECK. I felt my own neck self-consciously, concluding that if I was a given a 'no neck' brace I would be mortified. Why couldn't they call it something more flattering, like petite? In the background I could hear an old man who was lying on a trolley outside. He was calling, 'Help me, help me,' over and over in the same wobbly voice of desperation. I wanted to help him myself, the staff were rushed off their feet, but the presence of the policeman made me hang back, just in case I accidentally killed somebody.

Every five minutes a porter went by, winking at me or quipping with some daft remark. *Casualty* had got it spot on when they cast the porter as the jokey, light relief. The one that always pretended wheelchairs were sports cars and talked about the hospital as though it were actually a hotel, walking into a cubicle calling 'room service' or saying in a false butler's voice 'anything else you require madam?'

The doctor, also like in *Casualty*, was younger than me, flawlessly made up and fresh as a young daisy. I watched her come in, noting that it also seemed true that the higher up the staff rank, the posher the clothes.

She explained that I had experienced a concussion and would most likely be absolutely fine, although would experience some headaches for a few days. She advised that I should sit quietly at home until at least Wednesday, but must return immediately if I began vomiting, slurring, fitting, became drowsy, or I developed blurred vision. She didn't seem to think it was very funny when I joked that hospitals couldn't really complain that they were always full of drunks if they gave out advice like that. She prescribed Ibuprofen style painkillers the size of Maltesers and I took one straight away.

Travelling back in the police car I noticed that my headache was finally being numbed. The car slowed down on my street and I pointed out Harriet's house. The officer pulled over and I thanked him for all his help. I had agreed that he would come over the following day to take a formal statement, a task I didn't relish the thought of.

Leaving the car I noticed that Harriet was standing on the doorstep, emanating worry from every pore. Even the porch looked worried, if that was possible, with its gloomy lighting and dark surroundings.

I knew I should have called her. Stupidly, I decided not to tell anyone what had happened until I was out of hospital. I hadn't wanted them to worry about me and I didn't think I could face the gasps of shock and the multiple 'are you all right?'s'. I wanted to be strong enough to deflect their concerns so that they wouldn't fuss. Well, that and the fact that the phone was parked next to the old man who was begging for help as though he was about to breathe his last breath.

I should have known that word always had a way of getting around and Harriet would find out somehow. I did want to talk to her but mainly I wanted to talk to Nathan and Ed. I wanted to find out what was going on and if the police had discovered anything else. I wanted to see how Ed was feeling, make sure he was OK and assure him that I was, and I wanted to hear Nathan's voice, hear his concern for me, enjoy it for a while longer.

'Abby I've been so worried about you,' Harriet burst out as I approached the steps, unable to bite her tongue any longer. She ran out to me, hugging me tightly until I whimpered. 'Oh my God, you're hurt.' She quickly released me.

'No, no, you were just digging your watch into the back of my neck.'

'Oh, I'm sorry Abby, I'm just so glad to see you. I've been going out of my mind in the house. Nathan called from the station and told me what had happened. He called when he got home as well, twice, to find out if you were back yet. He gave up ringing you upstairs because there was no answer.' My heart skipped happily. 'Ed phoned here too. He sounded really upset.' The happiness faded as quickly as it had begun. 'Then Vicky called, wondering where you were and I had to tell her what happened because I was upset. I didn't know whether I should let your dad know what was going on.'

'You didn't. Please tell me you didn't.' The last thing I wanted was for him to be sitting at home alone, worrying about me.

'No, I figured that was your place. I thought you might have called him at the hospital, or the police would call him if there was any need. Oh Abby, you look so pale, you've had such an awful experience. I think you need to tell me all about it.'

'Can I get in the house first?' I said with a weak smile.

I sipped the lukewarm tea Harriet had made, trying not to spit it straight back into the mug. She had added twice my usual quota of sugar, presumably thinking it would help with any shock I might still be suffering from.

'What really bothers me is that he's still out there,' Harriet said. 'It's just awful. Some mindless animal with no regard for human life.'

I rolled my eyes at her. 'Do you want to give me nightmares?'

The doorbell rang and Harriet jumped up, alarmed, and peeked through the curtain to check who it was.

'What are you thinking, H? That the perpetrator has had an attack of guilt and has come over with a bunch of flowers and a get well card, or he has a personal grudge and has come to finish the job off? Because if it's the latter, I really wouldn't expect him to ring the bell.'

'There's no need for sarcasm,' Harriet said, skipping off to the front door and calling behind her, 'Ed's here.'

Ed walked into the living room and wordlessly came and hugged me tightly.

Harriet went to the kitchen and busied herself making clattering noises.

'Ed, not so hard,' I gasped and he let go, apologising.

'I'll never forgive myself.'

'You mustn't say that. You've got nothing to feel bad about, it wasn't your fault.'

'I should never have left you on your own.'

'You didn't, you left me with Tasha and Pete. You often do, it's no big deal.'

'I should have put CCTV in the shop. I had been meaning to.'

'You weren't to know.'

'I should have extra locks on the door.'

'Ed, I hadn't locked the door, so it would have made no difference.'

'I should have warned you to always lock the door when you're on your own.'

'Look, people who run shops on their own everyday would be pretty low on business if they locked their doors all the time, don't you think?'

He sat down on the sofa, rubbing his eyes with his fingers. 'You won't convince me Abby. I feel responsible for this, no matter what you say. Things will be different from now on. I'll kit the whole place up before you get back. You are coming back aren't you? I'd understand if you didn't want to.' He looked at me like a child that had just dropped his sweets down the drain.

I sat on the arm of the sofa and rubbed his shoulder, bending down to kiss the top of his head. 'Of course I am. I'm not letting anything like this beat me. Let's get this into perspective, only the float in the till was taken. There was a tiny bit of damage, and I have a bump on my head, nothing more than that. I wasn't held up at gun point, I wasn't tied up in the back and subjected to the kind of torture you see in Tarantino films and *EastEnders* hour long specials. It was just some little punk who saw an opportunity and took it; nothing personal. In fact, I thought it was quite considerate to make sure I was unconscious. It saved me a lot of embarrassment. You know what a coward I am, I wouldn't have wanted Nathan to find me standing in a puddle of pee, now, would I?'

Ed shook his head. 'I can't believe you can joke about this. God, if I could get hold of the little bastard I'd kill him.'

'Don't be daft. You wouldn't kill a fly if it sat on a swat and told you it had a painful, untreatable disease. You're hardly the violent type.'

'Well I'd wring his bloody neck then.'

'Ed!'

'Well, maybe I'd give him a really good talking

to, instil a bit of humanity into his fucked up little world.'

'Ed you'd run away and call the police and you know it!' I said matter-of-factly. 'There's no point making like some vigilante superhero. I don't want you to be like that. I love you just the way you are. Anyway, you don't know it was a he, do you? And, speaking of the police, what have they said? Have they found any evidence? Has anything else gone missing?'

'No more than what you saw really. They say he got scared off pretty quick. The scene of crime officers turned up and they've been looking around tonight but it doesn't look likely they'll find much more. They're looking over the CCTV footage from the Queens Road camera and I'm going to the station tomorrow to make a statement.'

I heard the phone ring in the kitchen then go quiet. A moment later Harriet poked her head around the door. 'That was Nathan, again. I told him you were with Ed so he said he wouldn't disturb you and would come over after work instead. He sends his love.'

I smiled at Harriet, disappointed that Nathan wasn't coming over. I had wanted to see him. When I turned back, Ed was watching me with a hurt expression and I guessed he sensed what I was thinking.

'Let's have a whisky and listen to some music, hey? Take our minds off it.' I jumped up and walked over to Harriet's hi-fi, turning on buttons.

'You hate whisky!'

'But people always have a shot of whisky when something bad has happened. And I wouldn't want to fly in the face of tradition now would I?' I got out three glasses from the cabinet and trooped off to the kitchen to blag a bottle off Harriet.

When I came back, Ed was sitting on the edge of his seat, tapping his fingers on the side of the coffee table.

'Ed, you've got to let it go. We won't let it happen again, so can't you relax? There's no point in dwelling on it.'

He took the drink off me and downed it in one, gasping and pulling a face. He looked at me and set the glass down on the table. 'Something's niggling at me though Abby. There's something I haven't told you.'

I sat down on the sofa next to him.

'They found a spray can on the floor. They thought that this . . . person, had been planning to deface the shop. They must have been scared off by something. Maybe he heard Nathan's car and ran out before he was seen.' He paused for a moment, staring at his hands. 'The police asked me if anybody had a grudge against me.'

I nodded, not sure what he was getting at. 'But lots of burglars trash the scene. I don't think it means someone's out to get at you. They could be on drugs, or bored kids, you know what it's like these days.'

'I know, I know,' he said. 'But, well, I told them about the guy who'd come in earlier. You know, the one trying to sell the stuff and called me a wanker. The police took it really seriously, Abby. They want me to look at a mug book on their computer tomorrow with an inspector, see if I recognise him from their photos.'

'Right, well, that's OK isn't it? I mean they are just exhausting all possibilities. I'm sure it's standard practice.'

'But don't you see Abby, it's my fault.' Ed's voice was wavering and he sighed, rubbing at his temples. 'I pissed him off with my smart alec mouth then I left you all on your own. I put you in danger, and if it wasn't for Nathan . . . Well, I'll never forgive myself.'

# CHAPTER ELEVEN

I took painkillers throughout the following day and my headache went through various stages of severity, from throbbing pain to barely detectable, depending on how long it had been since I'd taken the last tablet. I hadn't got much sleep, because the bump on the back of my head was so large and so tender it was hard to get comfy. I had a nightmare, the first I'd had in well over a year. I used to have them regularly. They started when mum first went in to hospital for chemotherapy. I used to dream that she was lying on a hospital bed, surrounded by machines. I would be standing outside the room, watching her from a window. I would look at her face, usually so animated and bright, and watch her slowly pale to grey. Her skin would begin to sag, wrinkling up as her soft flesh vanished and she became skin and bone. I would hammer on the window, trying to catch the attention of a nurse who was mopping the floor nearby, but she couldn't hear me. Mum would be staring across the room at a door, her eyes growing dark. I would scream at her to look at me but she never did, instead she would blink sadly and close her eyes. I always woke up in a pool of sweat, my heart hammering and my face damp with tears. This recurring dream haunted me for almost two years, continuing for months after mum had died. It gradually became less and less frequent until I couldn't remember the last time I had dreamed it. This time was different though, mum wasn't there, and instead I was all alone in the shop. I dreamed that the man that had come into Little Beat, the one Ed had been rude to, was attacking me. He chopped off my arm and hit me in the face with it. I woke up in the dark, frozen with fear and unable to feel my arm. I tried to move it but there was nothing, I felt for it with my other hand but it wasn't there. Suddenly it fell and hit my forehead and, still registering no sensation in my arm at all, I screamed, pulling it off me. That middle-of-the-night unreality made me believe that it wasn't a dream at all, that I was in the shop and it was all true. Sitting up, I realised that rather than having been gruesomely dismembered, I had, in fact, slept with my arm up over my head and it had gone numb, losing all feeling. I rubbed it until it tingled, shaking with relief.

'That's the sickest thing I've ever heard,' Ed said when I told him about my dream that morning.

'It wasn't my fault, I don't enjoy having Stephen King type scenarios playing out in my head you know.' I stared at the phone indignantly.

'Well, you must have a warped imagination then.'

'Thanks Ed, thanks a bunch. I feel so much better

now that you obviously think I have a secret blood-lust fetish that shows itself to me in dreams.'

'Well, try not to think like that in future OK? I don't like it,' he said firmly then after a momentary pause added, 'it's only because I'm worried for you.'

'Well, I'm fine. Just bored in the house.' I had forced Harriet into work, much to her protests. She wanted to stay with me but I knew she had an important presentation to give. She had been talking about it for weeks and I didn't want her to miss it on my behalf. Secretly I wanted her to stay with me. I didn't want to be alone, but I knew the police were visiting in the morning and Nathan was popping over after work, plus, I expected Ed to suggest coming over so I knew I wouldn't be alone for long.

'How about I come over when I've finished at the station? I'm not opening up the shop until tomorrow.'

'OK,' I said hurriedly, before Ed had finished his sentence. He laughed affectionately at me.

After PC McKillop left I knew it was time to call my dad and Vicky. I had to let them know what was going on, if I left it any longer they would be cross or hurt that I didn't talk to them sooner. I called them one after the other and their two very separate reactions made me smile. Dad was highly practical. He talked me through the incident with the man that swore at Ed, trying to get me to recall anything suspicious. He lectured me on the importance of CCTV cameras these days and wasn't happy to hear that I had left the door unlocked, also suggesting that I carry a personal alarm. I couldn't see how an alarm would have made any difference to what had happened to me though as I had been knocked out before I was even aware of anything happening. I flippantly suggested that I was thinking about getting a wing mirror attached to my chest so I could see who was behind me at all times and possibly with a blind spot mirror as well, for extra vigilance. Dad didn't appreciate the humour of the situation and answered me with a sombre silence. He was worried about my bang on the head and quizzed me ruthlessly about how I had been treated at the hospital and went through a string of symptoms I needed to watch out for.

'Dad, I know all this,' I said. 'The doctor went through everything pretty thoroughly. It's just a bump, nothing serious.'

'Well, I'm going to have a look on the Internet now, see what it says about concussion. I'll email you what I find.'

I groaned inwardly, ruing the day I had nagged dad about getting himself online. He had been an unstoppable font of knowledge ever since.

Vicky wasn't in the slightest bit practical and instead burst straight into tears. 'Oh, Abby, it's so awful,' she blubbed. 'Ever since Harriet told me I've been so worried. Why didn't you call me earlier? I would've come and looked after you. Oh, to think you were in the hospital all by your-self.'

'But Vicky, I had PC McKillop with me. I wasn't alone.'

'To think you were left on your own with a big scary policeman,' she continued. Her concern was making me feel guilty and I tried to play the whole event down, where normally I might have made it sound more exciting to make the most of a drama that doesn't come along very often. 'What is the world coming to? You can't trust anyone anymore. Where's the kindness? What happened to the days when you could leave your door unlocked and the only people that came by were neighbours with cookies?'

I stifled a giggle. 'Have you been reading the kids Enid Blyton by any chance?'

'Shall I come round? Do you need anything? I could come over and fetch you. You could stay with us and have dinner if you like.'

'Vicky! You have enough on your plate. The last thing you need is to be running around after me. Anyway, Ed should be here any minute and then—' I bit my lip faltering. 'Then Nathan's coming over. Just to check on me. He probably won't stay long. I think he just feels like he's a bit responsible, you know, because he found me. Then he'll go straight back and see Rebecca I'm sure, but I should be here to see him because I said I would be . . .' I most likely would have continued prattling on, digging myself into a deeper hole but my monologue was broken by somebody knocking on the door. 'Oh, Vicky, I think that must be Ed at the door. Listen, I've got the next couple of days off work so why don't I see you tomorrow?' Vicky hesitantly agreed after asking if I was *sure* I was OK and I was *sure* I didn't need anything, another half a dozen times and insisting I promise to call anytime, *day* or *night*, if I needed her.

I walked slowly and carefully down the stairs, holding on to the banister, and rather than pelting down the steps two or more at a time, I trod deliberately on every one. It wasn't that I was unhappy about seeing Ed, of course I wanted to see him, but having talked through every detail of what happened with the police, dad, and Vicky, I was beginning to get bored of the sound of my own voice. I was tired of reflecting on an incident I had no recollection of. I wanted to talk about something else now, I wanted to forget about it for a while.

'Hey,' Ed said with an easy smile. I leaned against the open door as he breezed past me, planting a kiss on the end of my nose then started to climb up the staircase. He had a giant dispatch bag slung across one shoulder which was bulging and clinking curiously. He turned and waved me away from the door. 'Come on Abby, we've got a whole day off work. Let's not waste it standing in draughts, looking puzzled, OK?'

I followed him obediently up the stairs to my flat and he let himself in, dumping the bag down on the floor and emptying out the contents. 'For you,' he said, presenting me with a bunch of flowers that were lying on the top. I was about to thank him when he handed me more gifts. There was a giant

175

packet of marshmallows, a tube of Jelly Tots and two four packs of bottled lager.

'Ooh, Jelly Tots and lager, now you are really spoiling me!' I cried with excitement, shaking the tube to make them rattle. Ed and I had discovered that magical concoction years ago and decided they were an even more complimentary combination than wine and cheese or even beer and nuts. Finally, Ed brought out a selection of videos; *Pretty in Pink*, *Ferris Bueller's Day Off* and *The Breakfast Club*.

'John Hughes films! Just what the doctor ordered.' I gave Ed an affectionate hug. 'Thanks. You're a star.'

'My pleasure. And I'm sorry for being so stressed out yesterday. I feel better about it all today. I've got somebody coming to fit CCTV cameras tomorrow and the shop's all cleaned up. I didn't spot that guy in the mug book and the police seem to think it was the same guy that has burgled a few of the other shops in the area so it most likely wasn't personal. So now, my only concern is keeping you happy.'

'Well, keep it up, because it's working so far,' I said, skipping off to put the flowers in water.

'Hey, people say that to me all the time,' he teased, raising his eyebrow in a mock James Bond gesture.

The credits were rolling, marking the end of *Ferris Bueller's Day Off*. Ed and I were singing along to Yello's 'Oh Yeah', taking it in turns to see who could make the most accurate imitation of the weird noises in the song.

'Abby, give up, you're hopeless,' Ed said, cracking

up. 'And besides, I really don't think he's saying "chicken tikka."'

I stopped the video and got up from the bed of pillows we had made on the floor, stretching. 'I really don't think I can manage a third,' I said.

'A third what? Lager or video?'

'Video of course, I finished my third lager about ten minutes ago and I've started drinking some of yours.'

'Oi! Get your own,' Ed cried, reaching defensively for the bottle by his side.

'I couldn't drink another whole one, I'm tipsy enough as it is. Besides, you shouldn't mind sharing a bottle with me, we're practically family.' I flopped back down on the cushions and buried my head in them. 'I think you'd better take me to the hospital,' I groaned.

'Why? What's up?' Ed sat up and reached for me. He shook my shoulder gently. 'Abby?'

I giggled into the soft velour that was smothering my face. 'Well, I'm feeling a bit dizzy, and I don't think I can get up.' I waved my hands around but stayed where I was. Ed was silent and I peeked up at him through a gap in the cushions. He was sitting close by, looking down at me. He was smiling, but it wasn't his usual broad cheeky grin, it was just a slight hint of a smile. My best friend, I thought to myself drunkenly. He reached out and stroked my face and I think if I was a cat I would have purred from the feeling of contentment that was washing over me. I sighed and closed my eyes.

'Shall I get you a drink of water?'

I frowned. 'Don't go.'

'Abby, I've got to, I'm desperate for the loo. I'll fetch you a water whilst I'm up.'

I nodded and rolled over, watching him leave.

Just after I heard Ed shut the bathroom door, his bag started ringing. I sat up, looking around, then went to the bag and took his phone out of the side pocket. 'Ed, your phone's ringing,' I shouted to the direction of the bathroom.

'Can you get it?'

I knew most of Ed's friends so well he never minded me answering his phone calls. 'Ed's phone,' I sing-songed cheerfully. There was a silence. 'Hellooo-oo, anybody ther-ere.' I stifled a giggle.

'Who's that?' An indignant woman's voice snapped eventually. I rolled my eyes. It must be Ed's mum. Probably wondering why Ed had a woman answering the phone when they had practically given up on their son ever having a girlfriend.

'This is Abby,' I said in my best voice. 'Is that Mrs Little?'

'No,' she snapped. 'It bloody isn't! It's his girlfriend!' The phone cut off abruptly and I sat gawping incomprehensibly at it.

'Here you go,' Ed said as he returned with a tray carrying a jug of iced water and two glasses. I swivelled around and chucked the phone in his direction. It hit him on the forehead then landed with a plop in the jug of water. 'Ow! Abby! What was that for?' He dumped the tray on a nearby surface and fished out his phone, looking back at me in disbelief, spluttering, 'What's up? You were . . . why? That was a new phone!'

'What the bloody hell is wrong with everyone these days? First of all Dad and now you! Of all people! What's wrong with you two? Do you think I can't cope with other people having relationships? I am aware that it happens you know, I can *cope* with it! Did you think I would just self-destruct at the thought of you being happy? Have you concocted some kind of conspiracy with the people I know to all pretend you're all sad, single losers too, just so I don't feel left out?'

'Abby,' Ed said slowly, holding his hands up in an effort to calm me down. 'What the bugger are you talking about?'

'I'm talking about your *girlfriend*,' I spat.

He laughed incredulously. 'I haven't got a girlfriend Abby, what makes you think that I have?'

'Well, perhaps the fact that she just called you up and *said* she was. I think that was my first clue! Then there was the fact that she sounded like she was going to go out and find a bunny to boil when I answered the phone. Sounds like the jealous type if you ask me, a bit *arsey*. Ring any bells?' I put my hands on my hips and tapped my foot, wanting an explanation.

Ed looked decidedly nervous then. He shifted from one foot to the other, swallowed hard and made several attempts at speaking, none of which proved fruitful.

'Come on Ed! What's going on?'

'Erm, I think I know who she is,' he said, clearing

his throat. I raised my eyebrows, waiting for him to enlighten me. 'I think it must have been Kylie.' He bowed his head and stared hard at his trainers.

I couldn't help but laugh. 'Kylie? With a name like that she must be, what, twelve?'

'She's seventeen,' he snapped defensively then, realising that it wasn't a fact he should be proud of, started watching his trainers again.

'SEVENTEEN? Are you mad? You have a seventeen-year-old girlfriend? Now I can see why you didn't want to tell me!'

'Look Abby, she's not my girlfriend okay? She's just someone I met at a club. I didn't know how old she was, I thought she was mid-twenties. You should see her, Abby. You'd never know, and you heard what she sounds like, she's all—' he waved his hands in the air '—Womanly! I had no idea. I couldn't believe it when she told me, I was mortified! And I'm not going to see her again. It was just one night. One stupid night, well, and an afternoon. But as soon as I found out, I finished it.'

'You slept with her? Isn't that illegal?'

'NO! No, of course it's not.'

I smacked my forehead with the back of my hand sarcastically. 'Oh yes, sixteen, I forgot. And a whole year makes all the difference. Anyway, aren't you old enough to be her dad? Did you tell her you were thirty-four?'

Ed looked at me. 'You know I never tell people my age. I don't *feel* my age.'

'No, just schoolgirls!' I snapped. I looked at Ed then, slouched over and looking like a scolded teenager. I had to admit he didn't look thirty-four, dressed in his usual, casual street style. He had on a baggy short sleeved shirt worn open over a long sleeved Quicksilver T-shirt and baggy trousers covered in pockets. He looked like he had just been skateboarding. It was one of the things I admired about Ed, his ability to defy time. It was those sweet boyish blue eyes that made it so difficult to stay mad at him. He was obviously doing a good job of beating himself up about it. I wanted to tell him it didn't matter but I was too hurt that he hadn't told me, to let him get away with it so easily. 'I thought you weren't really into girls anyway? I've only ever known you have relationships with men.'

He looked up at the ceiling, exhaling deeply. 'I really don't want to talk about this now.'

'But why not? I don't understand. When did you meet her anyway? What happened?'

Ed sat down on the sofa. 'Nothing happened really, I met her the night we went to the Mexican.'

I butted in before he finished talking. 'But, I thought you went home, you said you were tired.'

'I didn't really feel like going straight home. I went on to a club, which is where I met Kylie and we got chatting. She came back to mine and we swapped phone numbers in the morning. We met up again yesterday afternoon.'

I felt winded. 'Yesterday? When we were burgled?'

He nodded, not looking at me. 'I'm sorry Abby. I'm really sorry.'

The doorbell rang, breaking the increasing silence that was stretching between us. I looked at my watch, it was six o'clock. 'Nathan,' I said. 'I forgot about Nathan.' I looked at Ed, panicked.

'It's all right, I'll go,' he said, standing up and fetching his bag.

'Ed don't, you don't have to.' I followed after him feeling awful. I didn't want us to fight.

'No, it's OK,' he said, leaving the room before I had a chance to say anything else. I followed him to the stairs calling him back but he flew down them and swung the front door open. He walked wordlessly past Nathan and disappeared down the drive.

Nathan watched him go and then turned back to me, eyebrows raised.

'What's up with him?'

# CHAPTER TWELVE

Why was it whenever I saw Nathan I wanted to just throw myself into his arms and bury my head in his chest? It was almost as though I believed he was the answer to everything, a kindred spirit who could complete me, giving me the strength to cope with whatever unfolded around me. Or perhaps it was just the fact that his six foot stature caused my eyes to be naturally drawn to his chest, making it impossible to ignore. Whatever the reason, the urge was hard to repress.

'Is this a bad time?' he asked, looking behind me as though expecting another escapee to follow in Ed's footsteps.

I rubbed my eyes, still feeling woozy from the alcohol I had drunk. 'Do you fancy a walk? I think I need some fresh air.'

Despite it only being mid-September, signs of Autumn were all around us. The leaves on the trees that lined the paths and the hillside were beginning to hint at change and the horse chestnut trees in particular were already half glowing a golden-orange colour.

There was a chill in the harsh wind that blew across the downs and I was glad I had worn my jacket. I hadn't done it up but instead wrapped it around me until I was held tightly inside. We were sitting on a bench at a viewpoint, facing the valley that plummeted sharply in front of us. Nathan had bought us both a coffee from a nearby snack van and I blew on mine, taking a sip. The hot liquid scalded the roof of my mouth and I sucked in the cold air sharply, trying to soothe the burning sensation, whilst fanning my mouth with my hand. Nathan laughed and blew on his own drink, watching the steam rise off it in little clouds.

'I feel so much better getting out of the house. I really needed this.'

Nathan smiled, still watching the steam. 'Funny, that was exactly how I felt the other week. You know when I went for a walk by the harbour-side and saw you. All I needed was to get away and think. Take my mind off stuff. I suppose its fate that I can now return the favour to you.'

I smiled at Nathan calling us fate, it was how I had always seen us, drawn inevitably together. Meant to be together. I shivered. Why did I always have to think these things, torture myself?

'So, how's Rebecca?' It was the question I always asked him when I felt myself getting carried away. More to remind myself of their relationship than to actually find out how she was. Although I did want to know.

Nathan shrugged. 'Who knows? Probably hungover, almost certainly in fact. She didn't come back last night, after the leaving do. She slept on the floor at a friends house, she said she was too tired and drunk to make it home. She called me at about midnight on her mobile but the reception was so bad I could hardly hear her. I didn't tell her what happened, you know, about you. I guess I wanted to tell her to her face and our phone conversation was so brief. I thought I'd better tell you that in case you wondered why she hadn't phoned to see how you were.'

I nodded furiously. 'Of course, not to worry.' Actually I hadn't wondered why there had been no phone call from her. I hadn't thought about her at all, and I felt terrible about that. There was a time, when we were at school, when I would have called her about the tiniest piece of news, but these days I felt very differently. I hadn't spoken to her properly since her wedding, not in the way that intimate friends do. When Vicky married Alistair we spoke for hours and hours afterwards, dissecting the wedding night, the honeymoon, how it all felt, how it changed things between them. But Rebecca and I had only exchanged the briefest of conversations, the kind you share with people you hardly know. I hadn't even spoken to her about the miscarriage, it was pretty evident that she didn't want to dwell on that. I felt sad that we seemed to be drifting apart, but in a way, thrilled, because at the same time I was developing a closer relationship with Nathan. That afternoon when we went to the Piano and Pitcher, that was a turning point for us, and the way that Nathan had been there for me the day before, at Little Beat, had cemented that feeling. Whereas before we would chat and laugh together, I now felt we had grown closer, that we could talk, really talk, in a way Rebecca and I once had.

'Abby,' Nathan started, looking at me from under the curl of his dark eyelashes. 'Has Rebecca spoken to you lately?'

I turned to face him, drawing my knees up onto the bench seat and resting my arm on the back. 'Not really. I was just thinking that we haven't really spoken since the wedding. I think she talks to Vicky more than she does to me, these days.'

'That's what I thought,' Nathan said nodding. I felt a stab of hurt that Rebecca felt more able to talk to Vicky than she did to me, despite the fact that I felt the same way.

'I'm sorry Abby, I hope you don't mind me talking to you about her, it's just, well, you're really the only person I think I can talk to at the moment. You know Rebecca well enough to understand, but then, at the same time, I feel I can trust you.'

I nodded, letting him continue.

'I just get the feeling that she's ignoring me at the moment. Avoiding being around me, and I don't understand why. Things were so great before we got married, we were wrapped up together in the wedding plans and the baby. No one else knew about the baby. It was our shared secret and it felt really special, you know? Just us against the world.' He smiled sadly and stretched his long legs out before him, staring straight ahead at the view. 'Now I feel like I'm on the outside looking in, and she's not *letting* me in. She won't talk about the baby, says I'm getting too heavy and serious and it just depresses her. She just wants to have fun. She wants to go out almost every night with as many people as she can gather together, and I can't help but come to the conclusion that—' he bowed his head, sighing deeply then looked up again, still avoiding catching my eye '—that she only married me because she was pregnant, and now she's not, she wonders why she ever bothered in the first place. I think she's regretting the whole thing.'

I watched him, my heart hammering. He looked upset, as though hearing it out loud made it all the more real and painful.

'Have you tried talking to her?'

He shook his head, pulling a face. 'She cuts me down before I get the chance. I know she doesn't want to. I suppose I'm just giving her time, hoping that whatever this is about, it will work itself out. She'll get it out of her system and when she has, we can carry on as we were. Maybe she'll let me in again.'

I didn't know what to say. There were no words I could use to make him feel better. I didn't know what was going through Rebecca's head. All I did know was the way she had behaved in the past, and right now it didn't sound as though she had changed much. She was certainly a drama queen. She loved to shock people, to act on impulse and loved to create gossip, but she had always avoided confrontation and heavy, emotional scenes. She could never handle it. And although she had always had a boyfriend (sometimes more than one), she had never found one that she could really open up to, and if they got too demanding or too needy they bored her very quickly. I couldn't help but wonder if Nathan was right, that she had been swept away by the pregnancy and now couldn't handle the fall-out when it all went wrong.

Nathan looked up when I didn't say anything for a while. 'I'm sorry, I shouldn't talk to you like this, I'm putting you in an impossible position. You must feel really awkward now.'

'No, Nathan, honestly, I'm glad you talked to me, really I am. It must be so hard for you. But I think you're doing the right thing, giving her time. She's always been like this, it's nothing you've done. She just needs to get it out of her system, then I'm sure she'll calm down again. Things will get better.'

He thought for a moment then nodded resolutely, screwing up his polystyrene coffee cup and throwing it so that it landed perfectly in the bin, several feet away.

I raised my eyebrows at him, in a mock gesture and nodded, impressed at his shot.

He grinned back at me and said, 'Come on, let's keep walking before my arse freezes to this seat.'

'You know, you really are quite normal,' Nathan joked after I had finished telling him a story about a birthday party I had DJed for.

I looked at him, eyes wide. 'What do you mean, normal?'

'Well, just that I remember you from school. I

find it hard to believe you were the same person that used to follow us around at school.'

I felt my cheeks flushing and I stammered, not knowing what to say. Nathan noticed and laughed. 'I'm sorry Abby I didn't mean to embarrass or offend you. It's just that when you were at school, well, your dress sense was, well, let's just say it turned a few heads.'

'I wasn't that weird was I?' I couldn't believe this, I had always thought I was just a tiny bit different. Compared to some of the more Gothic kids at school, I was positively tame. I never realised that people at school would think I was weird.

'Well, my overriding memory of you is a very skinny girl in enormous army surplus boots and bright red hair, tiny skirts and bright stripy tights, and so much jewellery.' He laughed, remembering. 'Can you remember Neil? Neil Price? He was the other guy in Reverb that played the guitar.'

I pretended to think for a minute, then snapped my fingers as if just recalling. 'I think so, the guy with the long floppy fringe,' I said, when the truth was that I remembered them all as if it was yesterday. I had taken a great interest in all of Nathan's friends, not that any of them had noticed me. Neil Price was gorgeous, possibly more so than Nathan, but the difference was Neil Price knew it. I remember Rebecca saying that he was better looking than Nathan, despite my protestations.

'Well, Neil really fancied you. He was talking about you for ages before I even knew who you were.'

'Oh my God! I don't believe that. I never knew. Why didn't he say anything?' Nathan looked embarrassed then and looked down at his shoes. 'What? You can tell me, I can take it.' I egged him on with a smile.

'Well, promise you won't be offended?'

'Hey, it was a long time ago and I accept I was a weird dresser. I'm fine with that.'

Nathan winced, 'Well, it's just that Justin, the lead singer. He kind of took the piss. He thought that you, Becs and Vicky were really young and kind of like groupies. Neil was pretty shallow, he thought Justin and everyone would give him a hard time if he approached you.'

I covered my face with my hands, cringing with embarrassment. 'Oh God, we really were sad weren't we? Following you around like that.'

Nathan shrugged, smiling, 'I don't think I really appreciated it at the time. I was pretty shy at school. I think most of the time I just wanted to melt into the background. I was a nerd for ages and I can't believe how much everything changed when I joined Reverb. People treated me so differently, but I was still the same person. I was still completely incompetent around girls and still preferred to sit in my bedroom and work on the computer or listen to music rather than hang out at the Reccie with the other guys. All they wanted to do was buy cheap cider, get off their faces and snog any girl that was up for it.'

'But if you were so shy, how come you joined a band? Putting yourself up on a stage isn't exactly wallflower behaviour.'

Nathan laughed. 'We were hardly playing Wembley Stadium and landing interviews with *Melody Maker* though were we? We only played dark pubs and end-of-term discos and we were bloody lucky if we ever got a stage. I was rarely singing so wasn't in the spotlight much, but even when I was it was kind of different. God, I used to be shitting myself before we went up, but as soon as the music started I would get drawn into it. I'd be too absorbed in what I was doing to think about people looking at me and I'd just lose myself in the songs. That probably sounds really pretentious and stupid doesn't it?'

I caught his eye, and my heart melted. 'Actually, no, I don't think it does, I think I know exactly what you mean.'

Nathan looked over his shoulder then turned back quickly, grabbing the lapels of my jacket. He pulled me against him and we fell against a tree, me falling against his chest, as I had always dreamt of doing. It happened so quickly that I was momentarily flustered. Was he trying to kiss me? 'Nathan, what . . . ?' was all I could muster as I was breathless at his sudden close proximity.

Nathan looked deep into my eyes for a fleeting moment and my breath caught in my throat. He really did look as though he was going to kiss me.

'Sorry, no brakes!' yelled a man on a pair of in-line skates, who went whizzing past us, arms flailing. Nathan let go of my jacket. 'Sorry about that, I thought he was going to crash right into you then.' He dusted off the sleeve of his coat, which was now covered in tree moss and muttered, 'moron' under his breath, presumably referring to the guy on skates.

I stood back and ran my fingers through my hair, trying to compose myself. I looked back at the runaway man, who was executing a tricky half turn. He appeared to be trying to get a better look at me and had failed to spot a fast approaching litter bin.

'Look out!' I yelled at him as he collided with the bin and crashed to the ground. I ran straight over to where he lay groaning on the path.

'Are you all right?'

He waved one hand in the air at me and lifted his head up. 'Abby, I thought it was you! How're you doing?'

'Ben!' I cried, finally realising who he was. 'Interesting braking technique, I like it.' I stood over him, assessing the damage.

He sat up, wincing and turned his arm over. 'I think I hurt myself.' His elbow was badly grazed and bleeding. I pulled a face and searched in my pocket for a hanky. I hadn't actually owned a hanky since I was about eight years old so I don't know why I expected to find one then. I did however locate a piece of Mr Men decorated kitchen towel and I blotted up Ben's blood with it.

'Why am I suddenly reminded of Vicky's little boy Jack?'

'A man after my own heart is he? Do you usually kiss him better?' He grinned up at me, a twinkle in his eye. 'Abby J, why have you been ignoring my phone calls? I've been dying to bump into you ever since that night at Vicky's.'

'I've been far too busy for the likes of you,' I said, pretending to be stern. 'So what's your next plan then, wait until I'm under Clifton bridge and bungi into me? There are less . . . physical ways of bumping into me you realise?'

'Hmm, I hear you've had enough of that just recently as well. Alistair told me what happened at the shop, I couldn't believe it. God, if I could find who he is, I'd rip his bloody head off for laying a finger on you!'

I raised my eyebrows in surprise. 'You haven't been playing on a PlayStation today by any chance? Perhaps eating sweets with a bit too much food colouring in them?'

He ignored me, reaching out to hold my chin. He turned my face from one side to the other, inspecting me. 'Are you sure *you* don't need anything kissing better? Because I'm very obliging you know, excellent bedside manner.'

I stood up, unable to resist smiling at him any longer. 'I'm fine now, thank you very much.'

'Excellent, so you'll be all right to do a little gig for next week? I've been trying to call you for days to ask you about it. It's for my little sister's birthday. She's eighteen soon and my parents have agreed to let her have a party. It'll be really cheesy I'm sure, but then I'll be there to add a touch of cool. They've hired out the function room at dad's golf club for a week on Saturday and, well, I kind of told them I knew the best looking, most talented DJ in the area. If you can't make it I'll be forced to hire "Big Dan, muscle man", which, let's face it, could prove embarrassing.'

I laughed, knowing exactly who he was talking about. 'If you mean "Pec's on the Decks", he usually plays a set at the rugby club on Saturdays.'

He pretended to wipe his brow with relief. 'Well, that just leaves you then. Say yes, please say yes.'

I looked behind me at Nathan, who was standing a few feet away, watching us uncomfortably.

'I er . . .'

Ben clapped his hands together. 'Fantastic, I could kiss you! I'll call you about the details tonight.' He got up, holding on to my hand for support, then skated away, waving, before I could argue any further.

I watched him descend the hill and laughed as he circled an old lady, causing her to put a hand against her chest and exclaim, 'Oh, my!'

Nathan joined me then. He had also been watching Ben disappear. 'Was he your boyfriend?' he asked, seemingly surprised.

'Oh no. That was Ben. He's just a friend.' I started walking again, hoping that Nathan hadn't noticed I was blushing. My legs were still trembling from the nearness of him, just moments ago.

# CHAPTER THIRTEEN

The following day I had walked to the shop to clear my head. When I returned, I walked into the house and a smell of paint hit me.

'Harriet!' I called out, trying to work out which room she could be in. When I had left that morning none of the rooms were being decorated. Harriet had lost the urge months ago and several rooms had been left half finished. I could hear Madonna's *True Blue* album playing upstairs and I followed the sound until I discovered that the sounds and smells were emanating from her spare bedroom. I walked in and saw her wiping down walls with an old sponge in time to the music. She was dressed in an enormous old rugby T-shirt and a pair of shorts, her glossy blonde hair held away from her face with a paisley scarf.

'Hey, need some help?'

Harriet shrieked and jumped in the air, clutching her chest. 'Jesus, you just about gave me a heart attack then!'

'Sorry hon. What are you up to? You've haven't done any decorating for months and besides,' I checked my watch. 'It's only two o'clock. What are you doing back so early?'

Harriet flopped down on the dustsheets that covered the bare floorboards. 'I was feeling blue,' she said, lifting the lid off a tin of paint to reveal a pretty sky blue emulsion inside.

I nodded my approval. 'Gorgeous colour, I love the shade. And playing the *True Blue* album, I'm guessing there's a theme here, don't tell me, let me guess.'

'Funny,' she said, tilting her head to one side. 'The urge to paint hit me at about lunchtime and so I took the afternoon off on account of the fact that I'm completely sick of the place and if I didn't leave there and then I'd tell them all to stick it up their own arses.'

My jaw dropped in shock. 'Harriet! I've never heard you talk like this before, I thought you loved your job.'

'I do, that's the problem. I love the job, love the clients, the creativity, the challenge. I just can't work with those people any more.' With that her bottom lip began to tremble and her eyes filled with tears.

I hugged her, letting her cry. I was desperate to find out what had happened, but every time Harriet attempted to talk, she would dissolve into further bouts of tears. I was really worried. Harriet rarely cried about anything and I couldn't recall ever seeing her in such a state, not even when her parents split up. Eventually she pulled her hair-scarf out and noisily blew her nose on it. 'They all hate me,' she squeaked.

'Pardon?'

'They all hate me, always have. I know I shouldn't let it get to me, but I've ignored it and risen above it for so long and now I'm just tired, really tired.' Harriet, as if to prove her point, flopped onto her back and stared up at the bedroom ceiling, resting the back of her hand on her forehead. 'Ever since I nailed the tourism contract I felt I had to apologise for my own success. I still feel like they are jealous of me or something. Even the new ones, the staff that weren't there when I got promoted, they've all heard rumours, probably think I'm sleeping with the boss because he's the only one who treats me with any ounce of respect.'

'H, are you sure you're not, you know, being a bit paranoid?'

Harriet shook her head. 'It really has gone from bad to worse now. I could cope with them not inviting me to the pub at lunch times and whispering behind my back. They've even missed me off the birthday list for two or three years running now, so I don't get a cake. Everyone else gets a cake on their birthday, but that's all just petty stuff and I can handle that. If they're going to be bitchy and small minded about it then they aren't the kind of friends worth winning anyway, but now it's got really personal.'

'What happened?'

Harriet sighed, rolling her eyes. 'Well, I suppose the real problem is Sacha, you know, the office manager.'

I nodded. I had met Sacha once at a works party

Harriet invited me along to. I could tell within minutes of meeting her that she was jealous as hell of Harriet. She tried her best to undermine everything she said and flirted madly with every guy in the room that so much as looked at Harriet. The problem for Harriet was that Sacha worked directly under her, and in order for Harriet's day to run smoothly, they needed to keep a good working relationship. What made things even more complicated was the fact that Sacha's best friend in the company had been overlooked for promotion when Harriet started work there as a junior, and the managing director, seeing Harriet's obvious potential, took her on in a mentor role. Sacha's friend left the company in disgust and has yet to find herself in such a well respected company again, and Sacha was left with an axe to grind.

'Well, for ages now she hasn't been fetching my post for me. She's meant to collect everyone's from the mail room and put them on our desks at the start of the day, and she never gets mine. I have to fetch it myself. I've asked her several times but she just looks at me as though I'm a fascist or something. Then, this morning, I get to work and there's dust sheets over my desk and my computer and I can't find my work for looking and there's a couple of decorators in there painting the walls. I come out and ask Sacha why nobody told me about it and Sacha just stares at me with her arms folded, so I kind of lose it and shout at her. Stewart, the head of corporate accounts comes in asking what on earth is going on because there's a client in his office and they heard me shouting. Sacha then turns on the charm and goes "I don't know what's happening Stewart," in the most simpering voice you've ever heard. "I told Harriet weeks ago about the decorators coming in and that she'd have to work in the office across the corridor for a few days but somehow she must have forgotten, and then she just started shouting at me." Then she starts fanning her face like she's trying not to cry, for goodness sake. Why do women always do that? I told Stewart that it wasn't true and that Sacha never notified me at all. Stewart looked at Sacha and says "Is this true?" And Sacha pulls out a bulletin from her drawer and shows it to him. She told him that she circulated it with the post weeks ago and sent it out again several days ago as a reminder. It stated quite clearly that the decorating was to begin today, starting with my office as it was the area of most need, a nice touch on her part, making my office sound shabby. But of course I didn't get the bulletin because she never even brings me my post any more.'

I stared at Harriet wide-eyed. 'What a bitch! Did you tell Stewart that she doesn't bring you the post any more?'

'I didn't get the chance. Stewart gives the memo the once over then asks to see me in his office once his client has left. When I went in he pretty much gave me a lecture on how I should be more involved with the running of the office and not expect Sacha to take responsibility for everything that goes on around me. Those two have been flirting for weeks and I swear something's going on between them.

Anyway, Stewart suggested that I take the afternoon off and come in early tomorrow to sort out my work before the painters arrive.'

'So you thought you'd come home and do a little painting of your own,' I said smiling sympathetically at her. Poor Harriet had had a tough time trying to prove herself in that company and her job sounded stressful enough without the inter-office bitchiness that came hand in hand with it. 'So what are you going to do? You can't carry on like this.'

'That's what Robert said.' Harriet rolled onto her side and faced me, frowning. 'He's been encouraging me to quit for weeks.'

'Of course you should. He's absolutely right. You can't be expected to work with people like that. Sacha is going to make your life really hard. I doubt she's going to get any easier and if she's trying to make you look bad now just think what she could do; lose important paperwork, not put calls through, lose you clients. She could destroy your reputation. You have to get out now before things get worse.'

'It just pisses me off that if I do that, she's won. She's got what she wanted.'

'Don't think about her, think about what's good for you. Make her look bad by getting an even better job and reminding her that she's going nowhere. She's stagnating.'

Harriet nodded. 'So you think Robert's right?'

I hesitated for a moment. I didn't like siding with Robert about anything. That guy was fishier than Captain Birdseye, but of course he was right, and I was glad to see he had her best interests at heart. 'Of course I do.'

Harriet bit her lip. 'The thing is though Abby, Robert has been asking me to move to London. He's only got a one bedroom flat but he said if I want to be nearer to him he will find me something of my own, then when I'm settled and find a new job we can be together and find something bigger.'

'You mean he wants you to quit your job now, with no new job to go into? How would you manage? London is ridiculously expensive. You can't survive there without work.'

'I know, we've talked about it a lot. But Abby I can't work there much longer. It's just running me down. I've never felt as stressed as I have lately, I'm always tense, I'm getting headaches, I'm drinking more. I'm so frustrated because I know I'm good at my job, I get on great with the clients. I've made a lot of contacts. I'm not having petty office gossip hold me back. I need to start somewhere new where I'm not having to justify my position all the time. I think Robert's right. The only thing that stops me wanting to go to London is you.' She looked at me sadly and took a deep breath. 'You're my best friend in the world. But I love Robert. We're getting married and all I want now is to start my future with him. I'd miss you like crazy, but I'd only be a couple of hours away. I'd still get to see you. I'd come back and visit.' Her eyes began to well up with tears again. 'And I hope you'll understand, I really do. But I think I'm going to have to sell the house. I'll need all the spare money I can get my hands on to survive until I get another job. And I'll want to buy in London, you know how I hate renting. I couldn't afford to move there without selling the house.'

I stared at the floor, my heart sinking. 'It sounds as if you've made your mind up already.'

'There's no going back now, Abby. I handed in my notice today.'

'It's nuts, the whole thing's just nuts!'

'Is that what you said to her?' Vicky asked, pouring me a cup of coffee whilst whipping a bowl of cake mixture and using her elbow to knock Clarice's hand away from the chocolate goo.

I fetched the milk from the fridge and poured some into the mug. 'Of course I didn't. She was so unhappy, I didn't want to make things harder for her.'

'But you're going to talk to her about Robert?'

'Well, I'll try. Doubt it'll do much good though. Harriet knows her own mind, and once it's made up that's pretty much it. I'm certainly not going to win her round with the fact that I have a hunch, based solely on suspicious musical taste and bad vibes.'

'You have to try though. Even if you're wrong, you're her best friend. It's practically your duty to talk to her about it. You'll kick yourself if you don't and it all goes pear shaped.' She poured the mixture into a cake tin and passed Clarice the bowl to lick clean.

'The other thing is, my motives could be called into question. I mean, Harriet might well ask why

I didn't mention my doubts about Robert until she decided to move in with him and leave me homeless.'

'She wouldn't think that of you Abby. You're a loyal, honourable friend and she knows it.'

I smiled gratefully but didn't believe it for a second. There was a moment the previous day when I really thought Nathan was going to kiss me and I had lingered, waiting. I never pulled away, never thought 'this is wrong'. There was nothing loyal about my behaviour then.

'You can't kiss his bottom, that's just dirty,' Vicky cried in disgust and I looked up, surprised, only to see Clarice chasing their much harassed family cat out of the kitchen. Clarice returned to the kitchen a second later, grinning naughtily. Her face was smeared with the cake mixture she had licked from the bowl and sticking to the mixture were wispy white cat hairs. We laughed and marched her upstairs to get cleaned up.

Vicky and I stayed in the bathroom long after Clarice had struggled free of her mother's grip, face only half cleaned. I sat on the toilet and Vicky was balanced on the edge of the bath. 'So, what will you do if Harriet does end up selling the house and moving to London? Where will you live?'

I hunched over, cupping my chin in my hands. 'God knows, I could never afford to live in Clifton if it wasn't for Harriet. I guess I'll have to move downtown.'

Vicky pulled a face and whimpered. 'You'll be

further from us then. No more walking over the bridge for a visit.'

I sighed miserably. 'Don't!'

'Hey, you could always move in with Ed. He's got a spare room.' She wiggled her eyebrows suggestively.

The thought of Ed deflated my mood to new depths of despair. Perhaps we weren't as close as I thought. I couldn't shake the feeling that he had let me down by not confiding in me about Kylie. Why didn't he feel he could talk to me anymore?

'I don't want to talk about Ed either,' I moaned. 'Tell me about Rebecca instead. I haven't spoken to her properly since her and Nathan got married. How's she finding married life?'

Vicky picked up a bottle of Matey Bubbles and started fiddling with the top, avoiding looking at me. 'Oh, you know, we haven't spoken that much. I think she's had a lot on her plate.'

I knew Vicky well enough to know she was hiding something. 'I know about the miscarriage, Vicky, Nathan told me.'

She looked up surprised. 'When? I thought you didn't know anything about it. Rebecca swore me to secrecy. I don't think she could handle the pity. When did Nathan tell you?'

'It was when I was looking after the kids. Remember when I saw him at the harbour? I think that was why he was coming to see me when we were burgled. He wanted somebody to talk to. He's taken it quite hard and I don't think Rebecca has really wanted to talk to him about it.'

'No, she's been a bit funny with me too. Pretending it never happened. But you know what Rebecca's like, she's pretty tough.'

'So, she's OK is she? Her and Nathan are OK?'

Vicky nodded, tapping her fingers on the side of the bath. 'As far as I know. Right, let's see what Clarice has managed to cover herself with now, shall we?' She hopped off the bath and smiled at me.

I looked at Vicky's bright smile and knew it was false. She was attempting to change the subject and something told me it was because she knew something, that Rebecca had been confiding in her. I knew it would be pointless asking, Vicky would never divulge a confidence, but from the fleeting expression I glimpsed on Vicky's face, I sensed that Rebecca wasn't happy with the way things were turning out.

# CHAPTER FOURTEEN

Friday was my first day back at Little Beat since the burglary. It had only been three days yet it felt like returning to school after a long summer holiday (minus the tan and the new, brightly coloured stationery). So much had changed that I felt I was seeing everything through very different eyes. Even the way I saw Ed felt different. I could tell he had things on his mind. He was acting jumpy and distant. Guilt was making him fuss around me, trying to make up for what happened, but despite my best efforts to get him to relax I still sensed he was unhappy. He was pacing the counter and flicking through records with unregistering eyes, as though he was going through the motions, his thoughts far away.

The phone rang and Ed whirled around, picking it up abruptly. 'Yes?' he snapped into the receiver. 'Right, hi. Listen, I think I've said all I can say. I really don't want to talk about it any more, OK? It was a stupid mistake and I'm sorry, I really am, but that's it now. No more. Please, don't call here again.' He slammed the phone back down and slumped against the counter, groaning. 'God, Abby. If I had a rabbit I'd evacuate it to a farm in Devon, like those children during the war. Out of harms way.'

'Is she really that bad?'

'She's pretty scary, but it could be worse I suppose. At least she hasn't been able to call my mobile lately. It's still sitting in my airing cupboard in bits.'

I bit my lip. 'Sorry Ed, I shouldn't have . . .'

'It's all right. I deserved worse and besides, you probably did me a favour. I've tried to be nice to her and let her down gently but I'm just not getting through to her. She keeps saying we need to talk and she wants to meet up with me but I can't see the point. God, what a blunder.'

'Hey, don't beat yourself up about it,' I said, squeezing his arm. 'She'll get the hint. You just need to be firm and repeat yourself until she gives up. Kids these days are meant to have a low boredom threshold. Vicky swears by the broken record technique with Jack and Clarice. Not saying that Kylie is actually a child, but you know what . . .' I trailed off as the phone rang again. Ed looked at me imploringly. 'Or you could just get me to do it,' I muttered, reaching for the phone. 'Hello, Little Beat.'

I rolled my eyes at Ed to indicate that it was Kylie again. Ed waved his hands about, mouthing 'I'm not in!' and made like he would bolt to the door if I handed him the phone.

'No, Ed's not here at the moment. He's just popped out to fetch me some folic acid, he thinks it'll be good for the baby. He's going to make such a doting father. This is Ed's mum isn't it? Hello?' I put the phone down and shrugged. 'She hung up.'

Ed covered his face with his hands. 'Oh God I feel awful now, poor kid.'

'Well, she kept pushing. She's got to learn that she can't go harassing people like that. It's just not cool. Give her two days and she'll be fixated with someone else.' I smiled at the irony of me saying this, I was still in love with the guy I was fixated with when I was seventeen and I hadn't even had the bonus of sleeping with him.

Fortunately Ed didn't spot my own hypocrisy. 'If only all women were like you, Abby J,' he said, smiling at me properly for the first time that morning.

The phone rang again and Ed looked completely aghast. 'Surely she wouldn't.' We stared at the ringing phone, not sure whether to answer it or not until Ed eventually snapped, his face set in an expression of mischief. He picked it up and sing-songed, 'Stalkers Are Us, vacancy hotline . . .' His face fell and his jaw dropped open. 'Right, yes, hello Inspector. This is Edward Little. Sorry about that, a little private joke, silly I know, yes.'

He grimaced at me and I turned away, trying to hide my giggles as he talked to the Inspector. A customer came and asked me my opinion on a handful of records and when I had finished serving her, Ed was just hanging up, his face now serious.

'What's up? Has something happened.'

'Not exactly no. Just confirming what I suspected all along really. They've had a chance to have a look

208

at all the CCTV footage and the Queens road camera on the corner has caught a man walking in the direction of the shop just before the burglary took place. It's not conclusive, but they could see the back of the man's coat and it fitted the description of the guy who came in earlier. It was customised just the same, you know, with the drawing of the hand.'

I nodded, feeling goose pimples prickle along my arms. How could I forget?

'Anyway. They now have enough evidence to be granted a warrant to search his house, although obviously they don't know where he lives, so, if we remember anything we need to call them right away. We've got to be extra careful as well because it looks like I pissed him off, if he's got a grudge he might come back for more.'

That evening, after we had closed up, Ed insisted on driving me home. I didn't put up much of a fight. I felt vulnerable, not just because of the burglary, but because of everything. Life appeared to be changing at an accelerated pace just lately and I took comfort in being with Ed, despite his apparent pre-occupation. Pulling up outside the house, Ed took in a deep breath and looked at me, waiting for a reaction. I looked over to the house to see what he was staring at and saw the 'For Sale' sign straight away.

'Ha, she wasn't joking then.' My heart sank. She had warned me earlier about the sign going up, but seeing it for myself gave it an added reality.

'Abby, you know you can stay with me, don't you? If you've nowhere else to go then I'd love to have you stay. There's a spare room and storage space at the shop for your DJ gear. We could work something out I'm sure.'

I smiled gratefully. 'You see me enough at work, you'll end up hating the sight of me.'

He slapped his hand on his chest and said 'Never!' in a voice of Winston Churchill defiance. 'Hey, why don't we go for a drink?'

'Oh, you know Ed, I'm pretty tired. I think I'll just have an early night. I'm not really in the mood. Some time soon though.' I sighed, sadly, looking at the house that stood so grandly in front of us. It was a wonderful place, I'd miss it desperately, but admittedly I always knew it couldn't last forever. I just wished I had prepared myself a little better for the event. 'And thanks for the offer of the spare room, Ed, I might have to take you up on that. But let's see how it goes, I haven't given up hope yet.'

Harriet was sitting at the kitchen table, leafing through a London Property guide when I walked in. She looked up guiltily at me. 'Hi. Did you see the For Sale sign?'

I nodded, dumping my pack down on the floor. 'I still can't believe you're really doing this.'

'I know. Mad isn't it? And the prices in London are just unbelievable. If I want to live anywhere smart I'll be swapping my three storey terrace for a pokey little house that I'll be lucky to get a spare bedroom in, or a flat.'

I laughed at her. 'Yes, but knowing you, your idea of smart would be a house in Westminster or a flat above Harrods.'

She looked at me with mock disdain. 'Abby, I'm sure there are no flats above Harrods. At least not available to the general public. It's not like a Bristol corner shop you know.'

I pulled out a chair opposite her and sat down. 'Listen, H, I need to talk to you about something, but I want you to promise not to fly off the handle or go all defensive OK? I want you to know that I'm just looking out for you.'

Harriet looked up from the paper and frowned. 'What is it? You can tell me.'

'Well, it's just that I have a really bad feeling about . . .' There was the thumping noise of footsteps coming down the stairs. 'What's that noise?' I jumped up heart pounding and turned around. Robert was standing in the door frame.

'Abby!' he cried, 'Lovely to see you again.'

'Oh, right, and you,' I stuttered, looking at Harriet and then back to Robert. 'I didn't realise you were here.'

'No, well I popped up to see Harriet, just for the evening. I've got a spot of business in Bristol tomorrow morning so here I am. So, you sounded worried about something just then, is everything all right?'

They were both watching me with concern whilst I struggled to think of something to say. I quickly scanned the kitchen in a desperate search for inspiration. I spied a conical shaped strainer lying upside down on the draining board and blurted, 'Yes, well, I was just a bit worried about, er, Madonna, that's all. Yes, the Madonna party Harriet's having for her thirtieth. Well, I was just a bit worried that, er . . . that if she had it at her house then things might get a bit wrecked. What with the house being on the market, I was just concerned that nothing got broken, and wine stains on the carpet might put people off and . . .' I trailed off feebly.

Robert had folded his arms and was looking at me with derision. 'Oh, you shouldn't need to worry about that. I would imagine Harriet's friends are a pretty civilised bunch. Gosh, I haven't been to a house party in years where anything got damaged.'

That's because you're pushing fifty and look like the only parties you ever attend would have to be preceded by the words 'cheese and wine' I thought unkindly.

'Well, maybe you're right,' I said, embarrassed.

'I'm really looking forward to it,' Robert continued. 'It'll be a great way to meet Harriet's friends and I guess it will also be a kind of goodbye party also. The end of an era, and a celebration for the start of a new, London life.' He walked behind Harriet, resting his hands possessively on her shoulders. 'And besides, I just fancy the idea of being Warren Beatty for an evening.'

Figures. He was one of the few men in Madonna's life that Robert was the right age for, unless you also counted the Pope.

'Anyway, we were just going to order out for food and have an evening in. You're welcome to join us of course.' Robert stayed standing, despite there being a spare chair at the table and he looked at me, waiting for an answer. I got the distinct impression that Robert's invitation wasn't heart-felt.

'Oh no, that's OK. You'll want to catch up and well, I'm really tired. I've been planning on an early night.' I turned to Harriet. 'I'll talk to you tomorrow.'

'Well, if you're sure. You really don't have to go.' She smiled regretfully at me as I got up, bidding them both good night.

I went upstairs feeling annoyance practically spill over with every step I took. Why did Robert make me feel like a guest in the house I'd always felt so at home in? What was it about him that rubbed me up the wrong way? Once upstairs I shut the door firmly behind me and headed straight for the hi-fi, flicking it on. In a mood of angry defiance I picked out a handful of CDs; Skunk Anansie, Rage Against the Machine, Metallica and Lynkin Park. I made myself a coffee and stood, leaning against the kitchen counter, listening to the songs of disaffected youth and very gradually feeling my anger subside, exorcised by the music. Half an hour later I was getting the beginnings of a headache and I flopped on the sofa, legs dangling over the side, listening to Skunk Anansie's 'Infidelity (Only You)'. The phone rang, making my heart quicken. If that's Nathan then it's a sign, I told myself and got up to answer it.

It was Nathan. 'Interesting choice in music,' he said.

I grabbed the remote control and flicked it on to 'We Love Your Apathy'.

'Everything all right?'

'Fine, why?'

'Well, you're listening to the kind of music I listen to when I'm miserable, that's all,' he said wisely.

I lay down on the bed, smiling to myself. 'Very observant. But I was about to put something else on, I got a headache when I listened to Metallica.'

'Right, so you're definitely miserable then.' He sounded amused. 'I think I might join you. I'll bring my Limp Bizkit album. I can only usually listen to that in the car, Rebecca won't allow it in the house.'

'Well, I can see her point. Besides, I think that might just tip me over the edge.'

'You're right. Perhaps we should get out whilst the going's good. We could hunt out a good biker pub, passively listen to some REM with a Guinness or two. That way we could capture the mood without the suicidal undertone.'

'Good plan,' I said, laughing.

'Right, I'll be round in ten minutes,' he said and I laughed again, until the phone went dead and I realised he wasn't joking.

I had never been to the Highwayman before. It was a large old pub that stood alone on a main road out of town, surrounded by woodland. Getting out into the dimly lit carpark I had to admit it looked a little creepy and I hesitated at the entrance.

'Don't be shy, Abby. You'll love this place,' Nathan said, opening the door and waving me in.

He was right of course, it was a lovely pub. Down

to earth and rustic with a log fire crackling in an enormous stone hearth at the far end of the room. Just as he had predicted, REM's 'Find The River' was playing in the background and I looked at him, amazed. 'How did you . . . ?'

He grinned and led me over to an alcove by the fire. 'Evening,' the bartender called. He was a butch, middle-aged man with a weather worn face and long, dark hair, tied back in a low ponytail. He had a tattoo of a phoenix on his bicep, which rippled as he cleaned the pint glass he was holding with a white cloth.

'What can I get you and your lovely lady friend there?' He nodded in my direction.

I sat on a red velvet covered bench seat, slumping down so they couldn't see that I was embarrassed about him linking us as a couple.

Nathan returned with two half pints of Guinness. I wrinkled my nose, unconvinced. 'I've only had this once Nathan. I'm not sure I like it, it was quite sickly.'

'Well, you've not had it from here before. It's specially brought over from Ireland. Nearly as good as the real thing. Just try it, and if it makes you gag then I'll have yours and get you something else.'

I took a sip and nodded, pleasantly surprised as the cold, creamy liquid chilled my mouth. It was delicious. 'What a great place. How come I've never been here before?' I looked around, realising I had driven past it several times but having seen the motorbikes lined up outside I had swiftly dismissed it as an intimidating place.

'Makes all those bars in town look a bit character-less, doesn't it?' Nathan sat next to me, and I was very aware that the wooden slated partition we were sitting against was cutting us off from the rest of the bar, giving us complete privacy.

'I have to admit, it's not my usual kind of place, but it really is nice. Cosy and real, if that makes sense.'

Nathan smiled, glad of my approval.

'So, Nathan, I have to ask. What are we doing here? Where's Rebecca?'

He licked the white froth from his lips and pulled a face. 'I'm sorry Abby, you probably really don't want to be brought into this, I know you have a loyalty to Rebecca. I've just been so, confused. I really needed someone to talk to and you were the first person I thought of.' He took a long sip of his drink. 'I don't understand what she's doing. She's out all the time. I know she's avoiding me. She's out again tonight. A girlie night apparently with some people from work. Just for a change. We had a big row tonight because I tried to sit her down and talk this out properly but she wasn't having any of it. She shot out of the house as soon as she possibly could. But it's more than that. She's also acting funny, whispering on the phone and putting it down when I come in. It sounds ridiculous when we're only just married, we should be all loved up and into being together. When I think of how we were on the honeymoon, well, I feel like that must have all been a dream because I just don't feel like I have a wife anymore. And there's this niggling suspicion in the back of my head that's telling me she's seeing someone else.'

My eyes widened. 'Nathan, are you sure? That's pretty serious. I can't believe she'd do that!' Actually it didn't completely surprise me. Rebecca had never been faithful. But they had been so close before the wedding, so passionate together, I could see that Rebecca felt differently about him, and marriage. To commit to Nathan like that must mean something to her, even if she had been pregnant. She wouldn't have been so quick to agree to settle down with Nathan and have his baby if she didn't *really* love him. There would have been other options. 'It's early days though. You've not been married long. Perhaps she's finding it hard to adjust. Knowing Rebecca, she's probably just trying to prove that she can be married without forfeiting her social life. She doesn't want people thinking she's just a wife. I really think it'll get better when she's got it all out of her system.'

'Well, perhaps you're right. I just keep thinking about how many times I've heard people say that the secret of marriage is that you have to work at it, I never really understood what that meant until now. And it's a hell of a lot harder when I know that I'm the only one willing to put in the work.'

I took his hand and squeezed it, looking into his eyes. I didn't know what else I could do or say.

'Abby, will you talk to Rebecca for me? Find out what she's thinking.'

I let go of his hand, looking over to the flames of the fire. 'Oh, I don't know. I haven't spoken to

Rebecca since you married and I don't feel we're as close as we used to be. I'm not sure she'd really open up to me, and even if she did, well . . .' I wanted to help Nathan, I really did. But this was possibly above and beyond what I was willing to do. I didn't want to help them stay together, I didn't want to have to talk Rebecca around to staying with a man I would rather she had never clapped eyes on. I didn't want to be brought into it. What if Rebecca told me she was seeing someone else? I couldn't tell Nathan that, however much I wanted to. I cared too much to be an impartial go-between, I couldn't trust my motives.

'Please Abby. I don't know what else to do. I need to know what she's thinking. If she's regretting the whole thing. But she just won't talk to me.'

'Well, I don't think I should phone her. It would be too out of the blue. If I see her then we'll talk, but I don't know when that'll be. She hasn't seemed to want to do much catching up lately.'

'Thanks Abby.' He sat back against the bench seat and looked at me, a twinkle in his eye. 'Now, I want to hear all about why you were on such a downer that you listened to Metallica until you got a headache.'

# CHAPTER FIFTEEN

Ben was looking amazing, I thought as he leaned over the table, checking out my equipment.

'Nice set of decks you got yourself,' he said, winking at me.

I grinned back at him, suggestively. 'That's over two and a half thousand watts of pure energy I've got at my fingertips.' I put my hands deliberately on my hips, cracking up at the look on his face. Practically everything he said to me had an innuendo in it somewhere, if not in the words he used, then certainly in the way he said them. It must be catching, I thought, knowing I shouldn't be flirting with him, yet somehow unable to stop myself. Ben was attractive and a lot of fun to be around, but it went no deeper than that. He was so much like an impulsive kid, I could imagine him changing his mind a lot, getting bored quickly, falling in love easily. He wasn't deep enough for me, I wanted more than fun.

'You've got the most fantastic job, Abby. I'd love to do what you do.'

'Why do you say that?'

'Well, look at you, you're working the whole place.' He gestured behind him to the packed dance floor of the social room.

I laughed, seeing Ben's parents dancing to Destiny's Child's 'Bootylicious'. 'Do your parents always, er, join in like that?'

'Yep, they're cool,' he said unfazed and I looked up at him, impressed by the fact that he wasn't cringing with embarrassment at his parents, the way so many do. I could see now where Ben got his sense of fun from. 'Besides,' he continued with our previous conversation, 'you're your own boss. You can do whatever you want. Play whatever you want. It's barely even a job really, it's more a hobby that pays.' He grinned cheekily at me to show he didn't completely mean that, but I knew he did. It was just another reason why I couldn't see us working together. He was too much like me. He wanted to hide from responsibility so much that together we would never get anywhere. I knew it was hypocritical, but I couldn't help that. 'If you ever want to sell your stuff, I'd buy it.'

'You could buy your own anytime.' It was no secret that Ben's family were absolutely loaded. You could see it just by looking at them. Ben's dad was a typically successful entrepreneur. Ben had been telling me how his dad had started his own company at a young age and his mum had never had to work. They didn't mind sharing their wealth either and seemed quite happy to lavish it on their children.

'Well, yes, I could. But I wouldn't know where to

start. You've got all the gear already and it sounds great, you'd just need to show me what to do with it.' He raised his eyebrows wickedly.

'You, can keep your hands off my equipment. It's already spoken for.' I put on the latest Fatboy Slim single and when it started, Ben reached out and took my hands.

'Come on, you've got a few minutes to dance. *Please.*'

'Oh, I don't know, I . . .' I started to protest, but Ben pulled me around the table and out onto the dance floor. 'You've got one minute,' I said firmly and joined him, laughing as he started to dance manically.

I looked across the room to Ben's sister. You'd never believe she had just turned eighteen. She looked very much a woman and an amazing looking one at that. She took a sip of champagne and shook her blonde hair out behind her. She was obviously high maintenance, with well cut hair, expensive clothes and jewellery. She was also incredibly popular and was surrounded by a swarm of adoring friends. I was guessing that these were mostly school friends, half of which were probably under age, yet the champagne was flowing and her parents didn't seem to mind too much who drunk what.

'Hey, you're really not paying me enough attention,' Ben said, moving closer and wrapping his arms around my waist. I wriggled out of his grasp and danced further away, shouting, 'You can't *slow* dance to Fatboy Slim!' above the music.

He let go, looking exasperated. 'You are such a tease,' he said. 'And I love it.'

I grinned back at him, feeling truly relaxed for the first time in weeks.

The past week had been tough. Ed was still acting moody and it was beginning to get frustrating. We hadn't really talked much and I missed the closeness we had always shared. I didn't fully understand why he was acting so different. I knew he was upset about the burglary and what happened to me, but surely that would make him treat me even better, not ignore me and it didn't explain the long silences. Since I had answered the phone to Kylie that time, there had not been much contact from her. She turned up at the shop the following day, much to Ed's complete horror. Fortunately for him, he spotted her first and ducked down behind the counter, hissing, 'Shit, shit, shit!' under his breath. He had been serving a customer at the time, and I had to take over, guessing what was going on.

Ed was quite right about Kylie and seeing her in the flesh I could understand why he had thought she was in her twenties. When she walked in, the sunlight from the front room shone behind her, lighting up her auburn hair and making it glow strikingly. She was wearing a knee length coat, trimmed with fur around the hood and cuffs. Her face was naturally made up and a smattering of freckles decorated her nose. I could see that she was beautiful and had a natural style. Looking closer I could see her clothes were cheap, but the way she had put them together looked great. I felt a pang of jealousy. I should have known that she would have to be special for Ed to have gone for her. She was one of only a tiny handful of girls I had known him be attracted to. Ed was tugging at my trousers, trying to get my attention, most likely worried I would give the game away, but I didn't. I just smiled politely and told her that Ed would be away for a few days at a sales fair. I felt bad lying to her. She looked nice, not the obsessive girl I imagined her to be. She sighed and said, 'Forget it then. Don't tell him I came. I'm through trying to talk to him.' Then she walked out, her coat fanning dramatically behind her like a cloak.

After that Ed didn't hear from her again. I kept asking him if she'd been round or phoned but Ed just shook his head every time, not wanting to talk about it any more. I couldn't help wondering if perhaps Ed liked Kylie more than he let on, it would certainly explain his moods. Maybe she had really got to him.

The room fell silent and I felt several dozen pairs of eyes fall on me. 'Oh God, sorry!' I cried, racing off the dance floor back to my records, hurriedly putting on the next track on my list. My cheeks were burning with embarrassment, but Ben covered up the awkward silence by joking, 'Hey, that's my animal magnetism for you, the ladies lose all sense of time.' The crowd laughed, all in good spirits, and continued dancing as the next song began.

'I can't believe I did that. I've never done that before. Everyone will think I'm really un-professional,' I moaned to Ben.

He just shrugged, saying, 'They think you're fantastic. Everyone does.'

At eleven o'clock the guests were still going strong. Usually the crowd dancing would have thinned out by now as the older guests left, energy waned, and alcohol got too much for some, but not here. Instead there were more people dancing than ever, even Ben's dad was still holding his own. I put on the House of Pain's 'Jump Around' deliberately, knowing that it encouraged people to pogo up and down on the spot and tire easily. People always had to sit the next song out after that.

Just as predicted when the song came to an end the crowd shrunk noticeably and I was able to see Ben once again. He was talking to his sister Emma and some of her friends. They were all laughing at something he said. He looked up and winked at me and I looked away, trying not to smile. My attention was caught by somebody entering the room and I looked over to see who it was.

It was the hair that gave it away. The rich glossy red that was unmistakably Kylie's. She looked stunning in a tiny skirt and strappy vest top, a thin lacy black shirt hanging loosely over it. She had the curves of a true woman and several of the men in the room turned to watch her walk across the dance floor to Emma where Kylie presented her with a gift and a kiss on the cheek. Ben, whose conversation had been broken by Kylie's arrival looked unimpressed and wandered back over to join me.

'Do you know her?' I said as soon as he came within earshot.

'Who?'

'Kylie, the one with your sister.'

'Kylie Jackson? I think they were in the same class before dad sent Emma to the private school. They've stayed in touch. Why?'

'Oh, no reason. I've just seen her before, in the shop. Is she nice?'

'Hey, don't worry, I don't fancy her if that's what you think,' he said smiling.

'But, she must be pretty nice if Emma never lost touch with her,' I pressed, desperate to get a bit more background on her.

'I suppose. Best of a bad bunch.' Ben's mum came over and whispered in his ear before I could ask him what he meant by that. He told me he would be back in a minute and walked off with his mum.

Kylie spotted me not long after she arrived. Her face registered recognition at first, then she frowned at me suspiciously. I kept catching her looking at me from out of the corner of her eye then looking quickly away. She seemed determined to ignore me and I got the impression she was nervous. Maybe because she thought I was his pregnant girlfriend and worried that I knew about her. I tried to disarm her with a smile but it was in vain.

By the time Ben returned I was packing up my things and most of the guests had left.

'Sorry, sorry, sorry,' he said, rushing up to me and taking an amp out of my hands. 'Let me help you with that.' He carried it out to the Scooby and I followed him outside, passing him my CD players.

When he climbed out of the van he stood facing me and took my hands. His breath forming mist between us. 'Abby look, I know I'm perhaps a bit too flirty and full on and maybe I'm scaring you off a bit. You must think I'm a real ladies man.' I opened my mouth to confirm this but he carried on. 'Unless you hadn't noticed, you were the only girl I was flirting with tonight. You were the only one in the room who interested me. You're really special, Abby. I've never met anyone quite like you.' He cupped my face in his warm hands. 'I think I'm falling for you.'

I looked into his eyes and melted. I wanted to resist but I couldn't, it had been so long since anybody made me feel special. Ben drew me to him and kissed me. Gently at first. Small, slow kisses that made me tingle with anticipation. I reached up and stroked his hair, kissing him harder.

'Get your hands off me!' A voice cut through the night. I broke away from Ben who groaned in objection, bending down to kiss me again.

'What do you think you're doing following me around, acting like dad or something. What's your problem?'

I looked at Ben seriously then broke away from his grasp, peering around the corner of the Scooby to see what was going on. I saw Kylie standing by the entrance to the social club. She appeared to be drunk as she was swaying, fighting to stand straight. She was arguing with a guy I couldn't quite see. He was standing in the shadow of the door.

'Ben, perhaps you should go see if Kylie's okay. I think that guy's hassling her,' I whispered.

'Don't you touch me!' Kylie shouted again, pulling her hand away from the man and teetering backwards, holding on to the door.

'Oh don't get involved,' Ben said. 'It's just her brother. He's a right loser, always causing trouble.'

'I don't know why I bother with you Kylie, you're just a tart. An ungrateful little tart, getting drunk all the time, going home with anyone who'll have you.'

'That's not true!' she yelled. She sounded like she was crying. 'Just leave me alone. I don't want you hanging around here, showing me up in front of my friends. You're just embarrassing!' She lowered her voice until I could barely hear her. 'You'd better piss off right now before I do something I might regret.'

The man grabbed hold of the collar of her shirt and she squealed in fright.

'Stop him Ben,' I hissed.

He was just about to go over when his dad walked out of the door, and Ben faltered, watching to see what would happen next.

'What's going on here?' his dad said, all good humour gone without trace. He cut an indomitable figure in the doorway, a big man, dressed not unlike a Mafia member in his suit and long black coat. All he needed to do was crack his knuckles to complete the picture. The man hassling Kylie let go of her and stood back into the light.

I recoiled, as if winded, when I saw him. My heart started pounding violently and my head swam with confusion. I would never mistake him for anyone else. Never forget his face and even if I had, the coat I certainly wouldn't forget. The hand on the back with the defiant middle digit.

'God, Abby, what's wrong?' Ben said, seeing me turn away. 'You look like you've seen a ghost.'

'It's him,' I said, my voice barely audible. 'It's the man who attacked me. The one who robbed the shop.' I sat back against the Scooby, a thousand thoughts racing through my mind. It was all becoming clear now. He was Kylie's brother, that was why he did it. That's why he wanted to get back at Ed. He was an overprotective older brother that couldn't bear to see his kid sister growing up. He was also a bully, a frightening bully.

Ben's face slowly registered what I was talking about and he took off to the entrance, looking as though he was about to kill someone.

'Ben don't!' I cried, fear making my legs weak. I followed him around the van but there was no one to be seen. Kylie's brother had run off and I suspected Kylie had been led away by Ben's dad.

Ben ran out of sight, his face set in anger, but minutes later he returned out of breath, panting. 'He's gone.'

'Oh shit, Ben. What am I going to do?' I looked up at the dark, starlit night.

'Call the police, that's what you're going to do.' He passed me his mobile but I faltered.

'What? Do you want me to do it for you?'

'No. Don't call them yet. I think I need to speak to somebody else first.'

# CHAPTER SIXTEEN

'Ben, I'm taking Kylie home,' his dad said, leaving the building with Kylie in tow behind him. She was clutching a man-sized hanky and looking dishevelled. 'Can you ride with your mother in a taxi? I've already booked one. It's on its way.'

'Actually. I was going to suggest that I took Kylie home,' I said, stepping out where Kylie could see me. She looked up, alarmed. 'We've got a few things to chat about, haven't we?'

Kylie, with little other options available to her, nodded dumbly, accepting her fate.

'Well, if you're sure,' Ben's dad said. 'I'll take your mother home then, you can have the taxi.'

Ben nodded, turning to me. 'Are you sure you don't want me to come with you?'

'I'll be fine. I'll call you.'

He hesitated for a moment then turned around to see a taxi pull into the car park. 'Well, I'll see you then.' He cast me one last lingering look then walked off towards the taxi.

'Right,' I said brightly. 'Here's your ride.' I patted the side of my van. 'Hop on board.'

*

'I swear I have been trying to speak to Ed but either he won't answer my calls or he gets you to put me off with some ridiculous made-up story. I got to thinking, why should I warn him about Julian if he's the kind of person who uses girls like that then drops them without any thought at all.'

I looked at her, confused. 'Right, hang on a minute. Back it up sister. Just who exactly is Julian?'

'Julian. My brother.'

'He's called Julian?' What the hell kind of name was that for a violent headcase with a penchant for aggravated burglary?

Kylie nodded. 'Well, everyone who knows him, calls him Big J.' Right, now the name fits.

'So, how did you know? Why were you warning Ed?'

She looked out of the window, watching the houses pass by. I drove slowly down the streets, not sure where I was heading. Kylie still hadn't told me where she lived. I took a left turn towards Nathan and Rebecca's house.

'Julian is my half brother, he's twenty-four so he's pretty old.'

I tutted, annoyed at the suggestion that twenty-four was old.

'My mum's been married three times. He was the first child. His dad was a right sod and ran off when Julian was a baby. Mum was dead young when she had him. I'm the only other child and mum lives with my dad. Julian hates Dad and tries to make out like he's got more right to tell me what to do.

Dad argues with Julian all the time, tells him he's a good-for-nothing layabout. He's been in trouble with the police. Only small stuff, drugs, fighting in town, that kind of thing. He gets real angry. He went mental when he saw me with Ed. Followed us home apparently. I didn't even know he was there, but the next day, when I got home he really had a go, y'know? Wanted to know what went on, how old Ed was and stuff. I didn't tell him much but he'd figured out a lot for himself anyway. He found out Ed owns Little Beat and a few days later I found out he'd nicked all my CDs, tried to flog them in the shop. He sold the lot to Select a Disc. I went nuts. He told me I was bloody lucky he didn't do him over then and there and said he hadn't finished with him yet. That's when I figured I'd better warn Ed. Then I saw what had happened to you in the paper. I couldn't believe it, and it was just too much of a coincidence. I knew it was him, it was Julian. I didn't know what to do. I wanted to tell the police but I was scared.'

I looked over at Kylie and her face crumpled as she started to cry. I pulled the van over in a lay-by just before the entrance to the cul-de-sac where Nathan lived. I switched the engine off and turned to Kylie. 'Listen, it's OK. Of course you were scared, but you tried to warn Ed. It's not your fault. What you've got to realise is that your brother's out of control. He could have killed me, and God knows what he would have done if Ed had been in the shop instead. We need to tell the police what you've told me. He could do something much worse next time.'

231

More tears welled up in her eyes and spilled over. She didn't bother to wipe them away. 'I know. I know I need to tell them, but he's still my brother. No matter what he's done. Dad doesn't care about me. None of them care where I am at night. He's the only one that's ever looked out for me.'

I leaned over and put my arm around her. Stroking her long red hair. 'I know. But you know it's the right thing to do, don't you?'

She nodded, wiping her nose on her sleeve and I felt desperately sorry for her, thinking how lucky I was to have had such a stable family, to have been brought up in a house filled with love. I looked out of the window to the street where Nathan lived. I couldn't see his house but the nearness of it made me shiver. I thought back to my kiss with Ben and it seemed inconsequential now. Then my thoughts turned to Ed and I knew we had to tell him what had happened. 'Do you feel up to going to Ed's tonight? I think we should tell him what we know first.'

'Okay,' Kylie whispered, wringing her hanky nervously. 'Abby, I'm really sorry for all the trouble I've caused. Really sorry.'

'It's OK. I know, oh fuck!' I spotted a car I recognised pull up at the junction of the cul-de-sac. It was Chris's car, my ex's. Looking into the car I saw Chris sitting in the driver's seat. He was alone. I ducked down below the dashboard out of sight, hissing, 'Get down!' to Kylie, who was looking at me as though I had taken leave of my senses.

'It's my ex, he's a bit of an obsessive. I don't want him to know I'm here.'

232

Kylie obliged by ducking down next to me. Crouching in the foot well she whispered 'But Abby, isn't your name written on the van? Don't you think that's a bit of a give-away?'

She had a point, I thought, cursing the conspicuous nature of my transport. I listened intently and heard the car pull away, he couldn't have seen the Scooby. I popped my head back up and saw that the road was once again deserted. The clock on the dashboard told me it was gone midnight. What the hell was Chris doing over at Nathan and Rebecca's at that time of night? Nathan had never seemed to like Chris that much. I couldn't believe they were all socialising together, unless . . . I remembered the last conversation I'd had with Nathan when he confided his suspicions that Rebecca was seeing someone else. I put two and two together and the thought made me gasp.

'Abby? What's wrong?'

'Oh, it's nothing. I'm just being silly. Let's go and find Ed.' I started up the engine, trying to focus on the current problem of just what we were going to say to him.

Ed took it pretty calmly, considering. The look on his face was priceless when he opened the door, squinting with the effects of disturbed sleep. It took him a while to figure out who we were and when it finally dawned on him, he ushered us in, dumbstruck. In his kitchen he paced the floor, waiting for the kettle to boil. He scratched his head, trying to make sense of it all. He looked uncomfortable with Kylie and I being in the same room together and I wondered if I had done the right thing by bringing her over there, but I knew I had to sort it out whilst I had her on side.

Ed made us all a cup of tea and we sat in his living room. Kylie and I were silent as we waited for Ed to digest what we'd told him, waiting for him to come to some sort of decision. Kylie sat perched on the edge of her chair and looked around at the room, taking it all in. I suspected she hadn't seen much of it the night she stayed over. I was slumped on the sofa, fighting to keep my eyes open. The whole evening had left me exhausted and I didn't think I could cope with much more.

'Abby, why don't you go home? I can make sure Kylie gets back OK. We can sort this out in the morning. You look too tired to do anything now.'

'Right, yes, you're right.' The look on Ed's face told me that he wanted some time alone with Kylie. 'Are you sure?'

Ed nodded and I looked at Kylie, who had visibly relaxed at the thought of my exit. I picked up my coat and got ready to leave.

'I'll walk you out,' Ed said, standing up and following me to the door.

'Don't come out, you'll get cold.' I tried to push Ed back in the house. He was still only dressed in a pair of pyjama bottoms and a thin white T-shirt. His feet were bare and his arms were folded tightly across his chest. Ed ignored me and walked out to the Scooby, which I had parked up in the street, directly in front of his house.

'Listen, Abby,' he said in a hushed voice. 'I think that we've got to call the police tomorrow, and when we do it should just be me, maybe you too, but not Kylie. Let's not bring her into it any more than she needs to be. I don't want her brother having any more reason to have a go at her, OK?'

'Of course, that's fine by me. You are OK about telling them aren't you? You don't think we should forget it, for Kylie's sake?'

He shook his head fiercely. 'Absolutely not. He's not going to stop until someone does something about him. I can't turn a blind eye to what he did to you, he's scum.'

I lingered by the open door of the van, not wanting to go, jealous that Ed had wanted time alone with Kylie and not me. 'Shall I call you in the morning?'

'Yeah.' Ed hugged me briefly then turned to go back in the house.

'It's done,' I said, walking into Harriet's kitchen to find her bent over a chicken.

'Oh, hi Abby. I don't know if it is you know, aren't the juices supposed to be clear? I put the fork in it's leg and I think I hit an artery!'

I wrinkled my nose up. 'Yeah, Harriet, I think that means you need to whack it back in the oven and turn up the heat.' I sat down at the kitchen table. 'But that's not what I meant. I mean it's sorted. Ed called the police first thing and I went over. We've both given them a statement and they're going to search his house now and hopefully arrest him.'

'Thank God for that.' She slammed the oven door shut and joined me at the table. 'And Ed didn't worry too much about having to tell them about Kylie?'

'Well, he was pretty embarrassed. And he didn't like dropping her in it, but from what I saw of Big J after that do last night, well, I would imagine she gets hassle off him all the time anyway. A case of damned if you do and damned if you don't. And besides, Ed's priority is to protect me, not Kylie. He's only known her a matter of weeks.'

'Ooh, I sense a bit of jealousy going on here, a case of, "he's my man" possessiveness.'

I pulled a face. 'Don't be ridiculous. And why is it that now you've found yourself a man you've started making comments about me and Ed?'

'Since I saw you sitting on top of him in my front garden and every time after that when you've been together, well, there's just this thing.'

'What thing?'

She shrugged, smiling. 'Just a thing. A kind of closeness, a special kind of something.'

'Right. Very specific, well that just proves it then doesn't it. A thing. Now that would stand up in court.'

'Plus, he's proved without doubt that he does still have a taste for women after all.'

'Yeah other women. God, if you'd seen her. She is gorgeous. I can imagine a lot of gay men would make an exception for her. But anyway, I'm not getting into this discussion. I just can't think of him like that.'

Harriet looked at me knowingly and I frowned at her. She didn't know anything.

She jumped up from the table and grabbed a tea towel. 'Right, I've got to do the carrots. God, I can't believe how long this is taking me. We'll be eating at tea time at this rate.'

'So, where is Robert?'

'He's just popped out to get some wine, he'll be back in a minute. Abby, are you sure you don't want to join us for lunch? There's plenty.'

I held up my hand. 'Honestly, no, it's fine. I promised Dad. Oh shit!' I stood up, checking my watch. 'Oh my God I didn't realise it was so late. I promised Dad I'd go over for lunch. I haven't seen him in ages.' I stood up, shrugging my coat back on. 'I got the feeling he was going to come clean about his new girlfriend today. Shit, it's half two. He said he'd be serving up at one.' I rummaged in my bag for my mobile and found it switched off. 'Bugger.'

The phone in Harriet's kitchen began ringing. 'I bet that's him, he's probably tried my number already. Can I get it?' Harriet nodded and I picked up the receiver, but it wasn't Dad, it was a man for Harriet. I passed the phone over and collected my things together.

'Really? That's wonderful! And so quick! Right, well, I'll have to talk it over with my partner, have a think about it, and I'll get back to you later today. Yes thanks, bye.' Harriet put the phone down and looked at me, mouth open in shock. 'The man that came to look at the house last night is offering me the asking price. I think I've sold the house!'

I stared back at her, frozen. 'Someone came to see it last night?'

'Yes. Whilst you were DJing for Ben. He just turned up. He drove by and saw the sign, then called in on the off chance.' She looked at me sadly. 'I'm sorry Abby, I didn't know he was coming. But it was bound to happen sooner or later, wasn't it?'

I heard the front door shut as Robert returned with the wine. 'H, I'm sorry, I'm going to have to shoot off to Dad's. We'll talk later, OK?'

Harriet nodded and as Robert walked into the kitchen her face flickered with excitement.

I dashed out before I had to listen to Harriet telling Robert the *wonderful* news, waving goodbye to them as I went.

Walking down the drive to Dad's house I smiled to myself, glad to be home again. I was looking forward to having a long chat with Dad. Clearing the air. I was even coming around to the idea of him having a girlfriend. It was about time he started afresh with someone and let go of the past. Perhaps he would inspire me to seek out somebody new, open my mind to the possibility that there is more than one person in the world who is right for me. Just because Nathan is taken, doesn't mean there isn't somebody else out there, just as special, waiting for fate to introduce us. I just had to open my heart to the possibility and stop dwelling on old feelings. Perhaps Harriet leaving was the push I needed to dig myself out of the mental rut I was stuck in. Maybe I needed a shake up. I ignored the doubts about Robert that threatened to flood my head and ruin the positivity I was trying to create. I walked around the side of the house, planning on letting myself straight into the kitchen, rather than knock and disturb him. As I rounded the corner I could hear the clattering of plates being scraped and I knew I was too late for dinner. Poor Dad. I peered through the patio doors and saw him bending over the dishwasher. He stood up, turned to the sink and grabbed a lady who was washing up. She squealed with pleasure, batting him away with a soapy hand, and then Dad kissed her.

I watched from outside, uncomfortable at having seen their private moment. I hovered at the door, not sure what to do. I didn't want to embarrass them by walking in and disturbing them, but I couldn't stay outside much longer. Dad solved my indecision by breaking away and looking up. He saw me outside and let go of his lady friend. They checked themselves and in a swift movement, increased the distance between them, pretending to have been concentrating on clearing the plates all along. Dad smiled nervously and waved me in.

'Abby, how lovely to see you again. We were wondering where you were,' Harriet's mum said. She glanced nervously at Dad, who was now standing on the other side of the room and pretending to have just spotted a hairline crack in the kitchen wall.

I looked from Dad to Patricia, speechless with shock. Harriet's mum was dad's new girlfriend. Why hadn't I seen this coming? I should have figured it out. They were always so close, Dad had always said how much like Mum Patricia was. And the face cream in his bathroom was the same as Harriet's, a tip she must have picked up from her mum. It made sense and yet somehow it seemed all wrong. All the time we spent together when we were little. Our two families, merged into one, sharing holidays, Christmases. Patricia visiting Mum at home when she was feeling poorly, cheering her up with kind words and by treating her the way she always had, as a friend and confidant, not an invalid. Dad leaving them to it, busying himself elsewhere. When had he started to see Patricia differently? When did things change?

'Abby, I was going to tell you today,' Dad started. 'I wanted to tell you before Pat arrived. I've been trying to call you.'

Patricia bit her lip and picked up a wine glass, rubbing it furiously with a tea towel, unable to stand the tension any longer.

I turned around, closing the patio door quietly behind me and walked slowly around the side of the house. Once out of sight I broke into a run, passing the Scooby in the driveway and headed down the hill, away from the house. My feet pounded hard on the ground, my breath came in heavy gasps and my eyes smarted with tears.

# CHAPTER SEVENTEEN

'Where on earth have you been?' Harriet was standing at the door as I trudged up the steps to her house. 'Robert and I were worried about you.'

I pulled a face and walked in past her.

'Look, come in and tell me what's going on.' Harriet gestured for me to follow her into the living room but I ignored her and headed for the stairs, muttering sarcastically that I didn't want to disturb 'Robert and I'.

'Abby, Robert went home after lunch. He's got a meeting first thing. I'm on my own. Come on.' She took my elbow and tried to steer me down the stairs. 'God, have you been drinking?'

I shrugged and allowed Harriet to lead me back down the stairs and through to the kitchen.

'Abby, you can barely walk. How on earth did you manage to get home?'

'I walked, ha!' I pointed my fingers at her, laughing at the fact that I had proved her wrong.

'Where've you been?'

'I have been,' I said grandly. 'To the Hungry Horse.'

'Hey?' Harriet looked at me dumbfounded.

'Well yes, I've been told that's what they eat, H. But this particular horse was of the pub chain variety.' I found a kitchen chair and sat down on it. My feet throbbing from walking up the steep hill home.

'Do you mean that big family pub on the A4?'

'Yes. I have been to the A4,' I said, giggling uncontrollably.

'Were you on your own?'

'Oh yes, sad I know, drinking alone, but then I guess I am sad aren't I? Even my dad gets more sex than me these days. Hey, some nice man bought me a drink though. Said he likes a woman who likes her Guinness. He was pretty cute. I should have jumped him whilst I had the chance. They're getting snapped up pretty quick these days, bit like houses . . .'

Harriet was looking at me with complete disbelief as I ranted on. Eventually she butted in saying, 'You got drunk on Guinness? Since when did you drink that?'

I slumped forward, resting my head on the kitchen table and ignoring her.

'Does your dad know where you went?'

I raised my finger to my lips, shushing her. 'Don't talk about it.'

'Abby, I know about him and Mum,' she said gently. 'He told me this afternoon when he phoned up, wondering where you'd got to. They've been really worried about how you'd take it.'

'Did you know?'

'No, I didn't. But I guessed it was a possibility.'
Harriet sat down opposite me. 'Abby, why did you
have to go off like that and make them feel like
they're doing something wrong? Why can't you just
be happy for them?'

I sighed. 'I don't know. I couldn't help it, it was
just a shock. I felt disloyal being there with them.
I couldn't play happy families and act like it was
nothing to me.'

'Look, I know it's weird but you should at least
phone your dad. Let him know you're OK.'

'I don't wannoo,' I muttered, leaning forward on
my arms. I was tired and my head was spinning.

Harriet tutted, pushing her chair away crossly and
went to fetch the kettle. She stood at the sink, filling
it with water, her back to me.

I knew she was right, I was being ridiculous,
but I couldn't snap out of it, I was drunk and
incapable of thinking sensibly. 'Why do you have
to be so big about everything? So accepting? Don't
you find it just a little bit weird? You don't think for
a moment that they're being unfaithful to my mum,
your dad?'

Harriet shrugged. 'Not really no. I can see how it
would be harder for you to accept, of course. But I
don't know. I'm happy for them. You know nothing
happened whilst your mum was alive don't you?
You have to believe that. Our parents only got
together recently. Only a few months ago, they
said. And they must have a special bond. They
went through a lot together, they both loved your
mum and lost her. Maybe they understand each

other better than anyone else ever could. It almost seems natural.'

Everything she said made sense but in my drunken state her logic only served to infuriate me further. 'I suppose you're not bothered anyway,' I snapped angrily. 'You've got a new life now with *Old Man Collins*, you don't care what you're leaving behind. About all of us.'

Harriet turned around slowly, her arms folded. She looked as though she was trying not to lose her temper. 'What did you call him?'

'Old Man Collins,' I repeated. 'Haven't you spotted the likeness Robert shares with Phil Collins then? Haven't spotted the same receding hair line? Dreary taste in music? *Age* bracket?'

Harriet shook her head. 'What are you talking about?'

'Harriet, Robert is obviously lying to you about his age. He's pushing fifty and I don't understand why he's doing it, but if he lies about that he's most likely lying about other stuff as well.'

'What makes you think that?'

'Well, his taste in music really gave the game away.'

'Right, you hold it there. I don't want to hear any more about that Abby. When are you going to learn that you can't judge a person by their taste in music. It's narrow-minded. Stereotypical. Just because he doesn't like the kind of music that meets up to your rigid approval doesn't make him a no hoper. You know I couldn't care less about that kind of stuff.'

I tried to explain Robert's slip about seeing Depeche

Mode at the Bridge House Hotel but by that time Harriet was slamming about in the kitchen, saying 'I don't want to hear any more about it Abby.'

I sat quietly at the table, wishing I hadn't said anything whilst I was in such a state. I had been tactless and childish. The words had come out of my mouth before I had a chance to think about them. 'I'm sorry, I shouldn't have said that stuff about Robert. I'm just a bit worse for wear I guess.'

'I had noticed,' she snapped back, placing a cup of tea unceremoniously down in front of me.

'Thanks.'

'Yes, well I think I'll go and have a bath,' she said, leaving me alone in the kitchen to sober up.

'That's the first argument I've had with Harriet in ages,' I moaned to Ed. 'We hadn't argued in years before all this. I acted like such a horrible prat. I don't know what's wrong with me these days.'

'Well, you have been under a lot of pressure lately,' Ed said. 'I'm not surprised you're a bit stressed.'

'I am not stressed,' I snapped. The lead of the pencil I was using to write with snapped as I pressed down and I tutted, throwing it in the bin behind me. Ed raised his eyebrows at me, tapping his fingers on the side of his mug. 'I really need a holiday,' I muttered, ignoring him.

'So have you seen Harriet since then? How is she being with you?'

'Well, I saw her this morning and apologised so much I think I wore her down. She was OK, I think she understood. She told me she's accepted the offer on her house. The whole process could only take six weeks as the buyer is a bit of a property magnate apparently. Wads of cash in the bank and no chain to hold things up. He's pushing for a quick completion.'

'So, have you thought about what to do? Where you're going to go? Because you know I'd love it if you stayed with me. You're welcome for as long as you like.'

I smiled. 'Thanks Ed. Out of all the offers I've had, yours is definitely the most attractive. I just don't want to be a burden. I don't want to spoil . . .' I trailed off, feeling foolish. 'You know. We're such good friends.'

'We'd be perfect together,' he said seriously.

I felt a flush of pleasure, then a customer cleared his throat to get our attention. Ed winked at me then got up to serve him.

It was raining when I walked home and I cursed myself for not fetching the Scooby from Dad's house. Ed had offered to give me a lift but I turned him down. I didn't want to put him out any more than I had to. If we were going to be living together I wanted him to see me as an equal, rather than a burden or someone that needed looking after. Ed thought I was just being stubborn but I refused to be swayed.

When I rounded the corner onto our street I saw that Harriet wasn't home yet. Her car wasn't in it's usual spot. I also noticed that Dad had dropped off the Scooby and I felt guilt wash over me. I knew I would have to call him and apologise. I knew I was in the wrong. It was just going to take a while to get used to, that was all. For so long Harriet's mum had just been Harriet's mum, Mum's oldest friend and Patricia had been like a surrogate auntie. I was going to have to start seeing her in a different light.

Fumbling in my bag I took out my house keys and dropped them into a puddle that was forming on the bottom step. I bent down to pick them up but a hand scooped them up before I was able to.

'Hey!' I cried, righting myself.

Ben was standing in front of me, dangling my keys just out of reach. 'I win!' he said, grinning wickedly. 'Now, what's it worth to get them back? Perhaps a small token of affection?' He wiggled his eyebrows suggestively.

'Ben! I'm getting soaked here, give them back!' Why was it whenever I was with Ben, it felt like he was the younger brother I never had? I tried to swipe them back but he raised them higher.

'Oh go on Abby, don't tease me.'

'Me tease you? That's a laugh, you're the one dangling stuff!' I pretended to make a grab for them and whilst his attention was taken with fending off my hands I gave him a swift kick in the shin.

'Ow!' he cried, bending over. I snatched the keys from his grasp and ran up the steps, opening the front door.

'Ha! I win!' I shouted from the top of the steps, laughing as Ben chased up them.

'You're such a minx! You could have really hurt me then.'

'That's an old trick Harriet taught me, just enough force to momentarily take you by surprise but not enough to bruise. I'm sure you'll get over it. You have youth on your side.'

Ben leaned on the door frame, shaking the rain off his hair so it spiked up. 'You realise I now require compensation for that.'

'You can have one quick coffee, if you promise to behave.'

Ben thought about it, looking pained. 'Go on then. Two sugars in mine.'

'Why don't you pick some music whilst I make a drink?' I called from the kitchen.

I heard Ben say 'OK' and I smiled to myself. This should be interesting, I thought. Now, what would Ben choose? Young twenties, bags of energy and fun, fashionable and daft. Possibly Robbie Williams, although that's a little too obvious. Oasis? Maybe. The Verve, Travis, Ash? A studenty choice, more likely than Oasis. A boy band? God I hope not, but I wouldn't rule it out.

'Shit! You've got enough to chose from haven't you?' Ben called out from the living room, making me smile wider. 'Aha, got one. I haven't heard this for ages.'

Right, it would have to be more nostalgic then, perhaps Ocean Colour Scene? Yes, my final guess. I stopped stirring the drinks and paused, waiting for a guitar intro.

A guitar started and my mouth dropped open in surprise. I walked into the living room where Ben was standing back between the speakers listening to the song.

'Red Hot Chilli Peppers,' I said, appreciatively. 'I love this song.'

'Me too. I used to listen to this album all the time at Uni. "Under the Bridge" used to be my favourite but ever since the All Saints covered it I've found it a bit too popular. Now I always play "I Could Have Lied".'

'I totally agree. This is the best song on the album.'

'So, do I pass the test then?' Ben asked, smiling knowingly.

'You pass with a distinction.' I returned to the kitchen to finish making the drinks, looking back at Ben again only to see him playing air guitar in the middle of the living room. I shook my head, trying not to laugh. I knew it was too good to be true.

Ben took his coffee off me and we sat together on the floor, flicking through the rest of the album.

'Do you find that a good way of checking people out then? Seeing what they pick from your music collection?'

'It's a fairly good indication, yes. I think Harriet reckons I'm shallow. I would never go out with a heavy metal fan for example. But it's not that there's anything wrong with heavy metal fans, I'm just looking for someone who shares similar taste to me.'

Ben lay back on the floor, resting his head on his hand. 'So, what else would put you off?'

'Well. I wouldn't like to give the impression that I'm fussy. I think I've got pretty varied music taste.

But I suppose if I had to name a few turn-offs there'd be—' I counted off on my fingers. 'Michael Jackson fans, they make me a bit nervous; guys into UK Garage and the latest club stuff, it's good music but too limited; blokes that want to be Robbie Williams, there's a lot of those. And I don't think I could ever trust a guy that had a big thing for Jennifer Lopez, Britney Spears, Louise, anybody like that, especially if they had posters, ugh, men with posters, now that would be a turn off. Other than that there's not much that would put me off. So I'm not that fussy really, am I?'

'So,' Ben said, catching my eye. 'What about me?'

I sighed, looking down at my drink. 'What about you?'

'Do you think I'm suited to you?'

'Ben, you're like my little brother. You're excellent, but I think we're too similar.'

'Well you didn't kiss me like your little brother the other night. You can't deny you didn't enjoy that.'

I laughed, embarrassed. 'Well, yes, maybe. But I was caught up in a moment. I was wrong.'

Ben frowned, looking serious for a rare and fleeting moment, then there was a knock at the door and I breathed a heavy sigh of relief. I didn't want to get into a relationship assessment with Ben. I wanted us to be just friends. He was great company, but I wasn't attracted to him and I didn't want to jeopardise a possible friendship by having to spell it out.

'Come in,' I called.

Harriet walked in and saw Ben straight away. 'Oh, hi Ben. I didn't realise you were here. Shall I come back later?'

'No, no, come in and join us. Don't be daft,' I said, patting a space next to me. 'How was your day?'

'Not bad.' She took of her jacket and draped it over a chair. 'It's all so much better now I know I'm leaving. I feel like the pressure's off. Even Sacha's being nicer to me. Most probably delighted to see the back of me, but let's not talk about that.' She sat down on the sofa behind us and produced a bottle of wine, wrapped in tissue paper, from her briefcase. 'Can I tempt either of you into joining me with a glass of this?'

Ben and I both made appreciative noises and I sprang up to fetch some glasses and a corkscrew, grateful to see that Harriet and I were back to normal after my drunken outburst the previous night.

An hour later we were taking it in turns to pick songs we loved whilst the other two tried to guess in the shortest time what they were.

'Oh God, I know that song. They used to play it on Radio One all the time when I was at school. Oh, what is it.' She hummed something out loud, singing a few bars of a tune.

'Harriet, that's not even a song! It's the jingle for the Breakfast Show.'

Ben and Harriet burst out laughing when they realised I was right. 'Oh no, I'm hopeless at this,' she cried then reached for the bottle of wine but found it empty. 'Damn!'

'Out of wine already. That's no good.' Ben sat up, draining his glass.

'Hey, you can't complain. I only said you could stay for one cup of coffee. You've been here for ages,' I teased.

Ben pretended to look wounded. 'You're a right pair of heartbreakers, you two.'

Harriet lifted her head off the sofa's arm rest, suddenly interested. 'What have I done?'

'Maybe you should ask Jerry that question. He still talks about you, probably a couple of times a day. I've told him you're practically married but the poor guy won't let it drop. He seems to be using you as a standard to judge other women by. Every time I point one out for him he says something like, "But she's not as beautiful as Harriet" or "She's not as classy as Harriet" the guy's driving me up the wall.'

Harriet blushed, smiling to herself. 'He was nice. But meeting him was inopportune to say the least. Still, maybe I could make it up to him by inviting him to our Madonna party. I'll see if I can set him up with one of my clients.'

Ben looked confused. 'Madonna party?'

'It's for my thirtieth. And now I'm moving to London I guess it's also a good reason to get everyone over, say goodbye to an era. It'll be pretty big. I'm inviting loads of old clients, and Abby's going to get quite a lot of friends to come as well. It's kind of an Abby leaving do too as she'll be moving in with Ed when I've gone. Robert, my fiancé is coming so it'll be a good opportunity for him to meet everyone.

252

And it's a fancy dress. We're all dressing up in our favourite Madonna look or man linked with her. You want to come?'

'Absolutely! Girls in mad bras and corsets. What do you reckon?' He looked at me, arching an eyebrow. 'Why haven't I been invited before now?'

'We're only just getting around to organising it,' I said. 'We've been so caught up with other stuff that we haven't invited anyone yet.'

'Yes, we've got to start doing that actually. It'll be too short notice soon. Have you told Rebecca and Nathan yet?'

'Well, they'll remember from the night we were talking about it at the Mexican but I haven't told them what date it's on yet.'

'You really should. They might be busy that weekend.'

'I know, you're right,' I said, getting up to collect the empty wine glasses. 'I'll call them later on tonight.' I took the glasses into the kitchen, pondering on the idea of calling them. It would give me a great excuse to speak to Rebecca, to try and gauge exactly how she's feeling about married life. I checked my watch and hoped that Ben would be leaving soon. Suddenly I wanted to speak to Rebecca more than ever before.

# CHAPTER EIGHTEEN

It was almost a week before I finally worked up the nerve to call Rebecca. The night Ben had come over we ended up talking until late into the evening. Ben, I realised, was not too good at picking up hints. I had lingered at the door when Harriet left, waiting for Ben to follow her lead, to no avail. I had washed up the glasses and stopped offering him more drinks. I had yawned until my eyes watered but he had still not budged. Eventually I had to be blunt and show him the door. He had bent down to kiss me goodbye, gazing into my eyes for a sign that it was OK, that maybe I had been won over, but I pretended not to notice and kissed him quickly on the cheek, punctuating it with a cheery, 'Well, bye then. See you soon I hope, maybe at the party.' It was nearly eleven when I closed the door behind him. Too late to call Rebecca.

The following day I had lost my nerve and managed to talk myself out of it. I was frightened of what Rebecca would say. Not sure what I wanted to hear. And what if Nathan answered? Our friendship had deepened since the wedding and I was having to reassess how I treated him. I was scared of being alone with him. I felt sure my feelings were too difficult to hide when we were together. My heart would race and my hands became clammy. I was too aware of what I was saying and the way I said it, to be able to relax. I wanted to impress him. To be funny, clever, feminine and attractive, to show him what could have been. I knew it was wrong. I knew I should just treat him like any other friend, but the feelings were too strong to ignore and I ended up tying myself in knots, stammering nervously and floundering for things to say that didn't give away how I felt, making me sound too keen or flirtatious.

Friday came too quickly. It was almost a week since I discovered who robbed the shop. There had been the occasional phone call from the police station, letting us know what was happening. Big J had been arrested. The police found evidence linking him to several other burglaries in the area and he had admitted everything. He had made an appearance in the magistrates court on Thursday afternoon and they made a date for a hearing at the crown court for six weeks time. Ed and I were both glad to hear that we weren't required by the courts to give evidence as he had admitted guilt, and although Ed was a little jumpy at the thought of him being released on bail pending the court case, there was a general feeling of relief, that we could put it all behind us and get on with the future. A future, Ed was keen to assure me, that would not involve Kylie.

Ed was looking forward to Harriet's party. It was two weeks away and he was already planning his outfit, although he wasn't letting on what it was going to be. It was bound to be outrageous then, I concluded. Knowing Ed, he was going to want to create a stir and would most likely dress as her, rather than one of her men, possibly something from the Erotica era. I hoped he wouldn't go too overboard and embarrass me.

With so little time to go I knew I had got to call Nathan and Rebecca. I had already told Vicky and I didn't want them to think they were any less important. On Friday evening, after I returned from the shop, I finally plucked up the courage to pick up the phone.

Rebecca answered with a wary 'Hello?' and seemed to sigh with relief when I told her who it was.

'Abby! God, it's been ages. How are you?' She sounded really happy to hear from me, although it was always hard to tell with Rebecca. She could make the milkman feel he was her closest friend in the world.

'I know, it's been too long. How's married life?'

'Oh, you know,' she said vaguely. 'Abby, I really hate to do this to you when it's been so long, but I'm just about to nip out. Listen, I've just got off the phone to Vicky. We arranged to meet at her local for lunch tomorrow. She's bringing the kids. She did say she'd call and ask you along, so why don't we meet up then? Catch up properly.'

I wondered just how much of that was true. Perhaps she had been hoping to have Vicky all to herself. Having learnt that Rebecca had confided in Vicky about the miscarriage, I was beginning to wonder just how evenly spread this shared friendship was. Funny, I had always thought that Vicky and I had the closest relationship of the three of us. Maybe I had been wrong all along. 'Sure, OK. I don't think I'm doing anything. I'd love to,' I agreed with false enthusiasm.

'Great, see you tomorrow then. About twelve thirty?'

I agreed and said goodbye, aware that a sense of unease, possibly paranoia, was niggling at me, suggesting that I might have been an afterthought in this little get together, invited only because Rebecca had been put on the spot.

I walked around the side of the pub and saw that Vicky and Rebecca were already sitting on a picnic bench in the garden, leaning in together, seemingly lost in conversation. They both had an empty glass of wine on the table, evidence that they had been there for some time. Clarice was asleep next to them in the buggy. She was wrapped in a brightly coloured blanket and wore on oversized hat with a pom-pom dangling chirpily from the top, swamping most of her head. All I could see of her was a tiny window of her pale face, her mouth hanging open, emitting tiny puffs of breath, visible as it combined with the chilly, autumnal air.

I couldn't see Jack at first, then I spotted him under the giant oak tree which stood dominating the pub garden. He was standing precariously on a bench near the tree trunk, reaching for a rope swing that dangled from a sturdy branch, a loop tied at the bottom. He made a grab for it and put the loop over his head in the manner of a hangman's noose. 'Is this how you do it Mummy?' he called out. Vicky carried on her conversation with Rebecca, not hearing him.

'Jack, no!' I called out, running over to him before he tried to launch himself off the bench. Vicky and Rebecca turned around and saw Jack. They both sprang up, their conversation instantly forgotten and raced over to the tree, yelling at Jack to keep still. I got to him first, lifting him up into my arms and removing the rope. He looked at me, bewildered at first, then he broke into a dimpled smile.

'Oh, hi Abby. Do you want a go?'

'Jack, what a silly thing to do,' Vicky cried as she joined us. 'You could have strangled yourself!' She caught her breath and looked at me sheepishly. 'Thanks Abby. God, how embarrassing. That was my fault. I only took my eyes off him for a matter of seconds, but I should have been paying more attention. I'm so terrible. You can imagine the headlines can't you, "Boy hangs himself whilst mother sits drinking nearby".'

I couldn't help but laugh. 'Oh Vicky, don't be ridiculous. You would have spotted him. If you're a terrible mum then there's certainly no hope for the rest of us.' I put Jack down and Vicky and I both kissed him, ruffling his hair and laughing.

I smiled at Rebecca, who was standing further back, not quite sure what to make of the situation.

'Hello stranger,' I said, leaning over to kiss her cheek. 'How've you been?'

'Good thanks, really good. Busy though. There's been a lot going on. Sorry I haven't seen much of you lately.'

'That's all right, I guess it's a newly-wed thing isn't it? You and Nathan are probably holed up together being all romantic.' I searched her face for a reaction and I didn't have to look hard.

She wrinkled up her nose and said, 'Hardly. You've probably seen more of him than I have.'

I felt sure the colour was draining from my face as a rush of guilt left me tongue tied.

'It's OK, it's my fault,' Rebecca said, touching my arm and laughing. 'There's a lot of work dos on at the moment, I've been going out a lot. I don't really think Nathan likes that crowd. And this week I haven't seen him at all. He's had a management training course all week. They've put him up in a hotel in the lakes. He went up last Saturday morning and he won't be back till to-morrow.'

Last Saturday? That was the night I saw Chris driving out of Rebecca's cul-de-sac in the middle of the night, I recalled. I conjured up an expression of sympathy. 'You must really miss him.'

'Yeah,' she said absently, her attention now taken by a group of men who were all piling out of a BMW in the car park, laughing loudly. Vicky saw what Rebecca was looking at and frowned at her. I wondered if she too was worried about Rebecca's commitment to marriage.

Jack, who had been yanking my hand throughout my conversation with Rebecca, began to make
straining noises as he attempted to pull me back to
the rope swing.

'All right Jack, I get the message.' I let go of his
hand to take my gloves off. 'How about I show you
how it's really done, hey?'

'Yeah!'

'I think I owe you a drink,' Vicky said smiling
gratefully. 'I'll get this round. The usual?'

I nodded, thanking her and she walked back to
Clarice's buggy, extracting her purse from the net
bag that hung on the back. 'Are you okay with Jack
and Clarice for a minute?'

'Sure, no problem.' I climbed on a bench seat to
reach up for the rope whilst Jack cheered me on,
waving a stick in the air.

'I'll come with you,' Rebecca said, catching up
with Vicky, who had started back towards the
entrance of the bar.

When they returned I was swinging under the
tree, my foot wedged into the loop of rope, squealing
as I sped towards the tree. I narrowly missed it,
my thigh catching on some bark, making me spin
around precariously. I held on tightly, glad I had
worn my jeans. Jack laughed and I lent my head
back, pretending I was on a flying trapeze. I saw
Vicky and Rebecca, watching with a tray of drinks
and nibbles. They stopped talking when they caught
me looking, giving me that fleeting feeling of paranoia once again. I suddenly felt self-conscious and
dragged my heel along the ground to stop myself

swinging any more. 'There you go Jack.' I handed the rope over. 'I think you get the hang of it now, don't you?' He nodded, taking the rope excitedly and I went to join Vicky on the bench where they had been sitting earlier.

'Vicky was just telling me about the Madonna party, that you've set a date,' Rebecca said, handing me my glass of wine as I sat down opposite her.

'Oh yes, that's why I called you yesterday. You are coming aren't you?'

'Of course. It sounds like a great laugh. 'I've always wanted an excuse to dress up like Madonna, especially her Blonde Ambition gear.'

'Didn't Nathan say he didn't like her when she was blonde though?' Vicky said, surprised.

Rebecca shrugged. 'God, I'm not going to dress to please Nathan just because we're married. Maybe if I was trying to win him over, but then—' she smiled saucily, 'I've already done that.'

Vicky looked a little put out and I guessed that she was going to pull out all stops to impress Alistair, his approval had always been more important to her than anybody else's. Not that she needed to work hard for that, when Alistair, quite obviously, already had her up on a pedestal. She fiddled with the zip of the oversized fleece she was wearing, which I recognised as Alistair's.

'So, what do you think Nathan will go as?'

'Hopefully Guy Ritchie, he's gorgeous.' She took a large sip of wine and smacked her lips together.

'Oh, so it's all right for him to dress up sexy for

you then, just not the other way around?' Vicky teased.

'Absolutely, keep them on their toes, I say.'

She's doing that all right, I thought. 'Ed won't tell me what he's wearing, he wants to keep it secret.'

Rebecca rolled her eyes. 'Oh God, could be anything then. I bet he dresses as her.'

'Oh, I don't know,' Vicky said. 'He's not that bad. Besides, if keeping his outfit a secret means he's planning to wear something outrageous then I guess I'd better be worried too. Alistair won't tell me what he's wearing either. In fact, he just keeps laughing to himself and telling me I'm going to be very surprised.'

Rebecca and I exchanged a look of disbelief and shook our heads. 'You've got nothing to worry about there,' Rebecca said. 'He's one of those really dependable guys, he'd never embarrass you. I doubt he'd know outrageous if it mooned in his face. He's probably just winding you up.'

Vicky didn't look quite so sure. 'If you say so.'

The conversation turned to me and I filled them in on what had happened with Big J, about catching Dad with Harriet's mum and Harriet managing to sell her house.

'I can't wait to meet the mysterious Robert, its going to be really interesting,' Vicky said and I agreed. It was going to be interesting to see what Vicky made of him, she was a good judge of character and I valued her opinion. 'So much is happening to you at the moment,' she continued. 'It makes me realise how static my own life is. I got married, had children and that's it now, everything took on this very ordinary sense of normality. My whole life is routine and nothing happens to me any more.'

I looked at Rebecca, who was playing with a beer mat and frowning. Most probably worried that now she was married she was in danger of heading down the same path, but I saw Vicky's life differently, her family was a kind of protective armour. Security and happiness didn't restrict your life, it enriched it. 'You wouldn't swap though would you?' I said, comforted when the look on Vicky's face confirmed that she wouldn't. 'I'm beginning to wish nothing much happened to me anymore, it's been crazy lately and I'm having a hard time keeping up. Sometimes I think I really need to get away from it all, get a fresh perspective. Do you know what I mean? I feel like I just can't see the woods for the trees.'

Rebecca nodded furiously. 'God, do I know that feeling.'

Vicky and I both looked at her curiously, waiting for her to continue and after a long intake of breath she did.

'It's just that, before I got married, my whole life seemed like one long romantic episode. Me and Nathan were so caught up with each other, so intense, every day was exciting. It felt like it was just the two of us against the world.' She looked over at Jack, who was balancing on a series of logs set into the grass. She was lost in thought for a moment then shook her head and looked back at us. 'After we got married it changed the moment we got home. It got serious, grown up. It stopped being fun. I can't believe marriage can change a relationship so quickly. Just a piece of paper. One piece of paper and it's soured everything. I don't understand what's going on any more. What I've done.'

I sat quietly, not sure if she wanted advice, sympathy or encouragement to elaborate.

Vicky tilted her head to one side and patted Rebecca's hand. 'You've been through a lot, you're bound to be affected by it all. Don't blame being married though, you're still the same people. You can get it back. It'll just take a bit of adjustment. If you stopped trying so hard to prove you're still young and having fun, you might actually start to enjoy it.'

Rebecca groaned and stretched back. In one swift movement she pushed her slender fingers through her hair, gathered it together then let it fall back over one shoulder, where she twisted the ends thoughtfully. 'This conversation's getting a little too serious for a Saturday afternoon. How about I get another round in and then we can do some serious reminiscing. You know how I like to relive our school days.'

Jack saved me from that one by running up to the table, his face pink with exertion. He tugged the sleeve of my coat impatiently. 'Please come and play now Abby, please, please,' he begged, attempting, this time, to drag me in the direction of the obstacle course.

I shrugged at Vicky and Rebecca and got up, leaving them to discuss old times.

# CHAPTER NINETEEN

I picked up a heavy cardboard box that had been left at the top of the stairs and carried it across the landing into Harriet's spare bedroom. There were already several dozen boxes piled up by the window, ready to go. I put the one I was carrying down on the floor, next to the others and looked around the room, catching my breath.

Why did Harriet have to be so organised? I wondered sadly. Why couldn't she be more like me? She could leave everything until the last minute then run around in a state of frenzy, balancing belongings in her arms like a kid on Crackerjack and giving herself a stitch. At least that way I wouldn't have to see her things being gradually whittled down and packed away, reminding me that she was leaving and destroying any hope that somehow she would change her mind and stay. But that possibility was becoming less and less likely. The buyer Harriet had secured had visited the house several times now, always with a notepad, a tape measure and the cold confidence of a businessman in the middle of a profit-making venture. No need for sentimentality there. It was quite obvious that his plans were to split the house up again and rent, possibly to students, then sit back and let the money roll in. That was partly why I found it so hard to take. Maybe if it was going to be a family home, a place to be treasured and loved, I wouldn't mind so much. But this? This was like sending a pet to spend the rest of its days in a loveless kennel.

Harriet followed me into the room with a bulging black bin liner weighing down each hand. She dumped them in the corner of the room and looked at me. 'Don't look so sad,' she said with a consolatory smile. 'You're making me feel terrible. I'm only doing it early because of the party. I mean, if I've got to move all the stuff out of the way for tonight, then I may as well do it properly. I'll only have to pack them up later, so it's good . . .'

'Time management.' I finished for her with a smile. 'Yes I know Harriet, I'm used to your ways by now.' I looked at my watch. 'Right, it's half past three. We've got four and a half hours until people begin to arrive. What shall we do next?'

'How about you hoover up, I can start getting the food ready, then we'll both have time to get dolled up. The music can be done last minute can't it?'

'Sure.' Butterflies were beginning to emerge in my stomach, hatched from a mixture of fear and excitement. I always loved parties but this one was going to be special. I wanted to make the most of the time I had left here, my last few weeks with Harriet. I was also anticipating seeing Nathan. I hadn't seen him for several weeks now. Not since he asked me o speak to Rebecca. I knew he was going to ask me about that and I hadn't got a clue what to say. How could I tell him that the impression I got was that she was regretting getting married, hankering after her single, carefree life, and her late night visit om Chris whilst he was away? I sensed she was keeping secrets from him and from me, possibly confiding only in Vicky, but asking her what was going through Rebecca's head would be pointless. She was as loyal as it was possible to be and she would take a secret to the grave, rather than betray a confidence. My only option was to say nothing, let him find out his own way. If they were unhappy, they wouldn't be able to hide it for much longer. They needed to talk properly, to be honest with each other and decide for themselves if they had made a mistake by rushing into things. They needed to clear the air, if they hadn't already.

'Come on then, what are you waiting for?' Harriet called out from the top of the stairs and I broke from my daydreams, and followed as she descended the stairs.

'It looks so different doesn't it?' Harriet said, whirling gracefully around the living room, using up every ounce of space which had been cleared.

'It was never exactly cluttered though was it?' I laughed as Harriet danced around me, taking my hand and reaching it over my head, making me spin around. It was hard to stay gloomy when Harriet was so excited. Ever since she had given in her notice it was as though she had been given a new lease of life. Of course she admitted to being fearful, but then without a little fear, how could you ever take your life, shake it up and see it settle in a better place? Harriet was in love, her future was unknown yet exciting, and she was enjoying every minute.

The room looked great. We had taken out everything that wasn't essential and left only a bookcase, the pair of sofas, and left the cushions piled in the corners of the room for people to collapse in. It seemed gigantic, with its high ceiling and bay window only accentuating the space we had. My hi-fi equipment was piled up at one end of the room, ready to be set up, but that wouldn't take long. There was no need for my usual gear and I was instead using the separates I usually used in my bedroom. The only bit of disco kit I was using were my pair of tower lights. No disco was complete without at least a few flashing lights, I had told Harriet, who promptly counted them and informed me that 'thirty-two was rather a lot more than a few, but she'd let me off this time.'

The oven timer started bleeping, summoning Harriet into the kitchen to check on the batch of red pepper and basil flans that she had been preparing earlier.

I followed her into the kitchen, where I pinched a Gouda wafer from a basket and tried to eat it without Harriet seeing.

'What did you just pinch?' Harriet said, whirling around and pointing an oven gloved finger at me. The Gouda melted deliciously on my tongue and I opened my mouth to show her it was empty. Harriet gave me a knowing look and fetched a flan dish out of the oven, leaving it on the hob to cool. I wandered around the room, not quite sure where to start.

The kitchen was in a completely opposite state to the living room. There were bottles of wine, cider, spirits, lemonade and grape juice, a bottle of champagne (which Harriet had insisted she wouldn't have a party without), to name but a few, crowded together and practically obscuring the table from view. What remaining space there was, was piled high with giant packets of kettle chips, tortilla chips, pretzels and peanuts. The work surfaces were in a similar condition; assorted party essentials, packets of napkins, pots of dips, French bread and bowls of salad and crudités, jostled for space with the hot trays of fresh filo triangles, which were emitting a smell that was sending my taste buds into a heady state of over stimulation. Harriet had also insisted that we hire plates and glasses from the local pub rather than give out disposables, being convinced that even the most decent wine tasted like 'Barbie's pee' when served in a plastic tumbler. They were stacked high in crates in one corner of the room next to a keg of local cider and another of bitter.

The phone rang again making Harriet and I groan simultaneously. Barely ten minutes could pass by without the phone ringing at some point with people checking if it was all still on, could they bring a friend, asking for directions, blagging a piece of floor to sleep on or wondering if we knew any drivers they could get a lift home with. People wanted to know who was coming, what to bring, what time to come and what to wear, most of which had been written on the invitations Harriet had run up on the computer, but it was amazing how many people wanted to 'just make sure'.

'Your turn I think,' I said to Harriet, bending down to collect up one of the trays of glasses to take into the dining room.

Harriet flung a tea towel over her shoulder and reached across for the phone.

The dining room had also been stripped of anything deemed unnecessary and was bare except for dining chairs, a corner cupboard and a large table against the far wall, where all the food would be spread out. Harriet and I had hung up two trellis lights that spanned one wall, dotting it with tiny fairy lights. We covered them with a thin, purple muslin panel that hid the wires and let the lights shine through with an ethereal glow. There were two speakers on the walls linked to the hi-fi in the living room so that the music could just about be heard all over the house. The walls between the rooms were so solid we would never have done it with just one pair. There was a French door leading into Harriet's long corridor of garden, but I doubted many would want to go outside, it was a clear blue sky day, but a chilly north wind promised a bitter night that only the truly hardened or pissed to a state of numbness could endure.

Harriet appeared in the doorway and leaned against the frame, her arms folded and a frown creasing her forehead.

'What's up?' I said, quickly licking away the crumbs from another Gouda wafer off my lips, convinced Harriet was going to tell me off for eating the party food.

'Oh, nothing. I'm probably being silly.'

'What?'

'Well, Robert hasn't phoned me all day. He said he'd ring when he'd set off. I've tried the number of his flat but there's no answer and his mobile just goes straight to answerphone.'

'H, you worry too much. He's most likely already set off and his mobile's not on because he's on the motorway or something. I bet he'll be here any minute. What time did he say he'd arrive?'

'He didn't give me a specific time, just said it should be in the afternoon, but he'd ring first.'

I looked at my watch. It was half past five. The afternoon was almost over. I smiled brightly saying, 'He probably got held up and wanted to leave straight away rather than delay it with a phone call. Don't worry, if he's late it doesn't matter. It gives you time to get ready so you can wow him with your outfit.' I dragged her back into the kitchen and gave her some bowls and bags of nibbles to put out in an attempt to take her mind off him. I didn't like sticking up for Robert, but the last thing I wanted was for Harriet to waste time worrying about him. Tonight was going to be the first chance in a long time to really let our hair down and enjoy ourselves, I didn't want anything to spoil the convivial mood that had infected us both.

We carried on sorting out the food, laying it out

onto the table in the dining room or packing it into the over-laden fridge. When the kitchen began to look as clear as it could be and we were running out of jobs, Harriet decided that now was the time to get ready. We agreed to split up and meet back downstairs for a glass of bubbly before people started to arrive.

Getting dressed brought back memories of being in my very early teens. Harriet and I had both loved Madonna and would imitate her in our bedrooms in front of the mirror. Harriet, being older than me, had morphed into a woman before my eyes and I would look up to her with a mixture of jealousy and awe. She was confident and aloof where I was needy and insecure.

I loved the image of Madonna as the street kid, dancing in alleyways on the wrong side of Brooklyn Bridge, but Harriet saw something different. The potential, the starry quality hinting that she wouldn't stay there forever, she was different from the others and she was going places. I used to think I would become more like Harriet as I got older. But now I understood it wasn't age that made Harriet the way she was. It was attitude.

I pulled my black, cut off leggings, under the full mini skirt and viewed my reflection. I was pleased with the result. It had taken me a week to get everything together. The lacy gloves were the only things I had left from dressing up, years ago. The black leggings and skirt I had found in a charity shop and hemmed them up. I found a black string top to hang loosely over the tight, cropped black vest top, which was courtesy of Marks and Spencer. I borrowed a thick, black belt from Ed. The wide black material for my hair was a remnant from a fabric shop and the jewellery was all my own. I hung a silver crucifix from my waist and pulled on my fingerless gloves. I was all in black and was thankful that I still had the remnants of my summer tan. If the party had been held any later in the year my skin would have looked ghoulish with so much black next to it. My hair was back-combed so much I didn't think I'd ever get some of the knots out. I pulled the black band of material through it, tying a large bow at the top. My make-up felt unusually heavy with thick black eyeliner and deep lipstick, I had even given myself a mole above my top lip. I was afraid to touch my face in case I smudged it. I smiled in the mirror and danced about. There was no music in the room and the only sound was the clinking of my bracelets and the chains on Ed's belt.

I heard the phone ring downstairs and I stopped quickly as Harriet answered it, waiting to see if she would shout for me, but she didn't and the house was silent again.

I checked my appearance one last time. It was very authentically Madonna and I wasn't convinced that many others would go to such lengths to dress up, except for Harriet of course. She had decided that, as it was our party, we should set the precedent and have the best outfits, although I knew that was her way of justifying living out a long standing fantasy. Her outfit was incredible.

I had wrestled with my conscience for weeks after Harriet suggested the idea at the Mexican meal Nathan had said how much he fancied Madonna in the 'Like A Prayer' video and temptation taunted me ever since, suggesting that I get myself a tight black dress and dance in front of him, letting my bra straps fall down my shoulders suggestively. I kept asking myself if it would be obvious, if everyone else would also recall that conversation and see what I was doing. Fortunately caution stopped me in the end. That and the fact that I would have had to have dyed my hair dark brown and I was worried that my recently acquired highlights would turn a funny shade of orange.

I left my bedroom, hurrying down the stairs to see Harriet, I was dying to see how she looked in her outfit.

'Holy shit!'

'Do you like it?' Harriet asked, standing at the bottom of the stairs.

My mouth was hanging open in shock. I couldn't believe I was looking at Harriet. 'You look amazing. Just like her. I can't believe it!'

'So do you.'

'But your dress, it's fantastic!'

'I'm not sure pink is my colour,' she said, feeling the satin fabric self consciously.

'Believe me, it's your colour. It's stunning. You've done a fantastic job.'

Harriet had found a full, white satin wedding dress in a second-hand shop when we went into town several weeks ago. That was the last time I

274

had seen it as she wouldn't show me it again until it was finished. She borrowed her mother's sewing machine and worked on it in the evenings when I was out. I had no idea she was such a seamstress. She had taken off the straps and sleeves, leaving only the bodice. The skirt had been taken in to give it a more streamline shape and with the material that was left over she had made a huge bow for the back. She had bought some long gloves that stretched past her elbows and dyed the whole lot pink. It was an almost perfect copy of Madonna's dress in the 'Material Girl' video. The one where she paid homage to Marilyn Monroe's 'Diamonds are a Girl's Best Friend'. She had borrowed costume jewellery from me and a white fake fur stole from her mother to finish the look. Her hair was curled so it sat in soft waves off her face.

'God, forget marketing. You should really own a dress shop. You've got a real talent with the sewing machine. I never would have thought it was the same dress.' I felt the fabric and inspected her from all angles, shaking my head in amazement.

'I just hope that everyone else enters into the spirit of it. Imagine if we were the only ones dressed up. It would be so embarrassing. She swallowed nervously. 'Right, let's get the champagne open. I need a drink before I chicken out and put my "Italians Do It Better" T-shirt on instead.'

# CHAPTER TWENTY

'I can't believe how good everyone looks.' Harriet was looking around with a huge grin on her face. 'They've all put so much thought into it.'

The doorbell had been ringing so much that we had given up and left the front door open so that people could just walk in. They filed past, holding bottles of drink and presents for Harriet. There were several faces I didn't recognise and I assumed they were old associates of Harriet's. They greeted her affectionately, kissing her cheek and lavishing her with compliments about her dress. So far I had spotted a couple of women dressed like me, half-a-dozen men in Music T-shirts, aka Guy Ritchie at the *Snatch* première. There was a Michael Jackson, a Warren Beatty, several women in cowboy shirts and jeans, and a gorgeous looking woman with a sleek blonde bob, wearing a red tartan kilt and a black tank top.

I left Harriet to greet people and went into the living room to crank up the music. Drinks were beginning to flow now and I was anxious for the others to arrive. I wandered over to the bay window and looked out into the night. The headlights of a car lit the street with two yellowy pools of light as it drew up outside our house. I watched as a group of three spilled out of the back seats, they were laughing loudly and, as their car pulled away, a taxi pulled up behind them. I went to the door to find out who they were.

'Abby! You look amazing!' Rebecca cried, walking in and kissing me airily. She was wearing a tight black cat suit and had scraped her hair back into the long blonde ponytail Madonna wore for the Blonde Ambition tour.

'Oh my God, you've dyed your hair!'

Rebecca touched it laughing. 'Don't be daft, it's a hairpiece. Do you like it?' She twirled around, making her hair swing out behind her. 'This guy at work's wife did it for me. She's a hairdresser.'

'A miracle worker more like. It looks so real.' I looked at it really closely, feeling the ends.

'I know. I think I'm getting a taste for being blonde.'

Nathan stepped in behind her, holding a bottle of wine. 'Don't you dare,' he warned his wife. She ignored him and saw Harriet behind me. She squealed and ran over to talk to her.

'Hi Abby,' Nathan said, kissing my cheek. I breathed in his smell, a masculine mixture of spice and musk. An intoxicating smell, that made me want to lean in nearer and close my eyes. 'Where do I hang my coat up?'

'Oh, over there,' I said, watching as he took his denim jacket off. He was wearing a Music T-shirt as well, but it was closer fitting than the ones the other guys were wearing. It showed off the curves of his muscles and made his shoulders seem incredibly broad. I looked away and saw that Vicky was standing at the door. She had been watching me with narrowed, knowing eyes.

'Vicky, hi!' I said, enveloping her in a hug. The moment had gone and she rubbed my back then broke away to shrug off her coat. 'Wow, look at you!' I cried, appraising her outfit. She looked slimmer than I had ever seen her, and was wearing a stomach revealing pair of blue hipster trousers with a wide, sparkly belt and a white vest top. Her long hair was glossy and hanging loosely in soft waves and her cheeks sparkled with glitter. 'Slimmer of the month,' she grinned. 'Would you believe they're going to put my before and after photo in the class brochure. Ugh, how embarrassing.' She looked at me and touched the ribbon in my hair, laughing. 'And you look so cute. As if you've danced right out of the "Borderline" video. I love that song.'

'So, where's Alistair?'

'He said he'd join us later, our babysitter couldn't make it till half eight so he let me go on early. To be honest I think he secretly wants to make an entrance.'

'Do you know what he's wearing yet?'

She shook her head. 'No idea. I'm getting worried though. It's like he wants to prove to me that he's not square or something. Apparently all the guys at work call him Biddy.'

I frowned, not getting it. 'But that's his name, Biddles.'

Vicky laughed a tinkly laugh. 'Yes but that's not how they mean it. They mean it like "old biddy" because he's always drinking tea and reading the paper in the staff toilet.'

I cracked up laughing. 'Oh bless him.'

'It's true,' she continued. 'And what's making it worse is he's even started growing a beard this week.'

'Helloo,' a voice cried from behind Vicky and we both turned around to see who it was. Standing at the door were two very opposite looking men. One was tall and black, with huge dark brown eyes and the lithe body of a dancer. He was wearing the trousers of what appeared to be a very expensively tailored suit with a crisp white shirt, buttoned right the way up and a pin striped waistcoat, the back of which I could just glimpse, was made of rich gold silk. 'I'm the gorgeous one in the "Vogue" video,' he said. 'And may I congratulate you on your fabulous taste. A party in honour of—' he put a hand on his chest and said reverently, 'our lady. I can't think of anything more appealing.'

I realised who he was then. Ed had warned me that his friends, Spencer and Oscar had been so excited at the thought of a Madonna party that they had begged to be invited. Ed had already told me that his gay friends referred to Madonna as 'our lady.'

'And you must be Jean Paul Gaultier,' I said to his friend, who was a few inches shorter than me

279

and had hair bleached white blonde which was cropped close to his head. He was wearing a string vest and a kilt.

'Hi Abby,' he said, kissing me lavishly on both cheeks. 'We've heard so much about you.'

'Jesus Christ, check out the diva over there! I've got to ask her where she got that dress,' the first friend said and dragged Jean Paul off in Harriet's direction.

Vicky watched them go, laughing. 'Friends of Ed's I presume.'

'Of course.' I looked back at the open door. That was when I spotted Ed. He was leaning against the doorway in a casual pose, as though he had been there for some time, observing us. He was wearing a black suit and a white shirt. The first few buttons of the shirt were undone and he had a thin black tie hanging loosely around his neck. His chin was stubbly with a few days growth of beard and his hair was combed back off his face with a side parting. There was a cigarette hanging lazily from his mouth and I noticed he was holding an empty bottle of scotch. He struck an incredibly sexy image in the doorway and he reminded me of one of the old movie stars he idolised, Marlon Brando or James Dean. Rough, rugged and dangerously manly.

'Ed! You're in a suit!' I stared at him in disbelief. 'I've never seen you in a suit.'

He stood up from the wall and flicked his cigarette onto the floor, where he ground it out with a smart black shoe. He smiled slowly, raising an eyebrow. 'You were expecting something different?'

I had actually been expecting quite the opposite. Possibly cross-dressing or something outrageous. If not outrageous then definitely something humorous that would get people laughing and talking. Certainly not the coolly understated image before me. I shook my head, speechless.

Vicky was grinning at us both, then she spotted the empty bottle. 'Oh my God, have you drunk all of that?'

Ed drawled, 'No, ray of light. It's a prop. I'm Sean Penn. Drinker, rogue and womaniser.' He raised his eyebrows flirtatiously at Vicky, who put a hand on her chest and giggled, blushing. I pulled him inside, keeping hold of his arm protectively. 'Come on, let's all get a drink.'

An hour later the music was thumping in the living room and people were beginning to dance. Rebecca was already looking drunk and dancing wildly, her hair swinging as she waved her hands in the air. She seemed to be able to do this whilst still holding onto her glass of wine, which she took the occasional sip from. Nathan danced with her, but not with quite the same enthusiasm and he stopped often to fetch his drink from the bookcase or talk to people who were standing on the sidelines. I went into the kitchen, which was now bustling with people, to join Harriet and Vicky. They were sharing a bowl of Twiglets and looking gloomy.

'What's up girls? This is supposed to be a party.'

Harriet tried smiling but seemed to find it too

much of an effort and her face dropped again. 'Robert's still not arrived. I can't believe him. He knew how important this was to me.'

Vicky looked at her sympathetically. 'Don't worry, I'm sure he'll have a good explanation. Maybe something's happened to him.' She realised what she had just said, amending quickly. 'I mean, nothing serious, just something . . . unexpected, you know.' She looked at me desperately, her expression imploring me to back her up.

'Absolutely. And besides, you should be thinking like Madonna tonight. She wouldn't waste her time in the kitchen moping. She'd think, sod him, and party like there was no tomorrow.'

I saw a glimmer of a smile flicker on Harriet's face. 'I suppose.'

The doorbell rang and we all looked up expectantly. The door opened before anybody went to answer it, and in walked Alistair. At least I was guessing it was Alistair. It was hard to tell. I had never seen him with a goatee before. His outfit was even more surprising. He was wearing a bright yellow shell suit, yellow tinted sunglasses and a shower cap. He had a huge gold chain swinging from his neck and rings like knuckle dusters on both hands. At that point the music in the living room stopped as someone changed the CD and the house fell silent. Alistair spotted us all in the kitchen and walked into the hall, standing in a rapper stance with his hands raised. 'Katanga my friends!' he said loudly, then made a sound like a parrot screeching. Everyone stopped their conversations and stared at him, incomprehensibly. Vicky's jaw dropped open and several people peered around the living room door to find out what was going on. There was a smattering of embarrassed giggles as people exchanged glances. I heard someone say, 'If he's supposed to be Ali G, why's he talking like Lenny Henry?'

'Wus da matta wiv yous den?' he said in an accent that sounded vaguely Jamaican.

Vicky groaned and put her head in her hands with embarrassment, muttering, 'Oh my God!' under her breath. The music started up again and people picked up their conversations once more, casting the occasional bemused glance back at Alistair, who was coming our way and looking really pleased with himself.

'So, what do you's fink den?' he said.

'I think you need a lesson in Ali speak,' Vicky said, dragging him back out into the hallway before he embarrassed her anymore.

Harriet and I exchanged a look and cracked up laughing.

'Why are you laughing?' a voice said and Harriet and I both looked up. It was my dad, dressed in an old, stripy grandad shirt, unbuttoned at the neck with a cravat tied underneath. He had slicked his hair back off his face and looked oddly like Harold Steptoe.

'Mum!' Harriet cried, kissing Patricia, who was standing behind my dad. She looked as though she had stepped straight out of a classic war film, in a fitted dress, her hair swept back into a forties inspired chignon. I realised they were Eva Perón and Che from *Evita*.

'You look amazing!' I cried, staring at dad, who I had never seen in anything other than a pair of corduroy trousers and an M&S jumper.

He smiled shyly and tugged at his cravat. 'I don't think we're staying too long. Harriet invited us, and Pat was really touched that she asked her so, well, we thought it would be nice to make the effort.' He seemed worried that I didn't want them here and I felt shamed that I could make him feel that way.

'I'm sorry I haven't been over much lately, it's just . . .' I struggled with the right words to use.

'It's OK. You don't need to explain. I understand.' He smiled kindly.

'Patricia looks fantastic,' I said, my subtle attempt at a peace offering. He took it gracefully, nodding and watching her as she and Harriet poured drinks for a couple who had just arrived. The way he watched her told me everything I needed to know. She made him happy and complete. He needed her.

He reached across to the table behind me, helping himself to a can of bitter and a glass. 'Abby,' he started uncomfortably, clearing his throat and putting a lot of effort into retrieving, opening and pouring out his beer. 'About Patricia and I.' He carefully placed the empty can in the bin liner that Harriet had taped to the back of the door. 'I want you to know that, well . . . that it doesn't change anything. That all your memories, of your mother and me, of everything. Well . . .' He stood wkwardly with his beer, the only prop he had eft, that was now sitting redundant in his hand. He didn't dare take a sip of it until he had purged vhat was on his mind. 'I just don't want you to hink differently about that time, OK? It was still ust how you remember it. I still loved your mother ust as much. I always will.'

'Dad, it's all right. You don't have to explain. I understand exactly what you mean. I know. And I'm happy for you, I really am. It was just a shock, but I needed that, we couldn't carry on the way we were for ever and seriously, honestly, I'm glad for you.' I smiled at him and Dad visibly relaxed, taking a sip of beer at last. 'Come on, let's get some food. I'm famished.' I took his elbow and steered him out of the kitchen towards the dining room.

We pushed past Vicky and Alistair, who were leaning against the wall in each others arms.

'Booyakasha!' Vicky said loudly to him.

Alistair concentrated hard for a moment then said, 'Boo-sha-kia-sha!'

'No, no, no! Again,' Vicky instructed and they both burst out laughing.

Dad did a double-take when he saw Alistair's yellow Ali G outfit. 'Whatever happened to Vicky's husband? He used to be a nice, stable guy,' he muttered to me.

At that point Austin Powers entered the hallway, looked at me, and cried, 'Yeah baby, yeah!' Dad looked a little alarmed as a guy in a blue velvet suit and a white, ruffled shirt, sashayed over to me, grinning with false bad teeth. He saw Dad, stopped, and put his index finger on his chin, in a slow and exaggerated pondering gesture, saying 'Mr J, I presume. What a pleasure.'

Dad, who appeared to have been rendered speechless, allowed Austin to shake his limp hand.

'Ben? Is that you?' I peered closer.

He nodded, his teeth protruding with an unattractive overbite. 'Jerry's just coming.'

Jerry walked into the hall then. He was dressed as Dick Tracy with a camel coloured overcoat covering his suit and a matching Trilby hat, tipped over one eye. He was holding a toy gun and a Sainsbury's carrier bag.

Dad patted my hand. 'I'll be in the dining room,' he said and hurried away, clutching his pint tightly.

Jerry kissed me warmly, but I could tell he was looking past me, looking for Harriet. He spotted her in the kitchen, still talking to her mum, and his eyes lit up and lingered on her. 'So, where's the fiancé?' he said to nobody in particular.

I shrugged, shaking my head. 'Now that's anyone's guess.'

# CHAPTER TWENTY-ONE

Standing in the living room, I was reminded of those scenes in 80s, American films, where school kids surround a playground and chant and clap as the coolest kid, the one who can break-dance, body pops and windmills to an adoring crowd. Spencer, the guy that had introduced himself as 'the gorgeous one in the "Vogue" video,' was beginning to make me wonder if he had in fact been telling the truth. Not only did he look just like him, but he was also entertaining a crowd of guests with a 'Vogue' performance that would put Madonna to shame.

'He's brilliant,' Vicky said, jigging to the music.

I was beginning to notice that Spencer spent a lot of his time looking at Ed whilst he was dancing, checking that he was watching. Ed was leaning against a wall next to Oscar and staring moodily into his drink.

Spencer danced out of the circle, his cue to let others dance, and many took his place, trying out his moves, enthusiasm making up for what they lacked in panache.

Rebecca began dancing again and I stole a glance

at Nathan, who was standing next to the hi-fi talking to Ben. They were looking my way, causing me to flush with embarrassment, not knowing where to look next.

'I'm just going to check on dad,' I said to Vicky and walked out of the room.

Dad and Patricia were just putting their coats on. 'We're off now love,' dad said, seeing me come in.

'Oh but dad, you've not been here long.' I looked pleadingly at them both. I hadn't had a chance to talk to Patricia yet and I had been planning to all night.

'We never intended to stay too long,' Patricia said. 'We just wanted to make an appearance, wish Harriet a happy birthday, that sort of thing.' She trailed off and I felt sure she was thinking that she had also wanted to see Robert. It was ten o'clock now. It was looking less and less likely that he was coming at all. I looked at Harriet. She seemed to be putting on a brave face, smiling brightly but I imagined that she secretly wanted them to leave, humiliated by Robert's absence.

I kissed them both goodbye and showed them to the door.

'I don't suppose you'll be feeling up to a Sunday lunch tomorrow will you?' Dad said.

I pulled a face. 'How about next week? I'll make sure I'm on time.'

'Great. I'll call you.'

I watched them walk down the steps, reaching for each other's hand instinctively. When I shut the door Harriet said, 'Sad, isn't it?'

'What?'

'Well, that our parents have a more successful sex life than the pair of us.'

'Don't . . .' I said, smiling. 'I don't even want to think about that.' I put my arm around her bare, bony shoulder. 'Are you OK?'

Harriet nodded. 'I think I've gone past worry, anger, frustration, disappointment and now I'm into a new, and frankly quite exciting phase.'

'What's that then?'

'Well, you were right earlier about needing to capture the spirit of Madonna. I should be enjoying my moment, squeezing every ounce of life out of it.'

I looked at her nervously. 'You're going to get pissed and flirt with other guys, aren't you?'

'Damn right,' she said, fetching her glass from the kitchen and downing it in one.

'So, Ed, what's up?' I danced over to where Ed had been standing for the past hour and nudged his elbow chirpily. 'Are you looking surly and smouldering because you're perfecting the Sean Penn image, or are you actually a bit pissed off?'

Ed smiled tightly at me. 'Was I looking smouldering? Damn I'm good.'

He looked across the living room, his eyes settling on no one in particular and I sensed he was pretending. The wine I had drunk was beginning to unsettle my balance slightly and I leaned into him, resting my head on his arm. I felt him stiffen, then he patted me awkwardly.

'Are you all right, Ed? Really? You've been moody for ages.'

'Well I've been practising haven't I? I mean, passing myself off as a real man. Well, that's some challenge isn't it? Takes some perfecting.' His voice took on a clipped undertone and I lifted my head, looking at him properly.

'Are you annoyed with me about something?'

'No.' His voice was low and quiet.

I swallowed hard, hurt by his cold manner. 'I think Spencer fancies you,' I teased in a last ditch effort to lighten the mood again.

Ed put his drink down on the bookcase behind him and without looking at me, muttered, 'Back in a minute.'

'Where are you going?'

'The men's room,' he snapped. 'That all right with you?'

He walked off, leaving me to look around, not sure what to do next. The room was crowded with people and I began to feel smothered and breathless. I started to push my way out of the room, wanting to get to the dining room, where it was less crowded and the air was fresher. I trod on somebody's foot and turned to apologise. Pushing past next to me was a man in a suit, a lion mask over his head. At first I thought I was seeing things and I stared hard at him, setting the image in my mind. No, he was definitely real. The man's face was completely obscured, accept for two small holes for eyes. The mask went right over his head, making it impossible for me to even see his hair, which was covered in a fake, light brown lion's mane. He looked fleetingly at me when I apologised for treading on his foot, then looked away, carrying on through the crowd. He didn't speak and I had no idea who he was, or what a lion in a suit could possibly have to do with Madonna. This party was taking on a very surreal quality, I thought, heading for the door. I felt a hand rest on my shoulder, pulling me back and I turned around to see who it was.

Nathan stood behind me, smiling. He put his hands around my waist and leaned in towards me, saying. 'Abby, you look so gorgeous. You're taking me right back to my school days dressed like that. I'm all nostalgic.'

My body felt as though it had suddenly flooded with adrenaline. My heart was speeding, my breath laboured, my knees wobbly. I didn't know what to say. I wanted to return the compliment, because he really did look good, but that would seem too flirtatious. I just smiled back nervously and started to turn away again. He tightened his grip around my waist. 'You're always walking away from me. Avoiding me. Why don't you like me?'

I stopped still, listening.

'You've always been funny with me and I want to know why. Don't you think I'm good enough for Rebecca? Is that what it is?' His voice was slightly slurred.

I stared at him, surprised. He was looking at me as he often did, with the sad eyes of a puppy. I started to speak, but trailed off. Actually he was so far wrong it was almost laughable, it was Rebecca I had doubts about. How could he think that I didn't like him? I played with the bangles on my hand.

'Abby, can I talk to you?'

'Sure.' I had a fleeting image in my head of us going outside to talk, of Nathan telling me that he had realised he had been wrong. He had picked the wrong girl. He could touch my face, tell me that we were, in fact, so right for each other, so similar. And like the first time I saw him sing, his face would reveal everything, and I would understand and trust him. I would be the only person in the world and he would kiss me softly, gently. 'No. Not yet. Can it wait?' I gestured to the door, trying to tell him that I was about to do something, but unable to come up with a viable excuse. 'I'll find you later shall I?'

Nathan breathed out heavily and searched my face, frowning.

'Hey,' Vicky said, interrupting the silence and looking from me to Nathan.

Nathan let go of my waist as though he had been caught doing something wrong.

'Have you two seen Rebecca? She wandered off a while ago. Looked a bit worse for wear.'

'I haven't seen her for much of the night. She just wanted to dance.' Nathan sounded as though he was defending himself and Vicky frowned at him.

'Maybe you should find her, see if she's OK.'

Nathan nodded, glanced briefly at me, then walked away.

Alistair walked through the crowd towards us, grinning. 'Alo me crew,' he said, in an accent less like a Jamaican and more like Ali G. 'Dis is an wicked party, fer real. Me is feelin a bit ratted.'

Vicky leaned towards me saying, 'I swear the drunker he gets, the better the Ali G impersonation.' She linked arms with Alistair. 'Shall we get you another drink, love?'

Alistair looked Vicky up and down, nodding appreciatively and stroking his goatee. 'Yous is a fit bitch.'

'Watch it,' she warned, grinning flirtatiously and steering him away. She looked back at me. 'By the way, have you seen a guy with a lion mask? What's that all about?'

I shrugged and Alistair pulled her away, saying, 'You twos can natta lata. Respect!'

I poked my head into the kitchen on my way to the dining room, just out of curiosity. There were a couple of girls in there who I had met at a gig I DJed for. They were huddled over by a giant casserole dish like a couple of witches brewing a potion. 'Come on you daft bird, no one'll taste that. Stick the lot in,' one of them said, grabbing a bottle of vodka and tipping it upside-down so that the contents sloshed out, splashing the other girl's dress. 'Don't worry, it'll evaporate off in a sec,' she said and they both started cackling mercilessly.

I looked past them and saw that Harriet was sitting at the kitchen table with Jerry. They were the mirror image of each other; both sitting slightly to one side with opposing elbows on the table, both leaning in, looking completely engrossed in the other. Despite what she had threatened to do after our parents had left, she wasn't flirting. She didn't look conscious of herself at all, just utterly comfortable. As though she wasn't, in fact, in a Barbie pink ball gown, dressed up like Cinderella and talking to a man dressed like a comic book gangster, with a Tommy gun resting between them. Instead she could almost have been sitting in her favourite pyjamas, talking to a friend she'd known for years about the day's events. They looked happy and I was so glad Jerry had come. She needed someone to take her mind off Robert. Why hadn't they met sooner? I thought with regret.

I didn't want to break up their conversation and left them to it, wandering in to the dining room.

'Well hello,' Ben drawled lasciviously as I walked in. He put down his plate, which I noted was piled up dome-like with food, and came over, wrapping his arms around me. I hugged him back, unable to resist. He was like a favourite younger brother or an affectionate son. Impossible to refuse. He started making purring noises, nuzzling up to my neck and I cuffed him playfully across the head.

'Behave.'

'Look, don't fight the attraction. Just go with it,' he said.

I let go and wandered over to the table of food, picking up a stick of carrot and biting it. I held the remains of it in front of me like a barrier, feeling safer with something, however small, between us.

Ben leaned against the wall and watched me. 'When will you be mine?' he said.

I looked up at him, shaking my head. There was no point trying to convince him otherwise.

'Is there someone else?'

'Nope.' I finished off my carrot stick and picked up another.

'I think there is.'

I snorted, crunching. 'Chance would be a fine thing.'

'Do you have a thing going with Ed?'

I raised my eyebrows. 'What makes you think that?'

He shrugged. 'A vibe.'

I cracked up laughing. The sight of him standing there, his hair all brushed forward and the false teeth he was still wearing that were giving him a lisp. He looked ridiculous. 'Beautiful Stranger' started playing and Ben snapped back into Austin Powers mode.

'Yeah baby, yeah! They're playing our song. Come on, you can dance for me.' He growled, baring his teeth.

'I'll join you in a minute.' I laughed as he bounded out of the room, leaving me on my own. Looking around I noticed that the French door was slightly ajar and I wondered if maybe Rebecca had gone outside to get some fresh air. Vicky had said she wasn't feeling too well. I walked over to the door and felt the chilly breeze hit my bare midriff, making my skin prickle with goose bumps. I peered out into the night, scanning the concrete path and couldn't see anybody for a moment, and then my eyes rested on a couple sitting on the bench under the magnolia

tree. They were oblivious to me, kissing passionately, like teenagers at a school disco. Next to them
on the bench I thought I could see a cat, curled up
asleep in the dim light, then I realised it was in
fact the lion mask, now surplus to requirements.
I couldn't see the man properly, he had his back
to me, but the girl had long, straight blonde hair,
pulled back into a severe ponytail. She was dressed
as Madonna was in the Blonde Ambition tour and
the grim reality dawned on me that I was watching
Rebecca, kissing a stranger, who, now I thought
about it, was looking more and more like my ex-
boyfriend Chris. I stood frozen with indecision. The
best thing to do would be to turn around, leave
them to it and pretend I had seen nothing. But
what about Nathan? If it was Alistair out there,
cheating on his wife I would tell Vicky, I was
sure of it. I stepped back inside, closing the door
quietly behind me then rested my back against the
windowpane and closed my eyes. I couldn't believe
the audacity of her, doing that here, now, with her
husband only metres away. Maybe she wanted to
be caught? That had always been Rebecca's style.
Let them find out for themselves or wait until they
get the hint. So long as it didn't involve discussion, dissection or those dreaded words, 'We need
to talk'.

'There you are,' a voice said.

I snapped my eyes open and saw Nathan coming
towards me.

'Are you feeling all right?'

I nodded, pressing my body against the glass,

296

trying to block out as much of the garden view as I could.

'Have you seen Rebecca?'

I shook my head and made a sound as though I was being strangulated.

'Good. She's being a nightmare. I don't think I could face another scene.' He joined me by the glass door and leaned on it, looking at me for a long time. 'You know, she really is bringing out the worst in me at the moment. When I talk to her I sound like a nagging father.' He adopted the voice of a severe, domineering man. 'You're going out too much, you're drinking too much, what time do you call this? I can't believe I'm saying it sometimes. I wouldn't mind her being so sociable if she actually wanted to be with me whilst she was doing it but she makes no secret of the fact that she doesn't.' He looked down at the dregs of lager left in the bottle he was holding and swished them around, momentarily lost in thought. 'Have you had a chance to talk with her?'

'Oh, well, not really. We haven't exactly been alone.' I knew I sounded lame and Nathan looked at me as though he suspected I was covering for her, hiding a confidence. 'We're just not close anymore I suppose,' I added.

Nathan smiled bitterly and looked out of the window. 'I know the feeling.'

I stopped breathing, waiting for him to see them, but he didn't and instead looked back down at his bottle. I snuck a peek out of the window but with the door shut it was difficult to see anything outside. It was pitch dark out there and the dining room was lit with fairy lights. It occurred to me that if they looked up they would certainly be able to see the two of us and I was about to walk back over to the table, further out of sight, when a couple of Harriet's old colleagues walked into the room and began helping themselves to food.

'Hey,' Nathan said, moving towards me. 'Your bow's coming loose.' He reached up to my hair and untied it, then, swaying slightly, tied it up tighter, teasing out the loops to make them fuller. I stood still, looking up at him and felt a rush of affection as he concentrated hard on getting it just-so. I felt cared for and treasured, like when I was little and dad used to tie up my shoe laces. Nathan fluffed out my hair and appraised his efforts. 'Perfect,' he said, staying close to me. 'You look like a present. Perfectly wrapped.' His hands stayed touching my hair long after it was necessary and I started to feel jumpy. What if Rebecca could see? What would she think?

Nathan glanced across the room to the table where the men were still standing, deep in discussion. It was a furtive look that hinted at guilt. Like a burglar checking the street was empty, or a child about to raid the biscuit tin, he was up to no good. I stood back abruptly. 'Right, well, better er, join the others I suppose.'

Nathan looked disappointed. 'Don't you want to go outside? Get a breather?' He nodded towards the door.

'Oh, no! You don't want to do that, it's freezing.'

'Oh, come on. I feel like a change of scenery.' He reached for the door and I felt panic rise up.

'Look. You can't.' I pinned myself up against the door, blocking his exit, and he stood back, laughing at me. 'What? Why not?'

'Because . . .' My mind went momentarily blank. 'Because, we've not even had a dance yet and I really want to dance . . .'

He paused, tempted.

'. . . with you,' I added, looking at him with beseeching eyes. That worked. He looked touched.

'How could I refuse you when you asked so nicely.'

I began to walk out of the dining room, Nathan following behind, when the music changed. The pulsating beat of 'Human Nature' ended and in its place began the unmistakable introduction to 'Crazy for You'. I looked back at Nathan, embarrassed, but he grabbed my hand and pulled me near him. 'Perfect. Let's stay in here,' he said and put one arm around my waist and took my hand with the other. He began to move in time with the music and with stiff legs, I reluctantly let myself be led. My heart was galloping hard at the nearness of him. The smell of him. The feel of his chest against mine. I wanted to relax into it, close my eyes and enjoy a moment I had often imagined, but I was painfully aware of Rebecca outside, sitting on a bench not far from me. All that she would have to do was to look back at the house and she would see me, with her husband. But then what were we doing wrong? Nothing. Just dancing. OK so it was slow dancing, but then that was simply the equivalent of a hug, wasn't it? An extended hug with movement. Nothing more. A perfectly acceptable way for platonic friends to behave, unlike what Rebecca was doing outside with my ex-boyfriend. She hardly had a reason to be mad with me, did she? I heard footsteps by the doorway and Nathan and I both looked up guiltily. Whoever it was had gone. We exchanged a look and I thought I saw a flash of concern in Nathan's eyes. Perhaps he was worried that Rebecca had seen him. Seconds later he dipped his head back down again, nuzzling into my hair and I felt his warm breath. In another time, another place, this would have been such a perfect moment. I could have tilted my head up and kissed him, realising my teenage dream, but this didn't feel like a perfect moment. It was sullied with guilt and anxiety. His hand cupped the back of my hair and I suddenly felt as though all the nerves in my skin were wired and ultra-sensitive to his touch. I knew I would have to stop this. Rebecca could walk in at any moment. I stopped moving and looked at Nathan. Before I could speak he planted his lips on mine, kissing me, then pulled away, his eyes open, gauging my reaction. He hadn't parted his lips and it wasn't passionate, just affectionate, warm and moist. We looked at each other, both breathing deeply, our breath in sync with each other. Then I realised there was somebody standing at the door.

# CHAPTER TWENTY-TWO

'Ang on, me glasses is steamed up,' Alistair said, using the bottom of his yellow tracksuit top to clean his sunglasses. Nathan and I broke away quickly and I glanced guiltily at the window, wondering if anyone had seen. 'Thas betta.' He put them back on and grinned widely at us, arms outstretched. 'Big up me crew!'

'Oh Alistair, knock it off now, it's getting really annoying,' Vicky said, walking in behind him. 'Sorry about him. I think I've created a monster. A couple of girls in the kitchen said he actually sounded better than Ali G and it's really gone to his head. He's too drunk to get irony.'

'They was fit bitches,' Alistair said, nodding at Nathan then wandered over to the table where he grabbed a breadstick and munched on it, still grinning.

Vicky ignored him and looked at me. 'Can I have a word?'

I felt a sinking sensation in my stomach. She looked serious and I had a feeling she suspected something, perhaps she'd seen us. She would hate me for betraying Rebecca. She gestured to the hallway and I followed her out of the room, not daring to look back at Nathan in case Vicky saw me and my eyes gave away what had transpired.

'Where are we going?' I asked when we reached the bottom of the staircase.

'Just follow me.' She headed purposefully up the stairs.

Vicky stopped on the landing, outside the bathroom. The door was shut and she tapped softly on it. I heard someone groan quietly inside and Vicky pushed the door open, hurrying me in then locking the door behind us.

'Becca!' I cried when I saw her. She was curled up on the floor by the toilet, her head resting on the loo seat. She groaned again without lifting her head up. 'But . . . you're in the garden, well . . . I thought I saw you. You were kissing Chris.'

Rebecca finally looked up at me. The blonde hair piece she was wearing was slipping and I could see her dark hair underneath. Her eyes looked strikingly red and bloodshot next to her pallid face and her make-up was smudged. 'I wasn't,' she croaked in a frightened little voice.

'You were. I saw you, not long ago. But how did you get in here? Did you go in through the kitchen?' My mind was racing. If she came in through the kitchen she would have walked past the dining room. She could have seen me. Perhaps that's why she was crying.

Vicky sat down on the toilet and stroked Rebecca's

hair. 'She's been in here for ages. Why did you think she was outside?'

'Well, I saw her with Chris. At least I thought it was Becca. She had the same outfit on and the same hair, so I just assumed. And they were on the bench. He was the one that'd been wearing the lion mask. He probably used it to sneak in unnoticed because he definitely wasn't invited.' I sat down on the floor in front of Rebecca and put my hand on her leg. 'Bec, what's going on? And if it wasn't you outside kissing Chris then who was it? Surely it must have been you.'

She rubbed at her face with the back of her hand and swallowed hard, looking up at the bathroom ceiling as if to gain some control and stop herself from crying. 'Abby if I tell you something you've got to promise not to breathe a word of it to anyone. Especially Nathan.'

'Yes of course. What is it?'

'Oh God, I've been such an idiot.' I waited expectantly for her to continue. 'I had a bit of a thing with Chris,' she said eventually, looking down at the floor and screwing up some tissue paper in her hands. 'It's all over now. Well, it barely even got started. It was a few weeks after the honeymoon at a work do. I had been really low, you know—' her voice became quieter '—because of the miscarriage. I'd been off work and stuck in the house going over everything in my head. How we'd got married so quick because of the baby. Wanting everything to be right before we told my parents.' She laughed sadly to herself. 'I suppose I thought it was romantic and exciting, you know, keeping it a secret. I got so absorbed in it all I barely even thought about the fact that there was actually a baby inside of me. So then I started feeling guilty, wondering if I'd done the right thing, getting married, you know? If the reasons weren't good enough. The bubble burst and we weren't the same couple anymore. There was nothing uniting us, making it fun. And Nathan,' she shook her head and tears swam in her eyes. 'God I've been awful to Nathan. All he wanted to do was talk about it, get it out in the open. But I didn't want to. I just wanted to forget. I wanted us to be fun again. He was serious and hurt and I couldn't face all that. I've been avoiding him, going out all the time. Chris just made me feel like the old me, you know, fun and desirable. We kissed at a party and I went back to his flat. Nathan called whilst I was there wondering where I was so I told him I was on my way home and left. Fortunately.'

'So you didn't . . .'

She shook her head. 'No. Even if Nathan hadn't phoned, I don't think I would have done. Christ, I'd not long been in hospital. I wasn't up for that. I just wanted to have fun again.'

'Well then, you've not much to feel guilty about have you? All you did was kiss him. That's nothing.' I wondered just who exactly I was trying to convince with that.

'But the thing is I wanted to . . . up here.' She tapped at the side of her head with a long, false fingernail. 'If it hadn't been for . . . you know, the miscarriage, I might have jumped into bed with him then and there.'

'Bec, you don't know that, and it's only because of the miscarriage that you were in that situation anyway. That was why you'd distanced yourself from Nathan and wanted to feel attractive again. Things were great with you until then weren't they?'

Her eyes filled up with tears once more and she bit her bottom lip, nodding sadly. My heart ached for her.

'And was that it with Chris? You haven't seen him again?'

'Not in that way no, but you know what he's like.' She looked at me as her tears spilled over. 'He's a nightmare. He's been calling me up, hanging around outside the house. Just like he did with you. The guy can't take a hint. I can't believe he's turned up here, it's creepy. Then getting off with a girl dressed just like me. He was doing it on purpose, looking at me to get a reaction. He's so weird. He thinks that he'll make me jealous or something. Some chance. I just wish he'd sod off and leave me alone. I want to forget all about it.' She sighed and threw her shredded tissue in the bin. 'I want to start again with Nathan but I don't know where to begin. I've been such a bitch.'

Vicky smiled at her. 'You really love Nathan don't you?'

She nodded and I could see in her eyes that she was telling the truth. 'He's the only one I've ever felt comfortable with.'

'Well you'll be all right then. You can get over this, it's just a blip. A bad start.'

Rebecca looked worried. 'You're just born romantic though Vicky. You believe in happy endings. And anyway, I don't think I can shake this guilt. It's eating me up. Nathan's always been so good to me. So dependable. Every time I look at him I'm frightened he'll know.'

I remembered Nathan's kiss just minutes earlier and knew just what she meant. I touched my lips and felt consumed with guilt, wondering if Rebecca looked close enough would she be able to tell. If we hadn't been disturbed, how much further would it have gone? Would he have wanted to kiss me again? Would I have let him? I remembered how it felt and had to admit that it wasn't how I had imagined. It wasn't a perfect moment, it was scary and unreal, most likely brought about by Nathan having been drunk and being in need of affection. In my heart I knew that there was nothing more meaningful to it than that, it was no more than a kiss. And in a way I was glad. If I had thought that Nathan felt more for me than that, it would have left me in an impossible situation. I would have had to have made choices, and I didn't trust myself well enough to make the right ones. At least this way it was out of my hands.

'He doesn't have to know,' Vicky said. 'Just put it behind you.'

'But how can I with Chris sniffing around acting obsessive? It's impossible. He just won't go away. It's as though he's all smug about it and he's itching

306

o tell Nathan. Chris has never liked him for some reason. It'll come out eventually, it's inevitable.'

'You could always tell him first. It's not as if here's much to tell. Nathan would forgive you I'm sure. Then at least you could get on with your life with a clean slate.'

Rebecca let out a disconsolate sigh and looked down, not sure what to do. 'I can't see him like this, I'm a mess.'

'It's your choice Bec. What do you want us to do now? Do you want me to fetch Nathan for you?'

Rebecca shook her head, looking fearfully at us both. 'No, don't fetch him. Just give me a few minutes. Let me get myself together. I'll come down in a while. Maybe I can persuade Nathan to take me home. We can talk there.'

'Are you sure?'

'Yeah.' She picked herself up off the bathroom floor and looked into the mirror on the cabinet door, wincing at her reflection.

Vicky looked at me and I nodded. We walked out, leaving her in peace.

Vicky linked arms with me as we walked back down the stairs. 'What am I going to do with you two?' she said, almost to herself.

'What do you mean? What have I done?'

Vicky looked knowingly at me, then glanced back up the stairs, making sure we were out of earshot of the bathroom. She leaned in closer, whispering, 'I know how you feel about Nathan. Well, how you think you feel anyway.'

I looked at her, trying to appear puzzled, but my blushes gave me away.

'Ever since your mum became ill your whole life's been in stasis.'

I rolled my eyes. Not her too, it was bad enough getting this lecture from dad.

'You know I'm right Abby. You're trapped in this bubble, not letting anyone in, thinking you're in love with the same guy you fell for when you were fourteen. And why? Because it's safe, he's safe because you know you'll never have him and that way you can build him up in your mind as a perfect being and never have to know any different. And because you'll never have him, you'll never lose him, never be hurt. You can stay in your bubble and float about regardless thinking fate has put you there when in fact it was you all along.'

'What are you talking about?' I said, knowing full well what she was saying. I felt raw and exposed because she was telling me all the things I had been thinking up there in the bathroom, things that to me were a revelation yet came tripping off her tongue like simple, blatant facts of life that she had known for a long time.

'You've got to put that part of your life behind you. Give yourself a future.' She looked at me kindly and the glitter on her cheeks lit up her face, giving her the appearance of a fairy godmother figure, full of wisdom and understanding.

I smiled at her wordlessly, feeling empty inside and utterly alone.

Vicky looked as though she was going to say

omething else, something hopeful, when she stop-
ed and looked down. Alistair had run down the
all to the bottom of the stairs. When he saw Vicky
e said, 'You've gotta check dis. Chris an Becca in
la garden suckin face, you gotta do somefink coz
f you don't dey'll be a ruk or somefink.'

'Look, can't you just talk normally? I don't under-
tand what you're on about. What's happened?'

Alistair looked pained for a moment, stumbling
or words as though he'd spent so long in character
e had forgotten how he usually spoke. 'OK, Chris,
\bby's ex is here. He's in the garden with Becca,
:issing, I just saw them. You've got to do something
efore . . .'

I looked behind Alistair and saw that Nathan
ad just walked out of the living room. He had
eard everything. He whirled around, his face like
hunder.

'Nathan, it's not Rebecca,' Vicky called after Nathan
is he launched himself down the hall.

'How do you know?' Alistair asked.

'Never mind.' Vicky chased after Nathan and I
ollowed close behind.

As we ran through the doorway into the dining
oom, I just had the chance to see that Chris and the
olonde girl had come back inside. He was patting
er bottom as they helped themselves to food from
he buffet table. They had their backs to us.

Nathan didn't hesitate, he launched himself onto
Chris's back, throwing him forwards onto the food
ind they both crashed to the ground. The girl
:creamed.

Chris lay on the ground with Nathan on top of him, grabbing him by the throat. Chris held up his hands up saying, 'Easy mate, come on, I don't want to fight you.'

'I ought to fucking kill you for touching my wife,' Nathan spat.

'Who told you?' Chris said calmly.

The group of guests that were gathering by the door gasped. No one seemed sure whether they should step in and break them up or watch the excitement a while longer.

'I knew it!' Nathan cried and stood up, not letting go of Chris's collar as he dragged him up till they were face to face.

Alistair, having now realised that the girl wasn't in fact Rebecca after all tried to step in. 'Nathan, leave it, it's not her. Look, it's not Becca, I was wrong. Mate, I'm sorry.'

Nathan glanced away from Chris for the first time and looked at the girl. He frowned, seeing the girl's face. He was confused. 'But you just admitted it?' he said to Chris.

Chris grinned nervously. 'Shit. I thought you knew. I thought someone had told you. Look, it was nothing, really, it was over before it started. It was weeks ago.'

'You piece of shit!' Nathan snapped, pushing Chris back against the table. He stumbled, crashing headfirst in to a bowl of guacamole.

The 80s compilation that had been playing Fairground Attraction's 'Perfect' stopped mid-song and the Rocky theme 'The Eye of the Tiger' started up in it's place. The few sniggers from the crowd soon stopped and were replaced by an astonished silence.

Chris stood up, wiping the pale green dip from his eyes and licking it off his lips. It was a comical sight until you saw the anger in his eyes. He snapped, launching himself at Nathan so that they both crashed into one of the tables, scattering the buffet every which way. They both fell to the ground, scrambling to get the first footing so that they could get up and punch the other. Nathan managed to stand up first and put Chris in a headlock. Chris struggled to get free but, finding it impossible, reached for the nearest object to hit Nathan with, which turned out to be a French stick. I thanked God I had decided against putting the bread-knife out with it and watched helplessly as Nathan squeezed his eyes shut and the bread hit him in the face, breaking in several places.

Ben came up behind us, straining to see what was going on.

'Do something!' I begged him.

He watched them for a moment then said, 'Looks like Nathan's doing all right by himself. And besides, from what I've heard about that guy, he's had it coming to him for a long time.'

Nathan momentarily let go of Chris, who saw his opportunity and pulled away from Nathan, pulling the table out so that he could stand safely on the other side of it. They did a little dance for a moment, pretending to run one way around the table then change directions, like kids playing musical chairs, then Nathan grabbed a handful of nuts and threw them in Chris's face. Some of them stuck to the guacamole, making him look completely ridiculous. Chris retaliated by grabbing a bowl of potato salad and the gathering crowd gasped as he threw the whole thing, bowl and all, at Nathan. Nathan ducked and the bowl crashed to the floor, spilling some of its contents onto the carpet. Nathan narrowed his eyes and spat something inaudible as he launched himself onto the table, knocking whatever food was left out of the way and made a grab for Chris's collar again. He managed to get a firm grip, pulling him up close to his face and at the same time sat up and brought his fist back to punch Chris square on the nose. Chris looked as though he was struggling to breathe as Nathan tightened the grip on his collar. He couldn't move his arms well enough to get a swing at Nathan and scanned his eyes across the table, looking for something else to throw at him. He saw Nathan's half empty pint glass and swiped at it, picking it up and gripping it as though he was about to thrust it into Nathan's chin. The whole crowd took a deep breath, waiting to see if Chris would dare be that vicious in front of more than a dozen witnesses. The noise of the crowd made him think twice and whilst he hesitated, Nathan took Chris in both hands and pushed him, with full force, back against the wall, where he banged his head and slumped to the floor. The pint glass he was holding landed in his lap, spilling out its contents onto his trousers in an unflattering puddle. Nathan caught his breath

n an effort to calm down then stood angrily over
him. 'Come anywhere near me or my wife again
and I'll kill you,' he said, his voice was shaking with
rage. Chris sat dazed, saying nothing, and Nathan
turned away, pushing through the crowd. His eyes
fell on me and his face softened. He stopped in front
of me, wiping his forehead with the back of his hand.
'I'm really sorry Abby,' he said and left the room.

We all stood silently. No one seemed to want
to help Chris, who was a pathetic sight, covered
in food. The girl he was with had long gone and
I doubted he had a friend left in the house.

Alistair, who had stood watching the whole thing
with his arms folded and a big drunken smile on his
face now began to laugh, breaking the silence. He
wandered over to where Chris's lion mask had been
dropped on the floor and picked it up, approaching
him. 'Nil respect to da menstrual batty boy of da
jungle,' he said and dropped the mask on his lap.

# CHAPTER TWENTY-THREE

It's amazing how a fight can break up a party. After
Chris left, the majority of others followed, whispering
scandalously to each other and complimenting me
on the night's entertainment. They seemed thrilled
to be leaving with a story they could regale their
friends with on Sunday and I was told several times,
to my relief, that it was the best party they had been
to in years.

Ben and Alistair helped me to clear up the food
from the floor whilst Vicky went upstairs in search
of Rebecca. For a food fight there was surprisingly
little mess and it took the three of us only a few minutes to get it looking almost normal. Alistair bent
down to pick up several plates and groaned, lifting
his fingers distastefully to reveal the guacamole that
was now sticking to them. He was beginning to
sober up and wrinkled his nose, complaining that
he thought he was going to be sick.

'Hey! I made that,' I said, pretending to be
offended. 'And, well . . .' I looked down at where
it had come from and saw that there was a large
green splat of it, ground into the carpet. 'It does taste

etter than it looks, I can assure you.' I passed him
ome serviettes to wipe his fingers with and went
ff to the kitchen for a bowl of soapy water.

The kitchen door was shut and when I walked
n I found that there was a whole other mini-party
going on inside. Jerry and Harriet had been joined
y several of Harriet's collegues and they were all
itting around the table, drinking filter coffee and
aughing. Harriet, resplendent in her pink dress,
vas leaning with her hands cupped under her chin,
ooking at Jerry as if she was Sandra Dee in *Grease*.

'Hi,' she said sheepishly. 'We're being old and
oring, I know. But the kitchen was really warm
nd, well, we all fancied a coffee.' The others all
miled. 'We'll come and join you soon.'

'It's OK, a lot of people have gone home now.
Ve're kind of winding things down.' I squeezed
ast them to get to the sink. 'I'm just going to clean
p a bit. You carry on.'

'Clean up? Now?' Harriet looked confused and
ut her mug down. 'Has something happened?'

'No, no, everything's fine.' I flashed her a disarm-
ng smile and filled the bowl with soapy water, not
vanting to break up the gathering. I didn't feel like
going over the events that Harriet was obviously
lissfully unaware of. It would only make her feel
ad. The group picked up the conversation I had
nterrupted and I snuck past them, trying to make
nyself invisible.

When I walked back into the dining room I real-
sed that Harriet had followed me out.

'What's going on?' she whispered.

'Oh, nothing really. Some food got knocked over that's all. I was going to clear it up before it gets ground in any worse. I'll leave the rest till morning.

'There's no sign of her. Both of their coats have gone so I guess they must have gone home,' Vicky said, standing in the doorway with her hands on her hips.

Harriet looked confused. 'Who? What's going on?'

'Oh, it's a long story. I'll tell you later,' I said, dismissively. Scrubbing at the floor I was beginning to feel giddy and weak with exhaustion. I wanted to go up to my flat and hide from everyone here. I wanted to be alone. The 80s compilation had been left in and was playing in the background, quieter than earlier. T'Pau's, 'China In Your Hands', was adding to my despairing mood and making me want to start smashing crockery.

Vicky started filling Harriet in on what had happened. When she explained that Chris had hidden his face with the lion mask Harriet nodded, understanding. '"Like a Virgin",' she said to herself.

I looked at her, confused. 'What have lions got to do with virgins?' I asked, wondering if it was some sexual initiation costume I had never heard of.

'The video,' she explained. 'There's a guy prowling around in the background of the "Like a Virgin" video. This guy's done his homework.' She sounded impressed until she noticed that Vicky and I were both frowning at her.

Vicky took up the story where she had left off and I put my cloth down, wandering out into the

316

hallway to see who was left in the living room. I poked my head around the door and saw Ed's friend Oscar, the one dressed as Jean Paul Gaultier, sitting on the sofa with the girl dressed in Madonna's Drowned World tour outfit. They were comparing kilts, the girl feeling the fabric of Oscar's as he leant back on the sofa and examined her label, pulling a sulky face. 'Well, yours may well be from a better shop, darling, but I'm telling you, this tartan comes from a clan far superior to yours. This,' he said, standing up proudly, lifting up his sporran and gesturing underneath, 'represents thoroughbred breeding.' The woman cracked up laughing and Oscar turned around, noticing me for the first time.

'Hey Abby, has Ed not come back in yet?' he said. They've been gone ages and I told Spencer I'd give him a lift home soon.'

I looked at him, puzzled.

'Ed, you know, sexy music mogul? He walked out in a huff ages ago. Spencer went and found him and they've been gossiping in the street like old fish wives ever since.'

'I'll go and find him,' I said quietly and walked out.

'Tell Spencer to come and let me know if he still wants a lift,' Oscar shouted behind me.

I walked down the front steps of the house and out into the street. The air was dense with fine mist, making it difficult to see further than the bottom of our street. I stood at the end of the path, looking up and down the road, but saw nobody, then I detected voices floating through the air, coming from the direction of the green opposite. It was shrouded in mist and I couldn't make out who was talking, so I crossed the street, following the sounds. There I saw Ed and Spencer, leaning against a road sign, deep in contemplative conversation and smoking furiously. I stopped, watching them for a moment, uncomfortable at disturbing them, then Spencer looked up and saw me. He flicked his cigarette to the ground, whispered something to Ed, then walked over.

'Be gentle with him,' he warned. I waited for further explanation but none was given and he carried on, crossing the road to return to the house. I looked at Ed, who seemed fidgety, pacing back and forth and running a hand through his hair.

'Hi,' I called out.

He looked up, nodded, looked at the house, took a long drag of his cigarette then continued pacing.

I went over to the road sign and leaned on it, watching him curiously. 'Is everything OK?'

'I've got to give these up,' he said, ignoring the question and ground out the cigarette onto the grass with his shoe.

'You missed a great fight,' I said.

This caught his interest and he looked up.

'It was Nathan versus Chris over the buffet.'

'I didn't realise they liked food that much,' he said dryly.

'Well, they were fighting over Rebecca really, but just did it over a table of food.'

'Who won?'

'Nathan.'

'Figures.'

'Why?'

'The best man always does.' He kicked at something with his shoe.

'What do you mean?'

He ignored me again. 'I suppose that would explain why he left in such a hurry.'

'Did you see him go?'

He nodded, pointing up the street towards the main road. 'They headed off that way.'

'They?'

'Him and Rebecca. She ran out not long after him with their coats, she was calling him. Sounded upset.'

Sickness threatened to overwhelm me. I felt responsible for all the problems they were having, despite knowing that it wasn't me they were fighting about.

Ed was watching me intently. We fell into silence and the pause in conversation stretched on, becoming obvious and strained. My throat was aching and I wanted to cry. I wanted to tell Ed everything, like I used to. I wanted to hear his opinion, feel his understanding, but the awkwardness between us had been growing for some time now. Our friendship didn't feel the same any more, it was changing. Barriers had been put up. I desperately wanted to reach out to him, ignore the vibes, but his body language stopped me.

I watched the mist swirl around the trees and could see fine droplets in the air. I touched the ends of my hair, knowing the damp atmosphere would make it frizzy, then remembered it was back-combed anyway so it was pointless worrying about it.

'Ed, what's wrong? Something's been on your mind for ages. Why won't you talk to me about it?'

Ed stopped pacing and stood looking down at the ground. He sighed and rubbed his eyes with his fingertips.

'Is it Kylie?' I said.

He laughed, taken aback. 'What?'

'You really liked her didn't you?'

'Why do you say that?'

'Well, to start with, she's the first girl you've been with for years. I think it would have to take someone pretty special to change you like that.'

He looked as though I had disappointed him. 'Abby, I've not changed at all. You of all people should know that. You know I don't just date men, I've had relationships with women in the past. It's the individual I see, nothing else. I thought you understood me?'

I squeezed my hands together, aware that they were shaking. The last thing I needed was a confrontation with Ed. I needed a friend. 'Ed I do. I know that. It's just been a long time. All the relationships you've had since I left school have been with men. You always look at men in the shop. Never women.'

'That's because I don't need to, Abby,' he snapped suddenly.

'What?' I couldn't understand why he seemed angry. He was acting so out of character it was beginning to scare me.

'I don't look at other women because no one

320

ompares to you, Abby.' His voice was loud and he words tumbled out in a rush, almost echoing n the air between us.

I looked at him, eyes wide. I was speechless.

'Can't you see it?' He was bending down near o me, his hands spread out in front of him as hough he was telling me something that ought to be obvious, then his voice softened. 'You're the one. love you Abby. I have done for years.'

'Ed?' I laughed nervously, wondering for a brief second if he was teasing me.

'What? Why is it so ridiculous? You're my best friend. You're beautiful, funny, warm and caring. And passionate. Passionate about so many things. The things you love are the things that I love. We click so well, when I'm with you I don't need anyone else. I've never met anyone in my life that I wanted o be with more.'

I felt like I was winded. My mind had gone blank and nothing made sense anymore. It was as hough Ed had just gone inside my head, taken everything I thought I'd understood, that made me what I am, and turned it upside-down, leaving an unrecognisable heap of memories and feelings, hen stood back and said, 'Ta-ra! What do you think of that?' It made no sense, and yet, in a twisted, ncomprehensible way it made perfect sense. 'But, you never said before. All these years . . . you've never said anything.'

'No.' Ed looked sad, hurt. 'Well, perhaps I didn't want to spoil what we did have. Your friendship has meant everything to me. If I'd told you, you would have most likely felt uncomfortable with me. You would have moved on and worked somewhere else and I would have lost you.'

'What makes you think that?'

'I know that, Abby, because I know how you feel about Nathan. How you've always felt.'

I looked guiltily back at the house, hoping no one had heard him.

'I don't understand why you think he's so right for you. Why you keep hanging on to those feelings. Dragging it out like this. We're so close, I'm the one that really understands you. He could never love you like I do. But you just couldn't see me like that could you?' he said bitterly.

'He's married,' I said quietly.

'But that doesn't stop you having feelings for him does it? And anyway, I know.'

'Know what?'

'That you're seeing him,' he said simply, scrutinising my face. When I said nothing, he resumed his pacing, summing up his evidence like a solicitor in a court room. 'He's been calling you. You've met up with him without telling me, and you tell me everything,' he added, waggling a finger at me and carrying on. 'And tonight, I saw you. You were in his arms, dancing to "Crazy for You" for crying out loud. Inches away from kissing him.'

I stammered, wondering how I was going to talk my way out of that one. 'He needed a friend,' I said weakly.

'Yes, but he got something else instead, didn't he?' he spat nastily.

Tears spilled from my eyes, dropping onto my mini-skirt. I rubbed them away and stood up. 'How can you think I'd do that?'

He shrugged. 'You've wanted to for a long time.'

I shook my head, which was buzzing with confusion. 'I can't talk about this now.'

Ed stopped pacing and looked at me. His eyes softened and he reached out for my hands. 'Abby, I'm really sorry. There's so much I want to say to you and I'm going about it all wrong. Please don't be hurt. I understand, honestly I do.'

I pushed him away. 'Don't.'

Ed's eyes were glassy with tears, a sight which tugged at my heart, but I couldn't deal with him now. I wanted to get away.

'We really need to talk.'

'I know. But not now.'

'Will you come over tomorrow? Abby, please. I need to know that, you know . . .' his voice was hoarse and he looked upwards, blinking. 'I need to know that we're OK,' he whispered.

I turned away and walked slowly back to the house, deliberately not looking behind.

# CHAPTER TWENTY-FOUR

I couldn't believe I'd slept through until lunchtime. Well, perhaps it wasn't that surprising. I had stayed with half-a-dozen people, playing poker (using the non-strip rules, despite Ben's protestations) until four in the morning after all.

I hadn't told anyone about Ed's confession. For once my natural urge to gossip had left me and it felt disloyal to discuss it with other people before sorting it out with Ed first. I didn't want to reduce our relationship to just another topic for idle conversation. I also needed time to think. All I did know was that my initial reaction, apart from shock, of course, was that it didn't make me feel uncomfortable. It made me feel good. And although I wasn't ready to see him in a romantic light, I was relieved that whatever had been coming between us, was now out in the open. All I had to do was reassure him that nothing had happened between Nathan and I, and then we could start again with a clean slate. I was looking forward to seeing him later.

I pulled on some clothes, splashed my face with tepid water and ran my fingers, as far as they would go, through my hair. I could hear that somebody was up and about in the kitchen downstairs and there were the occasional muffled noises of conversation. Ben and Jerry had stayed over in Harriet's spare room and a woman called Geena, a friend of Harriet's, had slept on the sofa. I wondered if Harriet had heard anything from Robert yet and headed down the stairs to find them all.

In the kitchen, everyone was in various stages of dress. Jerry was standing by the sink, washing up, with a huge pile of clean crockery growing ever bigger beside him. Ben was passing mugs to Geena. He was dressed only in a pair of boxer shorts and a baggy Nike T-shirt, but didn't look remotely shy about showing off his body, and Harriet was sitting at the table, dressed in a pair of smart flannelette pyjamas. For possibly the first time in our lives, Harriet was in public and not looking groomed. The curls in her hair, so immaculate the night before, had dropped and matted together, making the two words 'hedge' and 'backwards' spring quickly to mind. And I was shocked to see that she must have gone to sleep with her make-up on. A rule she usually followed as religiously as the nuns at her old school followed the Ten Commandments. Her knees were drawn up close to her chest and she held a phone to her ear, frowning as she picked at the stitching on her slippers. She glanced up, acknowledging me, then clicked off the phone, dropping it onto the table.

'Still no news?' I asked, sitting down opposite her.

'Nothing. I can't understand it. It really isn't like him you know.' She checked her watch then got up, wandering over to a kitchen cupboard. 'I know I've got a Yellow Pages for London Central in here somewhere,' she said, starting to empty out a cupboard stuffed with paperwork. 'I'm sure I haven't already packed it. If I could find that then maybe I could ring around the hospitals.'

Jerry turned away from the washing up and caught my eye, sharing a sense of concern.

'Do you want a drink?' Geena asked me. 'I've made one for the others.'

'I'd love a tea, thanks.'

'Me too,' Ben said, plucking another mug from the cupboard.

Jerry laughed. 'Another one? That makes four cups of tea and half a cafetière this morning. Are you sure your kidneys are up to that kind of challenge?'

Geena joined in. 'I can't believe it's lunchtime already. It feels like about half past seven in the morning.'

'Well, that might be because we've only just opened the curtains,' Ben said. He turned a chair around and sat next to me, stretching backwards to reveal his tanned stomach. He looked like a completely different person from the night before, far more attractive. He caught me looking at his stomach and lifted his T-shirt up. 'Try and punch me,' he said, tensing his stomach and slapping it to demonstrate how firm it was.

Geena and I looked at each other and cracked up laughing.

'Go on, hit me,' he insisted.

Jerry finished washing up and dried his hands on a towel. 'That has to be drug assisted,' he taunted. The amount you eat at work. It just doesn't add up.'

Ben pulled his T-shirt back down, distracted by the thought of food. 'Do you think I should eat breakfast and lunch one after the other, because I slept through breakfast, or just have one huge meal?' He rocked back on his chair. 'Because I really fancy a traditional British fry up. You know, bacon, eggs, beans, mushrooms . . .'

'And fried bread, you can't forget that,' Jerry joined in.

'It's no good. We'll have to go to the shop. Get in some supplies. I can't miss the most important meal of the day.'

'I'll go for you,' I said, relishing the thought of a walk in the fresh air.

'I'll come with you,' Geena said, obviously as keen as I was to get out of the house.

'You little beauties!' Ben leaned forward to borrow Harriet's notepad and pen and proceeded to write us a list, complete with diagrams.

The icy wind whipped around us, carrying leaves that turned in the air then dropped, scooted along the ground, only to be picked up by the wind and circle us once again as we walked off towards the main road. Next to Geena I was suffering from a growing feeling of inferiority. Not from anything she said, but more from the way she looked. She must have been in her late thirties, early forties, but

had the kind of translucent skin which defied age
She was perfectly made-up and wore a classic, ye
still fashionable, long winter coat, neatly buttoned
against the wind. She had a pale blue scarf knotted
around her neck and her gloves matched. As she
walked, the heels of her brown leather boots clicked
confidently against the paving stones.

In comparison I looked a mess. My thin and
impractical military-style coat flapped open, chilling
me to the bone, and my stripy Doctor Who scarf
clashed blatantly with everything else I had on
Beside Geena I felt like a contrary teenager, delib
erately rebelling against a young mother's sense of
style and personal grooming.

'So, how do you know Harriet?' I asked.

'I work for Evo 8,' she said matter-of-factly, as
though the name should mean something to me. I
didn't and I looked at her blankly.

'We're a new cosmetics company. We've just had
a major promotional campaign to launch our winter
collection. Harriet's company helped put together a
marketing package for us, although, if I'm honest, i
was Harriet's idea's that really caught our imagin
ation. She has such a natural talent.'

I smiled, proudly. 'She certainly has.'

'Actually,' she lowered her voice in a mock whis
per. 'Don't tell her fiancé this, but I spent most
of last night trying to talk Harriet into forgetting
about London and setting up her own marketing
company over here. She would make a killing. She's
established quite a name for herself already and
there's certainly a gap in the market with someone

of her skills. And if she specialised in one area, say, women's products, such as ours, she wouldn't feel as though she was stepping directly on her old employers' toes. I know we would certainly be keen to offer her a contract.'

'That's a great idea. What did she say?'

Geena pulled a face. 'Well, she was flattered, and I'm sure she'd love to start up on her own, she's certainly got the drive to do it, but you know how it is . . . the pull of love . . .'

I nodded, feeling sad at the prospect of such a wonderful opportunity missed.

We rounded the corner of the busy road and walked into the shop.

The warmth hit me as soon as I was inside and my hair slowly came back down, no longer whipped up by the wind. I would have wanted to take my time, enjoy the refuge against the weather, except that the shop seemed to be playing a 'lift music' rendition of Steps Greatest Hits and the synthesised saxophone grated in my head like nails on a chalk board. I found Ben's list and started picking out the groceries.

Scrutinising the list I groaned. 'Ben wants the *Sunday Review*. How tacky is that?'

Geena grimaced and joked, 'Don't worry, I was going to get *The Times* anyway, I'll just hide his underneath. No one will see.' She took the basket off me and went to get the papers.

Whilst she paid with the money Ben had given her, I stood at the window, watching the people going by, wondering what Rebecca and Nathan were doing now, and if Ed regretted what he had said last night. I hoped that Harriet's guests didn't stay much longer. I needed to see Ed more than anyone right now.

Geena waved a hand in front of my face. 'Let's go back,' she said. 'After seeing all this food, I've decided I'm ravenous.'

When we returned to the kitchen, no one looked as though they had moved since we had left. Ben and Jerry were sitting at the table, looking at us expectantly and Harriet was still bent double, peering into cupboards with little sign of success.

'Thanks babes,' Ben said as we dumped our bags on the table. He jumped up, filling his arms with the food from the bags then made his way to the work surface where he began acting like Jamie Oliver, fetching pans from the cupboard with exaggerated arm gestures and juggling with the eggs.

I picked out the two newspapers and dropped them in front of us. Curiosity got the better of me and I skimmed over the headlines of the *Sunday Review*, flicking over the page.

'Shitting hell!' I cried, spotting a photograph on the bottom of page two.

Harriet stood up, peering curiously over my shoulder.

'What the fuck?' She grabbed the paper and skim read the story, then dropped it as though it had burnt her.

'What? What's the matter?' Jerry asked, looking from Harriet to me.

Ben stood holding a metal spatula which was frozen in mid-air and Geena was looking at the paper in confusion. 'What is it?' she urged.

I picked it up again, reading the article carefully.

## BLAIR BABE'S BUST UP

By Adrian Hackwell,
Political Reporter

'I WAS PERFECTLY safe to drive,' claimed attractive, blonde-haired Labour MP, Stephanie Lambert (41) following a driving incident after a West-End party she had attended on Friday night.

West Sussex police stopped Mrs Lambert at midnight when she was spotted driving erratically along the A40. Claiming she was suffering from asthma, she refused to take a breath test and officers at the scene took her to the station, where she was asked to provide a urine sample. An irate Mrs Lambert, once again refused to cooperate. She claimed in a later statement that she had been cruelly taunted by officers, who, an insider revealed, joked that perhaps they should also provide her with a pregnancy kit. Apparently they had referred to Lambert's political reputation for swinging so far to the right, that everything she does turns out blue! In an emotional outburst, Mrs Lambert revealed that she has been undergoing fertility treatment for several years without success, saying tearfully, that remarks the officers made were 'hurtful and insensitive, particularly considering her overwhelming desire for a child.'

Mrs Stephanie Lambert, who is a Member of Parliament for Bristol Channel South, is a junior minister in the Department of Health, where she has responsibilities for reducing the health damage caused by, you guessed it, alcohol. Mrs Lambert had been widely tipped for promotion, but after this weekend's upset she is likely to return to the back benches before the next election.

A spokesman for Mrs Lambert told THE SUNDAY REVIEW that a formal complaint had been made to the Chief Constable. Meanwhile West Sussex police are believed to be referring the case to the Public Prosecution Service for a decision on the drink driving charge.

Mrs Lambert is pictured here leaving the police station with her husband Robert (45). Neither were available for comment yesterday.

Beside the article was a photograph of Robert. Harriet's Robert. He was escorting a visibly upset woman to a car, his arm protecting her as he stared antagonistically at a photographer. I looked at Harriet, who had begun furiously searching through *The Times*. The supplements were being scattered across the floor and she tore a page in her haste, falling, eventually, on a similar story to the one in the *Sunday Review*.

LABOUR MP IN POLICE ROW, the headline stated. Underneath were two photographs. One was of Robert and the woman leaving a police station. The other was of them dancing. Both were dressed up and looked incredibly glamorous. The caption said, 'Stephanie and Robert Lambert, photographed before the incident on Friday night, attending a

arty to welcome the visiting parliamentary delega-
on from the Netherlands at Westminster Hall.'

I stared at the paper for a long time, not quite
elieving what I was seeing. It was Robert, there
vas no question about it, and the realisation was
auseating. I looked up at Harriet, not knowing
vhat to say, but my words would have been lost
n her anyway. She had already left the kitchen.
Three pairs of eyes all homed in on me, looking
or answers, and as I struggled for an explanation
I heard the thud of Harriet's footsteps above me as
he fled up the stairs.

# CHAPTER TWENTY-FIVE

I could have kissed Jerry, who stepped in to avoid further embarrassment by offering to cook Ben and Geena breakfast at his house. His car was outside and the others didn't argue as they gathered their things and bid a hasty retreat, passing on their best wishes to Harriet, despite not having the faintest idea what was going on. Jerry lingered at the door wanting to offer more. He gave me a card with his phone number on, asking me to pass it on to Harriet and I assured him I would.

I found Harriet in her bedroom. She was curled up in a ball with a pillow over her head.

'Rather like an ostrich sticking its head in the sand, I'm afraid you're not doing too well at making yourself inconspicuous,' I said, sitting on the bed by her side. 'In fact, in a room with four white walls, white curtains and a white duvet, perhaps red and green tartan pyjamas weren't the best camouflage outfit either.'

'Don't!' a muffled voice under the pillow cried.

'Come on H, talk to me.'

'It's too humiliating!'

I put my hand on her shoulder. 'Don't be ridiculous! You're the victim here. Why should you be embarrassed?'

She shrugged but still didn't take the pillow off her head.

The phone rang.

'Don't answer it!' she yelled, leaping up and hovering over the bedside table. She watched the trilling phone, wringing her hands like a woman on the wagon standing over a bottle of gin. She was desperate to answer it but fought against it as though her life was at stake. She looked at me pleadingly.

I wasn't sure what she wanted me to do, so I reached over to the side of the bed and unplugged it at the wall. The room went silent.

'I can't believe you just did that!' she spat and plugged it back in. The phone stayed silent so she picked it up and dialled one, four, seven, one. 'Robert,' she said sadly and put the phone back, her hand lingering on it. When it started ringing again it was her that unplugged it this time, whipping the cord away and dropping it as if it might bite her.

I smiled, glad she hadn't given in, and watched as she proceeded to race around the room like a possessed woman. She was gathering together some clothes, all the time muttering a scorned woman's monologue. 'I've got to get out of here . . . out of this house. I can't be in here, not with him trying to call me. I don't want to speak to him. He's a bastard. A fucking little bastard and if I talk to him I might just kill him or something . . . not

335

that you can kill someone over the phone, but I would if I could and I'd definitely threaten to . . . oh yes. Then he'd know not to go bothering me with his whiny-ass bastard excuses. He can't fuck me around like that and think I'll take him back . . . him and his smarmy, lying . . . sodding round-faced, short-arsed, fucking . . . middle-aged . . . God! How old is he anyway? Ugh! It's so humiliating! I hate him . . . I . . .' She disappeared into the bathroom, slamming the door behind her. I stared at it dumbfounded and a few seconds later she reappeared, fully dressed. She'd even put her shoes and a coat on. 'Come on,' she said, holding her hand out for me. 'Let's get some fresh air. If I stay in here a moment longer I'll go sodding nuts!'

Harriet walked past Whistles. Whistles was open. They even had a sale on. She didn't even notice. All she had managed to put into words was an extension of her earlier outburst. A diatribe of abusive words that, had it been aired on the television, would have jammed phone lines with complaints. Several passers-by had raised an eyebrow at her or looked at each other, whispering, 'Did you hear what she just said?'

I hurried along next to her as she walked briskly, her face tense and her hands balled into fists. I had never seen her so angry and had every confidence it wouldn't last much longer. I cast the occasional side-long glance at her, waiting for a sign that she was crumbling but there wasn't even a flicker. We walked across College Green, scattering pigeons as we went. Harriet's pace was unyielding, but my legs were throbbing and tired, still lethargic from the previous late night. We passed an empty bench opposite the cathedral and the lure of it was too great. I turned back and flopped myself down on it, my legs pulsing. 'I'm sorry H, I'm tired. Just give me a minute.'

Harriet looked unwilling to break the momentum of her march but seeing that I wasn't budging, she couldn't very well carry on alone, so she gave in and sat beside me.

'What are you going to do?' I asked her gently.

She exhaled hard, her breath forming a cloud that hung momentarily in the air then vanished. 'I feel such an idiot,' she said. Her voice was beginning to crack. 'I believed everything he told me. I thought they were separated. That he barely ever saw her.' She wrapped her coat around her so that it doubled over, holding her snugly inside. 'It sounds so pathetic doesn't it? You hear women say it all the time and you just think "How could you not have guessed? That's so naïve." But I really did.'

'You knew he was married?'

She nodded, looking up at the cathedral's tower, anywhere but at me.

'Did you know how old he was?'

She laughed bitterly. 'No. And how ridiculous. That wouldn't have even made that much difference to me. I mean, why lie about that? Still, I suppose he lied about everything else. He told me he was separated from his wife. That he walked out because she had become obsessive. She was a housewife, who didn't work and wanted desperately to have a baby. She was older than him and worried that time was passing her by. He said she'd lost her sparkle her life. She hassled him constantly and seemed to want him only as a means to provide a child. He felt used and lost respect for her. He made her sound like a nightmare. That the divorce was going through and he only ever her saw her rarely, and then only out of guilt, because she was alone and had no life outside the one they'd shared. He was worried she wouldn't be able to cope emotionally or financially on her own and that he was easing out of her life in a gradual way, to allow her to adjust to being alone. How much crap did he feed me? Turns out his wife's even more successful than he is. He probably had his ego trampled all over when she became an MP and reinvented himself to get a sense of male pride back. I was his midlife crisis, helping him feel like "the big man" again.'

I linked my arm with hers, squeezing her tightly.

'I bet you think I'm awful don't you?'

'Why?'

'You know,' she looked at me guiltily. 'Because I knew about his wife.'

'Of course not! You thought it was over. You had no reason to think you were doing anything wrong.' There was one thing still bothering me though. I wondered whether or not to ask her than decided, what the hell. 'H, why did you ask him to marry you though? I never even thought you were the marrying type. Why him?'

She frowned. 'God, I don't know. I was swept

338

way with it all. I felt like I was falling in love with him, I knew I could. Possibly the first time I've ever loved anyone. He was fascinating, and so clever. Everything he said was kind of poetic, you know? He's got this gift, and he had me on a string, hanging on his every word. He was making a big deal out of being a gentleman, treating me properly, wanting to know the whole me first. He didn't want me to feel it was just an affair. He told me he had fallen in love with me and I wanted to believe him. I knew about his wife and I was scared, I suppose. I was frightened of investing so much of my feelings in him when I didn't know for sure whether he still cared for his wife. I said it one night. Kind of like a challenge. If he said yes then I knew he was serious. I didn't want to waste my time with someone who wasn't. I didn't want to be his fling, or his rebound relationship. It was all or nothing. Turns out that a man can say almost anything he likes if it's going to get him a shag.' She buried her face in her hands. 'It's just so humiliating. I feel utterly stupid. The biggest mistake of my life and all I want to do is get so drunk that I can forget the whole thing. So that for just a short while I can obliterate it from my mind and not have to face up to what an idiot I've been.'

'Come on then.' I tugged at her arm. 'I'll help you.'

Harriet splayed her arms out wide and opened her mouth to sing.

'If you dare sing Gloria Gaynor's "I will Survive", I might just leave you in the gutter and see how well you survive alone on the streets of Bristol.'

'But iz the only song thas any good fer leavin yer luva to,' she sulked.

'It's too over used,' I said, steering her away from the window of Pizza Hut where she was already getting some concerned glances. 'If you want to sing about being a strong, single-minded woman then something by Destiny's Child might fit the bill. Just pick anything other than Gloria!'

'Hokay then . . .' she belted out the chorus to John Denver's 'Leavin on a Jet Plane' then petered out as she forgot the words.

'Well, that's more original I grant you, but with several major flaws. A: You're not leaving on a jet plane, and B: Nor are you standing in his doorway with a packed suitcase watching him sleeping, so it's possibly not the most suitable song to choose. Personally if you're going to pick a John Denver song, and I have to say, he wouldn't be my choice, then "Take me Home, Country Roads" might be a more fitting song, because at the moment I don't think you're going to make it to the next lamppost!'

Harriet waved her hand in front of my nose. 'Whadda you know anyway,' she slurred.

I couldn't quite fathom how she had managed to get so much drunker than me. We had pretty much drunk the same, and both on an empty stomach as neither had eaten breakfast or lunch. By dinner time we were both ravenous and had ordered food at the Pitcher and Piano.

Sitting there with Harriet I was reminded of the

340

last time I had gone there with Nathan. It seemed unreal now, that day. I couldn't imagine ever feeling that way about Nathan again. He had changed from my mental image of an ideal man, to becoming real, flawed, and more importantly, Rebecca's. That, I had finally come to terms with. People say you never forget your first love and I can see why that is true. I'd never forget how he made me feel when he sang, how my dreams of him kept me going throughout school and beyond, when all else round me seemed to be crumbling. He was a special memory. But now I knew that fantasy is sometimes better left that way. I had received a voice message from him on my mobile sometime that afternoon and I listened to it whilst we were sitting, eating.

'Abby, it's me, Nathan. I just had to call and say how sorry I am about yesterday. I hope I didn't spoil the party too much for you . . . anyway, I just wanted to say that Bec and I will be all right. We're sorting out some stuff, should have done it ages ago really. To apologise we must have you over for dinner soon. And Harriet of course. I'll get back to you about that. And thanks, for, you know. You're a good friend. We both think so. See you soon.'

I knew I'd be OK when I listened to that, because hearing his voice just made me think of Rebecca, of seeing her in a heap on Harriet's bathroom floor, racked with guilt and regret. He had forgiven her already and they would be stronger for it. I was happy for them both but particularly happy for her.

Harriet froze. She held up a hand to stop me

from walking any further. She squinted her eyes and listened carefully. 'Abby, I can hear moosic,' she cried happily and crept forward, following the sound. She cocked her head like a sniffer dog. 'Iz coming from ovuh here I fink.' She gestured at me to follow her.

'H, it's here,' I said, pointing out the grotty corner pub that she was creeping right past. The door to the street was open, emitting the sounds of a live band. A sandwich board outside informed us in squiggly, chalky writing that THE BLURBS were playing LIVE TONITE! The windows were softly lit and misted up so I couldn't get a look inside, but from what I could see, the place was packed. A couple of students walked past us into the pub and the sounds of the band were amplified for a moment as they swung the bar door open. The snippet I heard sounded good; rocking, in a cool 60s kind of way, rather than an '. . . All Over The World', terrible, Status Quo kind of way.

Harriet looked at me with pleading eyes and I relented without much struggle. 'But you're drinking coke,' I warned her.

I got the feeling I would be sleeping on Harriet's sofa tonight. At some point, I wasn't sure when, she had managed to fetch a blanket to cover me up. There was plenty of room for me to stretch out and I couldn't see the point in fighting it. The stairs are difficult to negotiate when your eyesight is impaired, giving everything the impression that it was floating about on strings. Even the floor was undulating.

Fortunately for us, as we had staggered out of the pub, a taxi had been parked up outside, waiting for no one in particular. He didn't look amused by us as we giggled all the way home, humming songs that the band had sung so perfectly.

The Blurbs had turned out to be an excellent band. I couldn't remember enjoying a live bond as much since Ed and I had seen Moby play at Glastonbury. Of course they weren't quite so polished, but they were great all the same. The lead singer had a long, shaggy mop of hair. It was thick, brown and falling in front of his eyes, giving him a sexy bed-head look. He sung a slow rendition of 'Wild Thing' with such tenderness that my knees began to quake uncontrollably. He had his audience in the palm of his hand. When he upped the tempo and sung a faster song, the crowd obeyed and danced without inhibition, and when he got romantic and sexy, the students that packed the pub looked like they could roger each other senseless, right then and there.

'He's got that thing, hasn't he?' Harriet said, unable to take his eyes off him.

'Definitely,' I enthused.

'He's not my type though.'

'No.' I wasn't sure what my type was any more. Watching the singer in front of me, so lit with passion, I wondered if I could have fallen in love with him when I was fourteen. The answer was, possibly. It was very easy to see someone singing like this and be drawn in by them. To feel you really know them, that they have spread themselves out before you, showing you their deepest, innermost feelings, loves and insecurities. That the words they sing could be written for you. It was easy to see why teenagers the world over fell in love with members of boy bands. The more I watched him, the more I was concluding that actually it wasn't him at all, it was the emotional power of the music and lyrics that was uplifting, touching. You didn't need to date the singer to feel the music.

We danced, sung along, clapped and cheered with the rest of the audience, lost in a moment of time, not worrying about what had come before or what would follow it. Just enjoying the music until the band packed up and the audience disbanded.

Lying on the sofa, watching Harriet as she clumsily mopped up the water she had spilled on the carpet, I pulled the blanket around my shoulders feeling secure and snug. 'Ed loves me,' I whispered.

'Tell me something I don't know,' Harriet countered and we both started giggling uncontrollably again.

# CHAPTER TWENTY-SIX

Walking to work I was suffering from a growing sense of anxious anticipation. I fiddled nervously with the beads in my bracelet, turning them around and around. I felt sick. The previous night's drinking had left me feeling as though someone had rung the moisture out of my brain like a wet dishcloth, leaving it parched and tender from misuse. If it hadn't been so publicly unacceptable, I may have dropped down onto all floors and crawled into work, croaking, 'Water . . . water,' like a prisoner of the desert.

I felt bad leaving Harriet this morning. Reality had finally caught up with her and she was looking upset and lost. The hangover didn't help either. She curled herself into a ball on the sofa, sipping at a glass of fizzy water and moaning. The phone rung several times and we both ignored it. Every time it rang I was tempted to answer it and see if it was Ed, but when we dialled one, four, seven, one it was always Robert.

'You'll have to speak to him at some point H,' I said to her after the third or fourth phone call.

'I know. But not yet. When I've got my anger back I know it'll come back, and then I'll be safe to talk to him. I don't want to cry, or give in, or anything else hopelessly weak. I want to be able to cut him dead without a shred of hope. Then I can get on with my life.'

I was glad to see that Harriet had retained her sense of organisation and self-control. She wasn't so much of a worry to me when she still had those I knew she would be OK in time. I pinned Jerry's phone number up on the notice board for her and left, promising to call at lunchtime to find out how she was and let her know what happened with Ed.

As I walked I tried to calm myself down with deep breaths; in through the nose – out through the mouth – but that just left me feeling light headed on top of everything else. I stalled, looking into the window of a bakery my breathing exercises had alerted me to, but I wasn't really interested in the food, delicious though it looked. I knew I was nervous about seeing Ed again. I never did manage to call or see him on Sunday and I felt consumed with guilt about that. Poor Ed. He had really put himself on the line at the party, risking a lot. It was obvious that he was anxious for me to reassure him, and to address our relationship one way or another. He would have waited for me yesterday and most likely would have misread my lack of communication as a sign that I wasn't interested in him, that I wanted to avoid the issue. He had tried to call me last night, when I was at the pub, he'd obviously given up waiting and playing it cool. I hadn't heard the mobile, the music was too loud and I was too drunk when I left the pub to have the sense to check for missed calls. I had seen it in the morning instead. He hadn't left a message. I'd tried to call him back, at his flat and the shop, but the phone just rang and rang.

I could see the turn for Little Beat in the distance. My heart sped up and my footsteps dropped back simultaneously. Seeing him in the shop didn't seem like the right place somehow. There were too many distractions. Too much pressure to fall back into our usual routine and simply act as though nothing had happened. Perhaps we could sneak off at lunchtime. We could go to a café to have some lunch and talk properly. I still wasn't sure what I would say though, or how I would feel when I saw him.

I knew as soon as I entered the shop that he wasn't there. Tasha was leaning against the till. She was chewing gum, reading the back of a CD as she listened to a So Solid Crew track.

I dropped my bag down on the floor. 'Where's Ed?'

'Didn't he tell you?'

I shrugged. He hadn't told me anything.

'He's gone to stay with his mum. Went late last night as a spur of the moment kind of thing. Said he needed a break. I'm not complaining though. I need the extra cash.' She carried on chewing gum, unaware that I must have been looking at her as though she was mad. 'He's so nice, Ed. He was talking about getting me to help out with the shop more, you know, he wants to go on holiday soon. Keeps ranting on that if he doesn't go to Thailand before the year's out he'll know he's past it, or something like that, he wasn't making a lot of sense, you know?' She looked up from the CD cover and saw my face. 'What?'

'So, how long is he going to be staying at his mother's for?' I was trying to keep the sarcasm out of my voice.

'A few days? A week? I have no idea. I don't think he knew. He said he'd call in a couple of days. Did he really not tell you? I thought you two were thick as thieves.'

I crossed my arms, frowning. 'So, where did he tell you his mother lives?'

'I thought you knew.' She was clearly confused. She wasn't the only one.

'I do know,' I said. 'She lives in Bristol, about two miles away, and Ed still tries to keep visitations to seasonal holidays and limit their duration to less than an hour. If he's staying at her house then I'm Geri Halliwell.'

I trudged across the shop floor to the phone and sat down. I was surprised to feel tears pricking at the back of my eyes. It was a huge anti-climax not seeing him in the shop. I hadn't realised how much I wanted to see him until then. I dialled his home number, praying he would be there, but it just rang and rang. I tried his mobile but it went straight to the answerphone. I didn't leave a message. There was no point. His phone was most likely still sitting in his airing cupboard. For a man who was so clued up about audio technology, I was constantly amazed at his inability to grasp the technological revolution in communication. I hung up, overwhelmed with disappointment. I considered calling his mother but I didn't see the point. I didn't believe for a minute that he was there.

'Are you all right, Abby?' Tasha asked, leaning on the counter and looking at me strangely.

'I'm OK. Just a mad weekend, that's all. I'm feeling a bit blown away.'

'God, yes. The party! I can't believe I missed that. Tell me all about it. I want to hear all the gory details.' She pulled up a stool and sat down, her eyes flashing with intrigue.

I didn't usually confide in Tasha but this time I just couldn't help myself. I told her everything and it felt good talking to somebody who would have a fresh perspective. She stayed silent, letting me talk. She took a sharp intake of breath when I told her about Nathan's kiss.

'Poor Ed,' she said when I finished. 'So you haven't spoken at all since the party?'

'No.'

She pulled a pitiful expression. 'He must be feeling really awful.'

'I know.'

'I mean, imagine really laying your heart on the line like that to your best friend in the world and then . . .' she paused, sweeping her hand out for dramatic effect. 'Nothing.'

'I know,' I said, feeling worse than ever. 'I feel so bad about it, but what can I do?'

Tasha cracked her gum, shaking her head. 'What *can* you do?'

I remembered why it was that I didn't usually confide in Tasha. 'I ought to open up I suppose,' I said, despondently. The thought of a day in the shop without Ed was a hollow prospect. I knew the time would drag.

By Wednesday I had to force myself into work. The past few days had been miserable. On Tuesday I had given in and called Ed's mother, but as I suspected she knew nothing of his whereabouts. Ed never phoned and I couldn't stop thinking about him. What if he just didn't come back? What if he decided to go to Thailand and was gone for months?

The shop had been quiet which only emphasised Ed's absence further. I missed talking to him about the average, day-to-day things, sharing a coffee when custom was slow, and joking and laughing together. We had rarely ever been apart and I understood now just how much I had taken him for granted. The longer he was gone, the more I realised that life was miserable without him.

I was leaning on the counter on Wednesday morning, listening to the Carpenters and staring into space when the phone rang. I pounced on it.

'Hello?'

'Abby, hi. It's me, Vicky.'

'Oh, hi Vicky,' I said, hoping I didn't sound disappointed.

'Still no word?'

'No.'

'Oh, babe. You're really missing him, aren't you?'

'Yeah.'

'Good,' she said, happily.

'What do you mean good? It's not good, it's awful! I can't stop thinking about him.'

'Even better. Listen, I think Ed going off like this is the best thing he could have done. You've been so wrapped in Nathan, you've been unable to see what's been right in front of you for so long now.'

Nathan? I hadn't even thought about him since Sunday. The name hung in the air, reminding me how stupid I'd been. I scrunched up my face, trying to erase the memory. I couldn't believe how long I had spent thinking he was right for me. The Nathan I had loved was the old Nathan, the Nathan from an era when life was different. Mum was alive and well, my life was full of possibility and I was just beginning to discover myself. That Nathan was in my past. I would never capture that time again and now I realised I didn't want to.

A customer approached the counter with a bag of records under his arm. 'I'd better go, I have a customer. Can I call you back?'

'Stop trying to avoid the issue,' Vicky said suspiciously.

'I'm not, it's true!' I cried. 'I'll call you back.' I hung up and smiled at the lad who was waiting for me to serve him. He was about sixteen. Tall and muscular for his age. He had a ripped denim jacket on and he reminded me slightly of Nathan when he was younger. I smiled at him kindly. He looked sweet.

'I was wondering how much you'd give me for these?' he said, taking out half-a-dozen records from his bag.

I spread them out on the counter. They were a collection of 60s rock and roll albums. The one on the top was the Beatles *Rubber Soul*. My heart skipped a beat.

'Don't tell me, you haven't got a record player. You have this on CD,' I said, picking the Beatles album up and peering inside, checking its condition.

'No, no. I've got a record player. I'm just not really into this stuff. My dad gave them to me years ago.' He smiled.

I smoothed the cover of the album feeling an overwhelming sadness. *Rubber Soul* was Ed's favourite Beatles album. He refused to be swayed by tradition and tout *Revolver* as their best work. If Ed was here now he would—

'Have you listened to "Nowhere Man"?' I asked, narrowing my eyes at him.

He shrugged. 'I don't know. Probably.'

I stared at him for a while, tapping the record with my fingers, then handed it back. 'I'm sorry I can't take these.'

The lad looked confused. 'Why? There's nothing wrong with them. They're perfect.'

'My point exactly. I think you should keep them. In fact, I think you should take them home, clean the wax out of your ears, and listen to "Nowhere Man", OK?'

The lad backed away, the tone of my voice obviously surprised him. 'Fine,' he said slowly. 'That's fine, I'll, er, do it now.' He walked out of the shop, looking over his shoulder at me as though I was a mad woman.

'You're lucky Ed wasn't here,' I muttered under my breath. 'I was easy on you.' Then I whirled around and grabbed the phone book, flicking through it with shaking fingers. I looked up Oscar's name first, but he wasn't listed. Then I tried Spencer. His number was there and I dialled it straight away, before I had time to really think about what I was doing.

'Spencer, it's me, Abby,' I said as soon as he answered. I was going to explain that I was Ed's friend but he didn't need further explanation.

'Abby, of course. How've you been? Did you clean up OK after the party?'

'Oh fine, no problems.'

'Excellent. I had a great night. You must do it again sometime. Sadly we're getting into that miserable age of "dinner parties" don't you think? The days of house parties are dwindling. It's nice to know there's a few of us still willing to burn the candle at both ends, so to speak,' he said in a voice that hinted at a double-entendre. 'Anyway, I guess you're phoning wondering where Ed is aren't you?'

'Right, yes. Do you know?' How did he know?

'Listen, Abby, I promised him I wouldn't tell anyone where he was. He needed some space and some time to think. If I told you, I'd be betraying a confidence. I think his pride has taken quite a knock.'

'Spencer, please. I need to talk to him. We've go
to sort things out. I can't leave it hanging in the ai
like this.' I felt close to tears. I had to find him. I had
experienced what life was like without Ed for long
enough now to know I couldn't stand it any longer
Just the thought of one more day in the shop withou
him left me feeling bereft.

'Look, Ed's always been a pretty sensitive soul
Personally, I think he's overreacting and I reckon
deep down, he doesn't really want to be left up
there on his own. So I'm going to tell you, on the
condition that you bear in mind that he loves you
more than anyone. He has for as long as I've known
him, and if you laugh at him, he'll most likely spend
the rest of his life sitting in a basement listening to
Radiohead or something just as miserable.'

For a moment my voice dried up. Hearing Spencer
talk about Ed's feelings so matter-of-factly made
it seem all the more real. I hadn't dreamed it. I
wasn't just something Ed had told me in a moment
of madness. Ed had confided his feelings for me
to Spencer a long time ago. How could I not have
seen it? I felt a sudden rush of affection for him as
I remembered how vulnerable he seemed when he
was attracted to someone.

'I give you my word. I'd never hurt him. You
have to help me find him.'

'OK,' he said, satisfied. 'He's staying in Hope.'

'Where?'

'In Hope.'

'I know, but where?'

'No, I don't mean Hope as in hopeful, I mean Hope

s in Derbyshire. It's a converted farm that belongs o Oscar's dad. It's on the outskirts of a little village alled Hope, well, in between that and Castleton?'

'Nope.' I still hadn't got the faintest idea where ıe meant.

'Chapel-en-le-Frith?'

'Derbyshire isn't in France, is it?'

'God, girl, Buxton?' Spencer said with a hint of lesperation.

'Mineral water!' I cried, triumphant.

He burst out laughing then. 'Shit, you really need o get out more, don't you?'

The cottage, according to Spencer, was gorgeous, ›ut sparse. One of those very rural places you go to ;et away from it all. It wasn't connected to a phone ine. Normally it wouldn't matter as most people, Spencer explained, had a mobile. But Ed, as far as ıe knew, hadn't taken his with him.

This didn't surprise me in the slightest, and I lidn't really mind. I needed more than anything to ;ee him. A phone call would never be the same, and vhat better way to restore Ed's confidence in how I 'elt about him than by driving up to surprise him.

I hung up, my heart racing happily at the thought of ;eeing him so soon. It must only be a couple of hours lrive away. I could even be there by lunchtime.

I told Tasha everything, bolting down a coffee she ıad made me whilst I was on the phone. When I ıad explained I looked at her, eyes willing her to ;ay what I hoped to hear.

'You have to go and get him, girl,' she said, flashing me a huge, pearly white smile. 'Don't worry about the

shop. We can call Pete in to help out. He's always up
for earning more cash and has no argument about
missing a few lectures. We'll hold the fort for you till
you get back. Take as long as you like.'

When I arrived home I went straight to find Harriet.
I was relieved to find her up and dressed for the
first time since we had returned from the pub on
Sunday.

'H, how are you feeling?' I asked when I saw her.

'I'm OK. I spoke to Robert this morning.'

'And?'

'Well, that's it really. We talked. He was apologetic, said he will leave his wife, blah, blah.' She
looked at me, smiling sadly. 'Don't worry, I didn't
fall for any of it. I told him it was over. I never
wanted to hear from him again, and if he pestered
me I'd tell the press.'

'Ouch!'

'I didn't mean it of course, but he's such a coward
didn't need to say much else. I think he got the hint.

'And you're sure you're OK?'

'I'll be fine. Don't you worry about me. Anyway
what are you doing back? What's going on?'

I filled her in as best as I could and as she listened
she began to perk up again, glad to be distracted
from her own crisis.

'That's fantastic, Abby. I'm sure it's the right thing
to do. You've been wretched without him.' She put
her hands on her hips and looked at me through
narrowed eyes. 'But what are you going to do when
you find him?'

I bit my lip. 'I don't know. I haven't thought that far ahead. But I know this much. Ed is my future. I just want to be with him.'

'Do you think you can be more than just friends?' I paused, grinning. 'I think so. In a funny way I think we always have been. Without the sex obviously. I think I've always fancied him, I always knew he'd make a fantastic boyfriend. I just didn't consider the possibility of him being mine because I really didn't think he was interested in me. Maybe because he was so much older than me when I first met him, he wouldn't have been attracted to me at first. I was still a kid. We became friends first and it became a habitual thing. It's sounds ridiculous but I never thought about it after that. I became preoccupied with other things. Other people,' I added sheepishly. 'Being without him now has really made me realise how much I need him. I love him.'

Harriet hugged me in a burst of spontaneous happiness. 'That's fantastic!' She let go of me just as quickly and dragged me out of the room by the hand. 'Come on then, you've got to go and find him. How about you get some things together, spruce yourself up a bit and I'll fetch a map. We can work out where it is you're going.'

As I was getting dressed I realised that for the first time in years I was doing something to change the course of my life. I wasn't just letting things happen to me, I was taking control, and instead of feeling pathetic about the future, I was filled with a sense of bravado and excitement. As I relished these new feelings an idea struck me. It was a crazy idea that a week ago I might have laughed off, but once had thought it I couldn't get it out of my head I leapt across the bed, without even bothering to finish pulling my trousers up. If I left it a moment longer I may have talked myself out of it and the last thing I wanted was for that old apathy to return. picked up the receiver and dialled Ben's number.

By the time I had finally made it on the road it was nearly lunchtime. I had taken longer than I'd expected to at Ben's house. The traffic was light on the motorway and I was making good time but I didn't dare go above seventy miles an hour Anything above that and the Scooby rattled so much I was frightened it would shake itself to pieces. I had begun my journey with Fiona Apples, 'Fast As You Can', trying to capture my mood and spur me on After that I progressed to playing pop music, trashy throw away pop that bubbled with happiness and sped me along with it's pacey beat. I had Harriet's map spread out on the passenger seat but I rarely glanced at it. I was heading North and for three hours that's all I did; follow motorway signs for North as though it was a place in its own right.

I didn't want to slow down or stop. I was frightened that if I lost my pace I would get to thinking about what I was doing and lose my nerve. What if Ed didn't want to see me? What if he wasn't there after all? What if he had lied to Spencer and taken Kylie away for a few nights of wild, undisturbed sex? The thought left me feeling choked remembered when Ed first told me about Kylie and how I reacted. I had been so angry and now I was waking up to my feelings for Ed, I knew why. I was jealous. Kylie was the first woman Ed had chosen to go with in so long I was shocked that he was still attracted to women. And there was a thought that niggled me then that I had tried to ignore because it seemed so crazy. What has she got that I haven't got? Why hadn't Ed gone for me? Because if ever there was a woman that suited Ed, it was me. At the time I didn't allow myself to put it down as jealousy. I told myself it was just because I was hurt that Ed hadn't confided in me and blocked the other thoughts from my head.

Another worry was also niggling me as I drove. What if I saw Nathan again and all those old feelings came flooding back? I tried not to think about Nathan, but the more I tried not to, the more he crept into my head; the image of him singing, touching the microphone; the shock of being introduced to him for the first time as Rebecca's 'new love'; of us splashing on the steps in Millennium Square and sharing a Guinness in his favourite pub. All these images played in my head like an epitaph. They were the old me. Dad had been right all along, I had been stagnating. Those images of Nathan, particularly the recent ones, were painful to remember. I felt foolish and embarrassed.

I concentrated on the road ahead, telling myself that from now on, I was looking only forward. I had an exciting future to look forward to and Ed was a big part of it.

# CHAPTER TWENTY-SEVEN

I had come off the motorway somewhere past Stoke-on-Trent. I wasn't quite sure where I was now. I had driven through a town called Macclesfield and was travelling on a road that felt as though it was heading to the top of the world. I had been climbing and climbing until my ears finally popped. The Scooby could only manage second gear, anything else and I suspected it would have started rolling backwards.

The countryside was beautiful. Wooded hillsides flanked either side of the winding road and there was a striking absence of housing. I lost count of how many hours I had spent in the car, stopping only once for a limp sandwich and a trip to the ladies. That was ages ago and I knew I couldn't continue any further without stretching my legs. I saw a viewpoint sign outside what looked like a picnic area and pulled into a car park.

I got out for a breath of air. It was fresh and dewy, smelling slightly of pine and I took in a lungful as I stood, staring at the view with my hands on my hips. I was parked on a cliff edge, looking down at a plunging valley, with a large town spread out n the distance. I had no idea what the town was. There were several high rises so I guessed it could ven be a city, possibly Manchester. My sense of irection had become confused as soon as I'd left he North signs behind on the motorway. I looked ip the road in the direction I was heading and saw hat clouds were quickly forming and dropping. The lense atmosphere made me think that perhaps a torm was brewing and a twinge of anxiety made ne return to the van.

I was about to start the engine again when a ouple of hikers knocked on my window. They were middle-aged couple dressed completely in water- roofs. They wore identical cable knitted woolly ats and had their hoods pulled up over them, he draw strings pulled tight around their necks. rolled down the window and smiled politely.

'A cup of tea, please,' the man said, fiddling vith the zip on his pocket and producing a couple of coins.

'Pardon?'

'A tea?' He looked at his wife, then back at me. You are a snack van aren't you?'

I rolled my eyes. 'No.'

'Ahh, you sell flowers?'

'I'm sorry, no.'

'Come on dear,' his wife said, pulling at the sleeve f his anorak. 'I think there's a storm coming anyway. Ve'd better start heading off.' She looked at me apolo- etically and I smiled back, starting the engine. I was eginning to wonder what on earth I was doing here.

\*

When I reached the top of the hill I may as well have been transported into another world. The cloud was now so low I felt I could almost reach out of my window and gather a handful. I could let it float around in the van; my own personal microclimate. The road I travelled along was flat and straight. I was driving across what seemed to be a plateau high above the towns and villages. It was barren and bleak.

My heart was pounding as the weather closed in and the rain began its inevitable drumming on the windscreen. In a matter of seconds I was sitting in the middle of a downpour. I had never experienced rain like it. It gushed across the road in front of me and poured on my van so hard I could no longer make out rain drops, they had merged together to form a never ending sheet of water. It was as though somebody was emptying a bottomless bath full of water straight down on top of me. It was deafening and just when I though it couldn't get any louder, I saw a fork of lighting cut through the cloud in front of me and a crack of thunder exploded around me vibrating the van as it rumbled on and eventually tailed away. I wanted to pull over and wait for it to pass but the rain was so hard and the cloud so disorientating, I wasn't even sure that I could distinguish the side of the road. My lights were on full beam and the car was rattling so much with the force of the rain, that for all I knew I could have driven off the road and right now be driving across a grassy hillside. Another fork of lightening struck unnervingly close to my car, making me jump. I riefly lit up the road I was on and I was at least eassured that I was still driving on tarmac. My eart hammered, keeping pace with the rain and wondered what on earth I was going to do. I vas too frightened to pull over and stop in case was hit by another car, equally blinded by the veather.

I turned off the music, I could no longer make it ut, and as I considered my options, a more terrify-ng realisation hit me. The Scooby was beginning to nisfire, jolting and bucking like a stubborn horse. pressed the accelerator, but it didn't propel me orwards, instead it slowed down to almost walking ace and cut out.

'Shit!' I hit the steering wheel with the palm of ny hand. I turned the key in the ignition, praying it vould start again, but the engine just turned over. tried again, pressing my foot to the floor of the ccelerator and to my joy, it began again. I drove on entatively, aware that it was struggling and I fought ard to keep it going. The drumming rain suddenly ased off and the water separated into raindrops nce more. As the sound of the rain also ebbed, could hear the Scooby's engine. It was revving rratically.

The clouds grew patchy, and as I drove through ne, a clearing emerged before me. Standing alone y the roadside, surrounded by nothing but empty illsides, was a pub. I looked up to the parting eavens and whispered a 'thank you', my hands ow shaking at the prospect of breaking down in he midst of the almost apocalyptic weather. The

pub was a matter of yards from where I was drivin
and on a slight downward slope, so I put the gear
into neutral and coasted into the car park.

I sat for a moment, scared out of my wits. I ha
seen *From Dusk Till Dawn*; I had heard of Roysto
Vasey and the sight of this gloomy pub, parked i
the middle of such a bleak landscape, was filling m
head with gruesome possibilities. I picked up m
phone, wanting to call Harriet, or the AA, anybod
that could help me out of this mess, but when
tried to dial it just bleeped at me. There was, o
course, no signal here. I stayed sitting in the var
eyeing the pub nervously, too scared to go in. The
I looked up and realised that the sun had broke
through the cloud and was lighting up a hillsid
in the distance. The contours of land were lit wit
brilliant shades of green and orange, all radian
after the soaking they had received from the rain
I watched the cloud disperse around me as quickl
as it had arrived, and within minutes the sun's ligh
had spread across the valley and reached the pub ca
park. The rain had gone, the clouds had lifted, and
patchwork of blue and grey sky was left. Suddenl
I could see for miles, and this inhospitable terrai
seemed friendly once more. The gravel of the ca
park was steaming as the rain evaporated and I go
out of the Scooby, awe-struck by the view.

I looked over to the pub and read the sign over th
door. THE CAT AND FIDDLE it read. Sounded harmles
enough. I was feeling braver by the minute and wa
about to go in until I finally noticed that the car par
was filled with motorbikes. There was every kind o

ike you could imagine; modern and old, stretched
out with long handlebars, compact and simple, red,
green, blue and black, but mainly black. Some had
sidecars, others were decorated with streamers or
flags, some were gleaming, some were rusty and
mud splattered, and one huge machine nearest to
me had padded seats like armchairs.

I stood still, taking in the scene and imagining
the one that would play out before me when I
stepped into a pub full of Hells Angels. I had a
feeling I wasn't going to blend in. I weighed up
my options and decided I had none. I couldn't go
any further without calling someone to fix my van.
I was stranded.

I reached into the passenger foot-well to fetch my
bag and as I was struggling to unhook the strap, I
heard somebody clear their throat behind me.

'Are you open love?' a gravely voice asked. What
is it with people thinking I'm a snack van? I whirled
around to see who it was and was greeted by the
sight of a growing crowd of bikers. They were
almost entirely male, dressed in black and sported
the most amount of hair I'd ever seen on a collective
group of men. The only sound I could hear was the
sound of leather creaking.

'I'm not selling anything,' I said in a small and
apologetic voice. 'I'm a DJ. My van broke down in
the rain. I don't even know where I am.' The more I
became aware of the sheer size of this guy, the more
timid I felt.

The crowd of bikers seemed to be dispersing
to their allotted bikes, preparing to leave. Only

half-a-dozen remained, interested to know what
had to say. Beside this barge of a man was another
shorter, but just as beefy. He said nothing and stood
looking menacing, as if he were a bodyguard.

'Where are you headed?' the man-barge asked
walking over to my front bonnet.

'Hope, near Castleton.'

He grunted, cracking his knuckles. 'Oh yeah?
We're going through there.' He patted the bonnet
which I took as an invitation for me to pop it open, so
I did, then left the van to peer over his shoulder.

'Try that,' he said after he had wiped part of the
engine with his handkerchief and sprayed it with a
can that his mate had fetched from his bike.

I turned the key and the engine chugged into life
again. I revved it and it sounded healthy, at least as
healthy as it normally did. I smiled at him.

'Water had got on your distributor, that's all it
was. Rain like that, not much you can do. Gets into
everything.'

'I'm really grateful, thanks so much.'

'Hope, you say?'

'Yes. Hope Dale Farm. You know it?'

He scratched his tatty beard. 'Oh, we know it.' He
nodded at his entourage, many of which were now
astride their bikes, helmets on, waiting patiently
with their engines thrumming.

The man-barge took the spray he had used on
my engine and put it back in his bag, returning
it to the box on the back of his bike. It was one
of the bikes with the low seats and long handlebars. There was an American flag painted on the

366

ngine cover and the writing underneath said CAP-
AIN AMERICA.

'*Easy Rider*,' I said, nodding at the writing and
miling. I had seen that film with Ed enough times
o remember that Peter Fonda road a bike, not unlike
his one, with the same name.

'You seen the film?'

'More times than I can remember.' Suddenly I
lidn't feel like such an outsider in this gather-
ng. Man-barge stroked the seat of his bike fondly.
There's no better film been made before or since,'
ιe said. 'Come on, we'll show you the way. Make
,ure you get there all right.'

My heart leaped. 'Are you sure?'

He mounted his bike, signalling to the others, then
started his engine and turned the bike around in the
:ar park until he sat just ahead of me. His friend
oined him, and I noticed that he had a tiny little dog
ucked into his jacket. The dog was also wearing a
eather jacket and his eyes were shielded by a pair of
iny goggles. His head poked out comically, and as
ιis owner manoeuvred his bike, the dog's ears blew
)ack in the wind. Ed will never believe me when I
ell him about this, I thought, wondering if perhaps
hadn't actually woken up this morning and this
vas some alcohol-fuelled dream. Actually, it was
ust the kind of dream I could imagine Ed having,
naybe I was just making a guest appearance.

The man-barge pointed to the road ahead, his
signal that we were off again and we started a
slow convoy out of the car park and on to the
ɔpen road.

Driving through Buxton I found myself beaming with pride at my leather-clad escort. People in the streets were stopping to stare at what must have been a bizarre sight. Fifty bikers roaring by, flanking a transit van painted with flowers. For those who looked closer, they also would have been treated to the sight of a tiny little dog, peering out of a leather jacket, it's ears whipping round in the wind. I wished I had a tape of rock music that I could play to capture the spirit. 'Born To Be Wild' would have been the obvious choice.

I saw a sign for Castleton and my heart-rate quickened. Soon I would see Ed. For a moment I thought I would never make it. I prayed that he would be there, the thought of turning up after driving so long, to find the farmhouse empty, filled me with dread. Maybe I shouldn't have been so impulsive.

The landscape became more dramatic still as we turned a corner and I was greeted with what a signpost told me was called Winnats Pass. It was a plummeting, narrow road that cut through dramatic limestone mountains on either side. Sheep roamed everywhere, skipping away as the collective sound of the engines got closer. It was a breathtakingly steep road that led to a pretty village of local stone and smoking chimneys below. There were walkers everywhere, enjoying the last of the afternoon sunshine. They were milling around at the bottom of the road, where a cattle grid marked the beginning of the village. We carried on through the people, who parted to let us pass.

Just a mile down the road, we turned onto a dirt
ack, where the man-barge and his friend pulled
ver. I trundled to a stop behind them.

He kicked his bike onto its stand. The others
emained seated.

'This is it,' he said, pointing to the large stone
arm building that stood alone at the end of a long
ravel drive.

'Thanks so much.' I smiled at him, sorry that my
mile could never quite convey the gratitude I felt.

He waved his hand in a gesture that said, 'don't
nention it' and returned to his bike.

I sat quietly, watching as they roared away, some
eeping or holding a hand aloft. When the last of the
ikers had gone, and the sound of roaring engines
ad faded away, I looked at the farm properly.
utside on the drive I spotted Ed's Astra and I felt
ny anxiety return.

# CHAPTER TWENTY-EIGHT

'What are you doing here?' Ed cried. He looked s
shocked I couldn't tell whether he was pleased to se
me or not. He had just walked around the side of th
farm, investigating the noise of the motorbikes an
was holding a small pile of logs. When he saw m
he dropped them onto the driveway, sending ther
scattering.

My journey had left me exhausted, and seein
him standing there I was overwhelmed with relie
and affection. I didn't know what to say.

He stood awkwardly, self-consciously brushin
away the wood chippings that were clinging to hi
old cable knit jumper. His jeans were torn under on
knee and he was unshaven. I had always thought E
was attractive, but today he looked better than I ha
ever seen him look before.

Ordinarily he would have swept me up in
gigantic hug and I wished he would. 'I misse
you,' I said.

He nodded. 'Me too.'

'I brought goodies.' I walked over to him, holdin
out my carrier bag as if it were a peace offering

nside were eight small bottles of lager and several packets of Jelly Tots I had bought from a service station on the motorway. They were meant to be a reminder of our familiarity, the things we loved and shared. I also didn't want to risk arriving to find that Ed had no alcohol in the house. I needed some to fuel my confidence and make me brave again.

He took the bag from me and put it down by his feet. 'You're a woman after my own heart,' he said. He rubbed the back of his neck and was about to say something else, but I couldn't stand it any longer. I went to him, wrapping my arms around his waist.

'How could you just go off like that and leave me, without even a phone call? I've been really worried about you.'

'I didn't think you wanted to see me. Not after what I said. I thought I'd ruined everything.' He stroked the back of my hair and I looked up at him.

'Don't do it again, will you? Leave me, I mean.'

'I won't.'

'I'm serious. It was horrible.'

'Good. I'm glad you didn't like it,' he said, smiling his boyish, charming smile.

Without thinking about it, I raised myself up on tiptoes and planted a kiss on his lips.

He looked stunned for a minute, then serious. He tightened his grip around my waist and kissed me back, his lips lingering on mine. The kiss deepened and I wrapped my arms around his neck. My knees turned to jelly and suddenly, all I wanted to do was kiss him all over and claim him, finally, as my own.

*

'Do you feel weird?' Ed asked, wrapping his arms around me as I washed up our plates.

'You mean about us?' I shook my hands dry and turned around to face him. 'No. Do you?'

'I feel great. Like everything is suddenly OK. Life is good.'

I knew exactly what he meant. It did feel right. At first I wasn't sure how it would feel to kiss someone who for so long had been my best friend. But the moment I did it all made sense. And Ed seemed different, in a good way. I thought I knew everything about him and that we were as close as it was possible to be. But now I felt I was seeing him in a different way. There was this whole added dimension to him and to how we related to each other. It was a chemistry that I hadn't allowed myself to see before. I wanted to share everything with him.

'I've got the fire going,' he said, nodding into the living room.

Spencer had been right about the farm being sparse. There was no telephone, radio or television. No shower, no gas. There was, however, an old fashioned, wood burning stove which Ed and I discovered made even better baked potatoes than he did, and a huge hearth in the living room, where Ed had been building a fire whilst I washed up.

I followed him in to the room. It was a huge, lofty space with floor-to-ceiling windows looking out on the hills and wooden beams criss-crossing the high ceilings. I wasn't at all surprised that Ed had wanted to come here. Everything seemed so clean, so simple. All you had to worry about was keeping warm and fed. It was the perfect get-away retreat. Looking at it now, with the sun having set an hour ago, and a fire now crackling in the hearth and casting shadows across the room, it was also the perfect romantic setting.

Ed had scattered cushions on the floor near the fire and lit the church candles that stood at either end of the mantelpiece. I fetched my rucksack off the sofa and joined him on the rug.

'So, Harriet's not moving to London now,' Ed said, carrying on the conversation we had been having over dinner, when I had explained my reasons for not getting in touch with him the Sunday after the party.

'No. I don't know what she's going to do now. Her job's ended and she hasn't got another lined up. But I think she'll be OK. You know Harriet. She's tough.'

'Poor H,' he said. 'We'll have to go straight back in the morning. She'll need you around.'

I leaned forward and kissed him. 'You, are nice, nice man,' I said, grinning.

He looked guilty. 'Right. I won't say the bit I was about to say then, about how it's a shame you won't be moving into my place any more. I don't want you thinking I'm only concerned about my own misfortune.'

I laughed and Ed picked at an imaginary piece of lint on his jumper. 'So, you won't be needing to stay with me then?'

'Ed!' I slapped his arm playfully and then sat back reaching for my bag. 'Actually, there was something I really wanted to talk to you about.' I bit my lip. 'I've done something crazy.'

'You mean crazier than driving hundreds of miles to see me then turning up with an escort of Hell Angels?'

'Crazier than that.'

'Go on.'

I took out the package that Ben had given me and passed it to Ed, waiting for his reaction.

'What's this?'

'It's money.'

'You've robbed a bank?'

'I've sold my stuff.'

'You mean the secret drug stash you've been keeping in the mattress?' he said, flicking through the notes in the envelope. 'And I just thought your bed was lumpy.'

I took a deep breath and braced myself. 'Ed. Please be serious. I've sold my decks. Ben bought them off me.'

'You did what?' He sat up, his jaw dropping.

I shrugged. 'It's no big deal. I wanted to.'

'Why did you do that? You love DJing.'

'I know, but I want to do something different now. It was the only way I could think of. And I still have the music. It's the music I love.'

'But what will you do?'

'I don't know yet. But I'm not worried. Something had to change. I've been stuck in a rut and I feel like I've finally woken up and I can see a future for the

rst time in years. There are so many things I want
o do.' I bit my lip and glanced at Ed. He looked
eally concerned, but he didn't need to be. 'I thought
could start off with a holiday. Thailand maybe, if
ou don't mind me tagging along?'

'You want to go to Thailand with me?'

'Yes.' I couldn't stop myself from grinning.

A smile began to appear on Ed's face too. 'Are
ou sure?'

I leaned across and kissed him, feeling heady.
Of course I was sure. When it felt this good, why
doubt it?

n the morning we packed Ed's things into the
cooby. Travelling back separately wasn't an option
now, and we had decided to leave his car for Spencer
or Oscar to drive back.

He sat down next to me, bringing the smell of the
fresh air in with him and I kissed him again, my lips
ender from a night of exploration and little sleep.

When we finally broke away I motioned to the
glove compartment which was filled with tapes.

'Pick a song, any song,' I suggested, starting up
he engine.

As I pulled away, Ed picked a tape, pushed it
nto the player and sat back, waiting for the song
o begin.

Driving back up the dirt track, the sounds of U2's
A Beautiful Day' filled the van.

I glanced at Ed, who had closed his eyes and was
inging along with the song. His voice was high
and off-key, making me wince, but looking at his

face I could excuse those minor flaws because th
feeling and the passion were there. I felt a shudde
of excitement rush over me. He definitely has tha
thing, I thought to myself happily.

I turned the music up and pulled over onto
secluded grass verge, undoing my seat belt.

'We're never going to get home at this rate
I tutted, climbing over to the passenger seat,
devilish grin on my face.